THE MUSIC OF MARS

YEAR of the BOOK

GEORGE G. MOORE

Year of the Book
135 Glen Avenue
Glen Rock, PA 17327

ISBN 13: 978-1-945670-70-1
ISBN 10: 1-945670-70-3

Cover design: Jay Aheer

Library of Congress Control Number: 2017962960

DEDICATION

This novel is dedicated to everyone who ignored those saying it can't be done.

Acknowledgments

In a variety of ways, many people assisted in molding this novel.

Kelly, my wife, offered endless encouragement. My good friend, Anne, gladly read every horrible bit of writing I produced (and some was quite awful) when I started down the writing path.

The Loudoun County Writers Group, especially Susan Jordan, Marissa, Mike Bresner, and Jeffery C. Jacobs, offered critiques week after week. The Round Hill Writers Group connected me to Pennwriters, all offering invaluable connections and advice.

My fearless editor, Demi Stevens, and her expert eye offered countless corrections and suggestions, some of which were difficult but highly rewarding.

And the biggest acknowledgment goes to my parents for instilling in me the love of reading, which has allowed me to experience untold adventures in a multitude of worlds.

1 | DRIVING DESIRES

"That didn't take long," Frank muttered. The vidcomm's chime had interrupted a gripping novel. He sighed... it was probably Sam, once again trying to cajole him into attending one of Mars City's pre-concert parties. Or it could be Erin, attempting to salvage a friendship from their failed romance.

Frank squeezed his eyes closed. Her refusal of his proposal still stung. The seven domes comprising Mars City might cover a lot of area, but when avoiding her, they weren't nearly enough.

It could be one of his engineers. He'd assigned himself the on-call duty while running a skeleton staff, so as many of his people as possible could attend the concert and parties. He craned his neck and glanced at the display.

As it turned out, all his guesses had been wrong.

He tapped the datapad screen to set a bookmark and took a seat in the comfortable chair before pressing the Connect button.

Under the MarsVantage logo, the screen displayed, *'Communication negotiation underway. Please wait.'* The message remained longer than usual, prompting Frank to mutter, "Damn solar flares." The Earther scientists still hadn't devised a means to stabilize the communication system's Morris-Thorne wormholes when the Sun was most active.

The reset seemed to take forever, but the on-screen clock indicated just twenty seconds for the M-T wormholes to realign and stabilize. The screen now displayed, *'Encryption handshake underway.'* Frank opened the vidcomm's maintenance panel, reached inside, and found the small device that he'd installed years earlier.

After pressing his thumb to it, the encrypted connection completed. A long-time Earth friend appeared on-screen and said, "Frank Brentford, you old Marsee."

"Jonathan Bank, you old news hound. You're the last person I was expecting to hear from."

As always, Jonathan was nattily attired in the current Earth trend—a sports jacket and thin-collared check shirt. Out of habit and out of view of the vidcomm's camera, Frank tugged the top of his steel gray jumpsuit to smooth it against his black t-shirt. On Mars, few people could afford to import the latest fashions. Regardless, he wanted to look his best.

In unison, they recited, "The knowledge I keep is true. I note the lies for what they are. I seek and safeguard information for prosperity, so humanity will never lose its knowledge, its history, or its essence. I do so, for a time when we'll need it the most."

Jonathan's smile faded. "I don't have all the pieces yet, but there's something brewing with Peter Konklin Interplanetary."

"Like what?"

Jonathan didn't request confidentiality, nor did Frank promise it; they were Knowledge Keepers—confidentiality was implied. "Interplanetary's pushing for stricter shipping regulations."

"They've been nibbling around that for years. They delay us, but we'll get our fleet certified for interplanetary shipments."

"Frank, they're taking shark-sized bites. I'm hearing major safety changes are coming down. They commissioned a study and strong-armed the Earth-based shippers to upgrade preemptively. Those shippers are passing the cost along, naturally."

"Of course. We'll just buy and install the upgrades."

"There's talk about new import/export taxes and fees, perhaps a quarantine period for your exports. My congressional sources think this is the start of a big push by Interplanetary to reacquire MarsVantage."

"What's different from their maneuvers over the past decade?"

Jonathan paused and drew his eyebrows closer together. "The staffers quickly shut down whenever the subject of Mars or MarsVantage comes up. It reminds me of when MarsVantage was originally spun off from Interplanetary. It's like they know what's coming, and they're just waiting for the paperwork."

Frank harrumphed. "I always knew Interplanetary would move against us. Believe me, I haven't been lulled into complacency by the dome they're constructing nearby. It's only an excuse for them to wander around Mars City to spy on us."

"If I had to bet, I'd say Interplanetary plans to shift public opinion and lobby the government for MarsVantage's return."

"Not if I have anything to say about it," Frank said, setting his jaw.

"I know after all these years you still haven't forgiven Konklin for what happened to Lori, but this is bigger than you. Interplanetary's too powerful. You can't take them on and win."

Frank forced a smile. Thirteen years ago, his wife Lori had been one of twenty-three people killed in The Airlock Accident. While the entire Interplanetary management team was complicit, the founder and CEO, *the* Peter Konklin of Peter Konklin Interplanetary, held the most blame. Given Frank's choice, he wouldn't have merely spun off MarsVantage, he would've spaced Konklin.

"Don't worry. I have an idea or two."

"Be careful, Frank."

Before disconnecting, they discussed other business, which, in comparison, was trivial. Rumor had it that a small band of archaeologists were investigating a boat buried in Antarctica. If true, it was a fascinating curiosity.

There were also whispers that an Australian scientist made strides in Heim theory. Numerous scientists had spent countless years trying to manipulate M-T wormholes for space travel, but they'd failed miserably. Now, a lone scientist working with a long-discredited theory might produce the breakthrough two worlds wanted. *Good for her if she's right.*

Frank stared at the ceiling, imagining a Mars-Earth trip taking only a couple of days, instead of a month—assuming, of course, the scientist could pull it off. Unfortunately, the Knowledge Keepers didn't have anyone close enough to either situation to get the details.

Frank looked back at the blank screen for a heartbeat. He'd been planning a project since shortly after his dad's passing, and its timing was tricky. If Chuck—MarsVantage's CEO—wasn't desperate enough, he'd never agree to spend the money to successfully complete it. If Frank waited too long, its completion wouldn't matter. Jonathan had never steered him wrong before.

Now was the right time.

At the wall next to his bathroom door, Frank tugged open the access panel to reveal a small combination safe nestled beside the pipes. He entered the eight-digit code, and the lock opened with an audible click. Within, he kept his encrypted Knowledge Keeper datapad and a few items that could make a huge difference to MarsVantage's future. He grabbed a small cloth bag sitting atop his dad's handwritten journal.

The bag contained a mineral fragment roughly the size of his thumb, designated Marsium121 by the Exploration and Mineral Rights Office. If he could access the cavern filled with Marsium121 stalactites and stalagmites, he'd solve MarsVantage's nagging energy problem.

And there was only one way to get it. He needed to convince Chuck to spend money they could barely afford on a consultant with skills ridiculously out of place on Mars. They needed to hire an archaeologist.

* * *

"Gretchen, honey, how did I know you'd still be here? I bet you feel vindicated, don't you?" Dr. Hawthorne, the expedition leader, asked from behind her.

Moments earlier, Gretchen Blake had heard the elevator motor's hum and the car's tell-tale creaking and squeaking as it descended fifteen feet into the carefully excavated Antarctic snow and ice illuminated by red floodlights. The night shift wasn't due to start for thirty minutes, and her shift-mates were a hundred yards away, enjoying a hot supper at camp. There could be only one person who would come to join her.

After looking one last time at the crude hatchets and wooden bowls, she stood and forced a blank expression to cover her disgust at his latest example of arrogance and condescension. "Finding these artifacts was unexpected. And their distance from the boat is intriguing."

"I'll send the astronomers an email to verify that they didn't disturb the boat."

A year ago, astronomers had discovered a surprisingly large three-hull catamaran held together with intertwined vines while preparing for another southern sky survey. They were scientists and wouldn't have tampered with it. And they certainly wouldn't have moved the bowls and hatchets thirty-seven feet away and buried them under fifteen feet of snow and ice.

Hawthorne had to know all of that already. He was toying with her. Or was he experimenting with her—probing for a reaction to a stimulus?

"Assuming they didn't, it's possible that ancient South American people were on the boat and lived here for a time." She didn't point to the artifacts as proof of her hypothesis, although her gut insisted it was true. Instead, she presented a possibility, hoping that'd be enough to placate his enormous ego.

Hawthorne shook his head. "Without food and heat? I'd sooner believe little green men from Mars left the artifacts."

"These artifacts may have become separated over time." That was his position, and although possible, it was highly unlikely. Gretchen couldn't imagine any natural process that could do so without scattering them about while shattering the boat. Yet, the hatchets and bowls had been found together, no more than five feet apart. She glanced across the excavation to the wooden hull, then focused on Hawthorne. "However, it's possible the boat was manned. I think it's worth investigating."

He leaned in closer. "If so, then where are the bodies?"

"The hull's been holed. If people came, they probably set out in multiple boats. They may have simply abandoned the damaged one and returned home on another."

"How'd you graduate high school, let alone college, without learning Occam's Razor? The simpler theory is the better one. The boat broke free and drifted here."

As hard as Gretchen tried not to, she frowned. "I can't argue that isn't a possibility."

A sickly, mocking smile formed on Hawthorne face. "You're young, and you want to make a big discovery. I understand. The truth is that there aren't any big discoveries left. Do yourself a favor and forget your pet hypothesis."

Gretchen hadn't expected such an explicit suggestion. He'd hinted that she should drop it, but he'd never said so outright. Until now. Ever since making a name for himself a couple of decades ago when he was about her age, Hawthorne somehow maintained an esteemed reputation without making another significant discovery. She'd always wondered how he'd managed it. And now it was clear—he bullied anyone attempting to capitalize on discoveries that had eluded him. "Sir, I still believe it's worth investigating."

"Do as you please, girl. I'm not wasting my time." He turned and waddled toward the elevator. In his parka, he looked like an obese penguin scurrying toward its next meal.

Gretchen shook her head and brought a gloved hand to her mouth to keep from laughing at the bizarre sight.

Regardless of his prejudgments, she'd do the work, research the boat and artifacts, and she'd understand how they'd arrived in Antarctica. She'd discover the knowledge for herself, not merely accept his interpretation because he had a title and position of authority.

Perhaps, it really was as simple as the boat breaking free and drifting here. But if it was something else, she'd add to mankind's understanding of South American inhabitants. Mankind would become more knowledgeable, due to her efforts.

The answers she sought weren't here, though. She'd have to find them on her own time between expeditions. It might take months, but with any luck, she'd make progress before her next dig, whenever that was. She hadn't heard anything from her inquiries yet, though several of her co-workers had already received offers.

A disturbing thought occurred to her. Hawthorne might have a hand in her not getting a new job, which would be a huge setback for her career. *No, that couldn't be it.* There were probably three emails waiting. She mumbled, "Quit inventing problems for yourself."

Gretchen forced her thoughts in a different direction. She should also have an email from her husband, Jimmy. She'd already sent two without a reply. By now, he should've been able to steal a few moments from covering the Socialist Republic of Kuristan's first open election since its founding 192 years ago. She was ready for a few days at their favorite South Carolina beach together, and he would be, too. She only needed to confirm the dates before making reservations.

As the elevator car carrying Hawthorne reached ground level, Gretchen protected the artifacts with a thermal blanket before shuffling to the elevator and recalling the car. When it arrived, she entered, closing and latching both doors before hitting the Up button. She cinched her parka's hood tighter as she rose above the dig area and turned her back to the never-ending wind, staring blankly at the stark, frozen emptiness of the crater. Although the scene was reminiscent of Hell, she hadn't been warm since arriving three months ago. Her next job would be in a jungle or a rainforest, anywhere hot where she could work up a sweat. Regardless, she'd never sign on to a Hawthorne dig again.

Yet, questions intruded upon her daydream. Why was she the only one wanting to understand the mystery before her? Why couldn't Hawthorne be troubled to do the work? Why couldn't her teammates? Did anyone want the truth?

* * *

An environmental alert interrupted the Caretaker's hibernation. He performed a self-diagnostic and determined that he was functioning normally. He then queried for the specifics of the alert and found a seismic event had occurred. It was the fifth over-limit seismic event detected in the 122,136 orbits he'd been in hibernation. The dead planet still held a surprise or two.

Bvindu protocol demanded a thorough examination of the city, so he transferred himself from the Master Control System to a mobile unit. The survey would require twenty-two days. Any repairs would take longer.

He rolled through the streets and corridors of the once vibrant, but now abandoned city, performing the inspection. He paid specific attention to the protective dome because it held back many orbits of slowly drifting sand. It'd never been intended to keep aloft so much weight for so long, but it exhibited no signs of distress.

Once completed, he'd correlate the results to determine the extent of any damage. He anticipated minor issues, at worst, because while the quake had been over-limit, it was weak, nonetheless. His activation had been the result of the overly-cautious Bvindu ensuring the totality of their civilization's accomplishments remained safe until they returned with news of a new homeworld.

But they hadn't returned. He'd expected them within 1000 orbits. He'd never contemplated that temporarily storing his consciousness within the Master Control System would become a permanent prison. More than anything, the Caretaker wished to see his people again through eyes of a body grown from his stored organic code.

Surely, they couldn't forget me or the treasures I safeguard.

2 | Marsium121

Frank exhaled as he stood before the door, holding a toolpac. He pressed the announcement chime below the nameplate bearing, "Charles O'Donnell." The next few minutes would decide MarsVantage's future, either as a viable, independent company, or as the eventual victim of an Interplanetary takeover.

The door slid open. "Frank, can this wait until tomorrow? I'm on my way to a party."

"No, Chuck. You're gonna want to see this. And you're gonna want to keep it quiet."

"It's been a long day. I just finished an unsatisfying board meeting, and I'm in no mood for riddles."

Frank chuckled. "A year from now, you'll look back on today as the best day of your life."

"That's a big promise." Chuck stepped aside and gestured for Frank to enter.

"I'll make good." Frank walked down the short hallway to the living room. Against the far wall stood a bookcase filled with paper books and *objets d'art* scattered among them. Chuck had spent a small fortune to find and ship physical books to Mars, a notable exception to his usual thrifty ways. Even though Chuck's quarters were identical to Frank's, the bookcase made his seem cramped.

After sitting on the couch, Frank pulled out a small bottle of brandy from his toolpac before depositing it on one side of the coffee table. Chuck's eyebrows rose, then he grabbed two snifters from the kitchen and settled into the chair catty-cornered from the couch. Frank poured a measure in each.

Chuck brought the snifter to his nose while he made small circles with his hand. He sipped. "Excellent. And quite illegal."

"I'll agree with the first and argue the second." Likewise, Frank swirled his brandy, allowing his hand to warm it. He inhaled the sweet aroma then sipped. It burned.

"So you expect me to believe you paid the taxes, levies, and fees to ship this to Mars? I'm paying you too much."

Frank grinned. "Perhaps the brandy didn't make it here through wholly legitimate channels."

"Fair enough." Chuck's eyebrows drew together.

For a moment, Frank didn't understand Chuck's concern. Then he felt it, like a rising and falling while he sat still on the couch. As quickly as it started, the sensation stopped. "Was that a Marsquake?"

"Sure was. I felt one much stronger years ago on a long-range exploration in the southern hemisphere. This one was weak. I'll bet most people didn't even notice."

Frank nodded. "I doubt anything was damaged."

"Good." Chuck sipped the brandy again, leaning back in the chair. "What's so important that I'm missing our monthly parties and concert?"

Frank unpacked the rest of his toolpac, laying out a Petri dish and a gadget the size of one of Chuck's books with two wires, one black and the other white, dangling from it. Lastly, he placed a cloth pouch on the coffee table. "Interplanetary and its Washington lapdogs have us boxed in. We're making money, but we're hamstrung by our energy production."

"Among other things. You're very knowledgeable about company business... for an engineering manager," Chuck half-teased, not for the first time.

"I'm out and about, and I see and hear things. For instance, June tells me that Energy Production is at a crossroads. Importing fuel cells keeps getting more expensive while building more solar panels means increased labor costs to clean and repair micrometeorite damage. And she's given up on getting approval for a nuclear reactor."

"Once the government split us from Interplanetary, that idea died." Chuck exhaled. "I've lost sleep over it. Energy Production has never run better than under June, but she's right. Unless we solve our energy production dilemma, we'll never be self-sufficient."

"That's why I'm here, Chuck. About thirty years ago, my dad was part of an exploration party in the Maelstrom Mountains where he came across crystal fragments like this." Frank pulled a blue-black crystal about the size of his thumb from the pouch and handed it over.

Chuck examined its every facet. At one point, it caught the light just so, and a faint rainbow appeared inside, as if painted with dull watercolors. Chuck returned the crystal to Frank.

"Per procedure, Dad submitted the crystals to the Exploration and Mineral Rights office, who examined, tested, and officially named it Marsium121. They also concluded it was valueless. Dad retrieved the crystals and incorporated them in various items. I understand that Konklin's office clock uses polished fragments for its hour markers."

"Sure, it's beautiful, but we're not going to become self-sufficient by selling pretty rocks."

Frank submerged the Marsium121 fragment and the gadget's wires in the Petri dish's water. Its LEDs leapt to life in ever changing patterns. "Dad spilled coffee on a sample once and received a shock while cleaning up. He experimented further and discovered that water was the most efficient medium to produce electricity."

Chuck's eyes widened as he leaned forward. "How much power are we talking about?"

"That fragment can power this room for the rest of my life and then some."

After using a cloth from the toolpac to retrieve the Marsium121, Frank replaced the Petri dish's lid and dried the crystal. He continued, "I have several fragments that fit together into what would've been part of a stalactite. I trained the Mars Scouts many times over the years in the area where this was discovered. We've taken ground soundings that reveal a large cavern filled with stalactites and stalagmites, and those soundings suggest the composition is Marsium121. That's centuries of power just waiting for us."

Frank pulled his datapad from his coveralls leg pocket, opened the screen, and showed Chuck the soundings and his analysis.

"Frank, tell me you filed those soundings."

"Of course. Everything's in the public records. We're covered legally."

"So we just have to excavate the cavern?"

"I drilled some test bore holes. The cavern's outer shell is composed of a tough mineral that I haven't seen on Mars before. But if we use explosives, we'll either bring the mountain down on ourselves or shatter the Marsium121 into a billion pieces. In that case, we'll only manage to recover a fraction."

"How do we get it then?"

"A cave fronts this cavern, and there are odd symbols carved inside. My dad found them on the expedition. He submitted an image along with the Marsium121." On his datapad, Frank showed Chuck a high definition picture of the entire cave wall. "Check out the faint lines on either side of the symbols. If you look closely, there's another above. I think they're the seams of a door and those symbols are the key to opening it."

Chuck looked to Frank. "You're treading dangerously close to suggesting there was intelligence here before us. We've never found any proof of that."

"These symbols are proof—unless you think bored employees were practicing their carving skills in an out-of-the-way cave."

Chuck raised his eyebrows. "Unlikely."

"The symbols' origin is beside the point. Unless there's incontrovertible proof of alien intelligence, let's avoid the subject entirely. Earthers already think we're half-crazy—we don't need to hand out more reasons."

Chuck traced his index finger around the snifter's rim and stared at the gadget. He frowned. "What's the catch?"

"You know me too well." Frank chuckled. "I had to fudge the power estimates, but they're as accurate as I could make them."

"Which means what?"

"Dad ran, and I replicated, several experiments. One powered a light uninterrupted for three months. Afterward, the fragment showed no degradation. The only water loss was due to evaporation. Contrary to the Laws of Thermodynamics, it appears energy was simply created."

"But that's impossible."

"Agreed, so I estimated crystal usage to be minuscule, just below what I can measure. The Marsium121 in the cavern can power us for centuries. And if the usage *is* somehow zero, then we'll have energy until the Sun turns into a red giant."

"Ideas like this are why I wanted you on the board of directors. You've accomplished what I've spent years unsuccessfully prodding them to do. You've provided us a path to prosperity."

Frank shook his head. "I'm not a paper pusher. I guarantee you I'm more hands-on than any other engineering manager you have because I love what I do."

Chuck gulped the last of his brandy and slid forward on the seat's edge. "What do you need? How quick can we get in?"

"Not so fast. We need to keep this quiet. I suspect we have an Interplanetary spy in the company, and we can't let him steal this."

Chuck pursed his lips. "What makes you think we have a spy?"

"Either we're the unluckiest people to have so many problems with our company, or someone is feeding sensitive information to Interplanetary. Luck has a way of balancing out over time, so I'm betting on the spy."

Frank pointed to the glassware on the top shelf, standing among volumes of paper books, and continued, "It wasn't a coincidence the government set a tariff just in time to scuttle Smithers' deal."

"He was upset, but I never heard the details."

"Jack put in a lot of time testing different sands and glass-blowing techniques suitable for high-quality mass production. Then Washington set the tariff that'd allow only the rich to afford his art. Jack was crushed when he realized he'd never turn a profit."

"That's typical. Washington takes that sort of action all the time." Chuck shook his head. "What's your plan?"

"We hire an archaeologist to translate the symbols, so we can access the cavern. I found one who should work out."

"Hold on. This is getting expensive. It'll cost a premium to get an Earther to Mars. I don't know if the risk is worth the reward."

"Chuck, if we don't take risks, Interplanetary will swallow us whole. I've been hearing rumors from well-placed friends that Interplanetary's making moves. Starting with shipping regulations."

"Information from your mysterious Earth friends?"

Frank didn't want to go down that road again. Chuck had always been suspicious whenever he'd mentioned receiving information from Earth because Frank couldn't reveal his sources, the Knowledge Keepers. "I know you see the writing on the wall. This is a great opportunity to break Earth's hold on us... or at least, loosen their grip."

After a few seconds, Chuck nodded. "Unfortunately, you're more right than I care to admit. But if I'm gonna spend this much money, I want to choose the best candidate."

"Most of the good archaeologists are already working on projects either directly sponsored or indirectly funded by Interplanetary. We'd have to wait months after we thumb off on the contract before our candidate would free up, which would give Interplanetary plenty of time to subvert them. Either they'd undermine us by feeding Interplanetary our findings, or they'd sabotage the project outright. We need a talented archaeologist, who's immediately available and doesn't have ties to Interplanetary."

"That's a tall order. Their influence knows few boundaries. How'd you find your archaeologist?"

"I used Earth's HR Acquisition Network."

Chuck's eyes flashed with anger. "You can't break into government computer systems! You'll bring down a mountain of trouble on us."

"It's okay. I didn't break in. I used proper credentials."

"Only Human Resources personnel are authorized for that system." Chuck shook his head. "I don't even want to know who you sweet-talked and what you promised."

"It's nothing like that. I used an Earth developer's credentials. I guarantee it can't be traced back to us."

Frank had connected to a Knowledge Keeper computer system, which had better safeguards than any corporation or government, before accessing the HR Acquisition Network.

Anyone attempting to trace his searches would discover their origin in a Buddhist temple in India, an environmental group in Iceland, or some other equally improbable location.

"I suppose you're not going to share how you have those credentials?" Chuck's expression was somewhere between anger and amusement.

"They're a friend's." The credentials were actually a fellow Knowledge Keeper's who worked for the contractor that had built and maintained the software.

"For someone who has never stepped foot on Earth, you sure have lots of friends there."

Frank had wanted to divulge his Knowledge Keeper ties more times than he could count, but doing so would color Chuck's view of him. The Knowledge Keepers perpetuated a reputation for being crackpots whenever anyone stumbled across their activities.

"Chuck, we've been friends since before the split. You know you can trust me. There's nothing much more to tell."

"Yet, I suspect I haven't heard the best part." Chuck looked him over for a few long seconds. "If it were anyone else, I'd demand more answers, but I do trust you. Perhaps, someday you'll share the rest of the story."

Frank nodded. "Perhaps."

"I take it that you don't trust our own HR department and that's why you went to all the trouble to find your own candidate."

While true, Frank had hoped the Knowledge Keepers could recommend qualified archaeologists. Unfortunately, none of the replies to his electronic bulletin board request had panned out. Most already had assignments and the others had ties to Interplanetary. Only as a last resort had he accessed the HR Acquisition Network.

Frank nodded. "I planned to select candidates from the beginning. I'm not about to give the search criteria away and telegraph our plan. More importantly, I was looking for a certain quality—something extra—but I wasn't sure exactly how to define it."

"Tell me about your archaeologist and the 'something extra' he has."

Frank called up a summary on his datapad and handed it over. "*Her* name's Gretchen Blake. She's nearing completion of a three-month expedition in Antarctica. She's done well on her previous expeditions, and her scholastic record is impressive."

"Yes, I see. But her current project leader gave her a poor performance review and blackballed her. Shouldn't that disqualify her?"

"Isn't it strange he'd evaluate her performance before the dig has even concluded?" Frank let the question hang there as he drank the rest of his brandy and set the glass aside.

"Chuck, we'll be betting a lot on this move, so I want you to have all the facts. Dr. Hawthorne's evaluation indicates he disagrees with Ms. Blake's conclusions. I don't have enough information to judge the particulars, but they're not important. What is important, is that she—a junior team member—stood up for what she believed, and she wouldn't back down. That shows me her heart. She values the truth. That's the something extra I was searching for, something I rarely see in Earthers."

"I know plenty of Earthers like Hawthorne. In some way, the problem always points to the ego." He handed the datapad back to Frank and folded his hands in his lap. "The regs require an in-person interview. I'll send Arnold. I don't trust our Earthside employment agency."

Chuck had just addressed another of Frank's concerns. "Me neither. Do me a favor. Wait until Arnold's underway to give him Ms. Blake's name, and don't share the task details."

"It'll raise Arnold's suspicions when I don't tell him why we're hiring an archaeologist."

Frank nodded. "If he's solid, Arnold will be confused and irritated. But if he's our spy, then you're saving the company. Let's err on the side of caution."

"You know the board will question the expense."

"We need to keep this to ourselves. Our spy could be on the board."

"I can't believe any board member would sell us out."

"Bunderbon's iffy if you ask me." Frank was relieved to finally share his long-held belief.

"He's a pain, but that doesn't mean he's a spy."

"I can see Konklin paying him to relay everything he sees, and he sees a lot as VP of Operations. Plus, he's a new hire since the split."

"I'll agree that anyone can be the spy, but I'm not gonna make accusations without evidence." Chuck looked at Frank for a long second.

"Fair enough, but he's ambitious, and ethics aren't his strong suit."

"Agreed." Chuck sighed. "You know our spy, or whoever's handling him, will target Ms. Blake."

"Damn, you're right." Frank had completely missed that angle. His disappointment over his failed relationship with Erin was still muddling his thinking. If he didn't snap out of it, he could blow this opportunity. "No matter how secret we keep the project, Ms. Blake will still be a new face walking around. People will notice."

"We're putting the company's future in her hands, and we'll have to share a lot of information with her that we don't want Interplanetary to have. You'll need to keep a close eye on her."

Frank nodded. "Yeah. We're walking a tightrope. One wrong step and we hand Interplanetary the Marsium121."

"Not only the Marsium121—eventually, MarsVantage itself."

3 | ENDINGS AND BEGINNINGS

After a late supper in their encampment's Mess Hall, Gretchen walked toward her quarters, her footfalls crunching the hardened snow of the path. Above her, the Aurora Australis swirled in brilliant shades of green and red with hints of yellow and pink.

She witnessed one of nature's wonders firsthand, something few people ever would. Along with the wondrous show, a hot meal put the Hawthorne confrontation into proper perspective. His laziness was his business, but she refused to feel bad about doing the job properly.

At the rightmost of the five Quonset huts, she entered, removing her gloves and unzipping her parka. She strode the hallway, as quietly as possible while wearing snow boots, past quarters where she overheard a couple having sex through the paper-thin walls. She reached a door with "G Blake" scribbled on a hand-torn piece of masking tape and opened it. Her spartan quarters held a cot with her guitar beneath it, a folding chair, an aluminum table with her computer and datapad atop it, and a folding stand holding her duffel bag of cold weather gear.

Gretchen stripped to her thermal underwear and pulled up *Earth Today* on her computer. The stories were much the same as every other day. A U.S. congressman proposed another grand plan to solve the budget deficit that other politicians would never agree to, and another holo star went on a three-day bender that ended in the hospital.

Finally, Gretchen found a Kuristan election article but was disappointed to see the opposition party had fared poorly. Jimmy hoped a more representative government would bring long-needed reforms. She desperately wanted to click on the three links to his video reports at the end of the story, but their limited bandwidth and the subsequent video buffering would only frustrate her. She skipped them. She'd see him soon enough.

Just before closing the news, a short article regarding the possibility of quarantining Mars imports caught her eye. Since the horrible tragedy over a decade ago, the Marsees had put up with ridiculous nuisances like this. The truth of the matter was that the vast majority of Mars imports were various types of mined ore used in orbital-based manufacturing, which couldn't contaminate anything. She shook her head at the waste of effort.

Next, Gretchen checked her email and reviewed the subject lines. There wasn't anything work-related. How could that be? She did excellent work. Why weren't any of the upcoming expeditions interested?

But she did have an email from Jimmy. The subject line read, "Our Marriage Contract." She glanced at the send date and held her breath as she realized her fifth wedding anniversary was only a month away. Thirty days was the legal notification deadline when one partner of a childless couple didn't wish to renew for another five-year term.

Barely able to swallow, she touched the Open button, as if it would burn her. The first paragraph was legalese stating his intent not to renew. Tears slid down her cheeks, which she wiped away with an open palm. The remainder of the email was a personal message:

While I still love you dearly, our marriage isn't working. We're not growing as a couple, and the reason is that we're rarely together. Either you're exploring a remote site, or I'm halfway around the globe reporting on a story.

You're a wonderful, amazing person, and I'm fortunate to have known you. Perhaps if we were more established in our careers, we would've been perfect together. But as matters stand, we're a couple in name only. You deserve more, and I need more.

I'm truly sorry to break the news to you this way, but the legal requirements are specific. I wish you all the best in the future. Take care.

Gretchen's analytical side forced her emotions to shut down. She composed and sent a dispassionate acknowledgment. Afterward, she leaned back in her chair, lacking the desire to move, her mind numb.

As the shock wore off, Gretchen's spine protested the ill-fitting chair. She turned off the computer and overhead light before retreating to the warmth of her cot. On her back, she closed her eyes, wishing for the release of sleep, but her thoughts raced.

As hard as she tried otherwise, she couldn't get Jimmy out of her mind. She fondly recalled their last vacation, laying on the beach beside him, and their visit to the expansive Cape Canaveral Museum. They'd had so many good times.

Now, it was all gone. They wouldn't share romantic meals and funny holos anymore. Never again would she laugh at their inside jokes nor feel his gentle, loving caress. It was over, in the time it'd taken her to read an email.

Without warning, she sobbed uncontrollably, her shoulders convulsing against the thin mattress. She pressed her hands to her eyes, unable to stem the flowing tears.

Her closest relationship had coasted along until it'd crashed. And why wouldn't it? She'd failed to put in the required effort. Jimmy was like a plaything she enjoyed until a new dig came along. Then she put him back on the shelf and was off.

Gretchen fought to regain control. The last thing she needed was for someone to hear and come investigating.

Did she have to choose between the field and a husband? Fieldwork was the path to leading expeditions or lecturing the next generation. What choice did she have? Give up her dreams for a man? No, not even for Jimmy.

When she returned to civilization five days from now, she'd be far busier than she'd planned. She'd have to move out of the house, not only because she and Jimmy were no longer a couple, but because the Housing Ministry would never approve of a single person assigned so much space.

Afterward, she'd have to find work. She had enough saved to get by for a few months, but when that ran out, the Housing Ministry would assign her to public housing, which was free, but the cost was high, for it was filthy, ill-maintained, and crime-ridden.

Gretchen wiped her eyes and cheeks with her thermal underwear top, leaving it damp against her chest. As she tugged her wedding band from her finger, her heart sank. She stretched to the desk and dropped it, hearing an unnatural clank. She slumped back down, feeling as if a part of herself was missing. Again, tears flowed down her cheeks.

She and Jimmy were no more.

4 | CONSPIRACY

"**D**amn. Of all the days to sleep through my alarm," Peter Konklin muttered as he glanced at his platinum Rolex watch with diamond chip hour markers. Today was the day that he'd take a giant step forward to reclaim what was rightfully his—MarsVantage, a company he'd built from the ground up.

He sighed. After twelve years of waiting, another thirty minutes wouldn't make a difference.

Dressed in a charcoal Italian suit, Peter stood on the Carrara marble landing, waiting for the private express elevator that linked his penthouse in Konklin Tower on Central Park West to the lobby below. When the door opened, he marched inside and ordered, "Proceed."

The doors shut and, twenty seconds and twenty floors later, they reopened upon the lobby. He hastened past the concierge, acknowledging him with a subtle nod before exiting through the glass double-doors.

A fire-extinguisher-sized police drone zipped by a couple yards overhead as Peter stepped on to the sidewalk. Not only was New York City on the cultural and business vanguard, its reputation for protecting its denizens' safety was known worldwide. He wouldn't live anywhere else.

A drunken derelict stumbled into him and collapsed. Peter stepped over the man's prone, shaggy-haired form as cheap vodka from the bottle he'd been cradling gushed onto the sidewalk with a gurgle.

Peter brushed his suit jacket to verify booze hadn't splashed on him and sniffed his lapel to ensure the bum's stench hadn't rubbed off, either. All was fine. He didn't need to waste more time changing clothes.

At the sidewalk's edge, he looked to the traffic signal a block to his left and picked out his black, stretched auto-cab from Elite Transportation nestled among the red, yellow, and blue auto-cabs used by the common people. Only a few, like powerful politicians, A-list celebrities, and influential business executives, could afford to contract with Elite. And that was the reason he'd chosen them.

When the light turned green, his auto-cab—gliding a foot above the guide rail embedded in the street—pulled to the curb and swung open its door. Peter stepped in and sunk into the rightmost seat facing forward. This model had room for six, three of which faced the rear. Even when traveling alone, he always ordered the large model. After all, appearances were crucial.

"Destination please?" the auto-cab requested in a pleasant, feminine voice.

If he didn't know better, he would've sworn he was speaking with a woman. "Peter Konklin Interplanetary Headquarters."

The auto-cab repeated the destination and merged into traffic.

After retrieving a datapad from his inside suit jacket pocket, Peter extended the screen and vidcommed his assistant. "I'm running late. Push the MarsVantage conference back a half hour."

"Yes, sir. Is there anything else?"

Out of the corner of his eye, he noticed Morton's Clothiers through the window. While fine clothing was sold in the front, for those in the know, the back room sold the best black market goods in the city. "I need more cigars."

His assistant's smile faded a degree. "Yes, sir. I'll take care of it."

Over the years, he'd surmised that she disliked running black market errands. She should thank him for not sending her to the seedy sellers that hopped among abandoned buildings.

Peter disconnected the vidcomm and contemplated MarsVantage. Once, it'd been a bright jewel in Peter Konklin Interplanetary's crown... before the government stole it from him twelve years ago, causing him as much pain as if they'd severed his perfectly healthy right hand.

He didn't *want* MarsVantage back—he needed it. No matter what the incorporation records indicated at the moment, it was his. With it, he intended to exploit Mars to become even richer and more powerful.

On the datapad's screen, Peter glanced over MarsVantage's shipped ore figures and grudgingly admired their efforts. They'd had their best month ever, achieving ninety-nine percent cargo utilization. They were producing more than he'd dreamed possible from their limited resources. If he were in charge with all of his capabilities, he could do things the Marsees could only dream of.

The auto-cab pulled up to his headquarters. Slowly and confidently Peter exited. Everyone—employees and public alike—should glimpse the upper-class life they'd never have. He wore the best clothes and rode in the best auto-cabs. More importantly, he belonged to the elite who created the rules for the masses to follow. He was their better, and they needed to be reminded of it at every opportunity.

With an easy, practiced smile, Peter strolled between fountains where red and green lasers displayed his diamond logo on water jetting upward. Once inside, he took an elevator to the building's top floor and entered his outer office where he nodded to his assistant.

Nancy Kaine, the head of Corporate Security, followed and took a visitor's chair while he settled in behind the desk. He vidcommed Tom Davidson, his primary lobbyist in Washington, D.C. After a second, the point-to-point encryption synced, and Tom's image appeared.

"Welcome, everyone," Peter said. "Let me start off by saying nice work. Our first step is proceeding as planned."

"Thank you." Nancy folded her hands in her lap atop her closed datapad as she said, "All the Earth-side shipping vendors placed their orders some time ago, and most have completed the safety upgrades."

"When Congress reconvenes next week, our friends will push through new legislation based on the safety study you underwrote," Tom added.

"Corporate Communications will then issue a press release announcing that our shippers are already upgrading, and that we call on the government to mandate it across the board," Nancy said.

Tom's image looked squarely at them. "If I may suggest, now's the right time to stage an accident on Mars. This time, you make it work to your favor."

"No, the timing's wrong." Peter's face was expressionless.

"It'll take forever at this rate," Tom said.

"Not forever, but months, perhaps years," Peter said. "Does anyone have anything better to do?"

Nancy and Tom laughed as Peter grinned at his own joke.

Peter continued, "Thirteen years ago, the public turned against us after an accident. That bad PR prompted the government to force our divestiture of MarsVantage a year later. Another accident at this time won't drive public opinion to us. No, we need MarsVantage to battle bad PR and struggle with rising costs on their own. When they're on the brink of bankruptcy, I'll buy them."

"I advise against that strategy," Tom said. "You're allowing the Marsees too much opportunity to adjust. Why not overwhelm them, buy them, and deal with the PR fallout afterward?"

Peter shook his head. "We can handle anything the Marsees can muster. It's not enough to have half of Congress in my pocket. I want the public and the press on my side, too. Otherwise, reporters will hound me, eventually prodding Congress to do something against my interests. Trust me, we'll manipulate the situation, the press, and the people to my liking."

On screen, Tom shifted in his chair. "The alternative is to funnel more cash to our congressmen and have them mold public opinion. It's a tried and true tactic that's worked for centuries."

"It may work, except the politicians will have to admit they miscalculated by splitting us apart," Nancy said as she looked to Peter, who nodded. "Peter's way affords them cover. They can say, 'We tried local rule for the Marsees, but they couldn't handle it.'"

Peter nodded, "Exactly."

Tom tilted his head slightly, keeping his face neutral. "It's your call. There are risks either way."

Peter leaned back and adjusted his silk tie to lie flat against his stomach. "We've kept steady low-grade pressure on MarsVantage for years. The shipper upgrades are the first move in reacquiring MarsVantage. Compliance is the next step. Tom, I'd like you to whisper in the right ears that the Taxation Authority should audit MarsVantage. I don't believe they've seen an auditor in years. Also, there are a half-dozen agencies with oversight responsibility, and I believe they're overdue in conducting inspections. Light a fire under them, quietly. Mars is a dangerous place. They're only independent because the government believed they'd handle safety better than us. It's time for them to prove it."

"Excellent, Peter. Just so you know, I've been inquiring along those lines already. I'll follow up on that."

"We should keep the space microbes scare going," Nancy said. "No one's seriously questioning it, and when there's a health scare, maybe we can tie it back to MarsVantage's mining exports."

Peter folded his hands on the desktop. "I like it. Nothing's lost if it doesn't pay off. But if it does, we can suggest a six-month quarantine. That'll throw a monkeywrench into MarsVantage's cash flow."

Tom scribbled a note. "I'll handle it."

"Remember, the hangman doesn't trigger the trapdoor until the noose is snugly around the victim's neck." Peter interlaced his fingers, placing his hands on the desk. "The steps we're discussing are necessary, but they take time. When MarsVantage is on the brink of failure, another accident will push public opinion in our direction. With enough bodies on the deck, Congress will follow like a tail on a dog. That's also a tried and true tactic. Trust me, I'll buy MarsVantage at a bargain basement price, and I'll hang my logo on the headquarters building myself."

5 | LESSON REVEALED

On the upper level of the Baker Street Club, Gretchen looked from the stage and empty seats below to Ashley, sitting across the table. "Thanks for coming down to Charleston. You wouldn't believe how much I needed a break from moving."

"It gave me an excuse to wear a nice dress," Ashley said, her eyes sparkling.

"And makeup, too." Gretchen smoothed her dress against her thighs. She never bothered with nice clothes and makeup on expeditions. Fossils and artifacts didn't care how she looked.

"Every now and then, I miss the nicer things when out in the field." Ashley took a sip of white wine.

"Isn't that funny? I only missed Jimmy." Gretchen looked away and exhaled. Instead of relaxing on hot beach sands with him at her side, she'd spent her time home packing, moving, and unpacking.

"I'm so sorry about you two. I had no idea you were having problems."

"Me neither," Gretchen said flatly. She ran her left thumb on the underside of her ring finger. The absence of her wedding band felt odd. "Sorry. I'm still adjusting. Apparently, I'm not succeeding."

Ashley reached across the table and gave Gretchen's hand a comforting squeeze. "You have every right to be upset. Jimmy never gave you an opportunity to work out your issues."

"I was so focused on my career that I didn't realize he was miserable. Ashley, I thought things were terrific. I was happy."

"Any chance for a reconciliation?"

Gretchen shook her head. "No. We spent more time apart than together, and he wants a marriage where his wife's in town when he is. I'm not willing to give up archaeology, not even for him."

Right now, her career came first. Because she didn't have connections, she paid her dues by working in the field. She'd never considered Jimmy's feelings or desires when taking a job. It'd never crossed her mind that he might've been unhappy.

Since reading his email, one question haunted her—had she really loved Jimmy?

Ashley asked, "How's the new apartment?"

"Good, a little bigger than I expected. I'm almost unpacked."

"I was surprised to hear that you moved so quickly."

It hadn't been quick enough. In the house, alone, packing her belongings, knowing she'd never see Jimmy again weighed on her, dredging up memories of their time together. *Enough of him.* Tonight was about breaking free of the negativity. "I contacted a high school friend who works for the Housing Ministry. She counseled me on how to complete the forms to get the best place available and then walked my application through the bureaucracy."

"Good for you—battling the bureaucracy with its own bureaucrats."

Gretchen uncrossed her legs and leaned in. "Did you get a chance to talk to Dr. Pacyna about the expedition?"

Ashley took another sip of wine, a bigger sip. She placed the glass on the table and flopped her hands in her lap before audibly exhaling. "He appeared interested in my recommendation to fill a slot until I mentioned your name. After that, he said that he didn't think you'd be a good fit."

Gretchen's shoulders drooped a degree. "I was afraid of that. I think Hawthorne asked his friends not to hire me."

"It looks that way. I'm sorry."

Gretchen had dug herself a deep hole, one she might not escape. After a few seconds, she said, "I let my enthusiasm get ahead of the data."

"You may have, but you found the artifacts and wanted to understand their significance. There's nothing wrong with wanting to expand mankind's knowledge of itself. Those ideals and your integrity ought to be rewarded, not punished. Hawthorne's being petty and abusing his authority."

"I'm considering publishing a paper."

Ashley looked straight into her eyes. "Be careful. You already pissed him off. You don't want to make it worse."

"How much worse can I make it?"

"Good point." Ashley chuckled. "But seriously, I'd do it only if I could reveal a compelling reason for ancient people to sail to Antarctica. Without that, your theory falls apart. And if you do publish, please be diplomatic."

Gretchen always appreciated Ashley's tact. At times, others had complained that Ashley came off distant and even cold, and perhaps that was true. At least, she'd never pissed off her project leader and found herself on the outside looking in.

Ashley added, "I know you don't want to hear this, but you could send Hawthorne a note apologizing and expressing your gratitude for his wisdom. It may salvage the situation."

"You're right." Gretchen pursed her lips. "I don't want to hear it."

Ashley leaned in. "It turns my stomach to suck up to such a pompous jerk, but it could get you back in the field."

Apologizing could solve the problem, but the idea of submitting to Hawthorne's will disgusted Gretchen. No one would ever know the truth behind the artifacts if she did. "I wonder how much mouthwash I'd need once I finished kissing his fat ass."

"A very large bottle. And a shower."

They both laughed.

Gretchen said, "I had a weird vidcomm earlier today. A hiring manager from MarsVantage wants to discuss a job—an archaeology job."

"On Mars? What'd you say?"

"We set up an interview. Apparently, there are regulations about conducting in-person interviews."

Ashley rolled her eyes. "Doesn't surprise me. Though, you'd think they'd contract with an Earth-based employment agency. It's expensive to travel from Mars."

"Yeah, like I said, weird. I was thinking about canceling, but considering the Dr. Pacyna news, I need to hear this guy out."

Ashley looked straight into Gretchen's eyes. "Be careful. You don't want to do anything silly and get labeled crazy like the Marsees."

"I swear if he mentions aliens or UFOs, I'll walk away."

"Good."

The waiter appeared with two seafood sampler platters. Before moving on to another table, he said, "Your NutriAccounts have been updated. Enjoy your meals."

Gretchen's mouth watered at the aroma, particularly the Old Bay seasoning. For the past two days, she'd eaten cold food, mostly sandwiches and fruit, because it'd been quick, giving her more time for moving. Hot, fresh-caught seafood was exactly what she needed tonight. She tried a bite of everything on her plate, particularly enjoying the shrimp, crab cakes, and scallops.

Ashley focused on the flounder and oysters. Over her shoulder, she glanced at the stage as a roadie made final adjustments to the microphones. She faced Gretchen and asked, "Who are we seeing tonight?"

"Magda Carr. She's my favorite singer. I was amazed when I first saw her during my freshman year in college. You're going to love her."

"I've heard some of her songs. She's pretty good." Ashley took a bite of crab cake.

"Not only will she perform her own songs, she often covers old ones, some written centuries ago. She does a variety of genres but mainly sticks to folk rock, retro-pop, and folk fusion. You know, I spent hours listening to some obscure genres because of what I heard her perform." Gretchen paused for a moment. Why was Ashley smiling? "I'm going on, aren't I?"

"Yes, and I don't mind. For a few moments, you actually forgot your troubles and were happy."

"I don't mean to be so self-involved."

"Don't worry about it. You have a lot of problems, but they're temporary." Ashley turned, glanced at the stage again, then turned back. "She'll have three band members?"

"Only two, a guitarist and a drummer. She plays the piano. And you're in for a treat. Erik Blount is her guitarist for this tour. He's amazing. I still remember the first time I saw him. He made a series of chord changes so fast that I swore he had extra fingers. That was when I knew I'd be nothing more than an eager amateur guitarist."

Ashley's eyes widened. "I'm surprised to hear that. You've never dodged a challenge."

"It's not like I gave up playing. I take lessons whenever I'm home, but I certainly don't have the time or the skills to perform for paying customers."

"Don't sell yourself short. I always enjoy hearing you play."

"Thanks."

They finished their meals and paid the waiter as the house lights dimmed. Men in tailored suits and women in stylish dresses, all holding drinks, started to fill the seats before the stage. Like others on the upper level, Ashley dragged her chair to sit beside Gretchen, so she could comfortably watch the show.

At last, bathed in blue stage lights, Magda appeared to applause with her supporting musicians in tow—Erik Blount, carrying an acoustic guitar, and a drummer Gretchen didn't recognize. Magda stood center-front before a microphone as her band took their places.

Unlike previous shows where she'd begun with "Some Still Dream," one of her well-known hits, tonight she began with a 300-year-old song written in the 1970s, accompanied only by Erik on the acoustic guitar. His picking was haunting as Magda sang of man's mortality.

Gretchen's sadness worsened as the words expressed the true nature of life: It begins. It ends. Always. She realized that what mattered was what she did in between. That revelation brought a sense of peace. Being upset with Jimmy solved nothing. Accepting the circumstances, moving forward, and learning from her mistakes was the only healthy choice. As the song ended, she grinned and applauded enthusiastically.

Magda performed many originals, spanning her twenty-year career. Interspersed between them were several covers, including a 22nd century swing-techna dance tune and a 100-year-old retro-pop anthem. Gretchen looked over to Ashley several times. She was enjoying herself, clapping to the beat along with the crowd.

Near the end, Magda—awash in yellow lights—wiped sweat from her forehead and stood before the microphone. "Those of you who follow me know I've been married seventeen years, and I'll tell you that every day is hard work. But the work is worth it. I cherish love, cultivate it, and most of all, give it priority in my life. My upcoming release is about discovering these lessons. This next song is from that album, and it's about encouraging and growing with love. It's entitled 'Love's Work.'"

Magda sang *a cappella*, softly at first, growing in intensity, until the drums joined, followed shortly afterward by an electric guitar.

Gretchen listened closely, riveted by the performance. Partway through, the words hit home, especially the lyric:

> *You'll only receive as much as you invest.*
> *You can never give too much love.*
> *And you won't believe how much you'll get in return.*

Gretchen had been foolish—she saw it clearly now. Every job she'd undertaken had been a choice with consequences, and she now understood. She'd never returned Jimmy's love as he had given it. Instead, she'd taken all of his until he was empty.

As reluctant as she was to admit it, she was responsible for her marriage's demise. Jimmy had recognized the problems and been wise enough to end it. He hadn't complained or guilted her into staying home, but he must've been unhappy for some time. He deserved a partner who would be equally invested in the relationship.

In the future, she mustn't make the same mistake. She'd find a balance between love and work. She swore to herself she'd work as hard on her next relationship as she did on her career.

Perhaps, she'd wait a few years until she was better established. She'd be in a better position to give a future partner the attention he deserved. She'd brought unhappiness to Jimmy, and she couldn't do that to anyone else.

By the song's end, she was dabbing tears from her eyes with a napkin.

Ashley leaned close. "Are you okay?"

"Yeah, I think I am. I really do."

6 | THE PAST'S LONG SHADOWS

The Caretaker approached the city's ruined manufacturing section. A new thought had occupied him while he searched for signs of damage. The treasures he'd sworn to safeguard, so long ago, were worthless unless reunited with the Bvindu.

Had the manufacturing section, in particular the Heavy Construction Factory, not been damaged beyond his ability to repair, he could've constructed a ship, like those used in search of a new homeworld, and found his people. When the intruders had crashed through the dome, that option had been lost.

Without choices, the Caretaker performed his duty, not knowing whether it was meaningful anymore. He longed for the Bvindu return with news of a new homeworld, but that hope was as dead as this planet.

In the center of the ruined manufacturing section, he inspected the dome repair he'd made 102 orbits ago. As he expected, it continued to hold at bay the slowly drifting sand.

Surrounded by several large chunks of rubble, the Caretaker struggled with memories of that time. Hardest to accept was the death of thirty beings. Although they weren't Bvindu, they were obviously intelligent and similar enough, though they only had two arms. Twelve of these beings, occupying two treaded ground transports, hadn't survived the plunge. The rest had been scattered among the reddish-brown sand and rubble of the ruined factory buildings, all exhibiting scorch marks from the intruder-control system.

While performing the repairs, he'd faced the prospect of death—an unusual occurrence for any Bvindu—when an actuator in his right tread had begun to overheat. Even if the Bvindu hadn't placed strict safeguards against the Caretaker copying himself, he never would've done so—he wouldn't consign another self to the virtual imprisonment he'd endured all these orbits. If he hadn't made it back to the Master Control Center, he would've perished after the mobile unit's power drained.

Is waiting for something that probably would never happen any better than death? Is there a difference?

7 | INTERVIEW OF A CAREER

Gretchen glanced at the clock. She had to leave in a few minutes for the interview. If it didn't go well, she planned to update her profile to add her willingness to perform service work. She'd lived off tips from rude people to put herself through college once, and she'd do it again to earn the remaining credits for her teaching certificate.

In the bathroom mirror, she checked her appearance, every aspect meant to project a professional image while reinforcing the impression of being comfortable in the field where niceties like tailored clothes and makeup were only fond memories. Her shoulder-length hair was pulled back into a practical ponytail, and her makeup was light. She chose a simple slacks and blouse combination, complete with black flats. After a few seconds, she shook her head and said to her reflection, "If your HR profile doesn't speak for itself, it doesn't matter how much makeup you wear."

Gretchen departed her second-floor apartment. Rather than waiting on the elevator, she took the stairs and exited the building through glass double-doors. Like most mornings, she walked past clumps of seedy-looking people smoking joints and drinking from liquor bottles. Their greatest ambition was to numb themselves day in and day out. Every year, the government programs, designed to provide for their basic needs, enabled their unfulfilled lives.

So much wasted potential—so many destroyed lives. *I'll waitress before turning to that.*

A delivery auto-truck bearing the NutriGroceries logo sped above the embedded guide rail in the road, which reminded her to change her food delivery address. She pulled her datapad from her pocket and made a note to do it later.

After crossing the street and walking a block, she entered The Roasted Bean, a conscious smile masking her doubts. At a corner table, she spotted the MarsVantage hiring manager, Arnold Janssen, and introduced herself. He bought her a coffee and a refill for himself before they settled in.

"We're pretty informal on Mars. Is it okay if I call you Gretchen?"

"Sure," she answered, her stomach tightening.

"Terrific, feel free to call me Arnold." He sipped his coffee. "You know, this is a real treat for me. Mars-grown coffee is bland, and it's too expensive to import Earth coffee for everyday consumption."

"It's a delicious blend." She took a sip, hoping it wouldn't make her stomach ache worse. "Actually, it's one of my favorites."

For twenty minutes, they discussed her schooling and work experience. Arnold focused on the working conditions. She emphasized her experiences in hostile settings such as the Arizona desert in summer and Antarctica, which were the most extreme places she'd ever worked.

"Good, good," Arnold said as he referred to his datapad. "Next, I need to cover some Mars-specific items. You understand this position requires that you travel to Mars, which will take approximately a month."

"Yes, I do."

"The duration of the task can range from two to six weeks. Will that pose a problem?"

"No. I'll need data and vidcomm access while en route, though."

"That's expensive. May I ask why?"

"I'm working on a paper related to my last dig. I need access to Earth resources to complete it."

"You can't put that off until you return?"

"No. The project leader and I interpreted the artifacts differently. I need to get my interpretation published. The sooner I do, the better the chance to attach myself to a new expedition."

Arnold placed his datapad on the table and audibly exhaled. "You may want to reconsider. You didn't hear it from me, but Dr.

Hawthorne has essentially blackballed you in his evaluation attached to your HR file."

"You're joking." Ashley had confirmed that Hawthorne's friends were avoiding hiring her, but Gretchen couldn't believe he'd make his displeasure official. If true, her future in the field as an archaeologist was basically over.

After a second's pause, Arnold said through an expressionless face, "I'm afraid not."

"That explains a lot."

"I expect that publishing your paper will only exacerbate the problem."

"Or resolve it." She took the last sip of coffee. She suspected Arnold was right. It didn't matter—she had to understand the truth and bring that knowledge to light. At least, she had to try.

"Perhaps so." Arnold made a note on his datapad. "We'll pay for vidcomm and data access. I have a few more questions. Do you get auto-cab or air-sick?"

"Is that important?"

"With Mars' gravity a third of Earth's, we have found people who experience motion sickness have more difficulty adjusting. It's not disqualifying but helpful for planning purposes."

"Oh, I never heard that. No, I don't get motion sick."

"One last thing. According to your profile, you're not certified in a spacesuit."

"Correct. I've never seen one in person, let alone worn one."

"Most people haven't. You can certify inbound to Mars. We'll pick up the cost, of course. And it'll pass the time." He made another note. "I only have a few more things. A fair amount of the job requires traveling by tractor outside the domes and spending a portion of your time underground. Are you claustrophobic?"

"No. You don't last long as an archaeologist if you can't work in cramped spaces."

"Excellent." He entered a figure on his datapad and showed her. "Here's the salary we're talking about. While on Mars, we'll pay you that sum per week. We guarantee a minimum of two weeks' work with any partial week afterward prorated up to a full day. We'll pay half salary for the trip to and from Mars. Also, we'll provide a private room, meals—no NutriAccount required—and clothing during travel and planetside. Do you find this acceptable?"

Gretchen performed a few mental calculations, assuming only two weeks' work, and figured the fee, including travel time, would cover nearly a year's rent. With a part-time job, she could pick up the outstanding credits for her teaching certificate. As a bonus, MarsVantage would pay her to write her Antarctica paper. It was almost too good to be true. "Yes, assuming I believe I can do the work. Which brings to mind my biggest question, why do you need an archaeologist on Mars?"

He laughed. "I honestly don't know. The project is so secret that our CEO, Chuck O'Donnell, hasn't disclosed the details."

"Wait. You mean to tell me this Chuck O'Donnell went to the expense to send you the whole way here, and you don't know what the job is?"

Arnold shrugged. "Yes. It's all highly unusual. Chuck doesn't like spending money unnecessarily, but he refused to use the local employment agency. So I'm here to satisfy the regs about in-person interviews."

"You're a trooper, traveling all this way to meet with a few people."

Arnold grinned. "We agreed to make the trip a working vacation. I'm planning to take in several baseball games, maybe do some hiking and sightseeing. As long as it's outside in fresh air, I don't much care."

Given in Antarctica that she thought she'd never be warm again, she understood. "What's next?"

"I need you to thumb-off on a nondisclosure agreement." He opened it on his datapad and handed it over.

She read the contract, which, when translated from legalese to English, simply stated that she wouldn't disclose anything discussed with MarsVantage representatives today. She applied her thumb, entered her contact information to receive a copy, and returned the datapad.

Arnold applied his thumb to complete the agreement. "We need to vidcomm Chuck for the remainder of the interview. We can use one of the meeting rooms in my hotel. I'll call for an auto-cab."

* * *

At the Grand Harbor View Hotel, Arnold led Gretchen into a conference room, which held six chairs around a U-shaped table opposite a large vidcomm unit against the wall. She took a chair directly facing the screen, and after closing the door, he settled into another next to her. As far as interviews went, this was the strangest she'd ever had.

After Arnold transmitted his credentials from his datapad to the vidcomm, he entered the comm number and annoyingly tapped his forefinger against the keyboard until the call connected. An image of a fit, middle-aged man with signs of gray at the temples appeared. Arnold made introductions, and Chuck and Gretchen exchanged pleasantries.

"Has the nondisclosure agreement been executed?" Chuck asked.

Arnold nodded, and Gretchen said, "Yes."

"Excellent. Arnold, I'll take it from here. Please wait in the lobby. Gretchen will let you know when we're done."

With a subtle frown, Arnold left. He mustn't have cared for the arrangement. And who could blame him? How awkward was it to interview someone without having the job's details? Being asked to leave was just plain embarrassing.

Chuck continued, "Gretchen, this task is of the utmost importance to MarsVantage, and secrecy is paramount. Only one other person knows the details I'm about to share, so please don't discuss our conversation with anyone, including Arnold."

"I won't." Gretchen shifted in the chair and breathed deep.

"I know it seems paranoid—believe me, it isn't. We're sitting on a power source, but we're unable to access it. Our competitor, Peter Konklin Interplanetary, would like nothing more than to steal it. It's in a cavern, fronted by a cave, but we can't open what we believe is a door."

"A door? In a cave? That's fascinating! I don't see why you need an archaeologist, though."

"There is writing carved into the cave door. You should be seeing it now."

Gretchen leaned in and examined the image. "It's grainy. I can't discern many details."

"The picture is two decades old. The photographer took it out of curiosity, not believing he was documenting anything valuable."

Gretchen said, "The markings appear artificial. The grooves are too straight and the circles are too symmetrical to occur through natural means. Do you have any more?"

"That's it. Those symbols were a minor detail forgotten until a maintenance engineer was sorting through his late father's things."

"Where's the door to the cavern?"

"We believe those dark vertical lines running from top to bottom, bordering the writing, outline a doorway."

"I suppose. It's hard to tell."

"I understand," Chuck said, nodding.

Gretchen had seen dead languages carved in stone, pictograms painted in caves, and hieroglyphics in ancient Egyptian pyramids, but she'd never seen writing like that. "What makes you think there's an energy source inside the cavern?"

Chuck recounted the details about the Marsium121 stalactite and stalagmites believed to occupy the cavern. He concluded with, "A few years ago, we discovered that Marsium121 produced electricity under specific circumstances."

"Are you sure you don't need a geologist?"

Chuck laughed. "Gretchen, I like how you think. You're not letting me double-talk you."

"No, I'm not," she said, staring directly at his image on the vidcomm. Things weren't adding up. "Couldn't you just tunnel into the cavern, or excavate it?"

"Excellent question. No, we tried drilling but couldn't penetrate the cavern's shell. We fear greater force will cause landslides, probably destroying the Marsium121. We get in through the cave door or not at all. These symbols are the key to solving our energy problems."

"So this is just about money and profit? Don't you care about who inscribed those lines and circles in the cave? Don't you want to understand how the Marsium121 got outside? I don't mean to offend you, but shouldn't we get answers before exploiting and potentially ruining a valuable discovery?"

Instantly, Gretchen wished she'd used more tact and a measure of Ashley's diplomacy. Her chances of getting this job had just gone down the drain, all because she'd spoken before thinking.

Chuck picked up a pen and examined it as if it held the answers to her questions. "I'm not offended. We have a practical need for the cavern's contents. On Mars, practicality is overwhelmingly important because we don't have the resources to do research for research's sake. Along the way—and I should've been clear about this—we want to gain all the knowledge possible, because knowledge is nearly as valuable as energy. If you can discover the answers to your questions, I'd love to see them."

"I apologize for jumping to conclusions. I shouldn't have assumed motivations without any facts."

"History provides plenty of examples where science was subverted or ignored for personal or political gain. Don't worry about it."

Gretchen nodded. She was certain Hawthorne was doing just that by suppressing her Antarctica theory. One sure way to hold on to the top position was to hold back the up-and-comers.

More importantly, Chuck was giving her an opportunity to salvage the interview. "I'm curious as to how a cave wall on Mars came to have writing carved into it. And if it's a doorway like you believe, I'd love to discover who created it."

Chuck set his pen aside, folded his hands, and placed them on the desk. "Are you curious enough to discover the answers for yourself?"

While the circumstances were odd, the money was good. And the symbols—what a mystery. Plus, taking the job would diffuse Hawthorne's criticisms in her HR profile, especially if she received a good review from Chuck. Not to mention that success in solving the symbol mystery would enhance her reputation.

"I am."

8 | THE HARSH TRUTH

The door lock beeped. Nancy Kaine opened her eyes. A single lamp in the corner left a good portion of the hotel room in shadow, including the hallway door. As the chrome handle caught enough light to show its rotation, she covered her yawn as she sat up straight in the only armchair. Arnold Janssen walked in, his hair disheveled and his eyes bloodshot.

Automatically, the door swung shut with a dull thud.

"Janssen, how good of you to return to your hotel room. Do you realize other people have lives?"

He snorted. "I never thought otherwise. I had no appointments, so I spent my time how I wanted. If that inconvenienced you, maybe you'll keep that in mind for next time and make an appointment."

What she knew of Janssen was based solely on her operatives' reports. The situation presented the perfect opportunity to better understand the man before her. She stood. "Perhaps you're not interested in continuing your relationship with Peter Konklin Interplanetary?"

"Perhaps I don't like your attitude at such a late hour," Janssen replied squaring his shoulders. He crossed his arms and stared at her. "Perhaps I believe you want my information more than I need the few luxuries you're smuggling to me. Perhaps, you can report your failure to Mr. Konklin and see what he thinks."

"Very well." Nancy returned to her seat, crossing her legs and smoothing her skirt against them.

"That's it? How about an apology for breaking into my room and harassing me?"

"My apologies."

Janssen's reaction was about what she'd expected. He had clear boundaries, even when tired. Though he was content to pass along information, she doubted that he'd willingly get his hands any dirtier by performing tasks like sabotage. Better to know now than wind up disappointed for relying on him later.

Janssen sat on the bed's edge, kicked off his shoes, and rubbed his toes through the socks. He was probably suffering side-effects of the stronger Earth gravity, which was the price Marsees paid for not running gravcomp decking like civilized people.

"What's so important that you waited half the night for me?" Janssen asked, half of his face in shadow.

"Who are the candidates?"

"There's only one—Gretchen Blake. O'Donnell offered her the job, and she accepted."

"What makes Blake so special?"

"Beats me. She's bright, energetic, and engaging. She has field experience but nothing especially noteworthy. One unusual fact, though, is that her last project leader, Dr. Hawthorne, blackballed her. Since then, she hasn't been able to get work."

"What'll she be doing?"

"We only discussed admin details. O'Donnell finished the interview after ordering me out of the room. Then he offered her a job on the spot. Without consulting me."

That sounded like wounded pride. When the time was right, perhaps Nancy could use that to her advantage. For now, she pushed him again. "Didn't you think to listen at the door?"

"The vidcomm took place in a conference room downstairs. Even I know you can't turn a corner on Earth without appearing on a security monitor. I'm not spending my vacation in jail because I was caught with my ear to the door."

"Fair point." At least, he was intelligent and wouldn't compromise their operation. "When does she leave?"

"The day after tomorrow." He rubbed his eyes. "Wait. It's after midnight. Tomorrow."

Nancy stifled a yawn, putting a closed hand to her mouth. "Does she have any MarsVantage ties?"

"Not that I can see. I think she's desperate for work, though."

"If we arranged for a job here, do you think she'd break the contract?"

"I doubt it. When she met me after the interview, her smile was genuine, and she had a bounce in her step. My impression is that she values the truth and her integrity. She'll go to Mars because she gave her word."

"For the right price, anyone can be bought." The question, though, was whether Peter wanted her to remain on Earth. "On a different note, is there any possibility the Marsees have found aliens or alien tech?"

Janssen's bloodshot eyes grew wide. "Alien tech? You Earthers complain we're obsessed with that nonsense, but I notice it's you who are constantly bringing it up."

She stared at him.

Janssen shook his head. "No one said anything about aliens. No one ever does."

Nancy stood and started to leave.

"Wait a minute," Janssen said.

"Yes?"

"Things are getting hot. All the departments are redoubling their efforts looking for your spy... for me. I need the Earth job you promised."

"I'll pass that along to Peter."

"See that you do. Part of our deal was that I receive a position with Interplanetary back here on Earth."

"I'm well aware—I authorized the deal. Let me ask you this. If we give you a job on Earth now, how can you help us retake MarsVantage?"

The color drained from Janssen's face.

"When MarsVantage is properly part of Interplanetary, you'll get your transfer. The more quality information you provide, the quicker it'll happen. You have a lot of control over the process. I suggest returning to Mars, so you can tell us what Blake's doing, assuming we don't convince her to remain on Earth."

Nancy exited the room. She purposefully strode to the elevator, breathing deeply the entire way, and pressed the call button. Not bothering to cover her mouth, she surrendered to a yawn. With her pinkies, she wiped excess moisture from her eyes, careful not to smudge her makeup. At last, the car arrived and she entered.

The elevator announced in a pleasant, feminine voice, "Please state your destination or use the buttons near the door."

"Lobby."

Janssen's impressions and conclusions about Blake formed a compelling picture. A rarity these days, she forged her own trail to achieve her goals instead of meekly following the path of least resistance, and hoping for a good end. Nancy knew many like Blake, all working at Interplanetary. Peter sought and encouraged those traits, which was why he ran the most successful business on- or off-planet.

Nancy exited the elevator and walked through the lobby to the sidewalk. She pulled out her datapad and requested an auto-cab. Thirty seconds later, one pulled to the curb beside her.

It opened the door, and in a computerized voice, announced, "Welcome to People Movers. Where would you like to go?"

"Charleston International Airport, Gate F."

The auto-cab repeated her destination and added, "Thank you. Estimated arrival time is thirty-five minutes."

From her datapad, she vidcommed Peter. It was late, but he'd insisted on a call as soon as she finished with Janssen. Peter answered on the second ring, looking as alert as ever. Nancy outlined her conversation and presented two options to address the Blake situation.

Peter leaned back and rested his elbows on the chair's armrests, steepling his fingers before his face. "Buying off Blake to remain on Earth temporarily handles the problem. Eventually, they'll get someone to Mars. No, I like the idea of O'Donnell spending a small fortune to hire her. When she's completed the work, we'll acquire it and use it against them. We'll get all of the benefits with little effort and expense."

"I'll have Heather and John make an offer once she arrives on Mars." It was the riskier option. It'd be harder to convert MarsVantage's discovery to their advantage, but ultimately, it was the more rewarding choice.

"Have them offer a position within Interplanetary. It'll be easy work for generous pay."

"Blake's willing to travel to Mars for an archaeology job. Everything suggests she loves her work. I don't think she'll accept a sinecure."

Peter steepled his fingers. "If she refuses the job, offer her a pick of archaeological digs here on Earth. It's nothing to pull some strings. I can finally get something besides good PR out of sponsoring them."

"Doctor Hawthorne has blackballed her in the archaeology community."

"If that becomes a problem, I'll speak to him personally. Trust me, he'll have a change of heart."

9 | DIFFERENCES AND EXPECTATIONS

"**W**atch your step, Gretchen. Entering the OTP is tricky. There's a small dead zone between the ship and station's gravcomp flooring," cautioned Trip Hendricks, Engineering Chief and spacesuit operations instructor.

Gretchen followed him into the Orbital Transfer Point. Although her basic spacesuit training was over, she continued to learn much from him. A week ago, he'd taught her advanced skills like how to perform a spacesuit self-test, swap oxygen vests, and patch a spacesuit tear. After she'd expressed her hope to never need that last skill, he'd said, *"Better to know than not, don't you think?"*

The OTP was nearly indistinguishable from the transport. It had ducts and piping—all painted shades of gray—running along the ceiling and exposed control panels on the walls. Here, those panels, along with caution signs, were placed between wide cargo doors outlined in black and yellow warning stripes. Even the atmosphere had the same reprocessed metallic taste. Gretchen was already looking forward to a long vacation under colorful sunsets on the beach, breathing the salt air.

"Welcome to Mars orbit. From here, you'll catch a MarsVantage shuttle to the surface. It'll be a little while until you shove off. First, we need to offload their ore containers and transfer a load of fresh supplies." Trip looked around and placed his hands on his hips. "Once the Marsees arrive. They're usually here, waiting on us to complete docking procedures."

Multiple clangs and thunks drew Gretchen's attention across the capacious transfer bay to the station's far side. Several seconds later, a woman and man entered, wearing spacesuits minus helmets and gloves. While the man worked a control panel, the woman, who didn't appear much older than Gretchen, walked toward them.

A large floor to ceiling cargo door rumbled aside, revealing the shuttle's packed cargo bay. A handful of people started to scurry about, preparing to offload standard bulk transport containers.

"Hey, Trip," the woman said. "How was the run?"

"Smooth, as always." He smiled broadly as his eyes twinkled. "You're running late today."

"Yeah. Routine maintenance on the landing bay planetside ran long."

"Where are my manners?" Trip said. "Gretchen, Erin Knox, pilot and Manager of Flight Operations. Erin, Gretchen Blake, your new consultant."

Gretchen shook Erin's hand. Business-like and quick, merely a matter of manners, not a genuine welcoming gesture, but it didn't matter. The next time Gretchen would see her would be in a few weeks when she returned home.

"Give me your datachip." Erin pointed to her left at six curtained stalls. "While I set up your datapad, put on a spacesuit for the trip planetside."

Gretchen fished the datachip from her coveralls pocket and handed it over before going to the changing booth. Once inside, Gretchen found a complete spacesuit and followed the instructions Trip had drilled into her. She emerged carrying a bag containing her boots in one hand and the helmet holding the gloves in the other.

Erin laughed at something Trip had said, and a few seconds later, laughed again, harder. Trip glanced Gretchen's way and nodded with a grin before returning to the transport.

After Erin joined her, she handed over a datapad. It was slightly larger than her model back home, though it still fit comfortably in her hand. Reportedly, standard Earth datapads couldn't handle Mars' harsh environment—the radiation, apparently—so Washington had established regulations preventing their transport beyond Earth orbit, which was inconvenient. It'd forced her to utilize the basic computer in her quarters on the transport, but better safe than sorry.

After she placed her helmet on a nearby bench, Gretchen extended the screen and familiarized herself with her new datapad. She browsed the info channels, but they were empty. The Marsees probably didn't waste money to uplink them into orbit.

The channel headings were telling, though: 'News,' 'Sports,' 'Weather,' and 'Entertainment.' Beneath were duplicates, except they were prefixed with 'Earth.' Obviously, the Marsees considered Mars home and Earth merely a place of interest. Apparently, there was something to all of the talk about the Marsees having problems with Earthers. She added that to the list of topics to be careful about. The last thing she wanted was to step on toes or worse, have them see and treat her as an ignorant outsider.

Gretchen spot-checked her personal information from her datachip. As expected, everything was there, including the research notes for the Antarctica paper as well as the paper itself that she'd forwarded to the *Journal of Archaeology* a week ago.

"Gretchen, follow me," Erin said. "We're shoving off. Don't forget your bag, helmet, and gloves. No one rides on my ship without proper equipment."

After shoving her datapad into a thigh pocket of her spacesuit, Gretchen grabbed her equipment and followed Erin across the transfer bay to the shuttle's hatch.

"Come up front with me," Erin said, directing Gretchen to the copilot's seat.

Gretchen settled in with her helmet on her lap and took in the outside view. Beyond Erin, who was already manipulating several controls, lay the transfer station's hull, cloaked in shadow. To her right were a thousand stars shining brightly. The copilot's console before her held more controls than she would've imagined necessary, so she consciously avoided touching anything.

"Try pressing your head against the side window and look down," Erin said.

Gretchen craned her neck and gazed at Mars, which appeared rusty like an old-fashioned, abandoned railroad rail. She made out darker areas and even some traces of white here and there, like faint wisps of clouds.

After Erin flicked a couple of switches, she said, "Wait here for a sec. I have to check the cargo before we detach."

So far, everything about the job was strange, from Chuck's interview to the idea of needing an archaeologist on Mars. And now, for the flight planetside, she was sitting in the co-pilot's seat next to a woman who barely acknowledged her. She'd tried to imagine and prepare for the strangeness of Mars, but she never expected this.

A couple of minutes later, Erin returned and donned an earset. "Flight Control, this is Captain Knox requesting approval for transfer from OTP to pad 1A." She paused for a couple of seconds, listening intently. "Copy that, control. I'm detaching now." Erin latched her five-point harness. "Gretchen, buckle up."

Gretchen found the harness' ends and strapped in like Erin. Gretchen's fit was loose, and she didn't see how to tighten it.

"Here, I'll get that." Erin yanked a strap on the harness, hard enough to make Gretchen cough. "Sorry. It needs to be cinched tight in case the ride gets bumpy."

Erin toggled three switches. A series of muffled thuds followed. She smoothly nudged the transport away from the station and started a gentle roll, bringing Mars into full view. "These next few minutes are the best part of the day, if you ask me."

"You should know that I'm not a pilot."

"Of course," Erin said flatly.

"Then why am I up here instead of in the passenger seats aft?"

Erin chuckled and shook her head. "Frank asked me to give you the VIP treatment."

"Oh." After a few seconds searching her memory for a mention of a "Frank" during the interview, Gretchen finally asked, "Who's Frank?"

"*Who's Frank?* He's running your project. You mean you never spoke with him?"

"No. I interviewed with Mr. Janssen and vidcommed with Mr. O'Donnell about..." Gretchen remembered the NDA she'd signed. "Well, what he needs me to do. I never heard of Frank."

Erin ended the roll and descended, performing a series of short maneuvers while relaying her status to flight control. "So how long do you think you'll be with us?"

"I don't know. Probably two or three weeks, perhaps as long as six."

Erin glanced over. "You spent a month traveling in a tin can, and will spend another month to return, all for six weeks of work? That's a lot of effort. Isn't there work on Earth?"

"Not for me, apparently."

Erin looked over, her eyebrows raised.

Gretchen hadn't even made it to the surface, and the Marsees were already prying into the last subject she wished to discuss. "My former project leader didn't care for my interpretation of our results. He put out word that I wasn't to be hired."

"Couldn't you go on unemployment until it blows over?"

Gretchen hesitated before saying, "I'd sooner waitress before doing that. I managed to get a nice apartment in a pleasant area. On unemployment, I'd be forced to move into free government housing. No thanks."

"Huh. From what I understand about Earthers, your attitude's unusual. Good for you." Her tone had a trace of warmth to it.

After Erin adjusted a few controls and spoke again with Flight Control, she maneuvered to a new heading. "Welcome to Mars. That bright speck in the distance is Mars City. Well, most of us call it that, anyway. Those seven domes are the only permanent outpost on Mars. We're just above the equator in the general vicinity of where the Americans sent their first probes, give or take a thousand miles."

Surrounded by red and brown sand, the fleck sparkled. As the seconds ticked by, it resolved into a ring of six domes surrounding one in the middle. Gretchen asked, "What's that off to the right?"

"That's our solar farm."

"Wow, it's huge. I've never seen anything like it."

"You probably never will again. It provides a sizable portion of our energy, but sand constantly gums up the tracking gears."

"I never would've guessed." Movement caught Gretchen's eye over to the left. It looked like a partially constructed dome set apart from the rest. Dozens of green-suited people were welding supports on its skeleton. "Why're you building a dome so far from the others?"

"It's not ours. Interplanetary's constructing it to compete with us."

Erin guided the shuttle toward a small box-like structure attached to the side of the nearest dome. After a few seconds, they touched down with a gentle thud followed by a harder one atop the fluorescent green cross on its rust-stained roof.

"Control, we're on the landing pad," Erin said. After several long seconds, Control lowered them inside, the tawny sky disappearing as the roof closed.

Erin pressed the harness release button, and Gretchen mimicked the action. After Erin tapped several controls and flicked as many switches, a deep thrum faded and a buzzing ceased. Finally, Erin passed along Control's all-clear signal. Gretchen followed Erin out of the cockpit, down the passenger ramp to the cavernous landing bay, and through the hangar door into a hallway.

The right side held a set of changing stalls. Erin pulled aside the curtain on one and said, "You can change out of your spacesuit here."

"Okay. What's next?"

"I'm not sure. Frank was supposed to meet you here. I'll send him a quick message to find out if there's a change of plan."

Inside her booth, Gretchen stripped off the spacesuit and put on her boots while questioning MarsVantage's commitment to the project. Already Erin had been late to the OTP, and Frank—who she'd never heard of until a few minutes ago—was late to meet her. These weren't the actions of people anxious to retrieve a new energy source.

10 | TIGHTENING THE NOOSE

In a soft and comfortable chair facing the floor-to-ceiling window, Peter Konklin sipped orange juice, freshly squeezed from black market oranges. Another hopper entered the landing pattern for LaGuardia Airport as the sun struggled to rise above the skyline.

A gentle rap on his open door stirred him. The workday hadn't yet begun, but he had his first appointment, the most important of the day.

"Nancy, come in." He looked to the ceiling and commanded, "Control. Lights, normal."

The lighting brightened to a social level and obscured the outside view. He showed Nancy to a seat before his desk and poured her a glass of OJ.

"What's the status on the shipper legislation?" Peter asked as he settled into his high-backed chair opposite her.

"The contributions to key committee members' reelection campaigns moved your safety legislation like crap through a goose. It's already sitting on the president's desk and will be signed today."

"Excellent. You know, I remember when I could personally get the regs and laws I wanted by simply promising and delivering favors."

Nancy tilted her head upward slightly. "There are only so many mistresses you can employ. Isn't it easier to just pay off the politicians with contributions?"

"I suppose," Peter muttered. Spending money in traceable ways, even though perfectly legal, opened the door for a crackpot to spin a conspiracy theory, shining an inconvenient light in a corner he'd rather remain dark. "So what's next?"

Nancy swallowed a mouthful of orange juice and nodded. "Delicious as always. Anyway, I discovered the safety equipment's supplier had inventory on hand. It's ready to ship to Mars, and it's enough to equip their entire fleet. The supplier's only waiting on the purchase order."

"Oh, that's not good, not good at all. I want the Marsees to spend money on the safety upgrades and waste manpower installing them. But more than that, I want them to request waivers to continue flying while waiting for the equipment. I want to draw out their interplanetary shipping license process, and have them battle the bad PR."

Nancy grinned. "I wasn't done. The warehouse caught fire an hour from now."

"I appreciate the way you worded that. Nicely done. Update me once you confirm the inventory is destroyed."

"If I may suggest, it may be beneficial to start a PR campaign with the main thrust being that you use the safest shipping available. Perhaps emphasizing that newly passed regulations haven't affected the shipping fleets you contract with because they were already in compliance. You can take the opportunity to point out that safety is your foremost priority."

"It may blunt criticism from the Marsees," Peter said as he looked to the ceiling, contemplating the possibilities. "Should they complain, the public will get the idea they oppose safety, which also works to our favor."

"Exactly, and it'll take the sting out of the accusations the pro-Marsee pundits and critics will level against our political friends."

With his glass, Peter saluted her and took another sip. "On the Blake front, once she discloses MarsVantage's objective, we can lock down our plan. Regardless, I want whatever the Marsees are after. It has to be valuable. Under no circumstances can we allow them to profit from it, though."

Nancy nodded.

Peter looked into her eyes. "Whatever it takes."

11 | THE FACTS OF LIFE ON MARS

Chuck rang the announcer at Frank's quarters, eager to show him the latest justification for their efforts. No one recognized how quickly they could lose everything they'd worked so hard for. Frank had a sense of it, but even he didn't see the precarious edge on which they lived.

Frank answered, freshly shaved, his hair wet. "Come in, but it needs to be quick. I'm already late to meet Gretchen."

"Sorry. I forgot."

"How could you forget?"

"I got distracted." Chuck thrust his datapad toward Frank. "The rumors are true. Washington's imposing new shipping safety regs. The bill passed Congress yesterday, and the President will sign it."

"They did it again." Frank shook his head. "What's the urgency?"

"Legal transmitted a summary of the regs. There's six month's work here."

"Six months! How're Earth's shippers handling it?"

"Very well, it seems. They already upgraded. Legal's requesting a waiver until we have time to order, receive, and install the equipment. It's bad PR, but we'll get it."

"PR's half the battle. Damn Konklin." Frank's datapad chimed, interrupting his complaint midstream. He withdrew it from his coveralls leg pocket and opened the screen. "Erin's back."

Frank showed Chuck the screen. *'We're at pad 1A. She's one of us. Where ARE you?'*

"Excellent," Chuck said. "We still need to keep an eye on her. I'm betting Interplanetary'll try something."

"No bet. I guarantee it."

"By the way, I know how hard it was for you to ask for Erin's help. It was the right move."

"No problem." Frank's flat tone and stony expression contradicted his words, though. "I really have to go. This isn't the first impression I wanted to make."

Chuck nodded and allowed the lie to pass. Asking for Erin's help was progress, but Frank hadn't been himself since they'd broken up. Frank had better snap out of it because Chuck needed him at his best, and the next few weeks were sure to be the most challenging since they'd split from Interplanetary.

*　*　*

Gretchen emerged from the changing stall, leaving the spacesuit hanging inside. The corridor was deserted except for Erin, who was sitting on a bench against the wall. "So, what's next?" Gretchen asked.

"Frank just sent a message. He's on his way."

Gretchen sat beside her. The Marsees mustn't receive many visitors. Otherwise, they would've decorated the hallway to engender a pleasant first impression, instead of leaving it strictly utilitarian.

Erin fidgeted, looking down the hallway. She acted like a desperate castaway searching for rescue on the horizon. Most likely, she had duties to perform, but wasn't allowed to leave Gretchen alone.

Apparently, Erin wasn't much for small talk, and it wasn't Gretchen's strong suit either. Trying was better than the awkwardness, though. "How long have you been a pilot?"

"Since I was a teenager," Erin said, pride filling her voice. "My dad taught me, not only to fly, but to do my own maintenance."

"That's impressive for someone so young."

"We can't afford dead weight on Mars. In fact, most of us wear many hats."

"Nice. Back home, it takes so much effort to land a leftover position after all of the connected people are taken care of. One time, I witnessed a cousin of a senator destroy a day's work because of his ignorance. You know what happened to him?"

Erin shook her head.

"He got a cozy desk job."

"I'm not surprised. It's the Peter Principle, promotion through incompetence. By the way, I meant to ask. What field are you in?"

"I'm an archaeologist."

"And she can't talk about what she's working on, Erin," said the man walking toward them.

"What else is new, Frank?" Erin stood. "You took your time."

"Sorry," Frank said, meeting Gretchen's eye. He looked back to Erin. "Chuck stopped by at the last minute."

"Problem?"

"New shipping regs."

"Safety?"

"Yep."

Erin's cheeks reddened. She bid them goodbye and departed, complaining Earth gave her more work to do.

By the sound of it, Earth had dropped a problem in everyone's lap. Perhaps she'd read too much into Frank's absence.

"Gretchen, I'm Frank Brentford, Engineering Manager. I'm running Chuck's project."

"Nice to meet you," she said as she assessed his handshake. Firm yet pleasant, not the limp, dead fish grasp that everyone back home considered stylish these days. "What's the plan?"

"We have a meeting with Chuck a little later. Until then, I thought I'd show you around Mars City while we have a little downtime. Starting tomorrow, we'll be busy."

"Sounds good." Rarely, had she ever started a project with someone taking the time to show her around. Usually, she'd received only an assignment and a map.

He directed her down the hallway toward the dome's interior. As they reached a large intersection, he said, "These are the express travel lanes, which encircle each dome like a belt. From them, you can pick up the Interdome Accessway that connects the dome to its neighbors."

A couple of bicyclists zoomed past. *Wow, people riding bicycles on Mars.* And without helmets and pads. Did Mars attract odd people or did it turn them odd? It didn't matter—she wouldn't be staying long enough to find out.

Frank continued, "Your datapad has a real-time map."

She pulled it from her pocket, extended the screen, and started the navigation program, which was just like the one on her datapad back home.

Frank pointed to their location on the datapad's screen. "You see, we're in an outer dome. Dome 1, actually. We're heading to the center dome."

"Got it." She glanced around. "Where's our auto-cab?"

He chuckled as he directed her onto the accessway. "Sorry, energy's too valuable to waste on moving perfectly capable people. Today, we'll walk to familiarize you with everything. There's a bicycle in your quarters that you can use to get around."

"It'll be a long trip to the far dome that way."

"True, but there aren't many reasons for multi-dome travel, though. Each dome has full facilities, like quarters, parks, hospitals, eateries, farmland, and such. If there's a big event, like the upcoming performance of *Atlantis' Valley*, it's held in the Admin dome, the center one, so it's only one dome away for everyone."

"Pardon me for saying so, but isn't that impractical in terms of manpower and resources?"

Two bicyclists passed on their left.

"On Earth, this arrangement is considered duplicative and wasteful. Here, each dome is designed to function independently. In case of a breach, the adjoining domes can lock down to limit the consequences. We can't allow a problem in one dome to endanger everyone."

Gretchen looked overhead and imagined an expanding crack. Her breath caught in her throat. The Marsees had placed considerable thought and effort into something that hadn't even occurred to her. Only human ingenuity and constructs were preventing an agonizing death. The tiny hairs on the back of her neck stood up, giving a tingly sensation.

"Gretchen, are you still with me?"

"It just struck me how dangerous Mars is. I thought Antarctica was tough, but at least I could always breathe," she said, her voice barely louder than a whisper.

He guided her to the side of the accessway. "It *is* more dangerous than Earth, but you adapt. On Mars, your actions have consequences that nothing—not even government regs—can protect you from."

Gretchen stared at the floor. What had she done? Was this job going to right her career? Her cheeks warmed from embarrassment.

"Remember, panic and instinct will kill while calm and thoughtfulness will keep you alive." Frank directed her attention to an array of green doors in the bulkhead. "Now's as good a time as any to show you this. All green storage doors in the corridor walls hold spacesuits. Above each one is a display that, when lit, shows details about the emergency. If it says 'Danger,' the current location is unsafe. If it says 'Warning,' the current location is safe, but somewhere nearby is compromised. As far as I'm concerned, if that display lights up, I'm putting on a spacesuit."

Gretchen opened the door, which drew a curious glance from a bicyclist. Frank waved his hand rapidly back and forth, and the bicyclist continued past them. "See, it's fully stocked. Since the Airlock Accident, these signs have only lit during safety drills."

"My instructor on the transport said the lockers were ill-maintained, but this one looks perfect."

"You can check any locker, any time, but you'll see the same thing. Many Earthers' perception of us doesn't match reality. I'll bet that your instructor never set foot on Mars."

With a sheepish smile, Gretchen said, "Thank you. That makes me feel better."

Frank removed her hand from the locker door's latch and closed it. "You'll draw a fair amount of attention accessing the lockers. People will think there's something wrong."

They continued on, eventually coming to, and passing through, the Interdome Accessway. It was a large tunnel with open double-doors on both ends. After they entered the inner dome, she was struck by its similarity to a small town. The scene before her was gorgeous.

The buildings were red-hued, almost like a magnificent sunset was painting across them. Instead, the midday sun shown through the transparent window encompassing a third of the dome starting about halfway up the side. She spotted trees planted at numerous places along the streets and what looked like a small park a couple blocks to her right.

They left the accessway behind and strolled the streets, which almost allowed her to forget she was millions of miles from home. Small details ruined the illusion, though. No one here was loitering while drinking booze and smoking weed. Auto-cabs didn't fill the streets, nor did graffiti mar the buildings.

Soon enough, Frank announced their arrival at headquarters, a nondescript five-story building with *'MarsVantage'* written in golden-hued block letters and a maroon-filled circle representing Mars resting atop the *'V.'* It was the opposite of the mandatory ostentatious displays of corporate headquarters back home.

As Gretchen approached the double-doors, she steeled herself. For the next few weeks, she needed to be at her best, so she could take her fee and move on to the next phase of her life. If only she could've deciphered the cave symbols during the month-long Mars passage.

12 | THE TASK AHEAD

On the fifth floor of MarsVantage headquarters, Frank showed Gretchen into Chuck's inner office. Gretchen spotted another dome nestled into the rusty Martian landscape through the office window and the current dome's plasti-glass. She fondly recalled a summer dig while in college. The Arizona sands looked just like the sand outside.

To her left, the wall behind Chuck's desk held a quote painted in script:

> *'If ye love wealth more than liberty, the tranquility of servitude better than the animating contest of freedom, go home from us in peace. We ask not your counsels or your arms. Crouch down and lick the hands which feed you. May your chains set lightly upon you, and may posterity forget that ye were our countrymen.'*

Gretchen forced a neutral expression. These days, finding anyone who'd heard of Samuel Adams, let alone who thought like him, was rare. Most didn't discuss such ideas in polite company, and they certainly didn't advertise them.

With Frank at her side, she joined Chuck at the conference table in the corner. Chuck stood, smiled broadly, and firmly shook her hand. "Welcome to Mars. How was the flight?"

They all sat as Gretchen replied, "Better than expected. I finished my Antarctica artifacts paper. I also tried to get a head start researching the symbols you showed me."

"Did you find anything?"

She pursed her lips. "No. I can tell you they're not hieroglyphics, pictograms, or any known written language."

"I wouldn't expect them to be a known language," Frank said. "I can't imagine someone from Mars City strolling over to an out of the way cave to practice chiseling."

"Oh, come on," Gretchen said, leaning forward. "You aren't suggesting little green men carved them? We've been searching for extraterrestrial intelligence for over 200 years and found nothing but static. There are no aliens."

"No one said a word about aliens," Frank said. "As much as Earthers love to believe we're kooks, we don't see aliens behind every other rock. I don't know who created the symbols or when, but they are there, and that's what's important."

"I can't argue that." Gretchen leaned back in the chair. *Who do they think they're fooling?* They were thinking aliens. Otherwise, they would've offered an explanation for the symbols. "I need a copy of the image to research them properly."

"We have more information to help with your analysis," Chuck said. He manipulated his datapad, and the table holo activated.

Frank walked her through the results of the soundings he'd taken over the years. He finished by displaying several more images of the cave's symbols and stopped on a crystal clear one.

Unbelievable—Chuck lied from the first word of the interview. Gretchen glared. "You said you had only the one picture."

Chuck's stone-still face guarded his thoughts for moments that dragged on. "Yes, I did. I lied."

"I don't particularly care to work for people who lie to my face."

"I apologize, Gretchen," Chuck said. "With all the precautions we took, I still had reservations about revealing too much. I didn't even want to show you the image, but I had to spark your curiosity."

While she sympathized with Chuck's security concerns, she hated deception. She reminded herself that the job was short-term. Soon, Gretchen would leave with a sizable payment, never to see them again. She consciously and slowly inhaled and exhaled, and wondered how her friend Ashley would tactfully handle the situation. "Very well. You need to understand that the more you withhold, the more likely your project will fail. Any piece of information may be useful, or even critical."

Chuck nodded. "You're right. You're now part of the team, and we're sharing everything."

Gretchen left her doubts unvoiced. Instead, she stood, leaned in, and examined the image. The symbols were precisely etched, with perfectly round circles and laser-straight lines. No natural process could produce them. Likewise, no person—not even one with the steadiest hand—could have carved them. A control mechanism had to have been involved.

"In the spirit of full disclosure, we need to explain the rules for claiming the Marsium121 and how they'll constrain us to work under certain conditions," Frank said.

Gretchen returned to her seat, filled with an odd mixture of concern and curiosity. The job was already difficult without putting more restrictions on accomplishing it.

For the most part, Chuck's explanation sounded like the basic children's rule—finders keepers—but one point confused her.

"I don't understand how Interplanetary could possibly claim the Marsium121. You've purchased the exploration rights, correct?"

"Correct," Chuck said. "And thirty years ago, Interplanetary purchased those rights and discovered Marsium121."

"Surely Interplanetary's rights have expired already," Gretchen said.

"After five years," Frank answered.

"And at that time, nobody knew Marsium121's value?" Gretchen asked.

"True." Frank shifted in the chair and leaned in. "We only discovered its energy producing capabilities years later."

"So, how can they dispute your claim?"

Chuck said, "Interplanetary can argue that thirty years ago, we withheld knowledge of the Marsium121's energy producing properties or we withheld how to access the cavern. They won't have any evidence because none exists. Still, they can lie. As a third party, you'll open the door, Gretchen. Between your involvement and the passage of time, I expect Interplanetary will let it go, or lose the Adjudication Board judgment."

"So, I came all this way, and you spent a lot of money, all so you could have... for lack of a better word... an alibi?"

"No, no, no—not at all," Chuck said rapidly. "We don't know how to open the door, and that's the truth. But appearances and truth aren't necessarily the same, especially when people like Konklin twist the facts to suit their purposes. We need your expertise to open that door just as much as your status as a third party doing it."

Gretchen sighed. Interplanetary couldn't have gotten to be the largest corporation on Earth by being kindhearted—that was for sure. This was an unexpected wrinkle, but it didn't affect her task.

"Fair enough," Gretchen said. "Understand that if I'm asked to testify in any sort of hearing, I'll tell the complete truth—no hedging or convenient memory lapses. If that's a problem, then let's break the contract, and I'll go back to Earth on the turnaround flight. You can't pay me enough to perjure myself into a jail cell. I'll still consider myself bound by the nondisclosure agreement."

Chuck glanced over to Frank, who nodded ever so slightly, and then focused on her. "Good for you. I know you need the work, and I'm glad you value your integrity more than money. You should know we're planning on running a continuous recording of your mission when you arrive on-site. The truth will be on our side."

Chuck and Frank clearly had a real concern for Interplanetary's devious tactics if they were willing to go to such an extreme measure. To Gretchen, it didn't make a difference one way or another. Whoever ended up watching the video would get bored quickly. "Okay."

"There's one more thing," Frank said. "Only the three of us know these details. There's at least one Interplanetary spy within the company, perhaps more. It's imperative you don't discuss our project with anyone else. If you have any questions or problems, speak directly with me. Don't even leave a message."

"A spy?" She just might've solved one of their problems without any effort. "During the trip planetside, the pilot asked a lot of questions."

Frank dismissed the idea with a wave of his hand. "Erin's okay. That's not spying—that's her being a busybody."

And that was why they had a spy problem—they didn't follow up on strange incidents and assumed people were 'okay.' Gretchen said, "Regardless, I didn't reveal anything."

"Good," Chuck added quickly. "In ten days, an exploration expedition will leave. You and Frank will drive a tractor to the cave where you'll get us in the cavern. After we take a sample and acquire the mining rights, you'll return to Earth paid in full with our heartfelt thanks."

"That sounds like a plan," Gretchen said.

The meeting ended shortly afterward with Frank and Chuck both transmitting their contact information and the project details to her datapad. Frank escorted her to her quarters on the opposite side of the accessway lanes along the Admin Dome's base, not in an individual building as she'd expected.

Inside, she found her luggage had been delivered already. She unpacked, which didn't take long, for she'd brought little more than necessities. Disjointed details related to the symbols, exploration rights rules, and conspiracies cluttered her mind.

The muddle was too much to digest. Gretchen pulled her guitar from its hard travel case. As she grasped its neck with her left hand, the familiarity of the cold, metal strings comforted her. Many would consider a guitar an extravagance, but for her, it was as essential as a toothbrush and toothpaste.

She sat on the bed's edge, closed her eyes, and warmed up with an old song from the mid-22nd century that started slow but ended in a flurry of chord changes. Afterward, she played a couple more songs until her mind cleared.

Her task was to decipher the symbols and not discuss it.

The rules and conspiracies that so concerned the Marsees were merely distractions. She understood their problems. She even sympathized with them, but in the end, they weren't *her* problems. She had enough of her own, without taking on the Marsees'.

13 | Questions Unanswered

Erin stormed into the hall leading to Frank's quarters. He wasn't in Engineering, and no one there knew where he was. Apparently, he'd shifted his duties to Sam and hadn't shown his face for three days.

For Frank to ignore work was bizarre. He might not be overly social these days, but work was work. Something was going on, something big enough to completely ignore his duties.

Erin pressed the announcement chime beside his door. She tapped her finger near the button, waiting an unendurable amount of time before pressing it again.

A few seconds later, the door slid aside. "Erin? What're you doing here?"

"We need to talk," she said while barging in.

As Frank closed the door, he looked amused, which further angered her. "I've got a lot going on right now. I don't have time to discuss it anymore."

"What? Oh, it's not that."

"The new regs, then? The parts will be on the next transport from Earth."

Erin shook her head. "They're backordered. Apparently, there was a fire in the warehouse on Earth, and our parts were destroyed. It's going to be months before they get shipped."

"You're kidding me."

"Do I look like I'm kidding?"

Frank's grin disappeared. Neither said a word for a few seconds until he asked, "What do you want me to do about it?"

Erin squared her jaw. "Nothing. I'm just irritated that, once again, we're facing an upgrade of negligible value, and we're one step further away from having our own direct-to-Earth transport capacity."

"That's Earth for you. What do you want me to do?"

"About that—nothing. I want to know what you and Chuck are cooking up."

Frank's eyes grew wide. "It's nothing."

Erin rolled her eyes. "You need to practice that line more—I'm not convinced. C'mon, you hired an archaeologist for God's sake. On Mars."

He paced. She'd seen him do this when he had to make a tough decision. Interrupting him would only delay the choice he'd make anyway.

Finally, he stopped before her. "Erin, I'd really like to tell you, but I can't. Not yet, anyway."

"I don't get it. You trusted me with your biggest secret. You trusted me enough to check out Gretchen when I ferried her from orbit. Until three months ago, we shared a bed. You *know* I'd never say a word."

"I know," Frank said in a monotone. "This is so important, only Chuck, Gretchen, and I know the entire story. If it gets out, it'll be one of us facing recriminations. There's nothing gained by bringing you into the mix."

"What about Arnold? You sent him to Earth to hire her."

"He interviewed her about HR matters only."

"Really?"

"Really." Frank smiled easily, like before she'd broken his heart. His fingers came ever so close to her chin as he gazed into her eyes.

He hadn't touched her since she'd turned down his proposal. He'd never returned to her quarters, they'd rarely spoken, and she hadn't seen him much. *Is he reconsidering?*

Before she could respond, she had her answer. He inched backward and his hand dropped to his side. His smile faded as his eyes dulled.

Frank wasn't avoiding her because he was angry. No, he was avoiding her because she tempted him to disregard his long-term desires in favor of short-term delights. She could've pursued it and had a thoroughly sensual and passionate time, but their circumstances hadn't changed. She'd only end up hurting him again, and she couldn't do that. Once had been more than enough.

Frank said softly, barely louder than a whisper, "If we pull it off, MarsVantage'll have an excellent chance to prosper."

"So that's it?" Erin said, unable to keep disappointment out of her voice.

"I'm sorry. I'm tempted to include you, but I can't."

"Okay, Frank." Pressing him would be useless. His mind was set. She'd have to do what she always found difficult—exercise patience. "Remember, if you need anything, I'm here and willing to help."

"Now that you mention it, there is something I may need."

For a moment, Erin couldn't believe her ears. She would've bet a lot on Frank politely declining. *What could he want from me?*

Frank explained what he had in mind should circumstances conspire against him. He let nothing slip that shed any light on his plans, though he did divulge that he and Gretchen would be going to the Maelstrom Mountains as part of the next exploratory expedition. It wasn't much of a detail because it'd be public knowledge soon enough.

Erin left his quarters, the backordered safety parts now a minor concern. Her role in Frank's plan was easy enough, though the rationale behind it was far-fetched. If he were anyone else, she'd call him paranoid. But not him—he was the most practical, even-headed person she'd ever known. Without hesitation, Erin had agreed to his contingency plan, doubting they'd ever resort to it.

* * *

On the top level of the restaurant court, Chuck focused on the latest mining report, the garbage from a late lunch pushed off to the side. Site 24 held more Marsium37 than previously estimated. Excavation of Site 31 was proceeding easier than expected, and the foreman anticipated extraction could commence within a week.

For every piece of good news, bad news awaited, however. In this case, reserve stockpiles continued to grow, now holding three full shipments for Earth. While Earth relied on Marsium37 to construct gravcomp plating and engine components, they refused to add extra transport runs. Chuck made a note to look into manufacturing gravcomp plating on Mars once the Marsium121 was in place and producing power.

"Excuse me, Chuck. Do you have a minute?"

He looked up to see James Bunderbon standing opposite him. He gestured to the chair. "Please sit down."

With a sardonic smile, Bunderbon sat with his shoulders squared. Chuck had seen this before—something was going on.

"Some discrepancies in shipping paperwork have come to light," Bunderbon said.

Chuck leaned back and consciously kept his expression neutral as he waited to hear what Bunderbon had found, rather than assuming the worst and giving him more ammunition.

Bunderbon continued, "There was an order for security software, approved directly by you, not Alan Greene. You collected it as soon as it arrived, and Security never saw it."

How did Bunderbon piece those facts together? He must be searching hard for anything to force out Chuck as CEO. A scandal or even the suggestion of one would make the task far easier. Fortunately, Chuck had planned for this contingency.

"James, everything you said is true. I'm willing to divulge that the software is being actively used and will eventually be entrusted to Security."

"Doing what?"

"Now's not the time to reveal those details."

"When will be the time?"

"I expect to give the board a full report at next month's meeting."

Bunderbon's eyes narrowed. "I look forward to your report. Also, I understand you ordered Arnold Janssen to Earth and together, you hired an archaeologist."

"Yes. In fact, she arrived this morning."

"At considerable expense."

"Consultants aren't cheap, but it's an investment in our future."

"Hiring an archaeologist to work on Mars is insane."

"The line between insanity and genius is very thin."

Bunderbon leaned forward. "You'll have to give me more than that."

"Actually, I don't. I'm purposely restricting the details, so our spy remains in the dark."

"No one has ever produced a shred of evidence pointing to the existence of a spy," Bunderbon said, once again dismissing the idea out of hand. "When will you provide us with the details?"

"When Interplanetary is powerless to stop us. I figure that'll be by our next board meeting."

The shock on Bunderbon's face was priceless. His lips formed an odd rictus, which reminded Chuck of a robin.

"With the way you're spending money, you could bankrupt the company by then. We need something concrete. Without it, I'll have to ask for a vote of no-confidence."

"You don't have the votes to oust me."

"Perhaps not at this moment, but with each unjustified expenditure, it gets easier."

Chuck pursed his lips. "You know, I suspected you of being the spy but eventually decided I was wrong."

"Why's that?"

"You wouldn't press me if you were the spy. You'd act like my best friend." Chuck smiled. "No, you're no spy. You're simply ambitious, and only one thing stands between you and my job— me."

"My ambition isn't the issue. Your idealism's sinking the company."

Chuck sat up straight. "Sinking? I'm rescuing MarsVantage."

"Fighting reality and antagonizing Washington doesn't help anyone, except Konklin."

"I don't know which is worse. Your inability to see the facts before you, or your inability to extrapolate the consequences of current events."

Bunderbon shook his head. "Chuck, your impersonation of Don Quixote is counterproductive. I've said it before, and I'll say it again—Konklin designed his Mars subsidiary, what is now MarsVantage, to be completely dependent on Earth. Fighting that fact is a losing battle and a waste of money from word one. We're better off working within the system."

"I have a different vision for us... One where we're treated as equals and don't have to live on food that's just good enough... One where we can take elevators to our offices and auto-cabs between domes. My goal isn't to survive—it's to thrive."

Bunderbon rose. "If your explanations aren't satisfactory to the board, it'll cost you your job. Count on it."

"If I fail, it'll be all our jobs." Chuck shook his head as he watched Bunderbon depart. *I'll just be the first to go.*

14 | THE PROPOSITION

In a hallway near Gretchen's quarters, Frank deposited a toolpac on the floor and opened a maintenance panel. He ran diagnostics on the control circuits for her quarters' door and vidcomm, finding no activity. Unless she'd used her datapad to communicate with someone, which was something he'd check later, she hadn't seen or spoken with anyone since he'd left her quarters.

Soon, Gretchen would leave for the restaurant court to make their scheduled supper meeting, so Frank acted busy at the maintenance panel while keeping an eye on the hallway intersection thirty feet away. As expected, a few minutes later, Gretchen walked through it, constantly glancing at her datapad.

He shoved the toolpac into the maintenance panel and, with his shoulder, forced it closed until the latch clicked. He set off after her, following at a discreet distance.

Perhaps he'd see why she insisted on meeting in the restaurant court instead of walking there together.

* * *

Gretchen looked up from her datapad's map and saw the restaurants lining three walls, a few trailing lines several people deep. In the center, a seating area, about thirty square yards, was nearly a quarter filled. According to a sign, the next two levels also held restaurants and presumably similar seating.

She grinned with satisfaction. Her first foray was a success. One thing she disliked about new places was that uncomfortable feeling of not knowing where she was or where she was going. Frank's tour had been helpful, but he couldn't show her everything.

She didn't want the reputation of a helpless Earther who couldn't get from "A" to "B" without assistance, so she explored the city by herself. There was no better means to learn her way around, and if she'd gotten lost, at least she wouldn't be embarrassed while trying to regain her bearings.

She closed her datapad's screen and looked up to see a man approaching. "Good evening, Ms. Blake," he said, "I'm Zach. Do you have a moment?"

"Sure."

"I have a proposition that I'm sure you'll find highly beneficial." He smiled broadly to punctuate his statement.

Zach's smarmy persona reminded Gretchen of salesmen in abandoned warehouses where the black markets thrived. They'd wander the walkways between tables, trying to entice potential buyers to their wares like precious metals, tobacco, and delicious snack foods, both the salty and sweet kinds. When she'd visited, she'd politely listened to the salesman but had kept her goal—usually milk chocolate—foremost in mind. That tactic ought to work here. "I don't have much time, and I'm not interested in buying anything."

Zach took a step closer. "Oh, I'm not selling, Ms. Blake. I'm buying. Let me explain. I'd like to know your project's details. In return, I'll make it worth your while."

It sounded as if Zach was proposing industrial espionage right here in the middle of the hall leading to the restaurant court. *Weren't these kinds of matters handled in dingy back alleys?* "So Zach, what does 'worth my while' mean?"

"A cash payment. Name the amount." He smiled again.

There it was—money for information. She was surprised that Chuck and Frank hadn't warned her about Interplanetary's boldness. "No, thanks. I don't want your money," Gretchen said as she started toward the restaurant court.

A second later, Zach caught up. "Perhaps you'd prefer a permanent job with Interplanetary. I guarantee it'll be easy work."

"No, thanks. I'm not interested."

"You're a tough negotiator. You don't want to be tied to a desk. I understand that. I can clear up your work status, so you can return to the field. Name the project and you'll get it."

Gretchen stopped mid-step and he smiled once more, this time raising his eyebrows. Lifting Hawthorne's blackball was exactly what she needed. She could get her career back on track and not have to worry about money. It was tempting, so tempting she nearly agreed, but then caught herself. No amount of money could restore her self-respect if she were to take his bribe. Her mouth was suddenly dry as she repeated, "No. I'm *not* interested."

"What would you like? Name it, and it's yours."

"You have nothing I want."

"You're making a mistake."

"Perhaps, but it's mine to make. Please leave me alone now." Once again, Gretchen continued forward. This time Zach didn't follow.

In the restaurant court, she gazed at the various eateries' menus, their offerings not registering. Eventually, she stumbled across Frank, who recommended a particular restaurant. They ordered and took their food trays to an open table. She gave little thought to her actions. It was as if she were wandering through a dream.

Or was it a nightmare? She might've just rejected her best opportunity to continue in archaeology upon returning home. She couldn't get Zach's words out of her head. *'You're making a mistake.'*

"Gretchen? Gretchen. You seem a million miles away. Are you feeling okay?" Frank asked.

She swallowed a mouthful of salad. "I'm sorry. I'm preoccupied with an odd encounter I had on my way here."

Frank mixed his steaming soup. "Tell me about it."

"A man calling himself Zach..." Gretchen exhaled, pausing, trying to postpone disclosing the encounter. "...offered me money, a position with Interplanetary, and the removal of Hawthorne's blackball in exchange for the details of our project."

After Frank swallowed another spoonful, he asked, still staring at his soup, "What'd you tell him?"

"I wouldn't be telling you about it if I accepted, would I?"

"I don't know," Frank said, finally looking her squarely in the eye. "Would you?"

Gretchen shook her head. "I turned him down."

"Why?"

The reason was obvious, but apparently, Frank needed to hear it. "Why? Because I thumbed-off on an agreement. I expect you to live up to your end, just as you expect me to live up to mine."

"Even though you'd easily solve all of your problems?"

"Yes. Because the price is too high. Because anything I accomplish afterward would be tainted by greed and betrayal."

As serene as ever, Frank said nothing but stared directly into her eyes.

Gretchen felt an urgent need to fill the silence. "How can you be so calm? You came this close to losing everything." She placed her thumb and index finger a fraction of an inch apart.

He leaned forward, his face impassive. "I'm convinced that if we fail, MarsVantage is already dead. The only question is how long it will take the body to slump to the floor."

"That's pretty graphic."

"That's what I thought when Chuck said it, but he's right. Anyway, I figured Interplanetary would proposition you eventually. While your education and experience are excellent, I hired you because of your integrity in dealing with Hawthorne. Clearly, the truth matters more than a good recommendation in your HR profile." He paused, averting his eyes momentarily. "Even so, I had to be sure, so I asked Erin to assess you."

"You mean Erin, the pilot." He'd arranged the entire situation, all of the awkwardness and discomfort. "The VIP treatment was a test?"

"She said VIP treatment? Huh, that's creative." Frank chuckled. "In case you're wondering, you passed."

Gretchen glared at him. "I couldn't care less if I passed your silly test."

"I don't want to offend you, but my experience with Earthers isn't exactly what you'd call stellar. They lie, cheat, and steal as easily as they breathe. I had to know for sure what sort of person I'm dealing with."

Gretchen pursed her lips. "I know plenty of people like that, but I'm not one of them. We're gonna have problems if you keep insisting on treating me like a typical Earther, instead of as an individual."

Frank's eyes grew wide, and he exhaled. "You know what? You're right. I didn't intend to insult you. You're unlike any Earthers I've encountered. I'm sorry."

They stared at each other, neither speaking for a time. He seemed sincere, but she wasn't ready to forgive him yet. This treatment had to stop here.

"Okay, Gretchen. Here's the thing. For the past couple of months, I've fallen asleep and woken up thinking about this project. At times, I've even dreamed about it. I'm doing everything possible to ensure it succeeds." Frank frowned and allowed the spoon to rest in the bowl. "But I lost sight of the fact that you're a person, not just a means of accomplishing our goal. I was thoughtless. I'm sorry. It won't happen again."

"So long as it doesn't." Words were one thing, actions another. She'd had her fill of working for people who lacked common courtesy and civility. If Frank turned out to be anything like Hawthorne, she didn't know what she'd do.

"Thank you." After a second's pause, he asked, "I'm curious why you didn't go-along-to-get-along with Hawthorne? I'd expect most in your position would have relented."

"It's hard to put into words. It matters to me that I make the discovery, find the answers, and reach my own conclusions. Having Hawthorne—who hasn't made a significant discovery since before I started kindergarten—denounce my hypothesis without a shred of evidence rubbed me the wrong way. I wanted to learn if my hypothesis was right or wrong, not make a snap judgment and allow my title to give it credence. I guess it's hard to understand."

Frank smiled. It was pleasant, a tad lopsided, but his green eyes sparkled. "Not at all, I understand perfectly. You think like a Marsee."

She swallowed, confused as to what he meant. "Uh..."

"Don't take that wrong—I mean it as a compliment."

"Well, thank you," Gretchen said. Glad Interplanetary's offer was now out in the open and that she'd cleared the air with Frank, Gretchen finished her meal while conversing about other matters. Much to her delight, Frank was well-rounded, able to discuss current events as easily as holos.

"On a different topic, I noticed you aren't wearing a wedding band. Don't be surprised if many of the singles ask you out," Frank said.

Gretchen raised her eyebrows. *That came from out of nowhere.*

"Mars is a relatively closed community, and there aren't many singletons here, but I noticed a few guys already checking you out while we ate."

"I see. Is there a problem if I date while I'm here?"

"MarsVantage employees? No. But considering the sensitive nature of your work, Interplanetary employees, yes. They're a problem. It's best to stay away from anyone wearing black and red coveralls."

Surely, he realized Interplanetary employees could change clothes. Zach had been wearing steel blue coveralls like theirs. There wasn't much sense fixating on that—it was beside the point. "And if I don't want to be bothered, I just need to wear a ring?"

"It'll dissuade everyone except the most desperate."

Gretchen swapped the emerald from her right hand to her left. It felt odd having something on that finger again, just as odd as when she'd removed her wedding band in Antarctica. The corners of Frank's mouth twitched upward ever so slightly as she performed the maneuver.

"Thanks for the heads up. My plate's full enough without having to deal with come-ons." She left unsaid that she wasn't interested in a fling. Frank was smart—he'd take the hint if he was contemplating such thoughts.

Frank checked his datapad. "Look at that. The time's getting away from me. I have some work to do before we start tomorrow, but if you like, I'll walk you back to your quarters. It's on my way."

She shifted in her seat. She still wanted the practice getting around, and she'd feel silly if she got them lost, but she didn't have much of a choice. After Zach's proposition, she wasn't surprised that Frank would want to stay close. "Okay, but under one condition. Let me guide us, so I can familiarize myself with the city."

15 | THE PROBLEM WITH ASSUMPTIONS

After John Reed closed and locked his office door, he slammed his palms against the wall so hard they stung. "Damn Earther bitch!"

He sat at his desk, stunned that Blake lacked the sense to grab a golden opportunity when offered. On his datapad, he reviewed her file, searching for an explanation of her behavior. Aside from her MarsVantage contract, there was no indication of another income. If money wasn't a concern now, surely, it would be soon. He rubbed his temples. How could anyone be so shortsighted?

John glanced to the darkened vidcomm and sighed. Nothing was gained by procrastinating. The conversation was going to be unpleasant whenever he had it. With the solemnity of a pallbearer, he opened a secure tunnel to Nancy Kaine's office on Earth. A few seconds later, the connection completed.

"Hello, John. I was expecting a call from Heather. What's going on?"

"Heather's at the construction site. A delivery shuttle from the OTP skidded into our dome while landing."

"We can't have accidents when we're pursuing safety issues to retake MarsVantage."

"She's managing the situation. No one at MarsVantage knows."

"Okay. I'll inform Peter." Nancy jotted a quick note. "What's the Blake status?"

"Heather delegated the task to me. She doesn't know how long she'll be away."

"And?"

"Unfortunately, Blake refused my offer," Reed said, anticipating an unpleasant backlash.

"How'd you approach her?"

"I laid out the proposition—money for information."

"Didn't Heather plan on you dating her?"

"She did. The dating approach is more of a long-term tactic. My best guess is that Blake will leave for the wild in ten days. It wasn't going to get us what we needed in the time available."

"Perhaps you're right. However, you're not negotiating a contract between two willing parties. You need to appeal to her ego or vanity. You can't just cut to the endgame. It requires the same mindset as when you're trying to bed a woman. You don't just walk up and ask, 'Wanna hit the sheets?' Pay closer attention to how Heather operates."

Heather Newton, the other Interplanetary spy handler on Mars, had voiced the same complaints many times, and he was tired of hearing them. He kept striving to improve, but he wasn't naturally skilled at recruitment. He covertly ran the already-recruited spies. Neither he nor his spies had ever been seriously suspected, let alone caught.

John nodded. "How do you want to move forward?"

"I'm not sure. I need to give it some thought. It's safe to say that you must avoid public areas. You don't want her pointing you out to MarsVantage."

John nodded again.

"It's a good thing she's a short-term consultant. Otherwise, I'd have to reassign you."

"Don't worry, Blake won't see me again." John had invested too much to position himself for Interplanetary's eventual rise on Mars. He wasn't about to allow one person to ruin his plans. "And if she does, I'll see to it that she doesn't tell anyone. In fact, if you like, I'll take care of her now."

"No!" Nancy commanded, her eyes growing wide. "She's still valuable. Sit tight, and wait for instructions."

After John watched the vidcomm fade to black from Nancy breaking the connection, he contemplated ways to discover the information she desired. Without Blake's cooperation, the task would become exponentially more difficult. More than likely, they'd have to resort to more extreme and quite possibly terminal tactics. Before it was all said and done, that idiot Blake might bitterly regret rejecting his offer.

*　*　*

In the corner of his living room, Frank sat before a borrowed computer running Security Data Analysis software—the same software many of Earth's large law enforcement agencies used— following up on Gretchen's encounter with the Interplanetary spy handler. He surreptitiously tapped into the security system and reviewed the footage from the Admin dome's restaurant court. The closest camera recorded excellent footage of Zach's back, never capturing a good view of his face. Other cameras either missed the encounter or were too distant to record a clear shot.

Zach apparently knew exactly where and how to stand to render the security recordings useless, and that couldn't happen by chance. *The damn spy must've passed along security camera locations, too.*

Frank programmed another scenario into the SDA for analysis, using Gretchen's visit to the restaurant court to filter the data. After thirty seconds, the SDA presented the results.

When given a firm anchor point, the SDA worked efficiently and effectively. His prior attempts since getting the software last week, lacking an anchor criterion, had been correlations creating a Cartesian product, which took incredibly long and produced a mountain of data, effectively making the results useless. Perhaps, the attempt to co-opt Gretchen was exactly what he needed to find the spy.

The only person in Gretchen's vicinity for an extended time, besides himself, had been John Reed, an Interplanetary employee. Frank accessed Reed's security profile and reviewed his background. He might call himself 'Zach' and wear MarsVantage's steel blue coveralls all he wanted, but he couldn't hide from the SDA.

He programmed another SDA scenario, focusing on John Reed. A slew of dates, times, and locations for the past ten weeks displayed in the time it took Frank to eat an apple. For close to two hours, he cross-checked the SDA results against security camera footage.

When finished, Frank leaned back in his chair, staring at the results list, allowing the words to blur as he considered everything.

All the contacts were innocuous. Most of the time, MarsVantage employees were nearby as Reed waited in line at a restaurant or as he walked a busy corridor. The software even flagged a handful of instances in the restaurant court where MarsVantage employees were seated nearby. In fact, it displayed his name from two weeks ago when he'd handled a routine maintenance check.

The SDA did its job, but it took judgment to interpret the results. Frank hadn't seen any hand offs, and none of the contacts were face-to-face conversations.

His hopes of ferreting out the spy and resolving a longstanding problem hadn't panned out. He'd continue to keep an eye on Reed, who'd eventually lead him to the spy. He had the key to breaking Interplanetary's spy ring. Now, it was only a matter of time.

An idea occurred to him—one that'd wreck schedules and create extra work. It should, however, force Reed and the spy to meet. Frank would have to get Chuck's approval to go through with it, though. That'd be an interesting chat, or more accurately said, *another* interesting chat.

His thoughts circled back to Gretchen. He'd chosen well, but until supper, he hadn't known how well. She'd kept her word by refusing Interplanetary's bribe. Telling him had only further proved her trustworthiness.

She'd displayed self-reliance, too. So much so, she desired to learn her way around the domes. Strange that she'd go to all the trouble since she'd be leaving Mars soon. A stereotypical Earther wouldn't bother.

Gretchen might be many things, but stereotypical wasn't one.

Truth be told, Frank could've easily mistaken her for a Marsee. She had the intelligence and attitude to make an excellent MarsVantage employee. *I wonder if she's interested in staying on?*

16 | Unwelcome News from Earth

After supper, Chuck settled into a living room chair with his datapad. He perused the news, reading several business articles in full. Afterward, as he switched to political commentaries, he yawned.

He was reviewing the list when a column, '*End MarsVantage's Free Ride*,' caught his eye. What a provocative title, especially because he recognized precisely how expensive their "free ride" was.

Chuck rubbed his tired eyes with his thumb and forefinger and selected the story authored by celebrated columnist Eleanor Klein. She was celebrated because she engagingly parroted the government's policies. When she wrote something, she was defending or advancing an established policy, or it was a signal of an upcoming initiative.

This commentary fell into the latter category. She proposed MarsVantage's inability to comply with the new safety regs in a timely manner, along with other issues long-since addressed, as justification for the government to oversee their operations more closely. She called for a financial audit first. Chuck shook his head trying to imagine how accountants pouring through columns of numbers would improve safety. Further on, she argued for inspections by various oversight agencies.

The concluding paragraph revealed the endgame:

Because the government has been negligent in its oversight, there's no definitive measure of MarsVantage safety levels. Considering their limited resources and the long-term free reign the company has enjoyed, it's reasonable to suspect a plethora of issues await revelation. In the end, the government may find they erred in divesting MarsVantage from Peter Konklin Interplanetary. If so, they must rectify their error before more blood is needlessly spilled.

Truly, her commentary was a masterful work of propaganda. Her deliberate selection of facts painted a compelling narrative, albeit a false one.

Chuck's supper felt like lead in his stomach as he imagined the events leading to its publication. Konklin had colluded with the government to press for regulatory oversight, and the government had in turn colluded with the news media to lay the groundwork. Naturally, instead of simply reviewing reports, the oversight agents would actively sift and probe until they uncovered something—anything, no matter how trivial.

The public would approve, ignorant of the machinations of the powerful to steal what they couldn't get through legitimate means. When it was all said and done, Konklin would wait with cash in hand to buy the tattered remnants of MarsVantage.

Chuck expected that once Bunderbon read the article, he'd use it as more justification for a no-confidence vote, no doubt insinuating that the current uncertainty was somehow Chuck's fault. Bunderbon simply didn't understand how MarsVantage's history informed their decisions regarding the future. Most people living in Mars City during the Airlock Accident wouldn't question a single decision Chuck had made. Bunderbon, having signed on afterward, had managed to raise doubts in a few of the weak-willed board members, though.

The door's announcer chimed. Chuck opened it and found Frank. "Come in. Is everything okay?"

"I had only good news until I read Eleanor Klein's commentary." Frank followed Chuck into the living room. He flopped on the couch as Chuck took the adjacent chair.

"I read it, too. I can use some good news."

"Interplanetary approached Gretchen."

"No, Frank—I said *good* news."

"They made their move, and Gretchen turned them down. That's great news in my book."

Chuck leaned forward. "She hasn't reported anything to me. Has she said anything to you?"

"She was distracted at supper. After I asked what was bothering her, she told me everything."

Chuck nodded, and he reclined. "That *is* good news. I think you found the one honest Earther."

Frank laughed while Chuck grinned at his own joke.

"Did you recognize who approached her?" Chuck asked.

"No, but the SDA identified him as John Reed. I looked into his background and found he's an Interplanetary software engineer, specializing in embedded systems and interfaces."

"I take it there wasn't any notation of industrial espionage in his HR profile."

"They failed to include that skill." Frank smirked. "I ran him through the SDA looking for MarsVantage contacts, but nothing stood out."

"Keep at it. We'll catch him with the spy eventually."

"Count on it."

In a somber tone, Chuck said, "The bad news is I think Klein's commentary is a trial balloon. The government will bleed us dry just proving compliance."

"Only if you're willing to play defense. When the Marsium121 is satisfying our energy needs, you can redirect the savings from buying fuel cells to hiring lawyers and lobbyists to take the fight to them."

Chuck shook his head. "It's funny to hear you say that. Bunderbon is insisting we shouldn't fight, just work within the system. You're saying we should fight using the system. Either way, we'll lose, and I can't do what I truly want—grow the company."

Frank leaned forward, resting his elbows on his knees as he looked to Chuck. "You're right. Fighting the system or working within it is a long-term loser, but you can play for time. You can look to capitalize on future opportunities."

"That's not much of a plan." Sadness reflected on Chuck's face.

Frank leaned back. "It's better than Bunderbon's, which is tantamount to surrender. Once we reduce our energy dependence, the landscape of opportunities will look entirely different."

Chuck tried to imagine the opportunities Frank was suggesting, but couldn't. He was too tired. "I can't help thinking I'm overlooking something."

"You're not considering declaring independence, are you?"

"No. That's suicide. We aren't anywhere close to self-sufficiency."

"Agreed. Look at it this way—three months ago, you knew nothing about Marsium121. Who knows what we'll know three months or three years from now. We're on the path to success. We only lose if we step off before we reach it."

Even though his heart wasn't in it, Chuck forced a smile. Frank was correct, yet hoping for a solution to magically appear compared poorly to the harsh reality of meddling regulators. He reflected on the commentary with apprehension and couldn't help thinking he had glimpsed the future.

With a gleam in his eye that Chuck hadn't seen in months, Frank said, "On a different topic, I want to force a meeting between Reed and our spy. What I have in mind is big and requires your approval."

17 | UNFORESEEN CHALLENGES

After breakfast, Gretchen arrived at the designated garage bay. Two rows consisting of five tractors each, people, tools, and spare parts filled the cavernous space. It smelled of lubrication oil, cleaner, and sweat. It reminded her of the airport hangars where she'd prepared equipment for archaeological digs.

She scanned the area for Frank, but didn't spot him. A passing maintenance tech, coveralls smeared with grime, directed her to the nearest row of tractors, indicating the second one from the right.

Gretchen approached as Frank stepped down from the rear cargo hatch. "Hi, Frank. What's going on?"

He leaned in close. "Loading some survey equipment, sampling tools and such."

"Survey equipment? We're going to need that?"

"No, but we want it to look like we're doing a standard survey."

The cargo containers were locked with activated tamper tags, like the ones she'd used when shipping expensive equipment to dig sites. They were elegant in their simplicity. Should anyone open the container, the broken or missing tag would testify to the tampering, and any replacement tag wouldn't have Frank's activation code. Unless someone wanted to steal the containers outright, they were as secure as sitting in a heavy-duty vault.

Standard survey equipment hardly required tamper tags, though. What was really inside the cargo containers? She didn't press the issue—it wasn't important. The last thing she needed was more friction between them. She was being paid to decipher symbols, not ask irrelevant questions. She needed to get the work done and return home with her payment.

"We might as well get this out of the way." Frank led her to the far side of the garage near the main airlock. "I need to confirm your proficiency with a spacesuit."

"I already certified in transit. The results were supposed to be transmitted ahead."

"We received them before you arrived, but—"

"Another test, Frank? I thought we covered this last night." She crossed her arms. *Do you truly think I'm not capable simply because I'm from Earth?* Tension or not, her pride couldn't allow it to pass unchallenged.

"It's not like that. Washington's regs are one thing, but we're going to be working in the wild for days on end. I need to assess your skill level."

"What makes you question my skill level?"

"Until a month ago, you never wore a spacesuit. Performing in one is a learned skill. Our children spend a couple of years near the domes gaining experience before they venture into the wild when they hit their teens, usually as part of the Mars Scouts. You haven't had that advantage."

"What about your Earth transfers?"

"The few that we have usually start out around the domes before heading into the wild after a couple of months." Frank shook his head and looked directly into her eyes. "Here's the thing. If you need extra practice, then I'll schedule time to get you up to speed. It's not a big deal. But I refuse to risk your life because you might be insulted by the question."

For a second, she put herself in his shoes and saw the situation from his perspective. She nodded. "Okay. I understand."

He activated a wall switch that lowered a shutter revealing the outside landscape. "Do you see the green marker flag straight out about a hundred yards away?"

It was a hideous fluorescent green isosceles triangle. "Yeah, who could miss it?"

"Good. Go out, replace it with this clean flag, and return with the soiled one. Part of the evaluation is to judge your dexterity with gloves, so you can't remove the clean one from the packaging until you're outside." Frank handed her a folded flag in a clear package.

Gretchen stared at him. "That's it?"

"That's it. I promise. I want to see how well you handle a practical task. No tricks, no agendas." He glanced around and hollered, "Hey, Sam. Come on over."

A clean cut college-aged man looked and waved, said a few words to another MarsVantage employee, and joined them. "What do you need, Frank?"

"Sam, this is Gretchen. Gretchen, Sam. He's covering my duties while I'm working on the expedition."

Gretchen shook his hand. "Nice to meet you."

"Sam, I need you to accompany Gretchen while she swaps the marker flag."

"Dexterity and proficiency?"

"Right." Frank pointed Gretchen to a changing stall where a green spacesuit waited.

Gretchen donned it per Trip's instructions. She finished by sealing the helmet and performing an integrity test. While it ran, she tucked the new flag in her suit's large thigh pocket on her right leg, so she'd have her hands free. She silently thanked Trip for the extra training. If he'd only required the minimum of her, she'd be fretting over the upcoming task.

The suit passed, but the air tasted somewhat stale. During one of Trip's sessions, he'd mentioned that this was a warning sign. She checked the air levels, which read one hundred percent, an estimated eleven hours remaining. She hit the reset and ran the self-test on the air vest. This time the air level displayed one percent available in flashing red digits. As she stepped out of the changing cubicle, she unsealed her helmet. "There's no air in this air vest."

Frank rushed to her side. "Let me see."

Gretchen showed him the wrist display. She struggled to keep to herself the suspicion that Frank had laid another test in her path. Even though she'd surely passed, her irritation level rose— she hadn't traveled to Mars to jump through ridiculous hoops.

"I have the same problem," Sam said, joining them with his helmet in hand.

At a nearby vidcomm, Frank connected to Master Communications. "This is Frank Brentford in Dome 7, Garage Bay Bravo. We have two air vests with bad readouts. Have everyone outside do a reset and self-test stat. Tell all sections to perform air vest checks immediately. I'll handle this one."

He turned around. "Sam, check the air vests awaiting refill, and I'll check the filled ones in the Supplies Room."

Gretchen followed Frank. Once inside, a large number of air vests hung, taking up one entire wall. "Is there anything I can do to help?"

"Yes. We've got around a hundred air vests to check, so I could use an extra set of hands." He handed her a bulkier version of the control panel on her left wrist. "Plug the vest's connector directly into the input, then do a reset and retest like normal."

Frank started his checking at the other end. His experience allowed him to move faster, but Gretchen was taking extra care to not make a mistake. He gave his undivided attention in testing the air vests. All other tasks took a backseat. Either he was a great actor or this issue was a mistake—one that could've been fatal. After forty-five minutes, they exited.

Sam approached with an air vest in each hand. "These two were fully filled. They probably got mixed up during the last refilling."

"We found no more empty vests," Frank said. "I don't know what to think. I want to blame Interplanetary, but this bay is secure."

What if the spy had sabotaged them? Gretchen kept that question to herself. Sensitive information like spies wasn't ordinarily shared with consultants.

Frank added, "I personally stocked the changing stalls this morning. Nothing looked suspicious."

"When we're done with Gretchen's evaluation, I'll check with Security for breaches or tampering in the Supplies Room, but I expect they'll find nothing. It has to be human error coupled with an equipment malfunction," Sam concluded.

"Stranger things have happened, I suppose, but it's hard to swallow," Frank said. "Let me know what Security says."

Sam handed Gretchen an air vest. After removing the empty one and handing it to Frank, Gretchen donned the fresh air vest, connected it to her suit, and sealed her helmet. She first ran an integrity test and concluded with a self-test. Her suit had integrity and the air vest was filled.

Gretchen resumed Frank's evaluation, departing the garage bay through the smaller personnel airlock off to the right of the main door. Sam followed, his sole job to ensure she didn't kill herself. Her suit fit better in the lower air pressure, almost as if she weren't wearing one. Absent were the binding, restricted movements she'd gotten used to during her training inbound to Mars.

About halfway to the flag, a rock shifted under Gretchen's foot, causing her to stumble.

"Careful! You don't want to fall and tear your suit," Sam said.

"Gretchen, are you okay?" Frank asked, his voice infused with tension as he watched through the bay's window.

"I'm fine. I stumbled over a rock, that's all. Walking on sand in the lower gravity is throwing me off a bit. I'll slow down."

"Good idea. You don't want to turn your ankle," Frank said.

Without further incident, she arrived at the flag and unclipped it on her second attempt. She unzipped her left thigh pocket, folded, and stuffed it inside. After zipping it up, she retrieved the new flag from her right thigh pocket. It was far brighter. The test was a necessary maintenance task. It might be minor, but it wasn't make-work, which made her feel useful.

After she tugged the pull tab on the new flag's package, she affixed the flag to the pole by its two clips. With a gentle tug, she pulled the packaging loose, placed it in the pocket, and zipped up.

In the reduced gravity and air pressure, the flag was still a folded lump, so she unfolded it to its full length of three feet, parallel to the ground. Mars' weak gravity took over when she released it, causing the flag to start sagging toward the pole. It was like watching a slow motion holo.

"Good job, Gretchen. You're done," Sam said.

"Thanks." She started toward the airlock with Sam trailing behind her, glad for the opportunity to get practical experience, though she would never admit it to Frank. The only annoyance was that the gloves didn't allow as fine of control as she would've preferred, but they were as good as the gloves she'd worn in Antarctica, so she'd make the best of it in the cave.

At the personnel airlock, labeled 7-B-2, Sam pressed the oversized button to open the outer door, and they entered. He closed it and equalized the air pressure to that within the garage bay. When the light above the inner door turned green, he opened it. They each removed their helmet and stepped from the airlock.

Frank was waiting with a broad grin on his face. "Well done, Gretchen. You're much further along than I expected."

"Thanks."

"Considering what we'll need to do outside, I don't see any need for further practice sessions unless you want them."

"I'll be okay." She unzipped her thigh pockets, handed the garish old flag and empty packaging to Frank, and went to the changing stall. As she stripped off the spacesuit, she contemplated today's schedule. They were prepping the tractor but were already an hour behind due to the air vest problem. On the plus side, the tractor was similar to those she'd used back home. She had a fair chance to leverage her experience and surprise Frank for a change.

18 | Lost Momentum

At the inner door of the personnel airlock, Heather Newton collapsed against the wall and punched the button with the side of her fist to cycle it. She yawned wide as its pressure started to equalize with Dome 4's garage bay, which Interplanetary was renting.

After what seemed like an eternity, the green light above the door lit, and Heather entered. She removed her helmet and scratched an itch on her cheek that had irked her for the past two hours.

More than anything, Heather wished to wash away the days of spacesuit-incubated sweat in a scalding shower and crawl into bed. But she needed to check on John's progress with Blake as well as file a preliminary accident report with headquarters.

After shedding her spacesuit, she wearily walked to her office where she locked the door and poured a well-deserved shot of vodka. She checked for vidcomm and email messages, finding an email from John and a second from Nancy Kaine mixed among several that could wait. She rubbed her eyes. All thoughts of a hot shower and sleep evaporated.

Heather sipped her drink while reading John's message, which briefly explained the events leading up to Blake's refusal. *What was Blake thinking? John offered her a blank check.*

Nancy's message indicated that she was disappointed in John's failure, but that was second only to her concern over the shuttle incident two days ago. She had insisted on an update as soon as possible, regardless of the time.

According to the wall clock, it was a quarter after two in the morning. Mars kept the same time as New York City, so she would surely be asleep. Heather followed instructions and vidcommed, using the secure tunnel.

Nancy answered, looking fresh, alert, and, most of all, tense. "Thanks for getting back to me promptly, Heather. First things first, tell me about the incident. All John knew was that a shuttle skidded into the dome during landing."

Heather glanced at her datapad. "There were no fatalities or injuries, except for the pilot, who has a broken arm. It was a simple fracture, so the docs mended it, and he'll be cleared for duty within the week. The shuttle is a loss, but we'll salvage the usable parts and dump the rest. The vast majority of the cargo is undamaged. There's about four weeks' worth of dome repairs, but thankfully, all the damage faces away from Mars City."

"So MarsVantage isn't aware of the accident?"

"All they know is that I changed the OTP offload schedule, but that's not terribly unusual. Shuttles get grounded for maintenance reasons occasionally."

"Good." Nancy exhaled and unclenched her jaw. "Fill out the accident forms for the Space Transportation Safety Ministry, and transmit them directly to me. I'll file them if the Ministry catches wind of the incident and my inside man can't head it off."

"Will do."

"What's the root cause of the accident?"

"I spoke with the pilot and the Flight Maintenance Supervisor. They both indicated that the aft starboard control thruster jammed during the landing sequence. The pilot did an incredible job to walk away from the crash. I recommend we give him a bonus."

Nancy leaned closer to her vidcomm's camera. "I planned to fire him. Heads need to roll over this."

Heather agreed as long as Nancy fired the person responsible. "This incident could've been far worse. We could be facing six months of repairs, deaths, witnesses, and government investigations. The Flight Maintenance Supervisor modeled the flight recorder data, which confirmed that the pilot did everything possible to address the emergency. When I fly, I want him at the controls."

Nancy's eyes grew wide. "I see your point. Write up the recommendation, and I'll take care of it. What caused the control thruster to jam?"

"The recorder data and the tests we conducted yesterday point to shoddy maintenance."

"Dammit," Nancy spat out through pursed lips. "That blunder nearly undid years of planning and months of careful execution to regain control of Mars. We can't use the safety tactic against MarsVantage if we're having accidents ourselves."

Heather had the same concern. The maintenance tech belonged back on Earth, separated from Interplanetary because his efforts fell below their standard. "I'll review the maintenance logs to determine the tech's identity, so we can fire him."

"Transmit his name, and I'll take care of it. I want to drive home to the other employees that incompetence has consequences. Now to the Blake business—John jumped into a *quid pro quo* and got rebuffed. He needs to lie low until Blake leaves."

"Of course. I'll take over running our assets for the duration."

"Assuming Blake's participating in MarsVantage's next exploration expedition, we're running out of time to discover exactly what her task is. If we can't figure that out, preventing MarsVantage from capitalizing on their prize will get messy."

"Messy" meant deaths, and Heather didn't wish to dwell on it. If MarsVantage had gone to the trouble and expense to hire a consultant, they expected a commensurate payoff, which could hinder Interplanetary's takeover plans. Everyone benefited by solving the problem before the messy options were necessary. "The time frame has always been problematic. I planned to befriend her and eventually offer to trade favors while John dated and charmed the information from her during pillow talk."

"That was an ambitious plan to execute in ten days."

"You're right, and John felt the same way. We never had a great option, but it was the best until I was called away. I spoke to him just before leaving, and he felt he had to use the back-up plan."

Nancy shook her head. "I can't believe Blake turned him down, but he still could've finessed it better. He should've stuck to his part of your original plan."

"Given the time frame, he didn't believe he could pull it off without me distracting her."

"Have him write up a detailed report and self-evaluation. We may be able to help him improve his technique." Nancy smiled broadly.

While Nancy might be pleased with her idea, to Heather, it sounded like nothing more than a punishment.

Nancy added, "If not, I'll reassign him. Make sure he's clear on that last part."

Heather dutifully nodded, even though John's reassignment would hurt their overall cause. Their skill sets complemented each other. She'd work with John on the report to placate Nancy if that was what it took to prevent her momentary anger from causing long-term harm. "I'll discuss improvement and work with him."

"Good, good. See what else you can do about Blake, but do nothing that links back to us."

"I can get everything we need by kidnapping, drugging, and questioning her. MarsVantage won't be able to prove a thing."

"That would tip them off, though. They'd change their plans and scream to anyone who'd listen that we're meddling in their business. We have the upper hand in public opinion, and we don't want to lose it."

"Very well. I'll think of something else." Heather stifled a yawn.

"Go and get some rest. You can't do anything about the Blake issue right now." Nancy broke the connection.

Instead of heeding instructions, Heather remained at her desk, evaluating the available options. She contemplated the dating approach herself, but decided against it because nothing indicated Blake had any interest in that direction. Besides, like John, she lacked enough time to manipulate Blake without her noticing. It was just as well—such liaisons didn't thrill her, but she would've grudgingly pursued one if it would've accomplished their goal.

There still had to be a way to get the details of Blake's task.

Hacking into MarsVantage's communications was out. Long ago, John had tried to tap into their vidcomms, but he'd detected a trace and abandoned the attempt before getting a chance to work on their encryption. Much of the same had happened when he'd accessed their email network. To Heather's dismay and

MarsVantage's credit, they maintained tight security on their systems.

In a few hours when the first shift was working, Heather would contact their operatives to see if they could glean any information related to Blake. It seemed unlikely, but one of them might have seen or overheard something useful. Unfortunately, Arnold was still in transit from Earth. Certainly, he could've contributed useful information.

As she finished her vodka, an idea popped into her head. Once Blake left for her shift, Heather could search her quarters. Perhaps the answers were there, waiting for her.

One setback wasn't going to derail Heather's long-term plans. She'd learn Blake's purpose on Mars, and she'd thwart the Marsees. Once Peter bought a failing MarsVantage, she would leave this sordid industrial espionage business behind and take over Interplanetary's operations on Mars.

19 | COUNTERMOVES

When Chuck entered his outer office, he expected it to be deserted since the first shift wouldn't begin for another two hours. Instead, James Bunderbon waited. His presence was inconvenient and sure to be unpleasant. Turning him away, however, would only antagonize him to no good end. As Chuck walked to his inner office, he asked, "What can I do for you, James?"

Bunderbon followed. "What happened with the air vests yesterday?"

"As best as we can determine, it was human error."

"Now isn't the time for human error. I received a vidcomm from the Safety, Standards, and Practices Administration last week. They're working on an inspection schedule."

"Excellent. An inspection only helps our cause by providing good PR We can spin yesterday's issue in a positive way. We discovered a problem, corrected it, and inspected all the equipment. Further, we alerted everyone who could've been affected to recheck their equipment."

"But it feeds the growing safety meme on Earth, and that isn't good PR. Frank needs to learn how to handle matters, quietly, off the record. This incident is official. It's my team that has to answer for it, and I don't have a good answer."

Chuck couldn't resist the opportunity to needle Bunderbon. "Try the truth."

"Do you really believe it was human error? You're the person who's been pushing the Interplanetary spy view for years. I'm sure Earth'll believe it, but I can't believe you do."

Chuck took a seat behind his desk. "We checked the entry logs and security camera footage."

"Which can be manipulated."

Bunderbon had a point. He must be feeling pretty satisfied with himself right about now.

"James, you're right. What do you propose?"

"Credentials refresh."

Chuck's first instinct was to argue about the suggestion's futility. They'd never catch anyone worth catching because Interplanetary was too smart to be tripped up attempting to re-validate an employee's cloned credentials.

Bunderbon's goal wasn't to catch Interplanetary, though. Instead, he was laying a trap to seize the MarsVantage CEO position for himself. Arguing about taking a positive step, even though it was likely futile, would only hand this opportunist more ammunition. Chuck nodded. "Good idea. I'll talk with Alan in Security as soon as the first shift starts. It'll be today's top priority."

After a moment's hesitation, Bunderbon replied, "Very good."

"Is there anything else on your mind?"

"No." Bunderbon began to leave but stopped and turned. "You make things so tough on yourself. Isn't it easier to accept our circumstance and work within the system?"

Chuck leaned into his chair's back. "Easier, yes. But would I be better off? No." The quote on the wall behind him came to mind, particularly the phases *'Crouch down and lick the hand that feeds you,'* and *'May your chains set lightly upon you.'*

With his right hand, he pointed over his left shoulder. "When you can read that 500-year-old quote and understand each line's meaning in the context of our current circumstances, then you'll understand why I refuse to accept those circumstances."

* * *

Chuck entered the inner office of the Vice President of Security, Alan Greene, and pressed the button to close the door. "I need a few minutes to discuss a sensitive matter."

After laying his datapad aside, Alan looked up. "Of course, what can I do for you?"

Chuck sat in a visitor's chair and folded his hands in his lap. "In addition to yesterday's air vest incident, our new consultant was offered a bribe the evening before."

"Where did it happen? And when?"

Chuck answered, and Alan immediately retrieved the surveillance video and learned what Chuck already knew. The security cameras hadn't recorded a clear image of the person offering the bribe.

At that moment, Chuck chose to withhold Reed's identity and by extension, the existence of the SDA. Chuck simply didn't want to deal with uncomfortable questions and hard feelings about why Security wasn't working with the SDA. All along, Alan conceded that Interplanetary was constantly seeking MarsVantage intelligence and even granted the *possibility* of a spy working within the company, but his team had never found any evidence. To Chuck's mind, Security had found exactly what they'd expected, which was why the SDA was Frank's side project.

"That's disappointing, Chuck. I thought we caught Interplanetary red-handed."

"No doubt they know exactly where the cameras are, but that's not why I'm here. I started my day with James Bunderbon."

Alan rolled his eyes. "Sorry to hear that."

Chuck snickered. "He suspects that Interplanetary got into our garage bay and sabotaged the air vests."

"If it were sabotage—and I seriously doubt that—it was an inside job. Bunderbon is grasping at straws, so he can replace you."

"I know."

"Do you know he's stirring up the board over the consultant? He's calling your secret project 'Chuck's Folly.'"

"I suspected, though I hadn't heard that he named it." Chuck grinned, recalling Seward's Folly. If the Marsium121 paid off half as well as William Seward's purchase of Alaska, Chuck would consider himself the luckiest person alive.

Alan leaned forward. "Here's the thing. Your friends trust you. We stand with you, but there are two or three weak-minded board members who're hearing Bunderbon's words. You can guess who they are. They need to hear your side."

Chuck shook his head. "I won't reveal the details of my project while we still have a spy scurrying about."

"Then don't, Chuck, but tell them something. Give them reassurance. Hold their hands if you have to."

Chuck nodded. He might not win them over, but it might keep them undecided, which was enough. "That's a good idea, thanks."

"So what do you want to do?"

"Bunderbon thinks we should recreate everyone's credentials. Given the air vest incident and the bribery attempt, I can't think of a good reason not to do it."

Under this plan, when an employee couldn't access a secured area after the credential switch, they'd have to submit their thumbprint and answer a personal question on their datapad. Security's systems would then transmit the new credentials to the datapad, and the employee could then proceed.

Practically speaking, an Interplanetary employee wouldn't risk exposure by incorrectly answering the question or supplying the wrong thumbprint. He'd just clone already-activated credentials, probably the spy's. That would be the smart move, and Interplanetary made a habit of making smart moves.

"Chuck, I know why we shouldn't do it. Ten percent of the employees will manage to foul it up, and we'll spend the rest of the day cleaning up employee access."

"Give me a list of who has problems. Maybe our spy'll show up."

Alan called in the watch supervisor and gave her the instructions. Without complaint, she left with much more work than when she'd entered the office. "It'll take a couple hours to create the new credentials. I'll send a notification that the switch will occur mid-shift."

Chuck wanted everyone, including Alan, to believe the credentials recertification was MarsVantage's response to the supposed security breach. However, by taking this step, Frank's plan would be that much more unexpected.

* * *

After she'd received Gretchen Blake's quartering assignment from Rogers in Janitorial Services, Heather, along with another Interplanetary employee, both disguised in MarsVantage's steel blue coveralls, chatted in the main corridor near the residence hallway leading to Blake's quarters. She didn't have to wait long for Blake to stroll past and get on the Interdome Accessway. After handing over her datapad, she dismissed her conversation partner, exhaled, and strolled down the hallway, acting as if she belonged. Less than a minute later, she stood before Blake's door.

From her leg pocket, she retrieved a datapad, a test device that wasn't linked to her or Interplanetary in any way. Though none of her informants had mentioned MarsVantage tracking Interplanetary datapads, she wasn't about to chance it.

She activated the lock defeater program on the datapad, which exploited a little-known flaw in the door's maintenance override circuit and bypassed the credentials validation. Several long, agonizing seconds later, the door slid aside.

Heather entered, closing the door behind her. She walked the short hall and reached the living area, where she remained motionless for several seconds while she took in the scene.

Nothing was out of order. If she hadn't known better, she would've sworn the quarters were vacant. She proceeded through the living area into the kitchen where the sink was sparkling and empty. Heather entered the bedroom, which at last, bore evidence of an occupant. Clothes—mostly MarsVantage-issued—hung in the closet, a guitar case stood in the corner, a toolpac sat along the wall, and the bathroom contained the typical necessities.

She rifled through the guitar case, betting Blake thought it'd be the last place anyone would look. It only held typical accessories like picks and extra strings but nothing else. Heather even shook the guitar, but nothing was hidden inside. Blake was softer than the usual Earther, unable to go a few months without her toy.

Heather replaced the case as she'd found it and inspected the toolpac, which held archaeological tools, mostly brushes and picks of various sizes. Undoubtedly, Blake was truly an archaeologist.

With the help of the datapad and a credentials cracking program, Heather gained access to Blake's computer after nearly an hour's wait. Blake had created no files. Likewise, her vidcomm messages and deleted messages were both empty.

Blake did leave behind a search history related to language theory and primitive languages. Heather didn't know what it meant, but she'd report it.

She departed Blake's quarters, heading toward her own in order to change before going to the office. On the Interdome Accessway, she overheard two MarsVantage employees grousing about a new security credential download that Security was about to implement.

Changing credentials wouldn't affect Interplanetary. They'd decided long ago that falsifying or cloning credentials was too risky in relation to the potential reward. Compromising MarsVantage employees was far more productive and incurred far less risk.

Something must've happened to arouse their suspicions. It wasn't anything Interplanetary had done. MarsVantage could chase imaginary problems and implement useless solutions as much as they wanted. It made her job all the easier.

20 | EXPEDITION'S EVE

On the eve of their departure, Frank's footsteps echoed through Dome 7's deserted garage bay as he scurried among the tractors under dimmed overhead lights. The crews manning these tractors tomorrow were attending the traditional send-off party at Taggert's. Frank needed to hurry—the party had already started, and his presence was expected.

From under the driver's seat of his assigned tractor, he grabbed a toolpac and slid beneath the tractor where he opened an access panel near the driver's side front tread. He withdrew a small flashlight from the toolpac to get a good view inside. With the toolpac's utility knife, he made two tiny nicks in the hydraulic line near the housing connection. A drop of hydraulic fluid formed. He replaced the access cover and repeated the same procedure two tractors over.

After returning the toolpac to his tractor, he brushed the dust off his otherwise clean coveralls and departed the garage bay. Outside, near the entrance, he opened the maintenance panel and transmitted his credentials to give him full access to the controls. He reactivated the door's security monitors and discontinued the looped video of the empty garage bay he'd fed the security system while performing the deed.

He closed the panel and hurried to Taggert's. When he'd told Gretchen he'd be late, she had seemed agitated, though he couldn't pin down why. She'd been getting around the domes like she was born here. Perhaps she simply wanted to attend with him, or perhaps she didn't like parties.

As he crossed into the center dome, he came across Arnold Janssen heading the other way. Arnold motioned to him, and they stepped out of the transit lanes. Politeness overruled Frank's schedule. "Arnold, glad to see you're back."

"It's good to be back," he said leisurely, like he had all the time in the world.

"I thought you were scheduled off for another week."

"I was. I missed Claire, so I returned early."

Considering the effort and expense to travel to Earth, Frank would've completed the trip as planned. It wasn't like Arnold could hop over to Earth whenever the whim struck.

Frank said, "It looks like you spent some time outside."

"Yeah, I took in five baseball games and hiked a couple days in the mountains. It was wonderful. Oh, how's Gretchen working out?"

"Terrific. She's been a great help in prepping for the expedition. She was a fantastic hire."

"I'm glad."

* * *

In Taggert's, one of the few restaurants with a dedicated dining area, Gretchen stood on the periphery of the party for the crews and maintenance personnel involved with tomorrow's expedition. She glanced around, absentmindedly fiddling with the datapad in her thigh pocket, not knowing what to do or what to expect next. Besides never feeling comfortable in large crowds of strangers, she had nothing to talk about. They shared few common experiences, and her contract barred her from discussing the assignment.

During countless hours of preparations over the past week, she'd developed a comfortable working relationship with Frank. So much so that a few days ago, they'd even started taking their meals, including breakfast, together and working through them. Now, when she needed a conversation partner the most, he had to attend to mysterious business.

Sam approached, interrupting her thoughts. "Hi, Gretchen. I expected Frank to be with you."

"He had something to take care of, but he'll be here shortly."

"Good. We can't go changing our luck."

"Changing our luck?"

"Sure. When crewmembers skip the Departure Party, the expedition runs into trouble. Always happens."

"That's ridiculous. One event has no relation to the other."

"We noticed the correlation. And when logic and human nature butt heads, logic loses."

Gretchen nodded. Most people had small habits and rituals that allowed them to get through the day. When she considered the dangers the Marsees faced, she wasn't surprised that they'd devised rituals and traditions of their own.

"Here, check out the snacks." Sam directed her to a large table that resembled buffets that bars back home provided as a requirement to maintain their liquor licenses. The table held vegetables like celery and carrots, various types of breads and crackers, and what appeared to be fried chicken, which was probably processed soy beans. The Marsees wouldn't incur the cost to raise livestock for food, nor ship large quantities of meat from Earth.

As Gretchen fixed a plate, avoiding the *faux*-chicken, Sam asked, "So what do you expect to find?"

"You know I can't say."

"C'mon, what's it going to hurt now?"

She glanced left, then right, and leaned in close. "Unimaginable treasures."

He stared at her with wide eyes.

"Gretchen, Sam, glad to see you."

Gretchen turned. Chuck sported a broad grin.

"Sam, can you find Frank, so we can get started?"

"Sure thing, boss."

Sam walked away, much to Gretchen's relief. If he'd pressed for more details, she didn't know what else to say without becoming rude.

"Please try some lemonade. It's really good. After numerous attempts, our agri people finally managed to grow palatable lemons," Chuck said.

Gretchen poured a cup from the jug and took a sip. "Thanks, it's tarter than I'm used to, but it's delicious."

Chuck smiled like a proud father. "For years, we experimented with many factors from soil nutrients to light filters, trying to grow worthwhile lemons."

"I never imagined it'd be so difficult."

"Sometimes, on Mars, what appears to be simple turns out to be difficult."

"And sometimes the hard tasks turn out to be simple?"

"In my experience, that's a rarity," Chuck said through a grin. "Hey, here comes Frank."

Gretchen turned and saw him. The tension in her shoulders eased. She wouldn't have to keep the lemon conversation moving forward by herself.

"Sorry I'm late," Frank said. "I ran across Arnold on my way here."

"He's back early. Is everything okay?" Chuck asked.

"Yeah. Says he missed Claire."

"Maybe next time they can arrange a trip together. How was his vacation otherwise?"

"He's sporting a tan. I don't think he spent a second longer than necessary indoors."

"Good for him. Get some food, and I'll get my speech out of the way."

As Chuck worked his way to the front of the crowd, Frank fixed a plate of food with Gretchen by his side. "Did you try the lemonade?"

"Yeah. It's good." Again with lemons—the Marsees were obsessed. She caught herself. Back home, lemons were commonplace, but here, they must be a luxury.

"Everyone, your attention please," Chuck said from off to the side of the room with his hands raised. The crowd turned to face him, and after a few seconds, a hush had fallen over the restaurant. "Tomorrow, you venture into the wild, looking for valuable minerals and water. Make no mistake, you're building our future. Every discovery you make directly translates into success for us and our company. And Ben Jacobsen, are you here?"

From the back of the room, Ben yelled, "Right here, boss."

"Good. Don't let anybody give you any guff about finding more water. I'd rather have a gallon extra than come up a cup short."

The crowd laughed.

In Gretchen's ear, Frank whispered, "Every time Ben heads out, he finds water. People are already betting about when he'll report his first find this time."

"Can I get in on that action?"

Chuck interrupted Frank's answer. "Good luck and good hunting to you!"

Gretchen set her plate and cup on the buffet table and joined in the applause. Once again, the chatter rose to its prior level as Chuck blended in with the crowd.

Frank pointed to a table tucked away in the corner. "Let's go over there, so we can hear ourselves think. There's one more thing we need to do."

After they sat, Frank pulled his datapad from his pocket, placing it directly before him while moving his plate off to the side. "We have a tradition before heading into the wild. In case anything happens, we leave behind a letter for the people who are important to us. They'll receive it only if we don't return."

Gretchen lost what little appetite she had. "Do you have many accidents?"

"We haven't had a fatality on an expedition since our inception. Still, it's a tradition, like this party."

"Will everyone do it?"

"They already have," Frank said after he swallowed a sip of lemonade. "It's your first time out, so you need to."

"Okay, I suppose." She shrugged her shoulders. "I really don't have anything to say."

"Some say goodbye to family and friends, some say the things left unsaid, while others leave instructions for their affairs. It can be anything to anyone you want. You have family on Earth, right?"

"Sure. My parents live in California a couple hundred miles apart, and my sister lives in the European Union of Socialist States. We're not that close."

Frank had already extended his screen and started typing. "It's up to you. You can say goodbye to someone else, a close friend, perhaps."

"Are you writing a letter?"

He stopped typing and looked up, his face expressionless. "Yes. My circumstances have changed since my last time out, and I need to compose a new letter."

She opened her mouth to inquire further but thought better of it. He didn't appear eager to discuss it, and she didn't want to pry.

As she turned her attention to her datapad, she decided she had nothing more to say to her family. Among other things, they'd blamed her for her marriage's non-renewal, saying she shouldn't have been traipsing around the globe and ignoring her husband. There might be a kernel of truth in those words, but when she'd needed sympathy, they'd only offered recriminations.

Instead, she would compose a letter to Ashley, who always had an ear when she needed to talk and a shoulder when she needed to cry.

Ashley,

Before venturing into the field—what the Marsees call the wild—they traditionally compose a letter should something unfortunate happen. I feel a little silly writing this, but here it is.

You're receiving this because I died on Mars. When I read that last sentence it looks harsh, but I don't know how to say it gently. Please know that I died doing what I loved. I have no regrets.

Don't be sad. The job that brought me here was irresistible once I learned the details. I couldn't pass it up.

You won't believe this, but the people I'm working with are fantastic, not at all what I expected of Marsees. They're nothing like their reputation, at least, not the ones I met.

There's one in particular, Frank Brentford. After getting off to a rough start, we ended up working well together, which is good because starting tomorrow, we'll spend a lot of time alone together in close quarters. I think you'd like him—he's smart, driven, and kind of cute. He reminds me a lot of Toby from college.

Remember fondly all the good times we had together. Live well, be successful in everything you do, and most of all, be happy.

Love,
Gretchen

The tips of her ears warmed as she reread the letter. She dismissed the minor annoyance as she considered the symbols awaiting her in the cave. She still hadn't deciphered them, and a twinge stirred in her gut.

After Frank completed his letter, he showed her how to save it. They finished their food as they discussed minor details related to tomorrow but neither broached the subject of their letters. Gretchen was thankful—the entire idea bordered on the macabre.

Afterward, as the party wound down, he escorted her to her quarters. They walked the vacant Interdome Accessway and the hallways. Frank was quiet, seemingly lost in thought.

"Is everything okay?" Gretchen asked.

"Uh, yeah. Why do you ask?"

"You haven't said anything since we left Taggert's."

"Sorry. It's been years since I had to write that letter. It started me thinking about my life, my mistakes and missed opportunities."

"I understand. Since my non-renewal, I had many of those same thoughts. You know, tomorrow's expedition is the start of a new chapter. Like Chuck said, you're building your future. That doesn't just mean for your company but for yourself, too. Every day, every decision creates the future. Create it to your vision. It can be whatever you want."

"Do you really believe that?"

"I wouldn't be here if I didn't."

21 | DISCOVERY AT DAWN

Departure morning arrived. Gretchen was glad to finally get in the field, though uneasy at not having an interpretation ready when she faced the symbols. She'd already discounted all of the possibilities.

She left her quarters and walked to Frank's. She had shunned the bicycle during her first days on Mars because it was easier to walk and read the map. Now, she ignored the map, yet still walked. It wasn't terribly far wherever she went, and it'd been easier to converse with Frank when he'd accompanied her, which had been often as of late. Plus, she never really liked bicycles.

He'd never complained about walking, kindly allowing her to lead the way while traveling throughout the domes. She was thankful—she now felt confident and comfortable traversing them. The irony wasn't lost on her. Soon, she'd head into the wild, fulfill her contract, and head home, never needing the skill again.

She rang Frank's announcement chime and heard a muffled "Come in" through the speaker. She activated the door and it slid aside, unleashing an unmistakable aroma.

As she walked through the living room, not seeing Frank, she hollered toward his bedroom, "Is that pancakes I smell?"

"Eah. Rhere's a rate on da table for yoo, if yoo wan some. Ra'll be out en ra rinute."

Gretchen understood perfectly. It wasn't the first conversation she had with a man brushing his teeth. She sat, removed the plate's cover, and inhaled, allowing the delicious aroma to tease her appetite.

She added her favorite toppings and ate. They were delicious, even the syrup, which she'd expected to be an inferior substitute.

Frank sat down across the table from her. "How are they?"

"Excellent. Did you import the syrup?"

"Nope, just the black maple trees decades ago. Over in Dome 4 there's a portion of a large park that we isolate to simulate New England winter, including snow."

"I'll skip that. I spent enough time in the snow lately. But you did a great job with breakfast. This is an unexpected treat."

"I thought you could use some decent food. We'll be eating FieldMeals for the duration of the expedition. The best I can say about them is the quality varies."

After finishing the last forkful of her surprise, she rinsed the dish, placing it on top of the other in the sink. "Thank you. That was delicious. You're a great cook."

"Wait for the meal I cook when we get back." He smiled easily, which she returned, hoping with all her heart she could give him a reason to celebrate.

Gretchen's cheeks warmed. Recently, it'd been happening at random times. She dismissed the annoying distraction as they departed for Dome 7.

When they entered the garage bay, full-fledged chaos enveloped them with people rushing in every direction, shouting orders.

Frank exhaled and smiled. "Here we go. I saw in your HR profile that you can drive, so start up the tractor. If you don't mind, I'd like you to drive out to Waypoint 1."

"No problem."

"Good. It's smooth, almost like riding in an Earth auto-cab from what I hear. When we hit Waypoint 1, I'll take over. Where we're going's less traveled, bumpier, but I've driven it many times."

Gretchen stepped into the tractor's cabin, transmitted her credentials from her datapad, and started the engine, hearing a familiar whoosh. Once again, Frank inspected the cargo behind her, paying particular attention to the "survey equipment" while she reviewed the status panel. After a few seconds, she noticed a flashing, low-pressure warning light for the front treads.

She grabbed a toolpac from under her seat and dismounted, intent on troubleshooting the problem. She crawled under the tractor, rolled over, and opened the access hatch. A wave of green liquid splashed across her chest. It was cold enough to take her breath away. And it smelled like dead skunk.

After Gretchen emerged, she stood, the hydraulic fluid seeping toward her waist. Once again, she stepped into the tractor's cabin and cut off the engine. She hollered to Frank in the cargo area, "You need to see this out here."

He looked her up and down, scowled, and exited through the back hatch, joining her by the front tread. "What happened?"

She recounted how she'd become a walking mess.

"Did you get any in your eyes?"

"No. Just all over my chest and arms."

"Good, good." Relief washed over his face. "Go change. There are clean coveralls in the lockers over there. I'll check it out in the meantime."

After finding coveralls that fit, Gretchen changed in a stall. As she finished, the garage bay's din died down. She emerged and saw everyone gathered around their tractor listening to Frank.

"Based on the problem I found, I'm concerned about overall safety, so I'm postponing this expedition until every tractor is fully inspected by Maintenance. Let's get to it, people."

The tractor crews exited the garage bay, leaving the maintenance crews with a full day's work. Frank approached with a half-smile on his face. "It's time to talk with Chuck."

She followed, waiting until they were out of earshot of the others before saying, "What's going on? The hydraulic line broke. It's a fifteen-minute fix. Even I can do it."

"It didn't break. It was cut." Frank pulled the line from his pocket and showed it to her.

There were two nicks near one end. "You mean we were sabotaged?"

"Yes."

Who would do such a thing? Don't they know people can die?

"Frank, shouldn't that credentials change a few days ago have prevented this?"

"Not really. Only an idiot would try to validate cloned or faked credentials. It's a sure way to get caught." Frank looked directly into her eyes. "Interplanetary doesn't hire idiots. They hire smart people who'd use other means."

"So why did you force the change then?"

"Part of it was politics. But Chuck and I hoped it would distract the spy and Interplanetary from our true plan."

"Which is?"

"Not here. Wait until Chuck's office."

As they continued walking, Gretchen tried to work through what Frank's "true plan" was. Many ideas came to mind, but she dismissed each as half-baked as soon as she'd thought of it.

In Chuck's office, they sat around the conference table just like the day she'd arrived. Frank explained the postponement and produced the hydraulic line.

Chuck inspected it with a broad, devilish grin. "You do nice work, Frank. A simple enough repair to make, yet serious enough to justify a postponement for a full inspection."

"Thanks," Frank said, adding a devilish grin of his own.

Nothing in this meeting made sense. Gretchen crossed her arms. "Okay, what's going on?"

"Our tractor wasn't exactly sabotaged. I did that last night to cause a delay and force a meeting between the Interplanetary handler and our spy." After a momentary pause, Frank continued in a sincere tone, "Let me now apologize. I'm genuinely sorry you got doused with hydraulic fluid. I never imagined you'd investigate the tractor problem yourself."

Relief flowed over Gretchen as she exhaled. *No one is trying to kill me.* Then, anger welled up. "Damn it, Frank! We could've avoided all this if you'd confided in me."

"Uh... I never thought you'd investigate."

"We've worked together for days. Haven't I earned your trust yet?" Gretchen glared at Frank.

"But... but... it's not like that," he said, looking from Gretchen to Chuck, who merely nodded toward Gretchen.

"From where I'm sitting, that's exactly what it is. I bet that's why you were late for the party. Instead of having Chuck distract me with inane lemon talk, you should've told me what you were planning. I would've even helped."

She stood as Frank said, "Gretchen, I—"

"Oh, save your excuses. I can't even look at you." Gretchen marched out of Chuck's office, her hands trembling in anger.

22 | Arnold's Perfidy

As soon as Heather Newton left another construction schedule meeting, she reached for her datapad. She'd expected to hear from John shortly after dawn but hadn't, and with lunchtime nearing, she still hadn't heard anything. Something was wrong—MarsVantage's expedition should've left already.

She returned to her office, locked her door, and vidcommed John directly. After a second, the screen went black because he lacked a video feed in the tractor. "Have you seen anything yet?"

"No. The equipment airlock hasn't cycled today. The personnel airlock has had only minimal activity."

"If they wait any longer they won't hit Waypoint 1 before nightfall."

"True, but it's due north on Main Street. They can safely travel it with lights."

"How often have they done that?"

"Once since I've been here."

"Exactly. Hold tight. I'll be in touch with further instructions." Heather broke the connection. From her lower desk drawer, she grabbed a triangular, fluorescent blue flag that typically marked cargo, and took the stairs to the ground floor.

Outside, she attached the flag to her bicycle's handlebars and pedaled to the Admin dome. She left it in the parking area next to MarsVantage's headquarters. Arnold would hopefully see the flag and remember its meaning, even though they'd never used that signal before.

She walked back to her office wondering what had delayed MarsVantage's expedition. For their schedule to slip this much, it had to be serious. Suppertime couldn't arrive soon enough.

* * *

114

With her back against the wall of the restaurant court, Heather sipped a cup of Mars coffee. Over the years, it'd improved. Only the premium beans imported from Earth tasted better these days.

At the Garden Emporium, Arnold Janssen got a meal and found an isolated seat, one where they could talk. It was off the main walkway, so they shouldn't have many people walking by. A handful of MarsVantage employees were enthusiastically enjoying their supper. That commotion should draw everyone's attention. He quietly read his datapad, not gawking around as she'd feared. He must've remembered the blue flag meant Interplanetary would initiate contact instead of following their standard procedure.

Heather gulped the last mouthful of coffee, rose, and tossed the empty cup into the nearest garbage bin before purchasing a salad. As she walked to Janssen and settled in behind and to his right, so their backs were facing, she patiently mixed the dressing into the salad. Her shoulders tensed, and she forced herself to relax by slowly canting her head from side to side as she focused on her datapad.

She felt exposed, as if MarsVantage was watching her every movement. Of course, multiple surveillance cameras captured the scene, but they weren't much of a concern because there was too much area to cover for them to clearly record fine movements.

She, as well as Janssen, had to remain alert for people watching them, but not appear as if they were on guard. Neither could they be overheard. Keeping it all in mind while getting the information she needed nearly overwhelmed her.

Long ago, she'd decided that hiding in plain sight would be the safest meeting method, allowing for believable excuses if they happened to get caught. John had agreed and had made conveying information an art form on the occasions that she'd watched. She much preferred recruiting where she could talk directly to the person and gauge their reactions.

The situation was what it was, though. The job needed done, and she had to do it. Nothing was served by focusing on her discomfort.

Without moving her head, Heather's eyes darted right to left. "Arnold, I'm your new contact. Call me Jane."

"What happened to Jacob?"

The "Jacob" he'd referred to was John, and she wasn't about to divulge his botched attempt to co-opt Blake. Janssen had no need to know. "He's involved with another task. I'm your handler until he's available again. When you leave, make sure you get a good look at me, so we can return to the regular arrangements. Just don't make it obvious."

"Don't worry, I have a good memory. I'll find you next time."

"Sssh." As a MarsVantage employee approached, she stabbed the salad and ate a forkful, chewing while he passed beyond earshot. "What's going on with the expedition? And keep it short. There's a lot of activity tonight."

"Two of the tractors were sabotaged. Security doesn't know how it was done, or who did it. Rumors are swirling that Interplanetary's responsible."

Heather fought the urge to turn around by grabbing the table's edge. "That's ridiculous. If MarsVantage has equipment problems, it's a maintenance issue, not our doing. We want Blake in the wild doing the task for which she was hired."

The table with five MarsVantage employees erupted in laughter. Everyone looked their way. Heather turned, looking over her shoulder, not really paying them much mind, but getting a good look at what else was happening behind her. She turned back to her salad and ate another bite. "When will they leave?"

"Tomorrow. Maintenance completed repairs within an hour of their discovery, but Frank insisted on a full inspection before departure. Maintenance crews will be working late into the night, and Security will be posted both inside and outside of the garage bay through tomorrow morning. The records with Exploration and Mineral Rights Office should be updated by now."

She would order John to return for the evening and start trailing the expedition tomorrow. While nothing would've been easier than to have him already waiting for Brentford and Blake, the tractor's energy constraints argued against it.

John's tractor's hiding place would block the sun for part of the day, which meant the solar panels wouldn't receive enough light to fully charge the batteries. Therefore, he'd need to partially power the life support systems from the fuel cell. That'd limit his time in the wild while MarsVantage wasn't likewise limited.

They'd decided not to exacerbate the situation by riding into the wild early. Given MarsVantage's delay, that decision looked brilliant.

John had to move in concert with MarsVantage to maximize his chance of success without resorting to extreme options. His trip entailed a certain amount of risk, but he was skilled and experienced enough to manage it as long as the destination was truly what the public records had stated.

"According to the filed plan, Brentford is heading to the Maelstrom Mountains," Heather said. "Do you know if that's his true destination or a deception?"

"It's his destination. Frank's been especially meticulous about procedures for this expedition."

"He's been there a dozen times. Why does he need an archaeologist this time?"

"My research indicates that there was an expedition about twenty years ago that found unusual markings in a cave."

"You mean Chuck O'Donnell hired an archaeologist, brought her to Mars, and paid her a handsome fee to decipher some marks on a cave wall?"

"Based on everything I know, that's my guess."

"Why?"

"Who knows? Chuck must have a good reason. He doesn't spend money without one."

"Okay. If you discover more, use the regular signals." She wished to vidcomm Nancy at headquarters immediately, but instead, she ate slowly to maintain the illusion of a casual meal. She heard Janssen get up ten minutes later. In response, she leaned back in the chair and studiously examined the datapad, which allowed Janssen a good view of her features. Several minutes later, her salad finished, she walked to MarsVantage's headquarters, retrieved her bicycle, and rode back to the office.

Once there, she searched the records as Janssen suggested and found the details. MarsVantage must be desperate if they were pursuing an explanation of those circles and lines. She vidcommed Nancy who didn't answer at her office. With a touch of uneasiness, she tried at her home, not wanting to interrupt her free time, but appreciating Nancy would want to know what she'd found.

On the second ring, Nancy answered. "Yes, Heather. What do you have?"

Heather recounted Arnold's theory and transmitted an image of the cave markings.

Nancy sipped from a coffee mug while inspecting the symbols. "Excellent. Now we've got something to work with. I'll have our people here look into it. Until I say otherwise, my original instructions remain. John is to acquire whatever they're after. If he can't, he must prevent MarsVantage from capitalizing on it. He's to use whatever means are necessary."

23 | SPY HUNT

On her bed's edge, Gretchen sat with guitar in hand, trying to forget her earlier argument with Frank. She couldn't.

Hours had passed, and he still hadn't contacted her. Not good, not good at all. MarsVantage would surely mark her as difficult to deal with when they filed their evaluation on the HR Acquisition Network. That, coupled with Hawthorne's evaluation, would seal the coffin holding her career.

She wished she'd ignored Frank's manipulations and slights. She should've. Ashley would've. She needed the money and the positive performance review. Yet, she'd allowed her emotions to get the best of her.

But she couldn't ignore his attitude. Besides the obvious safety concerns, she needed every scrap of information if she were to decipher the symbols, which meant that she needed to be a full partner in the task. She wouldn't get a positive performance review if she couldn't successfully complete the task, either.

Gretchen shook her head and played the video of the fingering technique on her datapad for the third time. With her left hand, she mimicked the technique on the fingerboard. As she was about to try it while picking, the announcer chimed. She set aside the guitar, took two steps to the panel by the bedroom door, and pressed the Speaker button. "Yes?"

"It's Frank. We need to talk."

There it was—he had come to send her home. It took him long enough to get around to it. There was nothing left to do, except face the consequences. She pressed the Open button. "Come in."

Gretchen met him in the living room where she sat in a chair while he sat on the couch, facing her, leaning forward with his elbows on his knees. She'd never seen him look so serious.

"After you left, Chuck and I had a very frank conversation, if you'll pardon the pun."

She nodded. "When do I leave?"

"Leave? You're not leaving, unless you want to."

"Oh." Her career may not be as dead as she'd thought. "What'd you discuss?"

"To be blunt, my misjudgment in excluding you from my plan." Frank looked down to his feet for a second before refocusing on her. "Chuck pointed out that I needlessly alienated you. Our entire project is in your hands, and telling you about our ploy was minor in comparison. He ended by saying, and I quote, 'Get your head out of your ass, and fix it.'"

Gretchen stifled a laugh. "I can't imagine Chuck saying that."

"It surprised me, too."

"What happens if you can't fix it?"

"Sam will take my place and accompany you to the cave."

"I see." As much as she'd mishandled the situation, by Frank's demeanor, he now recognized that he'd also committed mistakes. *That's a positive sign.*

He smiled weakly and stared at her. "I apologize. I have no problems with your expertise or in trusting you."

Teenage boys made more heartfelt apologies. "I hear your words, but your actions indicate differently."

He exhaled and rubbed his forehead with his left palm. "I'm so used to guarding information, especially on this project, that it never occurred to me to include you. We've worked together for days, and I should've brought you into the plan beforehand. You earned that much."

"I agree, but that isn't enough. If we're going to work together in the wild, you have to trust me. And I have to trust you. What's getting in the way? Is it because I'm from Earth?"

"I admit, at first, my expectations weren't high. You quickly showed me I was wrong."

Gretchen leaned toward Frank. "Then what is it? This morning's departure drama was clumsy. What's the problem?"

Frank leaned back and placed his hands in his lap. "Chuck also mentioned that I haven't been myself since... for a couple of months now. He referred once again to the need to reposition my head."

That was a curious tidbit of information, probably some sort of a personal issue. Before she could inquire further, he continued speaking.

"Anyway, in addition to running the Marsium121 project, I'm also Chuck's unofficial spy hunter. I'm trying to catch the Interplanetary spy while insulating you from him, so you can focus on the cave symbols. Clearly, I've done a poor job juggling all of these priorities."

Slowly, her shoulders relaxed. She hadn't realized that she'd been so tense. "Perhaps instead of protecting me, you should've let me help."

"That isn't what we hired you to do."

"Your machinations are getting in the way, so helping catch the spy may help me get my job done."

Frank smiled—this time, it was easy and genuine. Laugh lines around his eyes appeared. This was the first time she'd seen him truly happy. She liked it.

"Gretchen, you're remarkable."

* * *

In his quarters, Frank pulled up a chair for Gretchen to the standalone computer in the corner of the living room. He'd never expected help locating the spy. Gretchen might notice something he wouldn't, but the odds of that were slim. It didn't matter as long as she was still willing to finish the project.

They sat, and while he activated the SDA, he said, "With a little luck, there won't be much to do. If my plan has worked, we'll identify the spy tonight. Please don't say anything to anyone. Only Chuck knows about it."

"I promise."

Frank smiled. "I'm running a specialized data analysis program that uses Security's datapad telemetry information. It's looking for associations between MarsVantage and Interplanetary employees. Up to your arrival, I didn't have much luck. There was too much data, too many interactions. That changed when John Reed approached you."

"John Reed?"

"Oh, yeah. 'Zach' was an alias. His real name is John Reed."

"So, all you have to do is track John's datapad and see who's nearby?"

"Exactly. I expect he'll meet with the spy to learn why we haven't left as scheduled. I even delayed updating our itinerary for as long as possible to force an in-person meeting."

Frank ran the SDA, which indicated Reed had no interactions with MarsVantage employees today. That didn't make any sense. Undeterred, he retrieved Reed's full location data.

Gretchen leaned closer. "John Reed left his quarters early this morning in Dome 4, went to its garage bay, and hasn't been tracked since?"

"It makes sense if he worked outside all day. Security's systems don't track datapads beyond the domes. I'll start an all-personnel analysis, but it'll take some time." At that moment, Frank's stomach growled.

Gretchen chuckled. "I'm hungry, too. Let's hit the restaurant court while your program runs."

"I have a better idea." Frank rose and directed her to the kitchen table. He started heating water on the stovetop as she sat.

"Can I help?"

"No, thanks. I've been warming the sauce for a couple hours, so all I have to do is cook the spaghetti. There's nothing to do but watch the water boil."

* * *

A short time later, Frank and Gretchen sat facing each other eating a home-cooked spaghetti dinner. A couple months ago, Erin had sat across from him. The unwanted memory of her refusing his proposal barged its way into his thoughts. Again.

Before sadness consumed him, he focused on the here and now. "I'm truly sorry about the hydraulic fluid. Most employees would've called for a tech."

Gretchen took a sip of water and cleared her throat. "The tractors we used back home were similar."

"Makes sense. Similar problem, similar solution."

"You either handled basic repairs, or you walked a lot, which is downright dangerous in Antarctica."

"I see," Frank said, looking over to Gretchen. And that was the problem. Erin used to sit there—Gretchen was sitting there now. Living in the past was getting in the way of the present. He had to fight the memory. "We're good now?"

"Yeah, we're fine." Gretchen's cheeks brightened as she ate a forkful of spaghetti.

What's she thinking? Is she embarrassed? Is it something else? He didn't have time to contemplate further because she redirected the conversation.

"I noticed a plaque in your hallway junction commemorating employees' courageous actions during the Airlock Accident. I saw the name Charles O'Donnell listed. Is that Chuck?"

"Yes."

"Wow. I didn't know I was working for a hero."

"Don't let him catch you saying that. He won't hear any 'hero' talk."

"It must've been deserved." A question lurked in Gretchen's eyes, though she hadn't asked it.

She was curious enough to find out eventually, so Frank chose to get the story out of the way now. "Thirteen years ago, a seal failed on the emergency airlock in this residence hall. Decompression alarms sounded, and everyone put on their spacesuits. Many people found that their air vests were empty. Those seals had deteriorated, just like the airlock's."

"Even though I was a teenager, I remember the talk about equipment failure on the news," Gretchen said before taking a mouthful of spaghetti.

"To make matters worse, some people couldn't remove their helmets. Chuck and a few others helped pry helmets from spacesuits. Everyone who had been freed assisted others until the pressure doors were about to close. Even then, they dragged and carried people to safety. In the end, twenty-three people suffocated, including my wife, Lori."

Her eyes wide, Gretchen gasped and snatched his hand, cradling it between hers. "Frank, I'm so sorry. I saw the 'In Memoriam' on the plaque, but I didn't make any connections to the names underneath. If I'd known, I never would've said anything."

"It's okay, Gretchen. I accepted it a long time ago. All of these problems were failures in preventive maintenance, maintenance that Interplanetary pushed to the back burner. This is why it's so important this project succeeds. If it does, MarsVantage succeeds."

Frank smiled and patted her hand, prompting her to release his. He went to the computer, and she followed, neither saying a word as he retrieved the full-analysis results. "There's nothing unusual here. I've been seeing the same thing for weeks now. Lots of interactions, but nothing out of the ordinary. And nothing involving Reed."

"Wait a minute. I see Arnold Janssen's name listed. Why's he interacting with Interplanetary?"

"He's in the restaurant court. It's innocuous."

"How do you know that?"

"Early on, I checked out dozens of such interactions against Security footage. While we live and work separately, we do interact in places like the restaurant court. Here, I'll show you." Frank pulled up the security camera footage for Dome 2's restaurant court. In the lower right corner of the display, he pointed out Arnold sitting with his back to an Interplanetary employee. "See. A false positive. He's having supper and an Interplanetary employee happens to be nearby. They aren't conversing or sharing anything."

"How do you know they're not transmitting information using their datapads?"

"Our datapads are military grade, not commercial."

"I don't understand."

"Besides being ruggedized, any data transfer occurs through central MarsVantage systems, not directly between the datapads themselves. Security's been monitoring that since day one. If they tried it, Security would've already taken them into custody and arranged for prosecution back on Earth."

"Oh. What are you looking for then?"

"I'm expecting a face-to-face meeting in an out of the way place like a little-used hallway or one of our parks."

"Huh. But they'd be caught on camera. You have almost as many as most cities on Earth, counting the ones that you attempted to disguise. Don't you think they'd want to avoid that?"

You've managed to notice the hidden cameras? Perhaps Gretchen had used some to monitor prior dig sites for thieves and competitors. "They'd probably use the places that have spotty coverage."

"Instead of going to all that trouble, why wouldn't they meet in someone's quarters?"

"Eventually someone would notice and report a stranger who's somewhere they don't belong. It happens. Security has had a few reports about you."

"I should be surprised, but I'm not." She chuckled. "Perhaps we should look at Reed again. Maybe he met the spy after his shift."

Frank pulled up Reed's data. Since they'd last looked, he'd exited Dome 4's garage bay, had gone to his quarters for ten minutes, and afterward, had gone to Interplanetary's main office building.

Frank leaned back in the chair and rubbed his eyes. "We have nothing. And I wasted a day to get it. Dammit, nothing's ever easy."

"Come on, Frank. Ease up. It was a good try. Reed didn't go for it, that's all. Tomorrow, we're setting out to claim a huge load of Marsium121, and there's nothing Interplanetary can do to stop us."

24 | UNEXPECTED REVELATIONS

"Gretchen, back off a little. We'll get to Waypoint 1. I'd like to do it in one piece."

Gretchen glanced right. Frank's foot pressed into the center of the floorboard, as if he were trying to brake from the passenger seat. She eased up on the tractor's accelerator. "Sorry, it's a habit. During supply runs in Antarctica, we stayed close, especially during heavy snow squalls. You could get disoriented in nothing flat."

"According to Meteorology, there isn't a storm within a thousand miles. The terrain to tonight's waypoint is smooth and well-traveled. I promise we won't get lost." Frank added a reassuring smile.

Much to her surprise, he was more than upbeat today—he was enthusiastic. After last night, Gretchen had worried about spending several days alone in confined spaces with him wallowing in his failure to find the spy or worse, mourning the loss of his wife.

The "survey equipment" in the cargo area remained a curiosity, though. A couple of days ago—before their fight—she'd asked Frank about it. He'd said they were just-in-case supplies but hadn't said 'just-in-case' of what. She was tempted to ask again, figuring that she could pry a straight answer from him without much of a fight, but didn't wish to push her luck, at least not for something that unimportant.

About two hours out from Mars City, Frank said, "If you look off to the right, you'll see Baulnsville."

She looked over and noticed a small single rust-stained dome sitting on the Martian plain. "What is it?"

"That was the first permanent colony on Mars."

"I've never heard of it."

"Two centuries ago, a private group headquartered in the European Union of Socialist States—Germany specifically—led by Geoffrey Bauln, established a small settlement. They explored, conducted experiments, and forged a Spartan existence. Even by our standards. One day, about eighteen months after they'd completed the dome, a supply ship landed as scheduled. Its crew, expecting help off-loading the cargo, found all thirty colonists had disappeared without a trace."

Gretchen scratched her chin. "C'mon, without a trace? That sounds like an exaggeration."

"No exaggeration. No one was around. All the tractors were missing as well as most of the air vests. The supply ship searched and found only two of their four tractors abandoned in perfect working order about a day's travel north of here. The other two had vanished just like the colonists."

"No one since found a clue to what happened?"

"Nope, nothing. It's a mystery, though some believe Martians captured the explorers and made them slaves in a distant, hidden settlement. One popular variant of the story is that the explorers were turned into sex slaves." Frank flashed a devilish grin again.

"I see Mars comes equipped with ghost stories, regular and kinky." Gretchen couldn't help but chuckle.

"Just a mystery, maybe mixed with imaginative, wishful thinking."

"I suppose there's nothing left inside the dome."

"Nothing. When our first dome was under construction, the crews salvaged all the usable equipment. Why do you ask?"

"If I had some spare time, I would've loved to check it out."

Frank's grin disappeared as he said in a flat tone, "No one goes near there anymore. It's unlucky."

Gretchen glanced over at him. "You don't believe that, do you?"

"There are documented stories of people venturing over there and having freak accidents on the way back to Mars City or shortly after arriving."

"In my experience, if you believe an object... or a place, in this case... is cursed, you'll treat it as such and subconsciously sabotage yourself. I'm sure those people made their own bad luck." She savored the wonderful contradiction of a superstitious streak in someone so bright and accomplished.

As the minutes passed and the Baulnsville dome grew smaller behind them, Frank fidgeted, rubbing his left thumb over his fingertips as he stared out the side window. Had she not spent so much time with him, she wouldn't have thought much about it, but he hadn't even done that when he'd struggled to apologize for the hydraulic fluid fiasco. "Gretchen, I don't quite know how to broach the subject, but it's been something I've been thinking about for a few days."

Much to her surprise, her heart started beating faster, and her stomach sizzled with anticipation before it tightened. He was about to ask her out. She just knew it, even though the timing couldn't have been odder. She asked in as non-committal tone as she could muster, "What's that?"

"Would you be interested in staying on as a permanent employee? I'm not offering a job right now, but I'm sure I can arrange something with Chuck if you like."

Oh, he wants an employee. Her swirling excitement crashed into cold disappointment, surprising her again. "I'm not sure what I'd do if I stayed. It isn't like you'll need an archaeologist once you gain access to the cavern."

"You're right, of course, but you're bright, and you have what it takes to work here. I'm sure you'd be a great addition. Certainly, we could find something you'd enjoy doing."

"I'm sorry, but I'm an archaeologist, and I love my work. I wouldn't be happy doing anything else."

Frank sighed. "I understand. I thought you might be open to other opportunities because of your uh... *professional problems on Earth.*"

He had a point. She could easily return home to face the real possibility that employment as an archaeologist was impossible, especially if her paper didn't placate Hawthorne's enormous ego or shake loose opportunities in spite of his blackball.

She paid close attention to driving the tractor for no other reason than to avoid looking at Frank. "I have to try. If I don't, I'll never know if I could've succeeded, and I refuse to give up without a fight."

"Good for you," he said. "That attitude makes me want you on the team more."

"If things don't work out, I may end up vidcomming you." She glanced over and flashed a half-grin. "You know, all you need is to find—I don't know, a sphinx—and I'd stay in a heartbeat."

Frank laughed. "After we get into the cavern, I'll see what I can arrange."

* * *

Upon reaching Waypoint 1 six hours later, Gretchen parked the tractor with the remaining three tractors that hadn't previously peeled off toward their destinations. Frank switched the systems into battery mode to save the fuel cells.

The sky darkened, and a multitude of stars shined brightly. Not counting the trip to Mars, Gretchen hadn't seen so many stars since the desert nights in Arizona when she'd interned on a dig between college terms. Frank toggled a couple more switches, and red light washed through the cabin. She glanced out the window— the other tractors had done the same.

He pulled two FieldMeals from the storage locker behind her seat and handed one over. He showed her how to activate the heating element, and two minutes later, they were enjoying beef stew.

"It's not bad, but it makes me appreciate last night's spaghetti all the more. Thanks again, by the way," Gretchen said.

"I was glad to do it. It's been a while since I cooked for anyone."

Without thinking, she blurted out, "Since you lost Lori..."

Frank stared at his food. "No. Erin, the pilot who flew you down from the OTP. We dated for almost ten years. Until a couple of months ago, that is. Anyway, about once a week or so, I used to cook us supper."

That came from nowhere. It explained why he had to rewrite his letter. Suddenly, Gretchen felt her face flush again as she realized that she'd clumsily pried for personal information. "I'm sorry. It's really none of my business."

"That's okay. Gossip travels faster than light in Mars City. Everyone knows she turned down my marriage proposal. She said she didn't want to be tied down and unable to pursue her career."

Gretchen wondered if that was the entire story. At times, Frank had seemed reserved and had acted secretive. Maybe Erin felt he hadn't completely invested in their relationship.

As quick as she thought that, she considered how unfair the speculation was. She'd seen a small slice of his life, and it'd been under strained circumstances. *What conclusions has Frank drawn about me based on our interaction so far?* Probably that she was an easily angered hothead. But that wasn't her at all.

After a few moments, Gretchen solemnly admitted, "My ex didn't renew because I was always at a dig and never made time for him. The saddest part of it all was that I didn't realize it. I could've chosen different projects that required less time away."

"Now that you're aware of it, will you do anything different next time?"

"Yes, because it's unfair to everyone otherwise."

As Frank stared at the dash controls, he said, "I don't think that she believed she could do both well. In a perverse way, I think she didn't accept because she didn't want to hurt me." A few seconds lingered as he just stared ahead. "There's no sense dwelling on the past—I can't change it. Anyway, we need to turn in for the evening, so we can start at daybreak. The trip's going to get rough, and we have a lot of equipment to unload when we arrive."

Gretchen took the hint. It was just as well. Based on her track record, she hesitated to offer anything resembling relationship advice. Until she found someone she cared for and did the work to nurture the relationship, she had no business advising anyone.

She reclined her seat and closed her eyes. She'd surprised herself by opening up to him, and he'd surprised her more by doing the same. As sleep overtook her, she smiled at Frank's status. An unanswered question was her last thought. *Why does it matter?*

* * *

John Reed wore night vision goggles and drove north without lights on Main Street, which was nothing more than a well-worn path. His ultimate destination was in the general vicinity of where Brentford and the Earther were headed in the Maelstrom Mountains. The difference was that he'd hide across the valley at the base of the eastern range while they investigated a cave in the western range.

Already, a headache had started and his vision was blurry. Stopping and resting wasn't an option. He still had hours more to go. As much as he disliked extended travel, particularly at night, it was necessary. He had to beat the Marsees to the Maelstrom Mountains by hours, so he could set up everything unobserved.

Ahead, John noticed four MarsVantage tractors grouped in a loose semi-circle at Waypoint 1. He stopped, donned his helmet and gloves, and depressurized his tractor. Just as he'd practiced countless times, he attached the homemade apron to the tractor's rear mounts and tie-downs. The six-inch-wide tarp strips comprising it trailed on the ground and would erase his tractor's tracks as he drove forward. He tugged it with both hands, ensuring it was securely fastened before returning to the cabin.

After repressurizing and removing his helmet and gloves, he veered off Main Street to give the Marsees a wide berth. While he proceeded forward at a crawl over the uneven terrain, he kept an eye on the MarsVantage tractors parked for the night. Once Waypoint 1 was safely behind him, he picked up the route to the Maelstrom Mountains.

These days, few traveled there, which made for a rougher ride than Main Street. The Maelstrom Mountains had already been explored and little of value had been found. As John shook and swayed over the pockmarked ground, he imagined possibilities of what had changed.

* * *

As he entered his fourteenth hour of driving, only stopping for bathroom breaks or food, John arrived at his destination in the Maelstrom Mountains, parking in a spot hidden from view of the cave entrance MarsVantage had tagged for exploration. Driving alone in the wild and for so long without rest were both against regs, but he couldn't care less. Depending on how the next couple of days played out, he very well might be forced to break more than just regs.

After he set the alarm for two hours, he popped a couple of painkillers for his headache and dozed. When the alarm buzzed, though still tired, his headache had disappeared. More importantly, the sky had noticeably brightened. He could safely proceed with his next task.

John sealed the helmet and gloves to his spacesuit, then depressurized the tractor and opened the rear hatch, allowing it, with the attached apron, to swing aside. He quickly entered the cargo area and inspected the contents of two containers. Pleased everything was in order, he dragged them to the edge and dismounted.

He scanned the hilly terrain behind the tractor and located a suitably flat spot, fifteen to twenty feet high, with an excellent sight line across the valley. He grabbed the first container's handle and climbed the slope, at times using his right hand to steady himself, all the time careful not to damage his spacesuit. At his destination, he withdrew from the container a tripod and video camera, which he set up. He carried the empty container to the tractor and repeated the trip with the other container, which held a transmitter and fuel cell.

With the confidence of hours of practice, he connected the transmitter to the camera and the fuel cell to both. He adjusted the camera to point to the cave Brentford and Blake would explore. Afterward, he stood and stretched his arms wide before starting back to his tractor.

It was too bad that the tractor didn't accommodate in-field replacement fuel cells. He could've traveled here at a leisurely pace, days ahead of time. But no. The damn bureaucrats in their cozy offices on Earth decided it was too dangerous to swap fuel cells in the field. Just because *they* would blow themselves to pieces didn't mean people with an ounce of field savvy would.

Once in the tractor, he verified the video transmission before repressurizing it and removing his helmet and gloves. As he ate a FieldMeal, he kept an eye on the cave area via a monitor he'd hastily attached to the dash prior to leaving Mars City. Better still, he eavesdropped on the MarsVantage frequency, which was unencrypted per the regs. And MarsVantage abided by the regs. Always.

25 | RED SKY AT MORNING...

A t daybreak, Gretchen watched the other three tractors depart Waypoint 1. "Where are they going?"

Frank, now in the driver's seat, activated a small display on the dashboard. "Their exploration assignments are northwest through the western range of the Maelstrom Mountains."

"What's with the display?"

"It's the LandNav. It'll take me a second to enter our route to the cave."

"LandNav?"

"Mars has no magnetic field, so compasses are useless here. We can't afford satellites for navigation like Earth, but we installed numerous navigational beacons. As we push into new areas, we expand the beacon network. Between the beacons and the landmarks, we can safely ride to the cave." After he shifted the tractor into gear, he circled until they were heading north once again. "The ride's gonna get rough. Hang on. This is where the fun begins."

The tractor rocked and swayed as Frank guided it over the terrain. Frank hit a particularly large rut, sending a jolt through Gretchen's entire body. "This is your idea of fun? Anymore like that and you'll get a replay of breakfast."

"There's some motion sickness meds in the dash's top storage compartment. Take two now before it's too late."

Gretchen fished through the compartment and found them. She tore open the foil packet and popped the pills into her mouth, washing them down with a long gulp of water. "This is a far cry from auto-cabs."

"I'll take your word for it. I've never ridden in one."

"Really?"

"I've never been to Earth. I'm curious about something, though. How'd you learn to drive? From what I understand, Earthers rely on auto-cabs and auto-buses."

"On a summer internship before my senior year of college, I learned how to drive and perform simple vehicle repairs."

"So you learned just like that? In a couple of months?"

"Well... You should've seen my first lesson in the virtual trainer. I confused the brake with the accelerator and rammed a storefront."

"I'm glad you got better," Frank said as a grin formed. "You did get better, right? It's hard to tell because there aren't a lot of buildings around."

She swatted his leg. "I scored above average on my certification."

"Of course you did. You strike me as someone who won't stop until you master whatever you set your mind to."

"My guitar instructor says the same thing, sometimes to the bane of his musical sensibilities."

"You play guitar? When we get back, I'd love to hear you play. I'm sure I can borrow one."

"I brought mine from home, and I'd love to play for you. I have several songs that I perform well enough."

He glanced over, his eyes twinkling as he grinned. "I can't wait."

* * *

The alarm's din startled John Reed from a sound sleep. He scratched himself and glanced at the video monitor, which showed the deserted cave area.

His stomach rumbled, so he ate a FieldMeal while he waited for Brentford and the Earther's arrival. When he finished, he disposed of the packaging in a cargo container that had held the video camera and returned to his seat where the monitor showed a MarsVantage tractor entering the picture.

Surprisingly, Brentford didn't pass the cave and perform a U-turn. Standard MarsVantage practice dictated that he point the tractor toward Mars City upon arriving at a survey site. One reason

John had chosen this position was to observe the tractor's cargo area and the equipment they'd unload.

Brentford, instead, performed a right turn and backed up to the base of the slope leading to the cave entrance, which positioned the tractor broadside to his camera's vantage point. He'd only catch a quick glimpse of the equipment as they transferred it to the cave.

After several long minutes, Brentford and the Earther loaded a treaded hand truck and directed it inside the cave. The Earther must be a real winner if Brentford wouldn't even allow her to run a hand truck by herself. They repeated this routine for close to three hours. They completely unloaded the tractor, another atypical practice, and their cargo revealed nothing about their mission because everything was in generic cargo containers.

It was like Brentford knew someone would be watching. Of course, that was impossible.

Only one large container remained, and it sat at the cave's mouth. This one they unpacked in plain sight.

"Well, who would've guessed?" The Marsees were using an expensive portable airlock to seal the cave. Its typical use was as a stopgap during an emergency. They connected a power cable running to the tractor. Once it fulfilled its secondary function of providing heat and a breathable atmosphere within the cave, they'd be able to work in just coveralls.

What are they after?

Unless he missed his guess, they'd occupy the cave full-time, instead of eating and sleeping in the tractor like typical exploration crews. Unfortunately, John had planned to surreptitiously enter the cave to inspect their handiwork while they slept. That would now be impossible. "Dammit anyway."

Heather's instructions had been to acquire the cave's contents by any means necessary. She'd emphasized, as expected, that extreme measures were appropriate only as a last resort. The airlock provided Brentford and the Earther a measure of civilization while they accomplished their task, yet it eliminated his civilized options. For his mission to succeed, John didn't know how, but Brentford and the Earther needed to meet with a fatal accident.

26 | OPPORTUNITY'S THRESHOLD

An intermittent tone, much like a warning, awakened Gretchen. It had to be the vidrecorder that Frank had activated to document their entry into the cavern to counter any future Interplanetary contest to the Marsium121.

By the dim light Frank had kept running overnight, she glanced over to his air mattress, ready to complain about the vidrecorder, but he was missing. She rubbed her eyes and yawned. Where had he gone?

She sat up and looked to the cavern door filled with symbols, suspecting that he knew all along how to get inside. But ages of rust-colored dust remained embedded in the symbols and the surrounding seam. She shook her head. Did she merely distrust Frank, or was she insecure over not knowing the symbols' meaning? *Perhaps a little of both.*

More alert, much different thoughts rushed to mind. Why wasn't he here? Was there a problem? Were they in trouble? Before panic firmly set in, she turned in the opposite direction. The airlock door slid along its track, and Frank emerged. At last, the annoying alarm ceased once the inner door slid back into place.

He removed his helmet and gloves. "Glad to see you're awake. I hope the air mattress was comfortable enough."

"Yeah. What were you doing outside?"

"Opening the solar panels on the tractor. They'll convert enough sunlight to run the airlock's environmental systems during the day while recharging the tractor's batteries to power it overnight."

"I wish you would've said something. When I woke up and found you missing, I got concerned."

Frank frowned. "Oh. I forgot to mention it last night, and I didn't want to wake you this morning."

"So that's what you did last night. I thought you forgot something in the tractor and simply went to get it." Hearing the alarm while still not alert had caused unnecessary concern. She flashed a quick smile. "Anyway, I'm up, so I may as well get started."

Gretchen rolled off the mattress and stared at the symbols for a time. From her toolpac, which she'd placed near the symbols last night when they'd unpacked, she withdrew an electromagnetic spectrum scanner. She performed a detailed scan of the wall, making standard passes in the visual, infrared, and ultraviolet spectra.

For the next few minutes, she analyzed the results. They revealed nothing unusual, only showing the symbols had been carved into ordinary Mars rock. She'd hoped for an access panel to short-circuit, so she could bypass the translation issue altogether. *Damn, there goes my best chance for success.*

A thin seam surrounded the symbols. Like Frank, Gretchen suspected it outlined a door. If true, it would measure approximately four feet across by seven feet high. The circles and grooves were grouped together in three rows, a fact she'd failed to notice while reviewing the pictures. As she stood there, it was clear, though subtle.

Within a grouping, circles with corresponding lines of various lengths sat like they were on shelves. At points, two, and sometimes three, were positioned one above the other. She struggled to group symbols horizontally in an attempting to form words. She had no more luck now than she'd had in Chuck's office during their initial meeting.

Gretchen glanced across the cave. Frank was engrossed in his own task, paying no attention to her. She expected he'd be as impatient as a kid on a trip asking, "Are we there yet?"

She dragged an empty cargo container to the door and stood on it. With a small brush, she removed the dirt, starting near the ceiling at the seam's top. From left to right, she methodically brushed, careful not to damage the door or the surrounding rock. It was time consuming, but at last, the seam was clearly defined.

With a small flashlight and a magnifying glass, Gretchen inspected it. A few inches deep, both inside edges were smooth and even.

She repeated the process on the symbols themselves. The circles' centers were easily large enough to allow her to insert her pinky up to the first knuckle, but she could barely get a fingertip into the horizontal dashes.

Afterward, Gretchen took and analyzed a series of scans on the freshly cleaned symbols. The circles were perfect, and their depth uniform. The lines were laser straight and parallel. A precision machine had carved them. No one could've produced this result freehand.

As she looked to the airlock and back to the symbols, she figured the door was about fifteen yards away from the cave entrance. How had so much dust and dirt accumulated inside the symbols? "Frank, come here. This may be a hoax."

He joined her with standard sounding equipment in hand. "What's going on?"

"I brushed a lot of debris from the symbols, more than could have accumulated naturally. I think someone's playing a prank on you."

As Frank inspected the symbols, he said, "It'd be one involved prank, going on for two decades."

"Still, there was too much sand in the symbols for this far inside the cave."

"We're in the Maelstrom Mountains, which see heavy sandstorms once an orbit after Mars' closest approach to the sun. For the most part, they shelter this valley, but lots of sand gets stirred up."

"It would take strong winds to deposit so much gunk in the symbols."

"The winds get fierce, often reaching hurricane speed."

Gretchen pondered for a few moments. "Huh. Coupled with the low gravity, I can see that, I guess."

"Good." Grinning, Frank asked, "Gunk?"

She tried to keep a straight face. "It's a technical term commonly used among archaeologists."

"Same for maintenance engineers. Just surprised to hear you use it." They shared a long laugh. "Why don't you take a break? I'll do a series of soundings to get a better idea of what's on the other side."

Gretchen sat on a cargo container and drank a bottle of water, not realizing how thirsty she had been.

When Frank finished, he sat beside her and analyzed the data. "First off, there aren't any mechanisms in the wall. It's just stone."

"That's what my readings indicate, too. My bet is the door descends into the ground. I also think the door creates an airtight seal. The seam's deeper than the symbols, and it appears the rock backing the seam is part of the door."

"Check this out. There's a void for ten feet beyond the doorway. It looks like a walkway between the Marsium121 stalactites and stalagmites."

"And it just stops?"

"It's hard to tell because the Marsium121 is packed in tight, but if I had to guess, I'd say it turns right."

She brushed aside a strand of hair that fell onto her face, conscious of the act but quickly pushing the thought aside. "That suggests the formations are artificial."

Frank looked into her eyes. "Yes. It does."

Her jaw dropped, but no words came out. She shook her head. "You've been coy about the symbols' origin. You discounted alien origin, yet you can't provide a plausible explanation."

"I simply refuse to endorse alien involvement without proof. I'm not about to hand Earth another reason to criticize us."

They stared at each other for a moment.

"There has to be an explanation," Gretchen said with assurance.

"I'm open to all possibilities. Tell me where they came from and provide the proof."

"I don't know. Commonplace explanations don't fit, though admittedly, aliens are incredible."

Frank grinned. "Funny, I find tribesmen sailing to Antarctica for a source of fresh water because of an extended drought pretty incredible. Yet... your reasoning and proof were convincing."

Gretchen's eyes grew wide. "You read my paper? It hasn't been published yet. How'd you see it?"

He chuckled. "I have a friend at the *Journal of Archaeology* who forwarded me a copy."

Frank had never been off Mars, but he had a friend at an obscure scientific journal back home? That was so odd that it had to be a lie. *But why lie?*

Frank added, "By evaluating all the evidence buried in Antarctica and refusing to jump to conclusions, you advanced human understanding."

"And I'm prejudging the symbols. I'm making the same mistake Hawthorne did."

"I was trying not to say that."

Her cheeks warmed once again. She'd railed against Hawthorne for ignoring possibilities, and much to her dismay, she'd unwittingly committed the same mistake. At least she'd realized it, and it'd been an honest oversight, unlike Hawthorne, who was merely maintaining his position. "You'd like to find out more about the symbols and the cavern, wouldn't you?"

"Yes, of course. I'd love to learn its entire history, but our priority is to secure the Marsium121. I already have a couple of places in mind where we can install it. Manufacturing has produced and warehoused power cables that can connect all of the domes."

"You have definite plans."

"We didn't go to all this trouble without a plan." Frank smiled.

Gretchen forced a smile in return. *If only I can open the door...*

* * *

Once again, an alert revived the Caretaker from hibernation. He skipped a self-diagnostic and downloaded himself into a mobile unit. He rolled to a console where he found that the emergency water egress to Power Generator Three had an ambient temperature higher than had occurred in many, many orbits. Likewise, the atmospheric pressure was higher—far higher—than normal, and it included twenty percent oxygen.

Perhaps the Bvindu have finally returned!

He activated the egress' visual monitors, and after shrugging off his disappointment, he watched two strangers for hours. They organized several storage containers before resting.

After a significant fraction of a rotation, the most fascinating event occurred. It infused him with hope, something the Caretaker hadn't felt in longer than he could remember. The shorter one gently, almost lovingly, brushed the accumulated dead soil from the doorway's edge and the access's operating instructions. They must've deduced the writing on the doorway was the means to gain access and wanted to explore Power Generator Three.

More than anything, he wanted to meet them to request help reconstituting his manufacturing capability. His instinctual caution restrained him from traversing the underground power conduit to greet them, though. Any meeting must occur under favorable conditions where he had complete control of the situation. And complete safety.

The strangers could enter anytime—they only had to interpret the door's instructions. He hurriedly composed a message to arrange a meeting. Without enough time to learn their language, the Caretaker used simple pictographs along with basic words, both written and verbal, to provide a common frame of reference.

If they could help repair his manufacturing capability, he could construct a spaceship and find the Bvindu... or at least, learn their fate. His bodiless existence had to end. Either with completing his mission or forging a new future.

27 | One Answer and More Questions

"**A**aahhh! I'm no closer now than two days ago." Gretchen leaned her forehead against the stone.

Frank joined her, took her hand, and guided her close to the mysterious cargo. "Time for a break. You're pressing. You won't solve anything that way."

So far, Frank had busied himself with every conceivable chore around the cave, from monitoring the environmental systems to preparing FieldMeals. She would've preferred a suggestion or an opinion, especially now that she'd exhausted her ideas. "A break won't solve anything, either. I've tried everything, even Morse code, and nothing fits."

"I understand, so let's take your mind off the problem and talk about something different. It helps me when I'm stuck."

For a heartbeat, she stared into his eyes. A bit of chitchat appeared to be the only help she'd get from him. "If you insist... I know it's not important, but I'm curious. What's really in these containers we brought?"

He chuckled. "Are you sure you want to know? I haven't said anything because I didn't want to upset you."

Gretchen shifted to her right foot and wiped her palms against her spacesuit legs. "I really want to know now."

Frank stalled by rubbing his forehead with his left hand. "There's no reason to worry."

"C'mon, Frank. Just say it."

"Most are filled with air vests. Two contain a battery and a vidcomm unit, so we can call for help in case something... *unforeseen* happens.

She wrapped her arms around herself. "What exactly do you think's gonna happen?"

"I don't know... Nothing. Interplanetary has never interfered with an exploration expedition before, and I seriously doubt they're suddenly brave enough now. But Chuck and I aren't taking any chances." He stepped to her and softly asked, "Are you okay? You don't look so good."

"I'll be fine." Frank might not expect anything, but he and Chuck had contemplated Interplanetary interference, and thought enough of the threat to pack eight containers of air vests. Though slim, interference might be a real possibility, nonetheless. "I'm just not used to being in the position of needing such precautions."

Frank smiled. "Seriously, everything's gonna be okay. Trust me. You know the Mars Scouts' motto: 'Always prepared.'"

Gretchen returned his smile, wanting to believe him, hoping he was right. "Now that I know, I wish I didn't."

"Let's talk about something completely different then. When you return to Earth, what do you want to do for fun?"

She thought for a moment and smiled. "I'd like to visit Victoria Falls in Africa. When I was a kid, my parents took us to Niagara Falls, and I still remember the spray stinging my face and the rumbling roar of the water. Victoria Falls is supposed to be even more impressive."

"I've seen holos, but I suspect they don't do it justice. What else do you want to do?"

"I'd like to see a concert, perhaps my favorite artist, Magda Carr, again."

"She's talented. I really like 'Some Still Dream.' It's a shame you aren't staying longer. Several musicians perform at our monthly concerts, but you'll be halfway to Earth before the next one."

"It's just as well. I didn't pack a nice dress."

"I know that's how things are done on Earth, but we aren't much for formalwear here."

In an instant, fragments of theories, ideas, and facts coalesced. Her gut insisted she was correct. Gretchen grabbed his hand and pulled him to the door as she said, "I got it. I got it!"

"What is it?"

Gretchen pointed to the symbols. "I've been going about this all wrong. The circles and lines can't be grouped together to form letters, words, or pictures. They're pitches, musical notes if you will. I should've seen it earlier."

He stepped closer and studied the symbols. "Music. Okay, but there's no time signature, key signature, or measures. Nothing indicates tempo."

She squared herself to him and fought her instinct to call him an outright liar. "Sounds like you're pushing me away from music, which indicates you already know how to open the door. Tell me the truth—do you?"

"No."

Gretchen balled her fists against her thighs, her fingernails digging into her palms. She reminded herself that nothing was accomplished by yelling. For whatever reason, Frank wasn't forthcoming with an explanation, so she needed to draw one out of him. It's what Ashley would do. "Then, please level with me. You're using musical terms, but you don't strike me as the musician type."

"I'm not, though I often help some friends repair or modify their instruments. Along the way, I picked up a bit of their jargon. And I can play a mean 'Mary Had a Little Lamb' on the guitar." His eyes twinkled as he gave her a lopsided grin.

She shook her head. *Your charm is* not *going to distract me.* "What's going on then? You haven't offered a single thought about the symbols since we set foot in the cave. I expected you to hover like an expectant father, but you've barely paid attention."

"I have faith in you." His grin faded.

"That's not an answer. There's something else going on. I'm not making headway, and it's obvious I need help."

Frank flatly stated, "I've done everything I can."

"I don't get it. It's like you don't want us to get into the cavern. Or is it that you enjoy watching me struggle? Are you having fun? What kind of sadist are you?"

Frank's eyebrows rose as his eyes grew wide. "Fun? It breaks my heart, little by little, watching you struggle, knowing I can't add anything."

She inhaled and paused. Did he have nothing to say or was he just holding back? "So tell me what's going on."

"I'm stuck between my duty to MarsVantage and... I'm stuck. Of course, I have ideas. Any halfway intelligent person presented with the problem would consider solutions. But if I expressed those ideas, and one is correct, and Interplanetary challenges, they'll wind up with the Marsium121." He pointed to the vidrecorder to the right of the airlock. "This recording would clinch their case instead of proving ours."

"Frank, I'm not following you. Back up and explain." She tilted her head slightly. "Please."

"When we return, we'll file mission reports detailing our actions in the wild. If there's even a hint of a discrepancy between our reports—perhaps if I helped you and you tried to cover for me—Interplanetary would twist it into an elaborate scheme to steal the Marsium121 from them, starting two decades earlier. I think you've forgotten the conditions Chuck and I explained your first day here. *You* have to open the door."

Gretchen bit her lower lip, realizing the true meaning behind his words. He meant it in the most literal sense. She had to open the door, with no help from him.

All of MarsVantage's hopes fell on her shoulders. The burden had been heavy before coming to the cave. Now, the weight pushed down harder. She felt like Atlas straining to hold the world aloft.

More importantly, a second realization occurred to her. Frank's protests over the symbols weren't protests at all. He'd pointed out obstacles she must overcome in such a way as to bring the issue up without compromising the Marsium121 rights.

Gretchen nodded. *I understand, Frank.* "Your objections aside, I'll follow through on my idea anyway."

"If you think it's best. That's why we're paying you." Frank smiled again.

She saw his face anew. He'd tortured himself these past few days. Because she'd been too preoccupied with her work, she'd failed to notice the stress etched into his face—the worry lines in the corner of his eyes with hints of dark circles underneath. While he was protecting MarsVantage's interests, he was also helping her as much as he could, starting by pulling her aside to free her conscious mind from the symbol problem, which allowed her subconscious to work it through. She'd nearly overlooked it like she'd nearly overlooked his help in highlighting the obstacles. And he did it all without complaint.

Gretchen moved to the air mattress and propped herself against the wall. On her datapad, she pulled up her beginning guitar lessons where she'd been introduced to music theory. If she could determine the pitch of the first note, she'd be able to calculate the rest. The circles didn't vary like the notes on a musical score, but the adjacent lines did. She supposed the length difference indicated the time to hold the pitch. Although she needed to make several assumptions, she now had something to work with. *Finally.*

Gretchen transcribed the symbols into notes. As fatigue set in, her thoughts wandered, sometimes to Frank and what he thought the symbols represented, and other times to imagining what lay beyond the door. A vague feeling came over her that she'd overlooked something important. She just couldn't pin down what.

The next thing she registered beyond her datapad was Frank sitting beside her and handing over a beef stew FieldMeal. "How goes it?"

"Slow, apparently. I didn't realize it was so late. It'd be quicker if I had a full computer."

"Don't worry. We have enough supplies for another five days."

"The programming should be ready tomorrow morning."

"Excellent."

They ate in comfortable silence. Nearly finished with their meal, Frank inquired further about her impressions of Niagara Falls. Gretchen suspected that he was trying to give her another break from thinking about work, and she welcomed it. She closed her datapad while describing her memories of the falls, focusing on aspects that were difficult to capture in holos like feeling the rumble of the water down to her bones. He wondered aloud if MarsVantage could create a waterfall in one of the domes, pointing out that it'd provide some diversity.

In the middle of this important project, Frank was continuing to look for ways to make Mars a bit more livable. He was a true believer in Mars' culture and MarsVantage's mission. He was driven, unlike most of her peers back home. *Frank is one of a kind.*

With a little luck—and she was due for some—her idea would prove to be correct. Tomorrow, they'd unseal the door and enter the cavern.

28 | DANGEROUS DISTRACTIONS

Gretchen sat up and leaned against the wall, not bothering with additional lights so as not to wake Frank. Last night, while she'd translated the symbols into tones on her datapad, in the far recesses of her mind, something had nagged at her, something vague, something she hadn't been able to put her finger on.

This morning, with a fresher mind, that vagueness came into focus. She clearly recalled Frank saying, "*It breaks my heart, little by little, seeing you struggle.*" He cared, though he avoided saying it in so many words. Was it mere friendship or something more?

They'd become friends while working together these past two weeks. Oddly enough, their arguments had drawn her closer to him. For her part, the fuel to argue was that she cared what he thought of her. She was starting to have feelings for him, and she should never have allowed that. They had no future together—she was returning home shortly.

A part of her was tempted to surrender to this desire—it'd been months, after all. *Will I go home with fond memories or haunting regrets?*

Her desire and intellect wrestled, one seeking advantage over the other. Of her unsatisfying choices, her intellect won, though she wished things were different. She had to return home to continue her career. She loved archaeology too much to turn her back on it for a man. Sleeping with him would only erode her resolve.

After Gretchen glanced over to Frank, who slept peacefully, she forced herself to return to programming the datapad. The sooner she finished, the sooner they'd gain entry, and the sooner she could return home before her feelings complicated matters further.

Frank's datapad alarm rang. Gretchen jerked in surprise. He rubbed his eyes and rolled off the air mattress, then chugged half a bottle of water. "The worst part of these missions is that nothing regulates the humidity. It's dry as a bone in here, the spacesuits, and the tractor."

Frank prepared FieldMeals as she continued working on the symbol programming. After delivering breakfast, he ate while looking over the symbols and door. Today's fare was oatmeal, which she didn't care for. She was hungry, though, so she laid the datapad aside and ate without complaint.

Afterwards, she pushed away thoughts of Frank and continued with her program while he completed the morning solar panel chore outside at the tractor and ran diagnostics on the airlock's environmental controls inside.

Finally, it was ready. She rose and walked over to the symbols and verified them against the notes she'd transcribed. "Okay, I'm starting the program."

"Wait! Helmet!" He grabbed his own and twisted it into place.

"Oh, God." With care, she laid her datapad on the ground, staring as if it would strike like an agitated rattlesnake.

Intently focused on the helmet sitting by her air mattress, she walked to it, imagining the disaster she'd nearly caused. She grabbed the helmet and twisted it into place. With a small, quiet voice, she said, "All of our air would have rushed into the cavern, which is far larger, until the pressure equalized. The airlock couldn't possibly have compensated. We wouldn't have been able to breathe."

"It's okay now."

Gretchen sagged to the cave's floor, beside the mattress. She cradled her helmeted head in her bare hands. "I nearly killed us without a second thought. That's not okay."

The next thing Gretchen knew, Frank was pulling her hands from her helmet. "Gretchen, it's okay. C'mon, look at me. It's okay, really. Nobody's hurt."

"You don't know how close I was to pressing Start."

"About one second."

"Less."

"That's why we explore in teams, so we can look after one another. You've been focusing on the symbols and didn't think it through. It happens."

If only Frank were right. He didn't know she had been preoccupied with thoughts of them becoming a couple in both an emotional and physical sense... and he must never know. "This is serious. It's not like I forgot to pick up the laundry on the way home."

"It's been less than two months for you where air hasn't been omnipresent. You've adjusted better than anyone I've ever seen, and that's to your credit. You had a lapse, but it's okay—I'm looking out for you."

For a moment, Gretchen gazed into his eyes, taking in his words, allowing them to comfort her. "I suppose you better pay close attention then."

"There's worse duty." Frank smiled and went to the airlock. He toggled a couple of controls. "I've shutdown air recycling and heat."

After she donned her gloves, she rose, snatched up the datapad, and surveyed the cave, confirming there was nothing else she'd neglected to consider.

"Everything's set. You can continue," Frank confirmed.

Gretchen nodded and began the program. Muffled tones in the key of C sounded from her datapad's speaker. Nothing happened. She hit the Continue button. The tones sounded again, this time twice as fast. Again, nothing happened. "You might as well go back to what you were doing. This could take a while."

She played the tune several more times, increasing its tempo incrementally, but the door refused to budge. She switched to the next of the twelve keys, C#, and played her tune at various speeds. Nothing happened.

Gretchen stepped up to D, continuing the pattern through an entire octave. Still, no results. Now, sweat pooled in the small of her back. Her idea was failing.

Perhaps she hadn't transposed the notes properly. That would be the most likely problem. Still, she might not have picked a proper tempo or the correct octave. Perhaps there was an issue that she hadn't considered, like volume. Gretchen couldn't help but think about Frank's objections again—he'd only scratched the surface of the possible problems.

Gretchen worked her way down from Middle C toward Low C. At D#, with a tempo that played the tune in a second, the doorway cracked.

"Frank! Frank!" Gretchen said, looking toward the airlock.

He glanced up from his datapad. His eyes grew wide and a smile spread across his face.

A series of rapid tones sounded in response. Gretchen turned in time for the stone door to descend, leaving only the topmost inch exposed.

Excitement rushed through her body. The burden she'd carried since arriving disappeared. Frank and MarsVantage had something tangible because of her hard work, not because of her reputation, her name, or who she knew. This was true success, not the ersatz substitute that Hawthorne enjoyed.

"Great job, Gretchen!"

The cave air wasn't rushing into the cavern, which meant the cavern had been close to the same pressure level. *Interesting... What is the atmosphere made of?* Gretchen started an analysis from the control pad on her left wrist. She crouched down and inspected the doorframe and door's top. It operated within a track. The door's edge was thinner, leaving the face flush with the cave wall and producing an airtight seal. That explained how the cavern still had an atmosphere. It must be from ages ago when the door had last been closed.

Her control pad displayed the atmospheric analysis. "I read a breathable atmosphere—eighteen percent oxygen. The pressure's a tick low, and the air's a little chilly."

"I read the same. I just restarted the airlock's life support systems," Frank said as he joined her.

Gretchen stood, twisted her helmet, and removed it. "Oh, the air reeks in here."

Frank mirrored her actions and wrinkled his nose. "Congratulations, Gretchen! You successfully completed your contract. I can take it from here."

"Are you kidding? You can't think for one second that I'm not going inside."

Frank glanced into the dark cavern and back to Gretchen. "You're not required to."

Gretchen stared into his eyes and easily inhaled. *"Required has nothing to do with it. This is a once in a lifetime opportunity. I want to see it through to the end."*

"Good." Frank smiled broadly. "I was hoping you would."

* * *

For three days, John Reed had watched Brentford open the tractor's solar panels in the morning and close them in the evening. The Earther had never made an appearance.

Upon arrival, they'd checked in with Mars City as required by the regs, but hadn't radioed since. Typically, MarsVantage explorers checked in twice a day, once in the morning and again in the evening.

John had been unable to pick up any transmission from inside the cave, though he'd never expected to, because presumably, Brentford and the Earther weren't using their suit transmitters. He could only surmise that their efforts were proceeding slowly, at best.

To achieve Interplanetary's goal of converting the cave's value for themselves, he had to know when Brentford and the Earther revealed, discovered, or unearthed their prize. So he waited, as patiently as possible, for a sign of progress. The tricky part was to time his move for after they succeeded but before they pulled out for Mars City.

That assumed Brentford and the Earther finished before John's tractor ran low on power, forcing him to return to Mars City. Today, the fuel cell's power level edged below half. When it reached twenty percent, he would have to leave. Otherwise, he wouldn't make it back.

In any event, Brentford and the Earther would never leave.

29 | Unexpected Discoveries

While Gretchen explored further down the six-foot-wide path, Frank gawked at the towering Marsium121 stalagmites. They were packed close together, rising twenty feet from the ground, one identical to the next. He gazed upward. Stalactites hung directly over the stalagmites. As he shined his flashlight across them, dull rainbows appeared and vanished as the crystals refracted the beam.

He knelt, unzipped his left thigh pocket, and retrieved a small hammer and chisel. With his flashlight sitting on the smooth ground, its beam framing a vertical crack at the six-foot base of a stalagmite, he aligned the chisel, contemplating how best to strike Marsium121 to extract a sample.

"Frank, can you come here?"

"Can it wait? I'm collecting a sample."

"You should see this first."

"I'll be there in a sec," he hollered down the path before standing and sighing.

Thankfully, she hadn't sounded distressed. He should never have allowed her to wander off. In many respects, she acted like an experienced Marsee, yet in truth, she was new and required oversight, for her own safety. He needed to be a better teammate.

With a flashlight in hand, he started down the winding path between Marsium121 stalagmites and stalactites. Each successive row was slightly offset from the previous. From the soundings he and the Mars Scouts had taken over the years, he knew the cavern was about sixty feet in diameter and fifty feet tall. He was near the center, and Gretchen was nowhere in sight.

Where is she?

He rounded the third bend and his shoulders relaxed. Gretchen stood half in shadow, illuminated by her datapad's screen. "What'd you find?"

"That knee-high, black cylinder. See for yourself." Gretchen took his gloved hand and guided him forward. A six-foot-tall holo sprang into action before him.

"Incredible," Frank whispered.

After the holo finished, Gretchen played the reduced speed version on her datapad. "It's still too fast. I'll need a full computer to slow it further, though I can make out a couple of details. It appears there was a major city nearby, presumably a long time ago when Mars was thriving with life."

Frank shined his flashlight off to the side, so he could maintain a sense of Gretchen's presence while they conversed. "It looks like this cavern, along with two others, connect to it. Reminds me of power generating stations." Frank paused for a second. "Apparently all alien built."

"I can't think of another explanation. And I'm trying." Gretchen shook her head. "Yet all the signs point to aliens. The evidence is thin, though."

Frank nodded. "Agreed."

"Have you ever found anything resembling a city out there?"

"By the looks of the holo, it would've sat on the plain beyond the eastern mountain range. As a rule, we only survey rocky areas because they hold the valuable minerals."

"So a city could be buried, and no one would know about it?"

"Sure. Tractors may've crossed over it, but I doubt the area was properly explored. I can't recall it happening anyway."

"How much Marsium121 do you need to fulfill a claim?"

"Not much. Two or three finger-sized pieces will do. Why?"

"I suspect there's more of value here than just Marsium121," Gretchen enthusiastically said.

Unable to help himself, Frank smiled broadly. "You want a crack at the city, don't you?"

"Of course! It may hold untold treasures—art, tech, who knows what."

This city might be what Gretchen needed to stay. She already had the right attitude to live here. Now, she might have the desire.

And if there was alien tech, it might be the shot in the arm MarsVantage needed. Between the tech and Marsium121 power, they finally might wiggle free of Earth's tightening grasp.

Gretchen was both physically and intellectually attractive, and Frank envisioned a relationship, a first since ending things with Erin. As they moved forward, he wouldn't have to manipulate events as he'd done to get her here. He could be himself without first passing every word and action through the good-of-the-project filter. The future was bright if things settled out just right.

Unfortunately, right now, she had continued speaking, and he hadn't heard a word.

"...and if this is a power generator, you might be able to figure out how to use it as is. Maybe the answer's in the holo. Maybe it's in the city." Gretchen turned to face him. "There's a problem. You hired me to facilitate mining, which may render any greater value meaningless."

"We hired you to get us to the Marsium121. We can mine it anytime. The wisest course is to investigate the message's meaning to see if there's more value." Frank leaned in and gazed into her blue eyes. "That is, if you're interested."

"Yes!" She touched his forearm and met his gaze. "Frank, you're taking this much better than I expected. I figured you'd put up a fight."

"If you're correct, this discovery may change MarsVantage's future more than I ever imagined. Forget fighting—I'm embracing it." He placed his hand on hers.

"You're full of surprises," Gretchen said in a relaxed tone.

"You've been surprising me since you arrived. It was my turn. Anyway, let's head back, so I can get a sample."

As they walked to the entryway, Gretchen asked, "Do you think Chuck will want to go after the city?"

"He's always looking for opportunities. The Marsium121 is big, but the city may very well overshadow it."

She cast her eyes downward, hesitating for a moment. "Do you think he'd hire me on to help?"

You want to stay! "In a heartbeat. Get your thumb ready."

Gretchen looked up, wearing a huge smile. Her eyes twinkled in the glow of their flashlights.

Frank returned her smile. Today was a good day, the best in a long time.

They came to the door, which had risen without a sound after Frank had joined her. He looked to Gretchen, who was already working her datapad. In his excitement, he'd forgotten to jam the door open, or even test it before entering. It was a foolish mistake. With his heart beating faster and his mouth suddenly dry, he said in a monotone, "Please tell me we're not locked in."

"There's no reason the same sequence won't release the door from this side." Gretchen worked her datapad to run the proper melody from her program.

While he waited, he filled the awkward silence by asking, "Did you notice that the door is smooth on this side, just like the cavern walls?"

Her eyes glued to her datapad, Gretchen said, "Yes. Do you think it means something?"

"I suspect the cavern was filled with water to generate power for the city."

"Makes sense."

Gretchen played the tones, and for a split-second—longer than it ought to have taken, or at least it seemed so—the door remained stubbornly in place. Finally, a series of tones sounded in reply and the door descended.

They both exhaled.

That was too close—Frank needed to stay focused on the task at hand. He crouched down on one knee and collected a suitable Marsium121 sample to consummate their claim.

After he stopped the vidrecorder, he poured a small amount of water on the Marsium121 sample, touched it with a bare knuckle, and received a slight jolt. It was Marsium121, just like the sample in his wall safe. He wrapped it in a cloth from his spacesuit and deposited it into his right thigh pocket.

"Thank you again, Gretchen." He resisted the urge to hug her, though he wanted to more than ever. "It's time to radio home. Come on out with me. A change of scenery will do you good."

They exited the airlock after ensuring their suits were sealed. Long shadows extended before them from the setting sun. They hiked down the gentle slope and entered the tractor, him on the driver's side, her on the other.

Frank toggled several switches and checked the status readouts. "Everything's normal. Batteries are at full charge, and the fuel cell is at eighty-five percent. I tied our suits into the tractor's comm." She nodded as he manipulated a few more controls. "Mars City Control, this is Expedition Three. Please respond."

For a handful of seconds, there was no response. He repeated the transmission.

This time a man's voice replied immediately. "This is Mars City Control. We read you loud and clear."

"Please connect me with Chuck."

"Wait one."

* * *

After the Caretaker had returned to the main control center, he watched the two strangers in the infrared spectrum enter Power Generator Three. In due course, the short one found his message and presumably recorded it. The tall one joined and watched.

They spent more time looking at her device than watching his actual message. Something was wrong.

The Caretaker retrieved the egress' recordings and replayed them. His horrendous blunder quickly presented itself. He'd produced his invitation at the normal speed for his people, which seemed far faster than the way the strangers conversed.

He'd carelessly committed a mistake, one that could prove costly. In his haste, he might've squandered his best opportunity to escape this dead planet and search for his people.

30 | A Time for Action

On the couch in his office, Chuck held a book from his collection, his eyes scanning over the words but not comprehending them. He reread the page and sighed. After inserting a bookmark, he laid it aside. While he loved thrillers, he couldn't concentrate on it today.

He closed his eyes, leaned his head back, and willed himself to relax. More than anything, he wanted to accompany Frank and Gretchen in the wild and forge MarsVantage's future firsthand, but his duties chained him to the domes.

The vidcomm beeped. Chuck answered as he took a seat behind his desk.

"I have a call from Explorer Team Three."

"Put them through."

The video dropped out as Frank's voice announced, "Chuck, we have good news. Claim the mineral rights."

Finally, something is working in my favor. "I'll do so as soon as we disconnect. Is it what you expected?"

"Yes."

Chuck leaned forward. "Any problems?"

"Gretchen had difficulty accessing the cavern, but worked through it, mostly through trial and error."

"Sounds good."

"By the way, Chuck, thank you for the recommendation of *The Raven*," Gretchen interjected. "I enjoyed it, though I'm embarrassed that I never heard of it before now."

Chuck leaned back in his chair. *That's interesting.* "You're welcome. It's one of my favorites."

"It's late," Frank said. "We'll spend the night here, pack up tomorrow morning, and do a speed run to return tomorrow night."

"I agree," Chuck said. Once Frank hit Waypoint 1, he could open up the tractor to full speed—an option available when traveling on Main Street—and cut out a third of their outgoing Main Street travel time. It would be a long day but they wouldn't break any regs. The sooner they returned, the better Chuck would feel. "Remember a sample to certify the claim."

"It's already packed."

"We'll see you tomorrow night." Chuck disconnected the vidcomm, curious about what else they'd found. Gretchen's mention of *The Raven* was code for an unexpected and promising find. They'd worked out meanings for other Poe works depending on the circumstances. Chuck exhaled, thankful she hadn't referenced *The Tell-Tale Heart*, which would've indicated interference from Interplanetary.

Chuck glanced at the clock—it was late. Though, if he hurried, he could still file the Marsium121 claim today.

MarsVantage's future was bright, indeed.

* * *

The vidcomm chimed. From the armchair in his quarters, Chuck looked away from a power utilization report on his datapad. Peter Konklin was calling from Earth. He'd never expected Konklin to personally vidcomm... perhaps Interplanetary's Mars exploration director or an Earth lawyer, but not him.

The news must have traveled faster than expected. He'd only submitted the claim two hours ago, which meant the spy must be working overtime. If only Frank could've discovered the spy's identity before heading into the wild...

Chuck settled into his seat before the vidcomm and activated the connection.

The smug, smiling image of Peter Konklin in his luxurious New York City office appeared. "O'Donnell, I know you wouldn't go after and claim Marsium121 if it was worthless. You're too frugal to toss away good money, so I'm challenging your claim. That area was surveyed and Marsium121's discovery was under Interplanetary's watch. You've withheld the Marsium121's true value from us. The penalty is that it reverts to the original claimholder—us."

"I expected as much."

"My representative is waiting with the dispute as soon as your crew consummates the claim."

Chuck crossed his arms. "I look forward to seeing your evidence at the adjudication hearing."

Konklin's image grew larger as he leaned toward his vidcomm. "You expect the judges to believe that you only realized the Marsium121's value after our rights to the area expired? Then, you hired that Blake woman because you're too dumb to get into the cavern?"

Chuck leaned back in his chair and steepled his fingers. Konklin's last statement spoke volumes, more than he'd realized. He only knew of the Marsium121 claim but remained ignorant of its value. "I notice the clock on your credenza. It was assembled here and the hour markers on its face are Marsium121. In a number of interviews, you said, 'That's the only thing I have of Mars until my dome's constructed.' You still haven't figured out Marsium121's true value, and now you want to complain about how long it took us?"

At that moment, Konklin did something that Chuck had never witnessed before. He opened his mouth, but no words emerged.

"You personally had the same opportunity as us. A couple of years ago, one of my employees discovered Marsium121's usefulness. His son recently read about it when going through his belongings," Chuck offered.

Konklin asked, "Can you prove it wasn't twenty years ago?"

"No, just like you can't prove it wasn't the day before we started a search for an archaeologist. That's a game that'll get you nowhere. Anyway, based on that new information coupled with the public record, we acted on my employee's conclusions by hiring an expert and gaining access to a large deposit of Marsium121."

"Expert," Konklin snorted. "Gretchen Blake has been blackballed by Dr. Hawthorne, who is a bona fide expert. Your consultant won't cover the fact that you've been in that cavern long before you hired Blake, and that you knew Marsium121's true value while the original exploration grant was in effect. I'm not buying that you needed Blake to get in."

Chuck couldn't help but smile. "Your fantasies aside, she did the job we hired her to do. I'm aware of Gretchen's status. I also know the circumstances of Hawthorne's blackball. In my view, he acted unfairly. Regardless, that fact doesn't negate her work history, academic achievements, or the job she performed for us."

Their verbal thrust and parry continued a while longer without progress. Konklin finally asked, "Instead of wasting all the effort arguing about it, why don't we agree to share the Marsium121?"

"Okay. On one condition. Tell me what's so valuable about it."

Konklin's eyes narrowed and his jaw muscles tensed as he stared into the vidcomm.

Chucked lean forward toward the vidcomm's camera. "You've done nothing to earn the Marsium121. You've offered me nothing of value in exchange, except your promise not to dispute our claim, a dispute that'll surely fail given a reasonable hearing of the facts. I see no benefit in sharing."

The vidcomm went dark.

Chuck sat for a time, replaying and analyzing the conversation. Konklin's suggestion to share had merely been a pretense. Before ever placing the vidcomm, he must've known Chuck would never thumb off on such an agreement. *Does Konklin really believe I'd admit to withholding information until the mineral rights claim expired?*

He shook his head. No matter how Chuck assayed the conversation, Konklin's true purpose for the vidcomm eluded him.

* * *

Heather Newton disconnected the vidcomm transmission from Earth, stood, and reeled toward her kitchen. Nancy had explained that MarsVantage refused to compromise, so John was to follow through on his plan to convert the Marsium121 to Interplanetary's control.

More than anything, she wanted to recall him. The Marsium121 wasn't worth killing for, but she was the only one who felt that way. Nancy had expressed no qualms about John's plan, which meant Peter also endorsed it.

John's plan was wrong, and she was the only one who saw it.

In the kitchen, she realized that she had been staring at a cupboard for some time. She grabbed a vodka bottle and shot glass and wandered into the living area. After plopping into a chair, she poured a shot and gulped it down. Her throat burned as she searched for a way to get the Marsium121 without committing murder.

After the fourth shot, Heather closed her eyes, trying to recall exactly why she'd been so concerned.

31 | Targeted for Murder

The datapad alarm sounded by Frank's ear. He quickly muted it, eager to begin loading the tractor as soon as the sun rose. In the nightlight's dim glow, he stood and stretched. Before he could perform his morning routine, a yellow warning light on the airlock caught his attention.

The airlock's status panel indicated that it was running on internal battery backup and not receiving power from the tractor. The yellow warning light still blinked, so they had at least two hours of power left, though they'd drain the battery quickly by using the airlock or more lights.

He nudged Gretchen's shoulder. "You have to get up."

"C'mon, five more minutes," she said in a sleepy voice.

She looked so lovely, laying there peacefully asleep, her hair framing her half-visible face. He breathed out slowly. Now wasn't the time for such thoughts. "No, no. You need to get up now. We have a problem."

Gretchen sat up, eyes wide. "What happened?"

"Don't know. Put on your helmet." He pointed to the yellow light on the airlock's status panel. "We lost tractor power to the airlock and its air recycling system. I'm going to see what's wrong. I'll be back in a few minutes."

Gretchen nodded and donned her helmet and gloves.

Frank did likewise and opened the airlock's inside door. He closed it and evacuated the air. He opened the outside door and was greeted by the sun's first rays sneaking through the mountain peaks in the distance.

The tractor's power cable was still connected to the airlock. As he traversed the slope to the tractor, he inspected the cable, which was undamaged and still connected to the tractor.

Frank climbed into the tractor's cockpit. He attempted to activate the control panel, but nothing happened. He tried again, and still nothing happened.

He squeezed between the seats to the empty cargo area and began troubleshooting. Fifteen minutes later, the last power converter lay on the cargo bay's floor, all four displaying the same symptoms. The control chips had been destroyed by a power surge potent enough to char the circuit board. The tractor was rooted in place until it received at least one new power converter or a tow— neither of which was likely to occur anytime soon.

In all his years working with tractors, Frank had never seen anything like this. At worst, power converters degraded, requiring replacement. All of these converters had been on the new side and fully tested before leaving Mars City. None of them should've failed, let alone all of them at once.

The inescapable conclusion was that their tractor had been sabotaged. Interplanetary wanted to prevent MarsVantage from utilizing the Marsium121, and they were willing to murder for it. Chuck had been right in his concern.

From under the passenger seat, Frank grabbed the emergency-pac and withdrew a couple of rectangular, electric blue distress flags. He carefully climbed onto the tractor's roof and affixed one. Afterward, on the ground, he attached the other to the tractor's front.

Moments ticked by as he stared at the flag. Whoever had sabotaged the tractor was probably watching, and they certainly recognized that he'd performed an expected but useless gesture. No one was going to drive by and rescue them. The odds were only slightly better that an overflight would see the marker. But a one in a million chance was better than no chance at all.

* * *

From his tractor near the eastern range of the Maelstrom Mountains, John Reed watched Brentford enter the airlock on his video monitor. Brentford probably suspected sabotage. He was correct.

Brentford had spent time inside the tractor, presumably troubleshooting his power problem. Without the tractor, the MarsVantage team's air supply was finite and dwindling.

Shortly, the airlock's internal battery would run dry, leaving the cave with no more than eight hours of useful air. Their air vests held a maximum of eleven hours, and with the tractor inoperative, they couldn't recharge them. By dawn tomorrow, John could safely enter the cave and reclaim what rightfully belonged to Interplanetary.

A few minutes later, the airlock door slid open. Surprisingly, Brentford led the Earther outside. Brentford pushed a hand truck holding two cargo containers while the Earther carried a toolpac. They were attempting to repair the power converters.

John had applied a powerful current to the power converters' control circuits that rendered them irreparable. As futile as the repair attempt might be, he understood their need to try. If he were in their position, he'd try something—anything—no matter how far-fetched.

The Earther swung open the cargo hatch, and Brentford placed the containers inside. The Earther handed him the toolpac and walked around the tractor, gawking in all directions as if rescue would roll over the horizon.

Because his view of the tractor's rear was blocked, John couldn't see Brentford's efforts. Instead, he focused on the Earther climbing atop the tractor, a risky move for one not used to working in Mars' gravity. If she slipped and fell, she could easily damage her suit beyond repair.

In the end, it didn't matter. She was already dead.

It was merely a matter of timing now.

"Mars City Control, SOS," the Earther said. *"This is Explorer Three in the Maelstrom Mountains. We're in trouble. Send help. Please."*

She carried on like this for ten minutes, describing their circumstances in detail, circumstances more dire than he'd suspected—she'd said they would run out of air shortly after midnight. The delicate Earther was falling apart before his eyes. It proved the axiom that Earthers weren't prepared for the hazards of Mars.

Brentford finally emerged from the back of the tractor and said, *"No one can hear you. The suits don't have the power to broadcast back to Mars City. Nor can they broadcast to anyone in orbit. We can't connect the tractor's antenna to the suit. There's not enough power to drive it. I thought of it already."*

"Perhaps you're willing to give up and die, but I'm not," the Earther said.

"Neither am I, but I'm not wasting my time doing useless things."

"That's not true," John said to himself.

"That's not true?" the Earther mocked. *"Those power converters are fried. Even I know they need to be replaced."*

"Unfortunately, you're right," Brentford said with an audible sigh. *"We have scrap metal and burnt circuit boards that used to be power converters. Help me gather the tools and spare parts and take them back into the cave. Our best chance is to conserve our air and hope that someone sees the emergency markers."*

John leaned back in his seat and smiled. Their plan was logical and contained only one flaw. But it was a fatal one.

There was no one around willing to rescue them.

32 | RED SKY AT NIGHT...

Erin Knox emerged from the shower dripping wet, looking forward to the flights ferrying ore containers from mining sites to the OTP in preparation for the next transport from Earth. Although she didn't get as many flight hours as she wanted, she scheduled as many as possible within the confines of her other duties.

The vidcomm chime interrupted her toweling off her face and short hair. "Really? Again."

While entering the living room, she cinched her robe tight. The vidcomm screen displayed '*Mining Site 17*,' which was strange. *Seventeen closed months ago.*

"Dammit!" Erin smacked the Answer button and the screen displayed '*Video Unavailable*.'

"Erin, it's Frank. Can we talk?"

"Yes. I'm alone."

"I need your help. Interplanetary disabled the tractor's power converters. I'm sure they're nearby watching and eavesdropping on our standard comm frequencies. I need you to rescue us tomorrow morning."

"I'll be there in thirty minutes."

"No. Gretchen's making phony distress calls, telling Interplanetary exactly what they want to hear. I want to catch them in the act."

"Are you nuts? You could get hurt or worse. I'm coming now."

"Stick to our arrangement. Say you're shaking down a repair and come tomorrow morning."

He shouldn't confront Interplanetary from a position of weakness. By his tone though, his mind was made up. "I don't like it. Do me a favor—be smart, and watch your six."

"Will do. And one more favor, tell Chuck what happened, in person and in private."

"Do you think they cracked our vidcomms?"

"Probably not, but I'm not in a trusting mood."

"I'll see Chuck right away, and I'll see you tomorrow at dawn." She disconnected and closed her eyes, squeezing tears down her cheeks.

* * *

Once inside the cave, Gretchen helped Frank stow the transmitter and battery containers in the corner. They gathered the extra air vests from the "survey equipment" containers and deposited them next to the air mattresses. She flopped down, leaned against the cave wall with her eyes closed, and tried to digest the past hour's events.

Before long, Frank settled beside her. "Erin will arrive first thing tomorrow."

She registered his words but said nothing.

"Are you okay?" Frank asked with a concerned tone.

"I should've kept my mouth shut in Antarctica."

"You don't mean that."

"Considering the largest corporation on Earth wants me dead, it sounds like a good idea right about now."

"If you'd done that, we would've never met."

Gretchen opened her eyes and glared at him.

Frank took her gloved hand in his, which didn't comfort her. "I never expected Konklin to murder anyone."

"Yet you packed the extra air vests."

"Chuck insisted. I never thought we'd actually use them. Believe me, if I knew matters would play out this way, I would've canceled our expedition."

"I don't understand what's so important to go to all this trouble."

"Konklin knows Mars isn't a huge moneymaker, at least, not right now, not compared to his other companies. He only wants MarsVantage back to satisfy his ego."

"He went to all this trouble over a bruised ego?"

"MarsVantage was a very public failure. One he wishes to reverse. He didn't get to where he is by accepting failure."

On its face, Frank's explanation was absurd, but on a deeper level, it made sense. Konklin had lost the battle a decade ago and was re-fighting it now, using everything available to win. If people were hurt, well, it wasn't personal—they were simply in the way. "Terrific. What do we do now?"

"We wait. After Interplanetary thinks we've exhausted our air, they'll come to steal our findings, and we'll catch them in the act."

The air vests might've merely delayed the inevitable. "What if there's more of them than we can handle?"

"I'd like you to wait in the cavern where it's safe."

Frank's reasoning was muddled. The cavern held no safety. And one person against who knows how many sounded like a losing proposition. His instinct to protect her increased the odds of them both getting killed. "You didn't think that through."

He blinked. "I don't understand."

"The cavern isn't safe. If Interplanetary overpowers you, they'll either ignore the door while I wait inside, not knowing when it's safe to emerge, eventually suffocating. Or they'll blow the door, which means they'll capture me, before killing me outright. More likely, flying shards of Marsium121 will shred me to bloody pieces. Our best chance is to stay together."

Frank was silent for a few moments. "Damn, I didn't think about that. I should've let Erin rescue us immediately."

"She wanted to come right away?"

"I stopped her. I wanted to catch Interplanetary in the act." Frank exhaled and cast his gaze downward. "I've been selfish, and I placed you in needless danger. Help me with the battery and transmitter again. I'll have Erin get us immediately."

Frank walked to the cargo containers. He turned to face her, an expectant look crossing his face.

He was willing to abandon his plan, for her. MarsVantage would file a protest, but at worst, Interplanetary would hear a few harsh words. A court should hold Interplanetary accountable, really accountable, which meant they had to capture the perpetrators in the act.

His plan was risky. Plenty of times, she'd been in dangerous places, but the danger was nature, a force that followed specific, well-known rules. It killed the careless and the ignorant. This danger was different. It was ego and greed and would kill whomever stood in its way.

Yet the choice was clear—run away like a scared child or confront the danger head-on. She inhaled and straightened. "No. Playacting the victim is one thing. Being a victim is another. We wait until tomorrow like you planned. That gives us a chance to catch Interplanetary if they come. And I mean *we*, together, as partners."

With his lips pressed tightly, Frank sat beside her again. In a calm, even tone, he asked, "Are you sure? I don't want to see you get hurt."

He isn't arguing the point. She breathed easier. "I don't want you to get hurt, either, so we'll watch over one another."

"Okay." Frank looked around. "Let's arrange the cave to our advantage."

They pulled and pushed each cargo container to create a shoulder-high divider between the airlock and the cavern door. Before they hoisted the last container in place, he withdrew a shock-tab gun from it. Gretchen opened her mouth to ask how he'd managed to get hold of one but decided not to. Rumors circulated that certain black markets sold them, though she'd never seen one. After that, smuggling it to Mars would have been easy enough.

But where did he get the ammunition? Surely, MarsVantage didn't manufacture the rounds. They weren't easy to create like old-time bullets where patience, simple tools, and materials such as gunpowder, empty cartridges, and lead slugs were all that was needed. The shock-tab bullet opened like a flower upon impact. It held a small one-use power source that charged tiny contacts on each petal to shock and immobilize the target. The rounds were government controlled—even hearing rumors about their availability on the black market was rare. He must've gotten the ammo from a police or military contact, which was an interesting factoid.

After he placed the gun between the air mattresses, which were on the cavern side of the containers, he said, "This will even up things nicely."

As if to punctuate his statement, the light faded out as the airlock's battery finally died. Involuntarily, Gretchen stepped backward and whispered, "Damn."

After activating his helmet's exterior light, Frank looked around one more time. "It had to happen sooner or later. There's nothing more to do except wait. Let's get to the mattresses."

With her back against the cave wall, she sat on the mattress while Frank did the same on her left, next to the cargo containers. He extinguished his exterior helmet light, plunging the cave into utter darkness. He activated the interior helmet light and she did likewise. At least, that would give them some sense of presence.

She imagined Interplanetary coming for the cave. The two of them could handle a couple of intruders. Perhaps as many as three. More than that, they'd probably be overpowered. There was no other choice, though. They had to do the right thing. This time the right thing was hard and dangerous. Knowing that didn't keep her hands from shaking against her legs. "Frank?"

"Yes."

She hesitated. She hated to ask, but she wanted to feel connected. "Will you hold me?"

"Of course. Slide over." He opened his arm, inviting her to join him.

Gretchen scooted over and leaned back into him, her helmet resting on his shoulder. He wrapped his arms around her, placing his hands across her stomach. She placed her hands on his.

"Better?" Frank asked softly.

"Better."

33 | WHO WE ARE

While the clock on Gretchen's wrist control panel ticked past midnight, toward her advertised oxygen deadline thirty minutes from now, she reflected upon the events that led her to this cave. Her passion for archaeology had kept her in the field, dooming her marriage. Her training and curiosity had precluded her from kowtowing to Hawthorne, forcing her to take work beyond Hawthorne's influence. Upon learning of the symbols, she had to pursue them—the intellectual challenge was too great, not to mention her need for money.

She would've had to be a different person not to end up here. Obsessing about it wasn't doing her any good. She needed to divert her attention elsewhere. "Frank?"

"Yes," he whispered. "Is something wrong?"

"I was wondering what you're thinking about."

He cleared his voice. "A sentiment of Thomas Jefferson's, edited from the original draft of the Declaration of Independence."

She'd expected he'd be pondering the buried city and the message, or Interplanetary breaking into the cave... not something that happened five centuries ago. "Isn't that kinda odd considering the circumstances?"

"He wrote, 'We might have been a free and great people together.' One of our lawyers mentioned it in the aftermath of the Airlock Accident when we were opposing the split. It stuck with me ever since."

"I would've expected you to favor splitting from Interplanetary."

"I was angry, but we all recognized the difficulties in going it alone. We wanted a transparent and accountable management team with sensitivity to safety, not independence."

"Okay. Then why's that quote on your mind at a time like this?"

"Together is impossible. It's more true now than a decade ago. Konklin is who he is, and we Marsees are who we are, so here we sit." Frank's voice was little more than a monotone.

More than anything, Gretchen wished she could hold Frank as he was holding her now but without the spacesuits. "I hear your sadness. You need to stay focused on the goal."

"Oh, Gretchen, this isn't going how I planned, not even close. I nearly got you killed. And you're not clear yet. You didn't sign on for that."

"But we're not dead. A few hours from now, Erin'll rescue us."

"That she will." He audibly exhaled. "Something else bothers me, though. This attempt clearly shows Interplanetary's intention to destroy us. It's one setback after another, and I'm tired of it all."

"Trust me, Frank, I know about setbacks. I ruined my marriage with my career—which I also ruined. I traveled to Mars where people I never met want me dead. But you know what? When I was young, my mom used to tell me we experience failure so we'll appreciate success. Success is close. I just know it. When we return to Mars City and get some rest, things will look better."

He chuckled. "You're amazing. After everything you've been through, you're still able to cheer me up."

Before she could answer, an alarm sounded. She looked at the control panel on her left wrist. "It's me. My air's down to five percent."

She turned on her hand flashlight and sat it on the air mattress. She scooted forward and unzipped her air vest.

"Let me help you with the swap."

"I can do it. I passed the training." Before Gretchen could think, the words had escaped her lips. She looked in his eyes and saw hurt and disappointment.

"I didn't mean anything."

"I know, Frank. I really need to do it for myself."

He nodded.

After Gretchen disconnected the spent air vest from her spacesuit, she slid it from her shoulders and tossed it aside. Frank handed her a fresh one. She slipped her arms into it, making the suit connection with a twist and a click before zipping up. The diagnostic reported air and battery power at one hundred percent.

Frank took the opportunity to swap his air vest for a fresh one, too. "You did that like an expert. You must've paid attention in training."

"Thanks. My instructor was thorough." She turned off her flashlight and leaned back against him, pulling his arms around her. "Now, we're ready to catch Interplanetary if they show up. You know we're just assuming they will."

"I'm certain. Konklin's greed will drive them here as sure as the sun rises. I expect two Interplanetary employees are in a tractor waiting nearby. Your distress call provided them a timeline. If it were me, I'd wait for an hour or so after your deadline—just to be sure we're dead—then loot the cave and return to Mars City before anyone realizes we're in trouble."

He rolled his left arm, so they could both see the digital clock on his control panel. "According to your timeline, our oxygen supply will fail in twenty minutes. They'll be here soon."

"I'm ready."

"You know, Erin questioned my sanity for inviting the confrontation. It's strange because she would've done the same thing without giving it a second thought, yet I had to talk her out of an immediate rescue."

"It's not strange at all. She still cares for you."

"Perhaps, but not in the way that matters." Frank tenderly squeezed her hand.

Was it a signal toward her, reinforcing the point that he was single? Again, she fought her attraction to him, which was far more difficult when wrapped in his arms.

* * *

With dawn approaching, Gretchen concluded that Interplanetary wasn't coming. The oxygen deadline she'd broadcasted hadn't enticed them to trespass into the cave when it'd expired hours ago.

A weight she hadn't realized she'd been carrying lifted. Soon, Erin would pick them up, and they'd fly back to the safety of Mars City. The nightmare would be over.

And she could decipher the cavern message. She suspected—well, she hoped—it was an enormous discovery that'd take a lifetime to explore. Visions of an alien version of London, Washington, D.C., or Paris with their enormous libraries and grandiose museums danced through her imagination.

The path forward was clear. She'd delay her return trip to Earth until she fully understood the message's meaning. If her hopes proved true, the city buried under centuries of Mars' sands would alter MarsVantage's future and, perhaps, hers and Frank's as well.

Those thoughts vanished when the airlock door screeched in protest against its frame.

34 | THE THIEF IN THE NIGHT

Gretchen and Frank scrambled to their preplanned positions. Her pulse thumped in her ears, and her hands shook, mostly in anticipation. Behind the stacked containers nearest the airlock, she crouched, balanced on the balls of her feet.

Frank stood against the cave wall at the opposite end of the container row. He placed and removed his hand from over the air vest's green indicator, causing three flashes. She mimicked his action.

We're ready.

Overhead, shadows extended toward the cavern doorway, growing shorter as the murderers exited the airlock and approached the containers. Frank turned on his flashlight. A split-second later, Gretchen shouldered over the containers and turned on her flashlight.

"What the... Uhh!"

The plan had worked just as they'd hoped. Frank's flashlight had blinded the would-be murderer, and the containers had knocked him over. He now lay on the ground with his arms shielding his faceplate.

As the containers were settling, Frank slid over one and bobbed around two others to kneel on the intruder's chest before he could gather his wits.

"I can't breathe," the intruder gasped.

"I got this one, Gretchen. Check the airlock for his partner!"

She played her light along the inside of the airlock. "He's alone, and the outer door's shut."

"Good. We'll have plenty of warning if his partner enters." Frank pulled the intruder's arms from his faceplate. "It's John Reed."

"You're kidding." She looked to the prone figure. Apparently, Reed had decided to murder her and steal the discovery once she'd declined to spy for him. "Look, he's wearing an empty holster."

"Look for the gun. I'll tie him up."

After Frank placed his flashlight and shock-tab gun on the ground an arm's-length away, he pushed Reed onto his stomach. Frank planted a knee into Reed's back, eliciting a groan. From his shoulder pocket, Frank pulled a zip tie, spilling a couple on the ground. He bound Reed's hands together behind his back with the zip tie. After ensuring the tie was secure enough to prevent Reed from slipping loose, Frank rolled him over and pulled him up, propping him against the cave wall.

"Careful. You'll rip my suit!"

"What makes you think you're leaving alive?"

Gretchen couldn't believe what she'd just heard. Reed's face remained expressionless.

Next, Frank bound Reed's feet together with a zip tie that'd fallen to the floor. Afterward, Frank placed the remaining ties back in his pocket, and gathered his light and shock-tab gun. "There's a certain justice in allowing you to die by the fate you planned for us."

Where are his threats coming from? This wasn't the Frank she knew. *Would he actually mete out frontier justice?*

"I found the gun," Frank said. After he tucked his flashlight under his right arm, he reached over with his left hand and tugged it from under a container. He inspected it and placed his shock-tab gun in his thigh pocket. "It's a VLF gun with the intensity set to high. If we weren't dead already, he sure planned to finish the job."

She stared at Reed. How had he gotten his hands on a military-grade weapon? Very low frequency sound waves caused the target's internal organs to resonate, inducing headaches, disorientation, loss of bodily function control, and at the high setting—death. "You bastard!"

Frank gestured with the VLF gun as he asked, "Who else is with you?"

Reed chuckled. "Who are you kidding? We both know you're not going to kill me. How would you explain a dead body?"

"What makes you think anybody would ever find out about it? Mars is a big planet... and you're a small man."

Reed looked at Frank for several seconds. Frank's expression didn't change one iota. "Okay, okay. I'm alone."

"Are you sure you want to stick with that answer?" Gretchen asked. "We'll know soon enough if you're lying."

"I'm alone. My tractor's outside."

"That answers my next question. Now, sit still and behave until we get back."

After Frank righted a cargo container, Gretchen helped him retrieve the battery they'd used for the transmitter yesterday. Once inside the airlock, he connected it via an access panel. He closed the inner door and opened the outer door.

"Better than having to manually operate it," he said. "By the way, Reed was probably telling the truth, but keep an eye out for a partner anyway."

"What do we do if we see one?"

"Have you ever fired a shock-tab gun?"

"No..."

"I'm not surprised. Archaeologists don't have any need for such skills."

"And maintenance engineers do?"

Frank laughed. "Considering the past twenty-four hours, yeah."

"Good point. I'll add shock-tab training to my to-do list."

"Better to have the skill and never need to use it." Frank stepped out and activated his exterior helmet light. "If you start to feel nauseated, drop to the ground to reduce your target area. Don't worry about damaging your suit, we can always fix it."

Gretchen took her cue from Frank and activated hers. Additionally, they used their flashlights. She scanned to the left while he the right, searching for an Interplanetary partner.

"You aren't really going to kill Reed, are you, Frank?"

"Of course not. Maybe I can scare information out of him, though. I'll let him stew on my threats and then talk to him again."

Parked just beyond their tractor, Frank's flashlight beam found Reed's, pointing in the direction of Mars City. When they reached level ground, they walked side by side with measured steps. Gretchen played her light over it while Frank scanned the immediate area around it. Though the same model as theirs, Reed's had a hideous contraption hanging from its backside.

Two steps past their disabled tractor, Gretchen stumbled. She raised her arms as she took several heavy, awkward steps.

Frank snatched up what'd tripped her. Outstretched, it was four feet by three feet and appeared to be a tarp with foot-long cuts along one of its short ends.

"What's that?"

"Reed must've worn this around his waist to erase his footprints up to here. Beyond here, his footprints would become mixed with ours." Frank tossed the skirt toward their tractor. They continued to Reed's, Frank playing his light over its rear section. "He's using the same technique with the treads, too."

They entered the driver's side, Gretchen first, squeezing between the seats to inspect the cargo area while Frank stayed in the driver's seat. What looked like an old-time motorcycle with wide treads for tires leaned against the wall. On Earth, machines like this hadn't been used for centuries because of their inherent danger. "Check this out, Frank."

He turned around. "A monorider. Typically, construction site and mining supervisors use them to get around quickly. Reed used it too—I can see sand on and around the treads. I'll bet you that skirt outside was originally fitted to it."

Reed had probably used it when he sabotaged their tractor. It was small, difficult to spot if someone had happened to be outside when he'd been approaching.

Beside the monorider were four cargo containers. One was empty and another held FieldMeals and water. The third, Reed used for trash while the last held a surprise—five low-yield demolition explosives along with an empty slot for a sixth. "You aren't going to believe this. He's carrying demexes... and one's missing."

After a few seconds, Frank said, "I found the remote detonator. And I bet I know where the other demex is, but never mind that now. Come here. You have to see this."

Gretchen knelt directly behind Frank's seat, looking over his shoulder. He motioned to a monitor crudely attached to the dashboard, showing a darkened scene with only faint lights showing through windows... of a tractor.

She snorted. "Let me guess. That's us."

Frank waved his flashlight through the window across the landscape, which displayed on screen. "He's been watching us the whole time."

"By the amount of garbage back there, I'd guess since we arrived."

"Probably before. He wouldn't have wanted to chance us seeing him arrive." Frank stared at the ceiling. After several seconds, he looked her in the eye. "Assuming Reed was here before we left Mars City, I suspect there's at least one more spy handler."

"Why's that?"

"Interplanetary would want to know why the expedition was delayed, and they'd want to verify that we would still be coming. If I were in their shoes, that's what I'd do. I'll bet you anything the meeting I expected took place right under my nose, and I didn't recognize it."

"Don't feel bad, Frank. We'll get them. It's just a matter of time."

Frank looked at Gretchen with a broad grin on his face.

"What?"

"You said 'we'll', not 'you'll.'"

I did. It seemed so natural. But this isn't the time to discuss the implications. "The video camera must be in the mountains across the valley."

"Yeah, that makes sense, good sight line, far enough away that we'd never spot it."

Frank hadn't pressed the issue. A conversation about the future was premature. On a positive note, though, he seemed pleased that she'd sided with him. She filed that line of thought away for later. "He's been out there watching us, waiting for the right time to sabotage our tractor."

"Yes."

"He heard my broadcast and ignored it."

"Yes."

"Bastard!" she spat out.

Frank's eyebrows rose.

"What's so important that Reed would want to murder us?"

"Gretchen, now you see why we went to such lengths to protect the expedition and why I've been so secretive. We're used to their underhanded tactics, though nothing this low. The sooner we lessen our dependence on Earth, the better off we'll be."

"I understand. I really do." Gretchen looked at the monitor again and suspected that she already knew the answer to her next question. "Where's the missing demex?"

"I'd guess it's on our tractor's fuel cell. He probably placed it there in case we pulled out before he knew what we came for."

Gretchen shook her head. "That's what I thought you'd say."

"It's not going to do you any good focusing on that. Last night you reminded me to stay focused on the goal, so it's my turn to remind you. Stay focused on the goal." Frank opened the tractor's door. "Open up the cargo hatch. We're taking his demolition explosives with us as evidence."

At the tractor's rear, Frank met her. Together, they carried the container holding the five demexes to the vicinity of their tractor.

Gretchen followed him to their tractor's front where he slowly knelt near the passenger-side tread with exaggerated care. "Careful. Don't rip your spacesuit."

Frank leaned over, balancing himself on a gloved hand, to peer under the tractor with the aid of his flashlight. "There it is, just as I thought."

"You're not going remove it, are you?"

"I'm not letting it wait for whoever retrieves the tractor."

"Wait, Frank. Have you ever handled a demex before?"

"No, but I've read about them."

"Well, I have," Gretchen said evenly. "Let me do it."

"Gretchen! When did you mess with this stuff?"

"A while back, a group of us followed an expedition that collapsed a cliff face on their site. We trained and removed most of the debris with explosives similar to Reed's."

"That wasn't in your HR profile."

She carefully got on her knees to see the tractor's underside. "I know. A regulatory agent trained us. As part of the deal to receive training, the skill couldn't be listed on our profile, and we were required to notify Domestic Security if anyone sought us out for those skills."

"Isn't that something? The government redacts HR profiles. I didn't know that. It shows where their concerns lie." He sat the flashlight on the ground, pointing to the demex. "I'm already in position. I'll remove the explosive."

In the small of her back, sweat pooled. He must realize he wasn't actually protecting her. If it blew, it'd take them both, regardless of who was handling it. Fortunately, demexes were fairly idiot-proof. "Remember, squeeze it by the small ends. That'll release it from the fuel cell. Whatever you do, don't touch any of the controls on the top."

He tugged a couple of times to no effect. On the third, it came loose. "That got it."

He stood, slowly, not only in deference to his spacesuit but to the explosive he held in his right hand.

"Hold on a minute." Gretchen got up, leaning on her hands so she didn't drag her knees along the ground. She turned the arming dial counter-clockwise to the disarmed position and toggled the switch on the radio receiver. "Okay. Now it's safe."

"I'll put it in the container with the others."

Gretchen asked, "Do you think there's anything else we missed?"

35 | Replies Rather Than Answers

Not long after sunrise, though the sun remained behind the mountains, Gretchen and Frank made several trips, using the hand truck, transferring and stacking the cargo containers near their tractor. They returned to the cave, now empty except for Reed and the container that originally held the portable airlock. Once again, Gretchen looked at Reed, failing to understand what he valued enough to commit coldblooded murder.

"Are you going to leave me to die while you steal my tractor?" Reed asked through a smirk. "Won't that be difficult to explain?"

"Not at all. We'll just drag you outside and free you before we leave in *our* tractor, repaired with your working power couplings," Frank answered.

Reed's eyes grew wide. He mustn't have worked out that possibility.

"If you want a ride, tell me who the spy is and who ordered our murder," Frank offered.

Reed looked to the cave's floor.

"Have it your way." Frank turned and entered the airlock with Gretchen following. Outside on the cargo containers, they sat facing one another.

Frank looked skyward for a few moments, and then pointed. "Ah, Erin's right on time."

Gretchen peered up, straining to see what Frank was pointing out. Several seconds later, she caught a flash against the reddish-orange sky. It was a shuttle like the one that had transported her from orbit.

As it slowed, he said, "Be careful what you say about Erin around Reed. If he finds out she's landing because I contacted her—instead of responding to the emergency flag—there'll be serious consequences."

She was about to ask what was more serious than murder when Erin interrupted. "Explorer Tractor Three, are you declaring an emergency?"

"Yes, our tractor is non-operational. Our air supply is limited," Frank said while looking up as Erin circled overhead.

"Control, this is Captain Knox on a maintenance flight. I spotted an emergency signal from Explorer Tractor Three. I confirmed their distress via radio."

"Understood. Implement emergency protocol."

"Confirmed. Initiating emergency protocol. I'm landing now."

One hundred yards away, the shuttle settled to the ground, stirring the sand into a rusty-brown cloud, obscuring it from view. A minute later, Erin emerged.

"I'm here, Frank. And it better be good because it's my license on the line."

Frank summarized this morning's events without mentioning the cavern, Marsium121, or the message.

"Who says nothing interesting happens on Mars? How about we talk with this meathead?" Erin asked, though it sounded more like a statement.

"We tried a couple of times. He hasn't given us any names," Gretchen said.

Erin turned to Gretchen and smiled broadly. "Let me try. I can be pretty charming."

Gretchen could've sworn she heard Frank choke on a laugh. She looked over, but he was already following Erin up the slope to the cave.

First through the airlock, Erin crouched before Reed. "So, you tried to kill my friends. What do you think we should do with you?"

He merely looked at her.

For a couple of heartbeats, Erin stared back, not blinking. "Control has no record of any other tractors in the area. So you're out here, and no one officially knows, though I'll wager the higher-ups at Interplanetary do."

"You can ride back with us if you tell me who ordered you here and who your spy is," Frank said.

"I don't know what you're talking about."

Erin clapped her gloved hands together in front of his helmet. "Wake up, dummy. Either talk or die."

"You don't get it," Reed said, gazing from Erin to Frank. "I have two possible futures. I say nothing, and you leave me here to die. Or I spill my guts, and I return to Mars City. How long do you think I'll live once I betray Konklin?"

"That's the dull thinking of a limited mind," Erin said. "How about we load you in my shuttle and decide in-flight if you end the trip with us. Falling to your death is far worse than running out of air. Perhaps looking down on the landscape will loosen your tongue. If not, you'll get a great view of Mars. Until impact."

"Your threats are meaningless."

Frank raised his hand with two fingers extended. The MarsVantage employees switched to the second comm channel via the control panel on their left arms. A second later, Gretchen did the same.

How can Frank rationalize away Erin shoving Reed from the shuttle? He didn't have to be the one doing the pushing to still be responsible. "You aren't actually going to shove him out of the shuttle, are you?"

"That weasel deserves a lot more than threats," Erin said.

"Scaring him isn't working," Frank said.

Earlier, Frank had convinced her his threats were just talk, but seeing him with Erin... Was that all a lie? While she couldn't prevent them from doing anything they were planning, she'd at least have a say. "He can't tell you anything if he's dead."

Both Erin and Frank looked at her. She refused to back down and maintained eye contact with Frank.

Frank blinked. "We won't hurt him."

After a brief discussion over their next step, they packed the shuttle. Erin pitched in using a hand truck from her cargo bay, which made the work go much faster than when they'd arrived. For the last trip, they collected Reed from the cave, Frank holding him by his arms and Gretchen and Erin by the legs. They deposited him on a hand truck and pushed him to the shuttle. Once inside, Frank secured Reed with more zip ties from his suit to the passenger bench nearest to the cockpit as Erin settled into the pilot's seat. After a few seconds, several panels strategically placed near the ceiling changed from red to green.

"Atmo normal. Strap in. We're taking off shortly." Erin removed her helmet, donned a headset, and toggled a switch on the panel before her.

Gretchen sat opposite Reed and removed her helmet. She connected the harness' buckles and snugged the straps tight, eager to return to Mars City.

"Control, this is Captain Knox. The exploration team is unharmed. Their tractor is non-op. We'll arrive in fifteen, and we need Security to take John Reed from Interplanetary into custody. Frank caught him trespassing on the exploration site."

Reed smiled.

Gretchen hadn't been this tired in a long time. She lacked the energy to understand why Reed was happy. It didn't matter. He was their prisoner and couldn't harm them anymore.

Frank sat beside Reed, strapped in, and removed his own helmet before removing Reed's. He fastened Reed's harness with a snap of the buckle and two tugs of the strap. Reed coughed, but Frank ignored it. "There you have it, Reed. We're not tossing you from the shuttle, but you're in deep. If you tell me who the spy is and who ordered our murder, we'll request leniency and protection for you."

"Request away. There's no place safe from Konklin's reach. You, of all people, should know that."

Erin interjected, "I hope you enjoy your time looking at Earth through the bars of a cell."

"I love how you Marsees always abide by the regs," Reed said. He chuckled and shook his head.

"What does that mean?" Gretchen asked.

"Just as the regs require, she radioed Control that you had me in custody. As soon as she did, she created another future for me, the only one guaranteeing that I live. I thought I was going to have to give you the spy's name while staring down at Mars and then take my chances with Konklin. Instead, she handed me an out on a silver platter."

Frank exhaled loudly. "I get it. Reed remains loyal to Konklin, and Konklin buys the judge, prosecutor, or both to get him off scot-free."

"Shit," Gretchen muttered as she looked at Frank.

"Well played, Reed." Frank looked him squarely in the eyes. "But mark my words, we're gonna press charges anyway. And I'm gonna find the spy. Count on it."

36 | Working Within the Rules

Outside Pad 1A in Mars City, Gretchen emerged from her changing stall to join Frank. While she felt better finally getting out of the spacesuit, the fresh coveralls couldn't hide that she hadn't showered in days. Once they completed their duties, a hot shower was the first item on her to-do list. Right behind it was sleep.

They only needed to consummate the claim since Security had already taken their statements before escorting Reed away. At the Exploration and Mineral Rights office, the claim procedure was quick. Thankfully, Chuck had already handled most of the paperwork.

Afterward, they walked toward her quarters. Along the way, Frank's datapad chimed. He pulled it from his pocket and extended the screen. "I have a message from Chuck inviting us to a celebratory supper. Until then, he suggests some sleep."

"A good idea."

As they turned the corner to the hallway leading to her quarters, Frank touched her wrist. "What's wrong? You haven't said more than three words in a row since we landed."

Gretchen looked away from Frank. "It's Reed. I'm sorry. I know it doesn't help, but I'm sorry."

With his thumb and forefinger, Frank touched Gretchen's chin and guided it, so she faced him. "You have nothing to be sorry for. You were incredible. I couldn't have asked for a better partner in the wild."

"My concerns over his safety prevented you from using harsher means to get the information from him."

He looked into her eyes. "What more could I have done to get him to talk?"

"I don't know. Disconnect his air vest?"

189

"Gretchen! I'd never do that!"

"But you could've gotten the name of the spy and who ordered him to kill us."

"Perhaps."

"C'mon, Frank. Think about it. He spoke up only when he believed it'd save his neck. He admitted as much. I kept you—"

"I probably could've gotten the names. I probably could've even tracked it back to Konklin's New York City headquarters, but then I would've been forced to kill him. I'm not in the murder business."

She shook her head. "Forced to kill him?"

"I could get away with threats. But when the Washington prosecutors learned that I assaulted him, which they'd quickly liken to torture, they would've charged me."

"Ridiculous! He tried to kill us!"

"That doesn't matter. Washington strictly enforces every rule, regulation, and law as they pertain to us while Interplanetary flouts them at will. This is the situation we live with, and it factors into every decision."

"Even so, no reasonable person would charge you."

Frank shook his head. "It's funny. You were concerned about Reed's safety in the wild, and now you're pressing me for not being forceful enough."

Gretchen took a step backwards. She'd anticipated this conversation would be difficult, but she was unprepared for that turn. "Until Erin announced to Control that we had Reed in custody, I had doubts." She flashed a weak smile, trying to take the sting from her words.

"Like I said earlier, that was just talk to scare him. I went as far as I was comfortable. Lots of people would say that my concerns are unfounded, but I've seen too much. Relying on compassion or fairness from Washington is a sure path to ruin." Frank raised his eyebrows and titled his head slightly to the side. "Besides, I got all that I hoped for once I discovered our tractor was sabotaged. We captured the Interplanetary saboteur, which will garner Interplanetary bad PR, and nothing we did will distract from that news. As a bonus, we rid ourselves of a spy handler. This is a win, and I couldn't have done it without you."

She exhaled. Only one issue remained, a personal one, and she had to address it, or it'd nag at her until she did. "I feel bad I believed you could kill Reed."

Frank nodded and determination returned to his face. "Don't. I've given you plenty of reasons to doubt me. I want you to trust me, and I intend to earn it as we go after the city. I'm out of secret plans and hidden agendas. I promise." He stepped closer and kissed her on the forehead. "Go get some sleep. You'll feel better, and everything will look differently. I'll pick you up for supper."

He turned and walked away.

At that moment, she longed for him. Should she have invited him in? Would he have come? If he did, he wouldn't leave until supper. She yearned for intimacy and readied to call out, but he'd already turned the corner. She wanted to run after him but remained. *What if he isn't interested?*

Too exhausted to take the leap, she shuffled into her quarters. Her archaeology tools sat against the living area wall, no doubt delivered while she and Frank had attended to the claim. She placed her datapad on the kitchen counter and drew a glass of water from the sink.

As she drank, she stared at her datapad, contemplating slowing the cavern message. The lack of sleep and the stress of the past day made concentrating difficult. She set the empty glass in the sink and yawned wide, not bothering to cover her mouth.

After a long, hot shower, she set the nightstand alarm and crawled into bed. Her last thoughts before sleep were of the soft bed and smooth sheets.

When the alarm blared in her ear, she awoke in the same position as when she'd fallen asleep. It had been ringing for five minutes before she heard it, which meant Frank would arrive shortly. She was going to make them late for the most important meeting of her life.

Gretchen rolled from the bed, entered the bathroom, and splashed cold water on her face to wake up. Her hair had been wet when she had gone to bed and dried in a twisted bird's nest of a mess, so she ran a water-drenched comb through it and hoped this time it'd dry into something reasonably stylish.

She donned a fresh black top and steel-blue coveralls. The door's announcement chime rang, and her mind started racing at the possibilities on the other side. For an instant, she felt foolish— it had to be Frank. Anyone like Interplanetary or the spy intending to murder her or steal her work wouldn't ring the chime. However, memories of Frank announcing that they'd been sabotaged and Reed breaking into the cave flashed through her mind.

Frank was late, and that was unusual these days. Maybe something had already happened to him. She reached for the Speaker button on the bedroom panel, but stopped. First, she went to the living room and paused at her datapad just laying on the kitchen counter unprotected. Tired brains make poor decisions, but leaving it in the open unattended could've been a disastrous blunder. She grabbed a steak knife from the cutlery drawer. *Just in case...*

Then, she strode to the door, the entire time gripping the knife tightly, holding the blade flat against her right thigh. At the door, she pressed the Speaker button. "Who is it?"

"It's Frank."

"Come in." Gretchen closed her eyes for a heartbeat and activated the door. Frank entered. She turned and walked down the short hallway, hiding the knife from his view.

"Sorry I'm late. You wouldn't believe the number of little things I had to take care of before I had a chance to sleep. Then, I slept through my alarm."

As Frank had been speaking, she walked through the living area to the kitchen. She placed the knife in the metal sink as quietly as possible.

"We need to... Wait, you were ready to defend yourself, weren't you?"

She slowly nodded, feeling her cheeks warm. "After the announcement chime rang, my imagination ran wild."

To her surprise, he approached, hugged her tight, and whispered in her ear, "I understand. You're safe in Mars City. Nothing's going to happen to you here."

She forced a thin smile and broke the embrace. "I'll be fine."

"I can arrange for you to talk with a counselor. No one would think poorly of you if you did."

"I just need more sleep and a little time, that's all. We need to get going. We're late."

"Chuck can wait." Concern was etched on Frank's face as he gestured with his hand, palm facing the floor. "You answered the door wielding a knife. I can't overlook that. Talk to me. You aren't doing yourself any favors by bottling up your feelings."

For a moment, she said nothing, wanting to avoid the discussion but not seeing an alternative. "I felt vulnerable, okay? I grabbed the knife on impulse... I overreacted." Gretchen wrapped her arms across her belly. "I'm feeling better already. I just need a little time."

"You're safe now." Frank touched her shoulder and looked her in the eye. He said tenderly, "I won't press you about it anymore tonight. But if you're not feeling better, promise me we'll talk more."

After a second, Gretchen nodded. "I promise."

"It's time to give Chuck the surprise of his life."

37 | DECISION POINTS

Gretchen and Frank joined up with Chuck outside Taggert's Restaurant, and much to her relief, they entered a private room, which would make discussing the message easier. They sat at a small table already adorned with settings for three people.

Each wall showcased a painting of Mars vistas. The one off to her left depicted a verdant Mars, full of grass and trees. Looming in the background was a towering mountain, which had to be Olympus Mons. What a sight that would've been millennia ago.

After pouring everyone a glass of local wine, Chuck raised his glass, and began the meal with a toast. "Congratulations, both of you, on changing the course of MarsVantage's future. Frank, thank you for proposing the opportunity. Gretchen, thank you for securing entry into the cavern. Rest assured, we'll follow through and make the most of it."

She added her smile to Chuck and Frank's and sipped the wine. While she wasn't a big drinker, she'd tasted enough wine over the years to recognize and enjoy its uniqueness. "Have you considered exporting this wine to Earth? It'd be a hit with connoisseurs."

"Washington's tight import controls test for foreign bacteria, viruses, and parasites, making it prohibitively expensive," Chuck said. "There's even talk about quarantining Mars imports for six months."

"As if one sip would lead to growing a tail, an extra head, or something," Frank said through a smile.

She nearly spit her mouthful of wine on the table while attempting to hold back a laugh. Between coughs, she managed to swallow, and playfully slapped Frank's wrist. "Don't do that while my mouth is full."

In due course, they ordered, and while they waited, Chuck filled Frank in on current events. He finished by mentioning that Reed was scheduled on the next transport back to Earth to face charges. Further, they'd have to submit to an interview and testify at the trial, Frank via vidcomm. Gretchen nodded, hoping the case would make it that far but suspecting Konklin would buy his way out of the consequences first.

Their meals arrived, and Chuck allowed everyone several bites of their entrée before asking Frank for a full report on the cavern. Frank outlined the events, providing a fair amount of detail along the way, though he neglected to mention the cavern message. For the entire time, Gretchen ate her pasta and vegetables, barely registering the taste, preoccupied with broaching the topic of the cavern message.

"Do you have a timetable to start mining and utilizing the Marsium121?" Chuck asked.

"We don't want to mine it," Frank said evenly, giving Gretchen a quick look.

Chuck leaned in, looking deflated. "What was the point in buying the mining rights then?"

"Gretchen made a discovery inside the cavern." Again, Frank glanced in Gretchen's direction.

Does Frank want me to just jump in?

Chuck shook his head. "And we're supposed to put our plans on hold because you found a curiosity?"

Gretchen explained that she'd found the holo message and played both the real-time version and the slowed-down version on her datapad.

"What's it mean?" Chuck asked, staring at Gretchen.

"Without a doubt, we know Mars held intelligent life sometime in the past. Perhaps, aliens are still here."

Frank gently put his hand on hers. "Gretchen, such talk is a credibility killer, even with the symbols, the cavern, and the holo as proof. It's no better than saying you spotted Bigfoot or the Loch Ness Monster. The justification for our next move has to be more…"

"...Practical," Chuck added. "Alien talk is the quickest way for the board to lose confidence in me. I spent a lot of money on this project—we need to see a return on that investment."

Damn, the Marsees take the Earth joking seriously. "Okay. The holo, then. Even the slowed version is still too fast to glean much," Gretchen said. Better not to say what she truly thought the message suggested. *They'll think I'm crazy.* "Though, I suspect that you have a greater prize than you can imagine."

With his eyebrows pulled together, Chuck said, "Frank..."

"I made out what looked like an enormous city sitting on a plain of green vegetation. It must've been when Mars was habitable, way back when."

Gretchen added, "Back in the cavern, Frank suspected the Marsium121 was probably a power generator for that city."

"I couldn't tell," Chuck said firmly. "It doesn't matter. That city, if it exists, won't provide power—the Marsium121 will. We need to prepare for a mining mission, so we can benefit from our investment."

Frank stared at Chuck. "What? Don't you see? This is that opportunity we've been waiting for. Who knows what's in the city? At the very least, perhaps we can find the control center for the cavern and use it as a power generator instead of going to the expense of mining the Marsium121."

"Nothing I've seen supports your speculations."

"We're asking for the chance to gather more facts," Frank replied.

"How long before you can send a mining expedition?" Gretchen felt like an outsider wading into a family argument, but it had to be done. Frank was losing.

Frank answered, "We'll use the tractors that are currently exploring in the wild. It'll take two weeks minimum for them to return and undergo inspection and maintenance. We have flatbeds available, and the mining equipment will be lightweight and handheld."

"While you're prepping, let me borrow a computer, so I can slow the holo enough to understand it."

Chuck brushed a crumb from his coveralls. "Your transport to Earth leaves in five days, and we can't afford to keep paying your fee. Besides recommending ridiculous actions like refreshing everyone's credentials, Bunderbon is watching every dollar I spend. I'm boxed in. I'm sorry."

Frank's eyes grew wide.

Gretchen hadn't expected money to be a sticking point. Lately, her thoughts had been nowhere near her contract. "You're paying me until the transport leaves, so pay me to do something useful. If I can't slow the holo, or if I do and it's useless, I'll happily return to Earth."

"Let's say you slow it down. Then what?" Chuck asked.

"That depends on its contents. I'm guessing it tells us more about the city."

"And then what?" Chuck asked again.

"I... I'm not sure what you mean?"

"I assume that you want to explore the city. I'm not talking about a quick look-see, but a thorough exploration. I'm trying to get you to see everything involved to find out what that city holds."

She took a sip of wine for her suddenly dry mouth and swallowed hard. "Okay. Once we have an idea of the city's contents, I guess decisions would have to be made. I'd have to decide if it's interesting enough to stay. You'd have to decide if there's value for MarsVantage."

Frank interrupted, "Chuck, we understand the situation. This is the game-changing opportunity we've been looking for. I know it."

"No, Chuck's right, Frank. We need to get it all on the table." Gretchen looked directly into Chuck's eyes. "Then, you'll have to decide if you want me to help explore the city. If so, you'd be paying another employee, one who's not contributing to the bottom line, at least not initially. A snag on any one of these points means I'm heading back to Earth."

Frank sat stone faced, and Chuck nodded. Gretchen took another sip of wine.

Chuck folded his hands in his lap. "Gretchen, the odds are slim the city will interest both you and us."

Perhaps, but I'd like to find out for myself, not simply assume it.

Chuck continued, "Let's put that aside for the moment. After you slow the message, you said you'd see what's in the city. That seems like a leap. What do you think is in the message? You obviously suspect something."

"You're going to think I'm crazy, but you want it all on the table, so the hell with it. We're pretty far down the crazy boulevard already." Gretchen sipped her wine again and set the glass before her. "I think the message was recently created and left specifically for us. Something—I can't put my finger on it—tells me it's an invitation to the city. My guess is that someone's there waiting for us. And I think it's for more than just to say, 'Hi.'"

Both Chuck and Frank stared at her. *Well that's my guess. No one wants to say 'aliens,' so I won't. But it's aliens!*

Frank added, "Chuck, I'll bet it'll have manufacturing plants, at least enough to support whoever left the invitation. Just think what we could do with more manufacturing capability."

Gretchen could've kicked herself. Chuck needed practical capabilities, not imaginative notions of aliens. *Time to switch gears.* "If that city is anything like ours, it'll have libraries, perhaps containing the process to create Marsium121. Yeah, the stalactites and stalagmites are too uniform to be natural—they had to have been created. Imagine MarsVantage becoming an energy provider to Earth."

"*Now* that city sounds interesting." Chuck grinned. "And for the record, you're only crazy until you're proven right. After that, you're elevated to visionary."

She didn't know what to say. *Did Chuck just agree to another expedition?*

"I still have a problem," he said. "I can't pay your rate beyond the transport's departure. Bunderbon will have my head, and if I'm ousted, I doubt he'll pursue the Marsium121, let alone the city. You can't translate the message, get to the city, properly evaluate it, and return within five days—even if we had a tractor to spare."

Is the money worth more than a chance of greeting the invitation's creator, seeing the city, and revealing its secrets? Without another thought, she nodded. "You're on the hook for a month of half-pay to cover my trip to Earth. I'll investigate the city on that part of the contract."

"Are you sure?" Chuck's eyebrows raised. "It probably won't work out. You expect something like New York City or Paris. More likely, it's abandoned, filled with dirt. You'll be stuck on a transport unable to earn pay."

"Absolutely. My gut says that city is a treasure chest waiting to be opened. If you take a risk to pursue it, I'll join you with a risk of my own. Draw up an addendum to the contract, and I'll thumb off on it."

Chuck sipped his wine. He stared at the glass. A mouthful remained, and he gulped it down. He looked between Frank and Gretchen. "We've come this far. We may as well see what the city holds. We'll plan for a mining expedition, but you'll explore the city first. If it doesn't pan out, then we'll extract the Marsium121 from the cavern."

Frank smiled broadly at Gretchen.

Chuck joined in. "A couple of things. Wait until we know what we're doing about the message before filing your mission reports. When you file them, you must report the message, both of you. Gretchen, include the original recording but don't include any interpretation of its content. And lastly, Frank, assign Gretchen a workspace and make it secure—your kind of security. I don't want Konklin learning about the message until we know what it means."

Gretchen gave Chuck credit. He adapted to changing circumstances, unlike Hawthorne who made up his mind and nothing could ever change it. Of course, she and Frank dangled some serious prizes to induce Chuck, but still, he was going for it.

I hope the city pays off.

One curious question nagged at her, though. *What's Frank's kind of security?*

38 | UNWELCOME NEWS

While having a bowl of cereal in his quarters, Arnold glanced over an index of articles under the *'Mars News'* heading on his datapad. He selected one published late yesterday afternoon that was entitled, "Interplanetary Caught Interfering with Mars Expedition."

The article summarized how John Reed had committed several serious offenses—including sabotage, which amounted to attempted murder—against Frank Brentford and Gretchen Blake in the wild. They had eventually apprehended John Reed at their site, and Security had taken him into custody yesterday morning.

Interplanetary had gone after a MarsVantage team, and Jane had specifically asked about them. *That's not a coincidence.*

Upon scrolling, John Reed's mugshot appeared. It was Jacob, Arnold's original Interplanetary contact. Arnold's heart pounded, and his hands went clammy. His stomach soured as visions of Security taking him into custody flashed through his head.

Security couldn't link him and Reed together unless Reed talked. They'd never met privately, except for a couple of times, almost a decade ago, during the beginning of their association. Likewise, they'd never exchanged anything, except during those initial meetings. There was no chance Security knew about that.

And if Reed had already ratted him out, Arnold wouldn't be sitting at his table having breakfast. Security would've taken him into custody. With that thought, peace of mind returned.

Reed, and Jane for that matter, had used the information he'd provided to attack people. That wasn't part of the deal. It was one thing to destroy MarsVantage—it was entirely different to murder people.

His work shift was starting soon. Today, of all days, was the wrong day to be late. Without a doubt, Security would be vigilant for unusual comings and goings, and the best way to go unnoticed was to act normal.

Arnold rose and stopped by the bathroom. In a loud voice, so he could be heard over the shower, he said, "Hon, I'm off to work. I'll pick you up at your office for supper."

* * *

Once Arnold arrived at his desk, he checked his vidcomm for messages. Chuck had left one last night, requesting a tentative reservation for Gretchen on the next transport, which was leaving in four days.

Why not confirmed reservations? Something must've changed between Frank completing the claim yesterday morning and last night.

The second part of Chuck's message was unsurprising. He requisitioned equipment and personnel for a short-term mining operation, which would take weeks to organize. Chuck's two requests couldn't be related, considering the timing involved, but Arnold's instincts insisted that something more was going on.

After a few minutes of investigation, he confirmed his suspicions. Around the same time as Chuck's message, Frank had assigned Gretchen a small workspace in the Research, Engineering, and Maintenance building a couple of blocks away. They'd obviously found more than Marsium121, and it required a workspace.

He might be able to turn the situation to his advantage. He needed to inform Interplanetary as soon as possible to receive instructions.

Arnold pulled the window blinds' left corner halfway up. He hoped that Interplanetary would see the signal in time for lunch. If not, he'd have to back out of supper tonight, and he didn't relish listening to Claire's complaints.

When lunchtime arrived, Arnold bicycled to the restaurant court. After purchasing his meal, he searched the seating area and smiled upon spotting Jane. Like so many times before, he took the seat behind his contact, so that their backs faced. "I'm here."

As he chewed his third bite from a *faux* ham and cheese sandwich, Jane asked, "What do you have?"

"Tell me. Did you sabotage our tractor?"

"Why do you care?"

"I agreed to pass information so you could advance your business, not kill people."

"I'm sorry if it's too rough for you. Perhaps, if you gave us better information, we wouldn't have to resort to such measures."

Arnold closed his eyes. "You made me a party to attempted murder."

"Walk away then—give up on an Interplanetary job on Earth. I'm not the complaint department." She said nothing else. No apologies. No excuses.

Head downcast, he opened his eyes and stared at his meal. He took another bite of the sandwich, weighing Interplanetary's actions against his culpability and goals. He disliked his decision, but he had no other choice. Their arrangement was his only path to Earth. "Okay."

"Very good. If you're done with your soul-searching, tell me what you've got."

Arnold revealed his findings and started to relate his conclusions.

"Wait," Jane ordered.

He obeyed. A few seconds passed. A MarsVantage employee entered his field of view, walking toward the exit.

She ordered, "Continue."

"They must've found more than Marsium121."

"That's interesting. Find out what Blake's working on, and deliver it to me."

"I doubt it'll cross my desk."

"Then go after it. You're farther from Earth today than you were a week ago."

Arnold glanced around, using only his eyes. He'd had enough of Jane's attitude. *I'm risking everything, not you.* "I know Interplanetary suffered a setback, and I'm sure you're taking heat over it, but reconsider how you treat me if you want to continue this arrangement. The few luxuries you're delivering aren't worth putting up with your bitchiness. I'll signal when I have Gretchen's work. Until then, I don't want to hear from you."

His chair's legs scraped across the floor. He stood and discarded the remains of the lunch he wasn't enjoying before departing the restaurant court.

On the way to his office, he considered the best time to investigate Gretchen's workspace. He was breaking his rule about seeking information in person, but it needed to be done before MarsVantage profited on whatever they had found. That would only delay Interplanetary's takeover, which would in turn delay his permanent return home.

39 | A Path to Happiness

As the first shift began, Gretchen entered the workspace that Frank had showed her after supper last night. Upon opening the access panel by the door, she entered *7896* on the hastily-installed keypad, a special security measure courtesy of Frank. If the proper code wasn't entered within thirty seconds, she and Frank would receive an unauthorized entry alert on their datapads.

She sat at the desk holding an un-networked computer and vidcomm. Between the keypad and the computer not being connected to any other systems, her data was safe.

The room itself was a monotony of the institutional-green walls broken only by the door and a small window. It provided extra incentive—not that it was needed—to determine the message's meaning, so she would never have to work in here again.

She logged into the computer using her datapad's credentials and loaded the cavern message, which she'd transferred last night while Frank had installed the keypad. With a standard computer, complete with plentiful storage and proper software, she expected to need only a couple of hours to get results.

When she'd captured the message, she'd used the highest sampling rate possible, which left little free storage on her datapad to process it. She'd had one opportunity to record the message, so she had made the highest quality recording possible—the cavern was too far away to try again.

Gretchen sampled the recording by grabbing a frame every second. As expected, she'd missed content. She tried again by sampling every half a second, then every tenth of a second. With the last setting, she got closer, yet still the message wasn't clear. Some frames were duplicated, and some content seemed missing.

She exhaled. *So much for the easy way.* She'd hoped to avoid reviewing the message frame by frame, but she had no choice. She reviewed each frame, selecting the ones that changed, and finally after three straight hours had a version of the message that included all of the content.

It began with a series of images. Each contained a pictograph atop a small group of circles and lines—similar to those on the cavern door. They were like children's language lessons that displayed a picture and then spelled out the word underneath.

Afterward, the message displayed something akin to a surveyor's map, showing the city and three caverns. One, the cavern they'd explored, had two human-like figures, one smaller than the other, beside it. From the caverns were connections running through the Maelstrom Mountains' eastern range to a city on the plain. Next, several images showed the city's construction and growth.

The next few images showed the city's environs in decline, crops withering and trees dying. Another image showed a large spaceship departing the city surrounded by a barren plain. Finally, the last scene showed the two human-like figures at the edge of the city.

The scenes between the map and the human-like figures at the city's edge seemed to outline its history. The first and last scenes suggested that she and Frank were supposed to go to the city, but the middle scenes didn't track at all.

I can't go to Chuck with this. I need a splash... Maybe not a splash, but something more concrete.

Gretchen puzzled over the pictographs' relevance to the remainder of the message. Nowhere in the city's history scenes were there any symbols. It was as if several messages had been haphazardly spliced together.

I'm missing something.

Gretchen breathed deep, thankful she hadn't bragged to Chuck or Frank about how quickly she'd have the answer.

She rewatched the slowed message, seeing nothing new, but noticing a low, barely audible thrum. With another tool of the processing software, she enabled a graphical representation of the audio as she watched the slowed message once again. As one image transitioned to the next, the audio spiked. None of the spikes were identical nor were they evenly spaced.

She configured the computer to use the original audio, slowed to a quarter speed, while keeping it synced with the new hand-selected images video. She pushed the volume to maximum and replayed the message. The result was a rapid burst of tones similar to the cavern door's response tones, followed by a quick pause until the next scene displayed.

Now I'm getting somewhere.

Of course, the audio was part of the message. The cavern door's symbols represented tones. She'd played them to open the door, and the door's mechanism had responded with a series of tones. She shook her head at assuming the noise in the cavern had been wear from the playback mechanism. *Assumptions aren't science.*

The rumble of Gretchen's stomach prompted her to glance at the clock on her datapad. It was already past lunchtime. Her work drew her in again—she'd almost deciphered the message. She only needed a few more minutes.

Gretchen browsed through the pictograph images until she reached the one that resembled a city. With the associated sound, she searched for and found multiple instances in the rest of the message. *That's it!* The pictographs and their sounds were a vocabulary lesson to understand the message's second part. Suddenly, the message's structure became clearer. The sender had prefaced the message content with a language primer.

For most of the pictographs, she assigned a word or short phrase and then directed the computer to search the message and translate. For pictographs that she didn't understand, she instructed the computer to simply place a question mark symbol in the translation. Over the course of several runs, she translated many of the remaining pictograph symbols in the context of her previous work. Only a few untranslatable pictographs remained.

The last run displayed her best translation she'd been able to produce:

Civilization/sender's people build [many?/number?] cities [?].

Civilization/sender's people expand/enlarge cities.

[?] planet/world [proper name?] dies/dying.

Vegetation/trees dies/dying.

Food dies/dying.

Planet/world [atmosphere?] leave/depart.

[?/number?] [orbits?/cycles?] [?] civilization/sender's people leave/depart.

[?]

[Cavern dwellers?/explorers?/humans?] come to/arrive at city door/entrance.

[?] discuss [matters?/situation?/future?] [?] civilization/ sender's people.

As Gretchen read the translation, she scowled at the gaps and vagueness it still contained. It wouldn't win any writing awards, but as long as she and Frank traveled to the city, it'd accomplish its goal.

She watched the message one final time, as dispassionately as she could manage, to ensure she hadn't allowed her hopes and desires to color the facts. She hadn't. MarsVantage had stumbled into an historic discovery, perhaps the most important in human history. Gretchen's heart thumped in her chest as she copied her version of the message along with its translation to her datapad.

The door chime sounded. She pocketed her datapad and secured the computer before walking over and pressing the Speaker button. "Yes?"

"It's Frank."

After pressing the Open button, the door slid aside, revealing Frank in clean coveralls with a smile on his face. "How're you doing?"

She suspected he was referring to her jumpiness yesterday rather than offering a polite greeting. "Better, thanks. I had a good night's sleep. Trust me, I'm fine."

"Good. Do you want to grab supper?"

"Yeah. I'm starving. I missed lunch."

His smile faded. "I know you're under a time crunch, but you can't skip meals. A muddled mind never solved anything."

"You're right. I lost track of time." Gretchen sighed. "But what's one meal compared to deciphering an alien message?"

Frank's eyes grew wide. "You did it? Already?"

She nodded, trying to hold back a grin but failing.

"And?"

"Assign me permanent quarters. I'm here to stay."

Frank stepped closer, the laugh lines around his eyes becoming more prominent. "Seriously? It's that good?"

Gretchen embraced him tight, and he wrapped his arms around her. She closed her eyes. *I missed this...* "Frank, I don't have all the pieces, but I know enough."

"What's it say?"

Everything is coming together perfectly. "It's..." Choked up, she swallowed hard. "It *is* an invitation. Addressed to us."

40 | Goals Just Beyond Reach

Arnold's luck finally changed. While leaving the restaurant court, he caught sight of Gretchen and Frank sitting in a corner on the ground level. With a kiss, Arnold sent Claire home, saying he had to return to the office.

Careful not to draw attention to himself, he bicycled at a calm, steady pace to MarsVantage's headquarters. Once in his office, he deposited his datapad on the desk, and from the back of his bottom desk drawer, withdrew an unregistered one that Interplanetary had furnished shortly after he'd agreed to work for them. At the time, he'd complained that it was unnecessary because plenty of sensitive information would cross his desk. They'd insisted he keep it for a time when he'd need its resources. Tonight, Interplanetary would receive a return on their investment.

He encountered no one as he strolled to the Maintenance building. He used the datapad's lock defeater program at the main entrance. While it only took seconds to open, it seemed longer as he stared ahead, not giving the security cameras a good view of his face. He stepped inside. No one was around. He exhaled and smiled. With no cameras inside, he was home free. A minute later, at Gretchen's workspace door, he wiped his forehead with his coveralls sleeve as the lock defeater once again did its job.

Inside, after the door slid shut, he left the overhead lights off and activated a flashlight, keeping its beam at waist-level, so it wouldn't shine through the window. The room held only the basics and nothing related to archaeology. Even the trashcan was empty.

Likewise, the desk drawers were empty, which only left the computer. Arnold again used the datapad, this time activating the credentials cracking program.

Unlike the lock defeater, this program would take upwards of an hour to unlock the computer, according to John Reed's instructions. He had time to spare—Frank and Gretchen had just started their meals.

Very soon, Arnold would know Gretchen's secrets... and shortly thereafter, so would Interplanetary.

* * *

In a deserted corner of the restaurant court, Gretchen and Frank huddled close together at a table. She watched his eyes twinkle as she quietly related the message's translation.

Frank set his fork on the plate. "I can see that it's an invitation meant for us. I'm bothered that it's disjointed, though. Seems like a history lesson has been sandwiched into the invitation."

"That bothers me, too. It could be a tradition for the sender's culture, or maybe the unknown parts of the message, particularly the last line, ties it together."

"How so?"

"What if the sender wants help to make Mars livable again, so his people can return?"

"He's gonna be very disappointed. If we were capable of that, we'd have done it already."

"Perhaps he needs to be rescued."

"Huh. That'd be something."

Gretchen sighed at Frank trying to solve the mystery without all of the puzzle pieces. "I have a crazy idea. Instead of guessing, why don't we go find out?"

He reached over and patted her hand, smiling. "Fair enough. This could be a win/win for everyone. The message implies the existence of several technologies that could prove useful to MarsVantage. As the discoverer, you'll become a leader in your field with an unimpeachable reputation."

"And best of all, there's a reason for me to stay."

"There always was," Frank said softly as he tilted his head and leaned closer to her, a move that she mirrored.

Her datapad chimed. A split second later, his joined in.

Gretchen opened the screen and read the message. "Unbelievable! Someone broke into my workspace!"

She rose, tipping her chair over in the process, and raced for the exit.

"Terrific," Frank said sarcastically as he followed her.

Once they exited the restaurant court, they broke into a run, winding through the streets until arriving at the Maintenance building. With his datapad, Frank unlocked the main entrance. She followed him inside to her workspace door where the status panel indicated it was unlocked.

"The intruder is probably still inside," Frank whispered.

"No one steals my discovery."

"But—"

Gretchen activated the door and rushed inside, slapping the light control on her way in.

Arnold Janssen, sitting before the computer, turned and rose with a dumbfounded look on his face. "What the hell?"

Gretchen closed the five feet to him and pushed him away from the computer, toward the left wall. The chair rolled in the opposite direction.

Janssen shoved her aside. "What're you doing?"

To regain her balance, she grabbed his coveralls with her left hand. With her right fist, she punched him in the mouth. "You're not stealing my discovery!"

"What're you talking—"

Again, Gretchen swung, catching him square in the nose. He grabbed his face with both hands, blood oozing between his fingers.

"Crathy bitch, you broke my nothe," Janssen said, his voice muffled by his hands.

"I'll do more than that." She reached back to deliver another blow.

From behind, Frank grabbed her right hand and wrapped his left arm across her chest, pulling her aside. "He's had enough."

Janssen took a step toward Gretchen.

She steadied herself and pulled up her fists. "C'mon, thief."

Frank glared at Janssen and said sternly, "One more step and you're dealing with me. Now stay put while I vidcomm Security."

"Or don't, you thieving bastard," Gretchen hissed.

Frank retrieved the chair from the wall. "Arnold, sit and don'
move."

He did as instructed.

As Frank vidcommed Security, Gretchen positioned hersel
between Janssen and the door. She stared at him, searching fo
any excuse to take another shot.

Janssen remained silent and still, except for squeezing hi
nose to staunch the blood flow. After Frank closed the vidcomn
connection, he leaned against the desk.

No one spoke. Gretchen watched Janssen, who refused t
meet anyone's eyes. Frank alternated between watching her anc
Janssen. After a few minutes of uncomfortable silence, Securit
arrived and left with a suspected thief and traitor.

Frank gave Gretchen the chair. "You better check your work
I'll give Chuck a heads up about what happened."

To her left, he squatted before the vidcomm unit on the des
and connected to Chuck's quarters. Chuck's image appeared o
screen. "I have bad news. Gretchen and I caught Arnold Jansse
accessing the computer in her workspace. I think he's our spy
Security has him in custody now. You'll be hearing from then
shortly."

"Arnold? I can't believe he'd do that," Chuck said.

"There's more. He had to be restrained until Security arrived.'

Chuck exhaled. "How badly did you hurt him, Frank?"

Frank hesitated.

Gretchen leaned over, ensuring the camera picked her up
"Sir, Frank never laid a hand on him. I punched him in the face."

"Really?" Chuck's eyes grew wide while Frank subtly nodded
"Is there anything else?"

"Gretchen's made a lot of progress on the second task, but tha
can wait until morning," Frank said.

"Very good. I'll handle Janssen," Chuck said before closing th
connection.

Frank stood, a knee cracking in the process, and leanec
against the desk's edge.

"Janssen didn't access the computer," Gretchen said, glancin
up at Frank.

He nodded. "You really hurt him. Why?"

"I wasn't about to let him steal my discovery."

Frank crossed his arms. "You never gave him a chance to surrender."

"I ensured he didn't escape." Gretchen placed her hands in her lap, one atop the other.

Frank stared at her. "Or you dispensed revenge for nearly being murdered by his friends. You need to speak with a counselor."

"It's not like that." Gretchen shook her head and leaned back in the chair, rolling a couple of inches backwards. "It has nothing to do with the cave."

"Then what were you thinking about? You lost control." Frank gripped the desk's edge and leaned a bit closer.

"I know," she said softly. "Thank you for stopping me before I hurt him too badly."

He gave her a single nod and stared, waiting for more.

"I certainly wasn't about to allow Janssen to steal the only positive thing in my life."

"You're wrong."

"No, really. I can't get work on Earth. My ex non-renewed. My family has pushed me farther away, not that we were overly close to begin with. If Janssen stole my work, I would've lost the greatest archaeological find in history. That wasn't happening without a fight."

"He couldn't escape. I doubt he would've made it past me." Frank paused for a moment. A look of determination crossed his face. "But the city isn't the only positive in your life. You're allowing it to overshadow everything else."

"What's that mean?"

"Damn..." His voice grew soft. "I thought it was obvious."

Frank had provided an opportunity to discuss her feelings, and she'd missed it. Instead, she'd fallen into the habit of focusing on work and ignoring relationships.

Not this time.

Gretchen rose from the chair, allowing it to roll away, and sat beside him on the desk. She took his hand and inhaled deeply.

"I've pushed certain feelings aside because I was set to leave soon. Now, everything has changed..."

She leaned in and kissed him, pulling him tight. She savored the moment, pushing away her fears. After a time, while still maintaining the embrace, she slowly pulled back and opened her eyes. "I meant what I said, but—"

"There's a 'but'?"

"I don't want to start something I can't finish. Fundamentally our situation hasn't changed."

"I'm more sure than ever the city is valuable. Chuck will want us to go after it."

Gretchen broke the embrace. "I just assaulted an employee. That normally gets you fired from a job, not hired."

41 | THE WHEEL TURNS

"Let me see him," Chuck said to Alan Greene, Vice President of Security, who opened the door to a minimalistic room in the Security section. Mars didn't have a jail. There wasn't enough crime to justify one. Whenever they detained someone, the accused was held in a room much like an office except it only contained two chairs and a small table. No computers or vidcomms.

Chuck took the empty seat opposite Janssen whose coveralls were stained with blood.

"You're a lucky man, Arnold."

"How do you figure?" Janssen asked, sounding like he had a horrendous head cold. Gretchen's punch must've been hard and on target. In a couple of days, he'd look like a raccoon.

"I'd have bet a significant amount of money that Frank would've beaten our spy to within an inch of his life if he ever had the chance."

Janssen shifted in the chair, his black shirt reflecting more dried blood. "Huh. I'm lucky alright. Your consultant beat him to it."

"Better her than Frank. If he'd unleashed his anger over losing Lori in the Airlock Accident, we wouldn't be speaking right now."

Janssen grunted.

"So, why'd you do it?"

Janssen exhaled and his shoulders drooped. "To get back to Earth. Claire and I never wanted to live here. We came for the experience, intending to transfer back to Earth after a couple of years."

"But MarsVantage was spun off from Peter Konklin Interplanetary after the Airlock Accident," Chuck said, finishing Janssen's thought. "Why didn't you quit?"

"You remember what it was like back then. Experience with Interplanetary on Mars was anything but a career enhancer."

Chuck looked squarely into the eyes of a broken man sitting across the table. *There's nothing I can do about the past, but I can stop the spying in its tracks now.* "Here's the deal, Arnold. You're fired. That's non-negotiable. However, I'm willing to discuss charges. I have enough evidence to have you prosecuted for industrial espionage, conspiracy, and accessory to attempted murder."

"What do you want?"

"You'll overlook Gretchen... *restraining* you."

Arnold's eyes grew wide. "You're joking. That wasn't restraint. She has to answer for assault."

Chuck placed his hands on the table. "Perhaps you should hear my entire offer first. You'll make your usual arrangements with your Interplanetary contact, so we can catch them in the act. You'll overlook Gretchen *restraining* you. You and Claire'll leave Mars, and I'll only press the industrial espionage charge. You probably won't see any jail time. And if you do, it would be a minimal security facility without murderers and rapists."

"Is that all?"

Chuck nodded.

"No deal," Janssen said flatly.

"I'm sorry to hear that. I'll press conspiracy and accessory to attempted murder charges, too. The good news is that you'll probably never see the courtroom."

"What do you mean?"

Chuck leaned forward and stared into Janssen's eyes. "You have three people who are capable, both in will and resources, to see that you meet with an unfortunate accident. Your Interplanetary friends always say that Mars is a dangerous place. We can prove their assertion true."

"You wouldn't."

"Wouldn't I? For years, you undermined my company, and your friends tried to kill my employees, my friends. How about Frank? You partnered with the people who're responsible for his wife's death. As far as Gretchen is concerned, I think her actions speak volumes. Look into my eyes. Really look. Are you willing to bet I'm bluffing?"

Janssen sat silently and stared at Chuck's expressionless face. "Okay, Chuck, I agree."

Chuck smiled and rose. "Good. I'll have the doctor come by to fix you up. Then, you're going to explain in detail how your interactions with Interplanetary work—signals, code phrases, everything. And tomorrow, we'll catch your handler in the act."

* * *

Chuck watched Janssen carry a tray of food to an empty table in the middle of the restaurant court and sit. Seated behind him was a woman who must be Janssen's Interplanetary contact, known to him as Jane. Intent on arriving before they got down to business, Chuck veered around tables and chairs until he reached Janssen's table.

"Hi, Arnold. I'm glad I ran into you. This'll save me a vidcomm."

Janssen, his eyes showing the beginning signs of bruising, looked up with an expressionless face. "What do you need, Chuck?"

He sat opposite Janssen and watched Jane's back intently. She seemed oblivious to what was happening behind her, but she must be paying close attention. She probably considered it a stroke of incredible luck to get information straight from MarsVantage's CEO's mouth. "I don't want to wait three weeks for the tractors to return and undergo maintenance."

"I understand, but the regs are the regs. If I schedule them out and they break down, getting their crews killed, it's my neck on the line."

"You're right, of course. The loss of life would be horrible, and the PR problem back on Earth would haunt us for years. Frank suggested using tractors on routine duty around Mars City. They're within regs."

"That adheres to the letter of the regs, but bends the spirit badly."

Chuck feigned a long gulp from the cup he'd brought with him. It held a microphone that was transmitting the conversation to Frank and Gretchen hiding in a nearby equipment closet. He placed the cup on the table between him and Janssen and stood. "I'm okay with a little reg bending. This is too big to let the spirit of the regs get in the way. Let's do it."

"Very well. I'll get on it as soon as I finish lunch."

Chuck strolled from the restaurant court and, less than a minute later, unlocked a door labeled '*Authorized Personnel Only*' with his datapad. After a dozen steps, he addressed three people from Security waiting outside an equipment closet. "It'll be any moment now. I'll let you know."

Chuck entered, closing the door behind him. Frank and Gretchen stood among racks of equipment with blinking status lights. The receiver sat in an empty space on one of the rack's shelves.

"Frank, getting upset isn't helping," Gretchen said as she fidgeted with her datapad in her coveralls.

"They were meeting right under my nose, and I missed it. Multiple times."

"Hey, I looked at the same data, and I didn't notice anything unusual. It isn't like you're looking at close-ups of their faces."

"Sssh. Jane's talking," Chuck said.

"*What's happening?*" Jane asked, her voice distant but clear enough.

"*This is all based on the draft of their mission reports. Gretchen found a huge data storage vault. She copied a small portion and has been translating it. Based on Chuck's eagerness, I'd say she succeeded.*"

"*What's so valuable?*"

"*As best as I can figure, they believe the data vault holds information related to advanced technologies.*"

Jane asked, "*What sort of technologies?*"

"*Energy generation, at least. Chuck's betting that there's much more.*"

"I've heard enough." Chuck opened the door and ordered Security to take 'Jane' and Janssen into custody. Chuck turned his attention back to Gretchen and Frank. "Good work, both of you."

"I wish I recognized this was how they were passing information when viewing the Security footage," Frank said, shaking his head. "I could've stopped this whole mess weeks ago."

"Don't worry about it. Interplanetary put a lot of effort into how they went about spying on us. No one was supposed to recognize what was going on. That's the point."

Frank smiled, but Gretchen grimaced.

"Is everything okay?" Chuck asked her.

She pursed her lips and exhaled. "I apologize for my actions last night. They were inappropriate."

"Officially, I must say you were wrong, and Janssen has every right to press charges. If he did, there would be nothing I could do. You'd have to return to Earth to stand trial. However, part of our deal is that he won't."

Gretchen open her mouth, but didn't speak. After a long second, she said, "Thank you, Chuck. I appreciate you looking out for me. You didn't have to do that."

"This time, it's a freebie. Just don't do it again." Chuck smiled. "Unofficially, he deserved it. You saved Frank or me the effort. And neither of you heard me say that."

"I didn't hear anything," Frank said.

Gretchen finally smiled.

"Please forward the recording as soon as you can," Chuck said.

"Not a problem. I also have a list of suspected moles based on how Janssen interacted with Interplanetary. One person in particular is a problem, and I'm working on a plan to deal with it. I'll fill you in when I finalize everything," Frank said, displaying an easy smile, one Chuck hadn't seen in months.

He headed toward the office, considering his next move. On the way, Security sent a message identifying 'Jane' as Heather Newton. It was time to put Peter Konklin on the defensive.

When Chuck arrived, he got comfortable in his desk chair and placed a vidcomm to Konklin. After his assistant made Chuck wait for two minutes, the Interplanetary CEO finally appeared on-screen. "Are you calling to tell me you have reconsidered my offer?"

Chuck laughed. "I thought I'd deliver the latest news."

"There's nothing you can tell me that I don't already know."

"I went to all the trouble, Peter. How about I do it anyway? We identified your spy inside my company. His name is Arnold Janssen. We also recorded your handler receiving information from him. Arnold called her Jane, but we know her real name is Heather Newton."

"I don't know who you're talking about."

"Of course not. You better find out, though, because they're both in custody, and I'm filing a complaint with the Trade Commission. I'm also looking to see if we have enough evidence to tie her to Reed and the attempted murders."

Konklin looked like he ate bad fish, his bravado and confidence abandoning him. Chuck smiled before breaking the connection. He reclined. For once, he'd enjoyed a conversation with Earth.

42 | Teamwork

Gretchen settled in on Frank's couch. She'd been in his quarters several times before, but this was the first time she paid attention to them. The small touches, mostly 3D picts, made it homey. He'd placed them on the walls, shelves, and his desk. Each showed him with others at various locales around Mars City. They appeared to be group pictures recording significant achievements over the years.

"I'll be there in a sec. The coffee's almost ready," Frank announced from the kitchen.

"Take your time. It's nice to relax for a couple of minutes." Like Frank, she was rushing to prepare to get to the city before her contract ran out.

What a difference a few weeks made. When she'd first set foot on Mars, she'd looked forward to solving the symbol puzzle and returning to Earth as quickly as possible. Now, she was rushing about, so she could stay permanently.

She imagined a time when she'd sit here beside Frank, the lights low, the wine chilled, and soft music playing... and she smiled.

Frank joined her on the couch, placing two full mugs on the coffee table beside his open datapad. While they cooled, he summarized the logistics of the upcoming expedition. It would consist of five tractors, each with two crewmembers. Each tractor would pull a flatbed trailer. Three of the flatbeds would hold components for a mobile habitat while the remainder would hold handheld mining equipment. They'd caravan to Waypoint 1, the cave, and finally to the city.

"I wish we'd had a mobile habitat when we were at the cave. I would've appreciated showering," Gretchen said.

Frank smiled. "It takes two tractors to transport the minimum configuration, and I wasn't sharing our secret with more people. Besides, it wasn't that bad, was it?"

"No, but some comforts can go a long way in the field." She reflected his smile back.

"We'll have cots, showers, and a galley this time. The food will still be FieldMeals, though."

She shrugged her shoulders. "I appreciate you sharing the prep work even though I'm still only a consultant."

"A technicality. We have one shot at this, so we have to get it right. For instance, I'm assigning the best tractor drivers and equipment operators I have on staff. We're gonna have to dig out the meeting place at the city's edge where the message indicated."

She nodded. "Excellent thinking."

"There's one more thing. I'm assigning Sam, too."

She took a tentative sip of coffee. It was hot but not enough to burn her mouth. While tasty, it had been locally grown—the slight aftertaste was the giveaway. "I trust you know the right people for the job."

"That's just it..." Frank leaned forward and stared at his datapad. "The SDA indicated Sam had interactions with Interplanetary like Janssen."

Sam is a spy? She sat straighter and faced him. "Are you nuts? The last place he should be is on this expedition then. Dealing with whatever's out there is gonna be difficult enough. There's no protocol for what we're about to do... just common sense. We don't need a weasel with a hidden agenda popping his head up at the wrong time."

Frank swallowed a sip of coffee. "Gretch, understand, I'm shocked, too. I analyzed it three times. Sam's my friend and right-hand man. And he's been operating under my nose for *years*. If we don't draw him out now, he'll undermine us for years to come. If this city is as big as we suspect, he'll help Interplanetary make bigger plays. We'll never get what we should from it."

Frank's right. If they don't expose Sam now, when would they? How much would he steal? Gretchen rubbed her eyes. "Do you think he sabotaged the air vests?"

"I knew you'd bring that up. I struggle to believe that he'd do it, but I can't deny the possibility either. If he did, I don't actually think he wanted to hurt anyone. Remember, he came to me to report the problem. I think he was counting on me to officially report it, so we'd get bad PR on Earth. Regardless, you can't go punching him. You have to promise me."

And that's how you get a reputation. Gretchen forced a smile. "You know I usually don't go around punching people."

"I know, but there's a good chance Sam is following in Janssen's footsteps, and we can't have the same outcome. We got lucky that Chuck cut a deal. Janssen almost didn't go for it." For a few moments, there was nothing but silence. "Will you help me keep an eye on Sam?"

"Isn't there another way?"

"If there is, I can't think of it. I know it's a risk, but it's the best shot we have. I can't do it alone. I need your help."

"It won't do us much good to get the city, and then have him undermining us at every turn. So what's your plan?"

"I don't have one," Frank said as he rubbed the back of his neck.

"Wait, you always have a plan." Gretchen smiled.

"Ever since you arrived, my plans have tended to go sideways." He matched her smile. "Seriously though, we don't know what we're going to find out there. I know how to set everything up, but we're going to have to play it by ear. We can catch him in the act if we work together."

"Why don't you just send Sam back to Earth?"

Frank sighed. "You mean fire him? He's excellent at his job. I don't have cause without solid proof of industrial espionage. And reassigning him still leaves a spy in our midst, even if he isn't working directly with us."

"I'll keep an eye on him," Gretchen said softly. "I won't be obvious about it. I don't want to scare him off."

"Thanks. I'll brief Chuck first thing tomorrow morning."

She reached over and took his hand in hers. "Thank you for discussing it with me beforehand and not waiting until he revealed himself. That means a lot."

"I promised you I'd earn your trust. Together, we'll meet this situation head on."

"Still, there are so many ways this can go wrong, I can't even count them."

Frank took her hand in his. "I know."

"After our initial meeting in Chuck's office, I promised myself that I'd avoid all of your side issues and concentrate on deciphering the symbols. Now look what I'm doing."

"Yes, look at you now." Frank's eyes sparkled. "You're making huge strides to build your future—one that'll eclipse Hawthorne."

"Forget Hawthorne. I have bigger aspirations in mind."

* * *

Five days later, Gretchen again wore a green spacesuit and sat to Frank's right in a tractor as they approached the cave. MarsVantage's tractor, abandoned just over a week ago, remained firmly in place, but Interplanetary's had already disappeared, probably an attempt to limit the incriminating evidence.

The caravan of tractors passed the disabled one and parked side-by-side twenty yards beyond the cave. The eight crewmembers joined Frank and Gretchen in front of their tractor. Two maintenance engineers, who were Jackson's passengers at the tail of the caravan, lugged toolpacs and parts toward the disabled tractor.

"Everyone, your attention please. You already know there is Marsium121 up there." Frank pointed toward the airlock that filled the cave's mouth. "What you don't know is that we'll only mine it as a last resort."

Crewmembers looked among themselves. Sam asked, "Then why the mobile habitat and mining equipment?"

"Now that Interplanetary's spy has been apprehended, I can tell you the rest of the story. We found definitive evidence that there was once a city beyond those mountains." Frank pointed toward the mountain range across the valley of rust-colored sand and rocks.

Jackson said, "Shit, Frank. You should've said. We left the alien traps back at Mars City."

Everyone laughed, even Frank.

"Okay, okay. Keep a lid on the alien talk," Frank said. "Like I was getting ready to say, I believe the Marsium121 powered that city, and a control center for this power station is buried over there. So, we're going to expose the power transfer conduit here where it's near ground level and determine if we can tap into it. If so, we're going over there to find and activate the control center."

"Incredible, Frank," Sam said. "We'll just need to lay power cable back to Mars City, and we'll have free power."

"Exactly. Now, grab your shovels—no picks—and meet here in five minutes."

The crewmembers scurried to their flatbed trailers. Gretchen met Frank at their trailer and handed him the sounding equipment as she winked. He smiled before returning to the rally spot.

"Okay, people. Follow me." Frank led the crews to the power conduit, which according to the surveyor's map in the invitation, was one hundred yards beyond their position. Along the way, he issued detailed instructions on how he wished to proceed. He was keeping the crewmembers' minds occupied with immediate concerns, so they wouldn't notice her absence. All according to plan.

Gretchen leaned against her tractor's rear, out of sight from Frank and the crewmembers. Their flatbed carrying mobile habitat components hid her from the maintenance engineers repairing their original tractor. Twenty minutes passed until they signaled Frank that the tractor passed its diagnostic. *Good. Reed didn't do more than destroy the power converters and attach the demex.*

Frank authorized the crew to return to Mars City. They drove off, trailing a red-brown dust cloud.

Gretchen smiled. Frank had had qualms about her next actions but had reluctantly capitulated after she'd pointed out it would be the safest way to implement their plan. *Safe for the plan—a bit risky for me, operating alone in the wild.*

She quickly retrieved the suitcase-sized holo generator from the tractor and hustled to the cave. At the airlock, she manually cranked the door open. While it was strenuous work, it was better than hiding and lugging around a bulky battery.

Sweat beaded on her forehead as the vertically-sectioned outer door slowly slid back into the airlock's wall. Inside the airlock, she repeated the action to close the outer door, which left her out of breath in utter darkness.

She activated her exterior helmet light via her wrist control panel. She cranked the handle to slide the interior door aside to gain entry to the cave.

In her helmet's lights, the symbols waited and welcomed her like an old friend. She strode to the door and played the tone sequence on her datapad. In response, the door descended and the reply tone sequence played. She took a step inside the cavern and glanced around. Her light shown on and around the blue-black Marsium121 stalactites and stalagmites.

She walked the winding path until reaching the alien holo projector. It activated, showing her the same images that she'd slowed and later deciphered.

Beside it, she laid her own holo projector and activated a message she'd created after capturing Janssen. At a comfortable speed, not at the pace of the sender's invitation, the holo displayed the English words as her voice spoke them: *"Thank you for the invitation to your city. We shall arrive soon. We wish to share knowledge in friendship."*

Next, it played the pictograms she'd interpreted with the English equivalent written underneath as her voice pronounced the word. Afterward, it played children's language lessons that displayed a picture, the written word, and its pronunciation. Her message would loop until the holo projector's battery died, a week from now. Hopefully, the sender could learn enough English to communicate because her efforts to learn the sender's language had been a failure.

She withdrew from the cavern, through the cave, to the airlock, once again manually cranking the airlock doors open and closed. She marched across the sand to the tractor crews, who'd already removed six feet of sand near where the power conduit connected to the cavern.

Gretchen caught Frank's eye and nodded. He subtly returned it.

Shortly afterward, two crewmembers exposed the black conduit. They exited using a flexiladder. All eyes were on Frank as he climbed down and manipulated the controls of the sounding gear. After a few minutes, he joined everyone at ground level.

"The conduit is about ten feet in diameter. We could easily walk through it."

Sam asked, "What's it made of? Can we cut through it?"

"Our shovels nicked it. The sounding doesn't indicate any surprises. Yes, we can cut into it."

"Excellent," Sam said. "All we have to do is determine how the power regulation controls work."

"Indeed," Frank agreed. "Phase one is complete. We camp here tonight and head to the city at dawn."

Everyone walked back to their tractors, happily chattering away. Frank and Gretchen, trailing behind the others, remained silent while carefully observing Sam.

Once inside the tractor, Frank repressurized it. They removed their helmets, both smiling.

"The invitation is still in the cavern."

"Good."

"I set up our message and left it playing."

"I expect the sender monitors the cave and the cavern. It's the only way that invitation could've been left for us. Whoever it is should notice your visit and the holo playing. Hopefully, we can communicate without too much trouble."

Gretchen nodded. "Language translation programs work well on Earth languages because their grammar rules and vocabulary are well defined. I only had a fraction of what I needed from the sender's language to plug into a language translation program. If we have to use it, we'll get mostly static, at least to start with."

Frank took her hand in his. "Don't worry. We'll make it work."

She smiled. "Did anyone notice my absence?"

"Nope. I kept them busy."

"Good. It'll be easier to catch Sam red-handed if his guard is down."

43 | WORKING TOWARD REVELATION

A gain, an alert roused the Caretaker from hibernation. He downloaded into a mobile unit, rolled to a control console, and discovered that the egress door to Power Generation Three had been opened again. He activated the power generator's monitors and switched to the infrared spectrum, finding a lone figure approaching the holo generator.

He analyzed the figure's height, proportions, and movements and compared them to his prior records. He calculated with ninety-five percent certainty that the figure was the smaller one from earlier—the one who was called Gretchen.

His holo activated as she approached. She ignored it and placed a device beside his, activating it once his holo had concluded.

The Caretaker zoomed in and raised the audio sensitivity.

Perhaps he hadn't missed his opportunity after all.

* * *

At dawn, Gretchen rubbed the sleep from her eyes while Frank led the caravan of tractors. As they traversed the valley and cut through a pass in the eastern range of the Maelstrom Mountains, she tossed a foil packet of motion sickness meds back in the storage compartment—she didn't need them. The ride was far smoother than leaving Main Street at Waypoint 1. Once through, they headed northerly, arriving late afternoon in the vicinity of a large cylindrical landmark near the meeting spot.

While the other crewmembers assembled the mobile habitat, Gretchen and Frank methodically took soundings based on her calculations from the invitation's map. For an hour, she couldn't locate the tower or match anything from the soundings to the city map.

Without determining their location, they would never find the invitation's meeting location. They could be miles away from where she thought. The map itself might not have been to scale. The landmarks she'd used in her calculations might've shifted since the city's construction. Or something she hadn't taken into account could've led them in the wrong direction. If so, they might never find the city.

With the sun sinking, Gretchen finally caught a break and pinpointed their position. "Bingo. There's the tower that's not far from the city's edge."

She closed her eyes for a moment, breathed in and out. When she opened them, Frank smiled at her.

"We can find the meeting location now." Frank looked across the rusty plain. "It'll be east, past camp."

Gretchen also glanced around, amazed that the sand under her feet was hiding a vast city, and no one had ever suspected. "Let's see if we can get it mapped before dark."

"Sounds good. Just out of curiosity, how close was your map in comparison to the city's actual location?"

"About two thousand yards."

"Considering how much interpretation you had to do, I'll call it a bull's-eye. Great job, Gretch."

"Thanks, but the invitation's sender gets most of the credit. I'm just happy my math was right."

After they returned to their tractor, they raced the setting sun to the city's northern edge, near the designated meeting spot. They walked in opposite directions, performing soundings.

Ten minutes later, Gretchen announced that she had readings. Frank joined her as the sun flirted with the peaks of the Maelstrom Mountains. They took more readings and planted fluorescent green markers to guide tomorrow's excavation. Afterward, they hurried to the tractor.

As he climbed aboard, Frank said, "We won't make camp on time."

"It'll be close," Gretchen said, closing the door.

"We're breaking regs by driving in unfamiliar territory at night. That'll be a fine." Frank started the tractor and repressurized it.

She considered the situation for a moment. "Is it really unfamiliar if we just drove over it half an hour ago?"

"How literal of you."

They both laughed.

On the control panel, the atmosphere status light changed from red to green. They removed their helmets, and Frank donned an earset.

They drove back to camp, riding over their earlier tracks, reducing speed and activating the lights when twilight engulfed them. After twenty minutes, he pulled next to the other MarsVantage tractors, facing the mobile habitat.

From his tractor, Sam transmitted, "Nice of you to join us. Just in time, give or take. The mobile habitat is assembled. The batteries haven't charged enough to last through the night, so we'll be in the tractors again. We also need to perform the safety checks. The good news is, tomorrow we'll have supper together and sleep in cots."

"Good work, everyone. We start again at dawn. Tomorrow's going to be a long day, especially for the plow crews. Get a good night's sleep."

Frank removed the earset. "Tomorrow, we'll have full use of the mobile habitat. They only have the safety tests to perform. Two crews will do that while the other two help us plow out the meeting place."

"I can't wait. I don't know if I can sleep."

Frank slid between the front seats and entered the tractor's cargo area. He inflated two air mattresses and arranged them between the seats and the cargo containers. "Come on back and get comfortable while I get a couple of FieldMeals."

She unrolled two sleeping bags, putting one on each mattress. She settled in next to the cargo containers as Frank handed her a hot meal.

"So the anticipation is getting to you?" Frank asked.

"A little."

"Perhaps you should concentrate on something else," he said with a mischievous grin.

She suspected he meant something more intimate, but now wasn't the time. In a carefree, playful tone, she said, "A good idea. So tell me, what're you hiding?"

He exhaled. "Again? Didn't we settle this in the cave?"

"Yes, again. The more I think about it, the more I can't believe that a maintenance engineer knows so much about so many subjects."

"Like what?"

"Let's see. Organizing an archaeological expedition. Hacking into security systems. Remembering obscure historical quotes."

"You're twisting the facts a little," Frank interjected.

"Receiving unpublished archaeological articles from *friends* on Earth." She made air-quotes when she said 'friends.' "And your explanation concerning your music knowledge is iffy. I suspect there's more I haven't noticed, but all in all, it's an impressive skill set."

He inclined his head ever so slightly and smiled. "Thank you."

"And an uncanny ability to change the subject."

"C'mon, I know many people who're good at that. You aren't so bad yourself—take right now, for instance." For a moment, he looked at her as if performing a series of calculations. "Is it really that unusual? On Mars, we need to wear many hats out of necessity."

Gretchen chewed and swallowed a bite of meatloaf. Even though it wasn't real beef, it still tasted good. "I'd believe you, except..."

"Except what?"

"The way you look at everything."

He raised an eyebrow.

"Yes, like that. You watch, evaluate, and categorize. Everything. From the simplest situation to the most unusual. It's like you expect knowledge to be lurking everywhere."

"Don't you?" he said as he chewed his supper. "So many people stumble through life oblivious to what's happening around them. There's a wealth of knowledge ready for the taking by just paying attention. That's how I acquired many of those skills you question."

"I can't disagree. It's just unusual."

He exhaled and set his FieldMeal aside, turning his entire body to face her. "You pay attention, too. I'm keeping something to myself. It has nothing to do with this project or MarsVantage for that matter. And before you ask, I won't tell you. Not yet. Perhaps in a couple days."

Her mouth opened. She hadn't been prepared for such a blunt admission. "What's so special about a couple days from now?"

"We'll know a whole lot more about what's happening beneath our feet, but most importantly, I'll know what's happening by my side."

* * *

Morning arrived, and Frank pushed sand with a plow blade attached to his tractor. The other two tractors sported excavator arms and buckets. Frank led the way by plowing aside a long stretch of sand adjacent to the green flags marking the city's edge. The two excavators dug deeper into Mars, transferring buckets of sand away from the city's edge, and Frank pushed it out of the way. Gretchen, supervising on foot, choreographed their movements.

Around mid-morning, Gretchen took a moment to evaluate their progress. The excavation was going quicker than she had expected. Frank had chosen his people well, even Sam, who was skilled at operating the excavator's arm and bucket. It was a shame he had divided loyalties.

They spent the rest of the day digging deeper into Mars. When Gretchen stopped the operation, they'd dug a crater, roughly shaped like half of a bowl, over twenty yards deep and about two hundred yards wide.

In the crater, she stood admiring the day's effort. Only a couple yards of Mars' sand now stood between her and the city.

The two other tractors remained at ground level while Frank drove his to the bottom and joined her. "Impressive dirt. If you would've let us dig a little closer, we could've been looking at architecture that predated human civilization."

"Or we could've been looking at newly-created ruins that originally predated human civilization."

He winked. "Just checking. Your professionalism has controlled your enthusiasm."

She took the sounding equipment he'd proffered and approached the dirt-encrusted wall.

"Gretch, we have fifteen minutes before we have to go."

"It'll be enough."

They probed the freshly exposed dirt with the sounding equipment. Every so often, she referred to the map on her datapad. After ten minutes, she announced, "This is it."

Frank placed fluorescent green markers as she directed to indicate where the final excavation would be performed by hand, slowly and carefully.

"Frank, Sam here. We need to return to the campsite pronto. We're losing daylight."

"Mounting up now," Frank said. "We'll be at ground level in two minutes."

Gretchen reviewed the marker placement one last time. Everything was in order. She returned to the tractor, satisfied with their day's efforts.

Frank drove up the incline and led the other tractors to the campsite. As they parked facing the flatbed trailers supporting the mobile habitat, the last rays of the sun sneaked behind the distant mountain peaks.

* * *

At dawn, Frank and Gretchen drove to the dig, yesterday's tractor tracks showing the way. Gretchen tapped her right foot, looking forward to finally getting inside. "Don't the others think it's odd that we're investigating the city alone?"

"Several routine tasks need to be done. I also told them that our exploration needs to conform to archaeological standards, so we can methodically find the power generator's control center. We can't have ten people blindly blundering about, getting in one another's way. Besides, they need to get some rest—they'll be busy again soon enough."

Frank and Gretchen arrived at the crater and traversed the slope to arrive at the bottom. Gretchen blinked several times, not believing her eyes. "That isn't how we left the site. Look, the entryway has been exposed."

44 | THESAURUS CITY

The freshly dug crater swam with the shadows of sunrise. Gretchen dismounted the tractor and met Frank at its front, each carrying an extra air vest. She examined the ground and pointed to fresh tread marks, much thinner than those produced by their tractors. "This sand has been plowed away... and by the looks of the tracks, it originated from within."

She glanced around, searching for more clues as to what had happened overnight. More than ever, she was sure someone was waiting for them. *Inside, somewhere.* She didn't know how or why, but she was sure.

"It's your dig." Frank smiled broadly. "Welcome to Thesaurus City."

"Thesaurus? What do synonyms have to do with anything?"

"It also means repository or treasury. We both believe that's what we're about to enter."

"It's an apt name, I suppose. I'm adding 'knowing obscure word meanings' to your list of uncanny skills."

Frank chuckled.

After a few steps, she crossed the threshold, expecting to enter a building. Instead, she stood in an open space, much like a wide city street. She examined the walls. At her feet, a long, flat bar ran the width of the hallway. "This is a larger version of the cave door, though it looks to be made of some type of clear material."

"It's probably the alien version of plastiglass," Frank replied. He deposited his extra air vest near the entrance while she placed hers atop it. Although they had enough air for a full day's exploration, the spares provided peace of mind. It was another example of the just-in-case mentality the Marsees held.

From his thigh pocket, Frank withdrew a locater beacon, a six-inch-long cylinder with three extendable legs. He deployed it next to the spare air vests.

With his help, she configured her datapad for it. Now, if they got lost, they could always home in on the beacon. If events worked out, she'd place dozens of them across the city to create an accurate, real-time positioning system for their datapads. She'd used such a network exploring a complex tunnel system in the Unified Islamic Republic from the time when that region had been known as Pakistan. It'd worked well. She'd never been lost for long.

After a dozen steps, the light from the entryway faded, leaving them facing complete darkness, except where their exterior helmet lights and flashlights revealed. Rectangular and cylindrical structures of various sizes bordered the street, each having closed doorways level with the ground and what appeared to be windows scattered across their faces. A few structures abutted while others resided on alleyways or streets.

Gretchen shuddered at the sand suspended overhead, and feared an imminent avalanche. She shook off the sensation. The city was enclosed in a transparent dome. If it hadn't collapsed already, it was unlikely to give way now.

She calculated her needs to process the city. It'd have to be explored in phases like all large sites, but first, they'd have to excavate the dome. With plenty of natural sunlight, she'd only need artificial lighting for inside the buildings.

With Frank at her side, Gretchen approached a huge structure that occupied a standard city block, as best as she could make out. She followed its face upward, shining her helmet light and flashlight to the top. In the murky shadows, the building nearly touched the dome. Back at ground level, a dim, blue glow spilled through an open doorway. Not only was it the only open doorway she'd seen so far, it was the only sign of power usage.

"I think we should go in," Frank said.

What if this is all for nothing? What if no one's here?

"Gretch, you okay?"

Please, let it be... everything it should. She steeled herself, taking a deep breath and exhaling loudly enough for the helmet's microphone to broadcast. She looked at him and forced a smile. "Let's do it."

They cautiously entered.

Before her stood row upon row of chest-high, opaque units, which reminded her of library datacard shelves. However, these units contained a myriad of faint, pulsating blue lights with blue-white sparks intermittently jumping among them. Above, a series of lights illuminated a portion of the room, perhaps fifty yards square.

The power for the room had to originate from somewhere other than the power generation cavern they'd explored. Perhaps it was from one of the other two or a reserve generator located elsewhere.

Frank asked, "What do you think—" He never finished the statement because a rumble from behind interrupted him.

She hadn't heard it, but rather, felt it through her feet. She turned in time to see the entryway disappear as the door slid into the top of the door frame. She rushed over to examine it closer, noting it was free of symbols or nearby controls.

On her datapad, she accessed the command that'd activated the cavern door. She played it three times, each time the door stubbornly remained in place. "Looks like we're locked in."

"Gretchen, I need you here," Frank said evenly. "The door can wait."

She studied her datapad and the door. "Hold on a sec. I'm trying something here."

"No, really. I need you over here. *Now!*" He'd stressed the last word like he'd grunted it through clenched teeth.

Irritated at being interrupted, she walked toward where Frank had been standing, but he wasn't there anymore. He was two rows over. She came to a cross-aisle, turned left, and joined him.

Then she noticed it... standing ten yards away... partially hidden in shadow. It was seven feet tall and dark gray, almost black. Its head—twice the size of a person's—held four round structures, presumably visual and auditory sensors. The inner two glowed amber while the outer two were black voids.

The head rested directly on a larger sphere of a body containing four arms, two to a side. Each arm ended with a hand, which was comprised of four fingers. As best she could tell, they were of equal length. Instead of fingers arranged like a human hand, two fingers opposed the other two. Lastly, two thick legs, ending in treads for locomotion, supported the body.

She inhaled as Frank stepped backward, bumping into her as the thing before them gathered its arms to its chest.

"I get it. The door can wait," Gretchen mumbled. Her spacesuit started to tug around her knees and elbows. "I think we have an atmosphere."

"I feel it, too. I'll check. Let me know if... whatever that is... gets any closer." Frank manipulated the control pad on his wrist. He glanced up once as he waited for analysis to complete. "The air is breathable."

The machine before them said in English, "Please remove your helmets." Its message hadn't been transmitted through her suit's comm system, but rather through the atmosphere.

She looked over to Frank, reached up, and twisted her helmet off. He followed a second later.

"This will make it easier to communicate," it said. "I am pleased that you came to help."

"I'm sorry," Gretchen said. "Help?"

"You received my message. You are here to help," it said.

"Yes and no. I translated your recording as best I could, but I didn't fully understand it."

"That is unfortunate. I hurried to create my message. It was before I understood your language and your slow pace of communication. But you arrived, so I believed you had overcome those issues."

"We still may be able to help, if you explain the problem," Frank said.

"Follow me. I will show you." The machine turned and rolled farther along the row. It stopped beside a break in the row, but instead of a cross-aisle, it appeared to be a control station. A moment later, the machine, using the lower set of hands, manipulated the controls.

A hologram appeared—it was the surveyor's map from its original message. The machine narrated. "The Bvindu built thirty cities across this planet, *Opilus*, once we rejuvenated it."

The images of the city's growth and expansion appeared. "We thrived in the cities until the planet failed again, leaving the vegetation and food to die. *Opilus'* atmosphere dissipated."

The scene with the spaceship departing displayed. "After 200,127 orbits living here, I became the caretaker for our accumulated knowledge and treasures. The Bvindu left to search for a new home but failed to return. Explorers—you two—come to the city entrance to discuss ways to help me rejoin my Bvindu brethren."

The holo disappeared.

"How long have you been waiting?" Gretchen asked.

The machine's arms dropped to its sides. "For 122,136 orbits."

"When did you lose contact with your people?" Frank asked.

"I hibernate inside this control center unless there is a matter that requires my attention. Then, I transfer to a mobile unit like the one before you."

"When will your brethren return?" she asked.

"They expected to be gone for one thousand orbits while they established a new homeworld. Something must have happened."

That last statement had been tinged with sadness. Even though it was a machine speaking, a consciousness dwelt within. Gretchen no longer thought of the alien as an 'it'. She caught Frank's eye, not voicing her suspicion that the Bvindu were long dead. "Why didn't your people go to Earth, the third planet from this star?"

"We found conditions for intelligence favorable, but our sad experience demonstrated that two intelligent species competing for limited resources could only end in tragedy. We nearly caused an extinction on the prior planet we inhabited."

"How do you think we can help you?" Frank asked.

"Before I answer, allow me to ask. Why did you enter the power generation cavern?"

Again, Gretchen and Frank exchanged glances.

"Outside of it—we found fragments of the same crystals that are within," Frank said. "We discovered they can generate power. We intended to mine these crystals and put them to use."

"But when we realized it was part of something bigger," Gretchen added, "we halted our plans and came here." She was pleased with Frank's honesty, though she felt it best to underscore that their plans had changed when the circumstances had changed. They needed to start on the right foot with the city's caretaker.

"Perhaps we can reach a mutually beneficial arrangement. As the city's caretaker, I can restart the power generation caverns in exchange for your help repairing my manufacturing capabilities."

"Why do you need the repairs?" Frank asked.

"To construct a ship to search for my people."

45 | THE VAULT OF THE AGES

After Frank and Gretchen reattached their helmets, the city's caretaker lowered the control center's door. Outside, Gretchen climbed aboard a flatbed vehicle that was waiting, glanced around, and found no seats. She followed Frank's lead and sat in the cargo area.

The Caretaker rolled on and took the controls, and the vehicle lurched forward. She caught and braced herself with her gloved hands. As he guided them through the city, ashen flashes of abandoned buildings streaked by in their helmets' lights.

They were racing toward a dim, gray area, which brightened as they grew closer. When they stopped, they were surrounded by ruins illuminated by light panels embedded in the dome's overhead support beams.

"This is what is left of the Manufacturing Section." The Caretaker guided them through the ruins, outlining each building's purpose and damage.

Frank made copious notes on his datapad and asked thoughtful questions along the way. He'd explained to the Caretaker that he couldn't agree to help unless he knew that his team could perform the work.

As they toured the area, they came upon a severely damaged building that looked as if a bomb had hit it. Gretchen followed Frank onto the rubble and found the cause: An older model tractor stood on end, half-buried and noticeably twisted.

Frank turned to the Caretaker, who hadn't followed, and asked, "How did this tractor get here?"

"Two of them fell through the dome and caused all of the damage you see. There were thirty of your kind inside. The city's monitoring systems revived me. I came here, and all were gone.

Most did not survive the fall. I am sorry that the internal security system neutralized several who did."

Frank asked in an even tone, "Where are... the remains?"

"On the other side of the dome," the Caretaker said, his top left arm pointing to the dome above, which had obviously been crudely repaired.

Frank turned toward Gretchen.

At last, they knew what happened to the Baulnsville explorers. She looked up from her datapad. "I made a notation on the map, so we can recover them."

"Thanks," he said softly as he patted her shoulder.

* * *

With the survey of the damage concluded, the Caretaker returned Frank and Gretchen to the control center. Frank removed his helmet, set it atop one of the glowing blue units, and started estimating the scope of repairs needed to the Manufacturing Section.

Meanwhile, a couple of rows away, so as not to disturb Frank, Gretchen recorded a conversation with the Caretaker on her datapad. She hung on every word as he chronicled Bvindu history, relating so much information she'd have to listen to it a dozen times to fully comprehend everything.

But she already understood a great deal. The Bvindu could travel interstellar distances in relatively short times. Mars was the third planet they'd inhabited since escaping their homeworld's dying star. Each of their relocations weren't measured in months or years, but rather centuries. And Mars was the second planet they'd molded to suit themselves.

The Bvindu were long-lived. Though the Caretaker hadn't explicitly said so, she gathered they were practically immortal. The medical and ethical implications were both auspicious and ominous.

And the knowledge to perform all of these feats and more resided here. "Can I access your information systems?" Gretchen asked.

"Why do you want this? You said you came for energy."

"We did, we do," she quickly said. "The energy is our primary goal. I find your civilization fascinating. I'm interested in how you lived, what you created, and what you believe."

"I understand." The Caretaker spread his arms wide. "What you see in this room are the control circuits for the entire city, our Vault of the Ages. I can access every city function from here. The levels above hold our information systems, which are also accessible from here."

She adored the Bvindu name—the Vault of the Ages. It captured the true grandeur of the city and its contents. She'd carry it forward rather than using Frank's suggestion of Thesaurus City.

The Caretaker interrupted her thoughts. "Could I get a spaceship? I can modify it with my technology much quicker than constructing a new one. I am eager to start my search."

"Maybe there's something we can arrange."

Frank chose that moment to join them. "Arrange what?"

Gretchen repeated the Caretaker's request.

"A ship is a big thing to ask for."

"In addition to restarting the power generator caverns for repairing my manufacturing capability, I will give you full access to the city in return for this. I only request that you do not remove anything. We will eventually return for our cultural heirlooms."

Frank contemplated the request for only a second. "And we can use your Manufacturing Section?"

"Yes, that and everything else."

"I believe I can secure a spaceship." Frank glanced at his datapad. "And I can repair the Manufacturing Section with guidance from you. It'll take a full crew several weeks."

"Very good, on one condition. Once the repairs are completed and I have the ship, you must delay your occupation of the city until I depart. I do not want to be distracted by outsiders."

"Agreed," Frank said. "I'll have to clear it with my superiors, but I doubt it'll be a problem."

They worked through the details regarding the repairs and accessing the city's controls. It took hours, but Gretchen loved every minute of it. She and Frank were laying the groundwork for their future. She had taken this job, in part, to rebuild her reputation, so she could get work on Earth. Yet, with this unprecedented discovery, her reputation would be solidified beyond her wildest dreams, and it didn't matter anymore. Earth held nothing for her now.

The Caretaker suddenly announced, "I am detecting a nearby transmission on a frequency you have not been using. I will play it."

After an audible click, the transmission played from the Caretaker. "...*explore the city while everyone's asleep and report back. Whatever they say they found, don't believe them. They're most certainly lying,*" a woman's voice said.

"*Understood,*" Sam replied. "*No one will ever know I was gone.*"

Frank and Gretchen looked to each other.

"The woman sounds like she's on Earth. The highs and lows of the transmission tend to get clipped when relayed into the wild." Frank stared at the Caretaker. His eyes expressed a sadness that words fully couldn't. "I didn't want to believe the SDA's results, but it's true. Sam has been betraying us to Interplanetary."

"I can handle this intruder," the Caretaker offered.

"No, thanks. We'll take care of it ourselves," Frank said with authority.

Simultaneously, Gretchen said, "Uh..." The Caretaker's offer would be a simple solution to a messy problem, and it'd send a strong message to Interplanetary. If they took the hint, she'd be able to devote less time to thwarting their machinations and more to her work.

"Gretchen, we'll handle it, right?" Frank stared at her, his eyes accusing her of the unthinkable. He had to have guessed what she'd been thinking.

She couldn't believe that she'd considered the Caretaker's offer for even a second. No matter how inconvenient Interplanetary's interference was, death wasn't a suitable punishment. "Uh, yes, of course. We'll handle it."

"As you desire," the Caretaker said. "I must inform you that if this intruder approaches a sensitive area, I must take action."

"We understand," Frank said. "We need to leave now to deal with this."

Gretchen reattached her helmet while Frank did the same. The Caretaker lowered the door, and they exited the control center.

As the glow from the open doorway faded, Frank asked in a concerned tone, "Why'd you hesitate when answering the Caretaker?"

"I wouldn't say I hesitated..." she answered, her voice trailing off.

He stopped and faced her. "Gretch, *you* don't even sound like you believe that."

She looked into his eyes for a handful of heartbeats and then turned away. "I'm so ashamed. Days ago, I was upset thinking you would kill Reed, and now I'm calmly contemplating a stranger killing Sam. How can you look at me?"

Frank wrapped his arms around her. "Don't beat yourself up. What matters is that you arrived at the right answer."

"It's not like I got caught with illegal chocolate bars. I nearly sanctioned murder. You know that's what he was suggesting, right?"

"I know, but everyone gets tempted at one time or another. Decent people like you rarely give in to it."

If he hadn't been there, what would her answer have been? She'd never been tempted like that before, not even by Reed. She pulled away and looked into his eyes. "Have you ever been tempted?"

Frank clasped his hands before him and looked down. "After I lost Lori to the Airlock Accident, I wanted revenge on Interplanetary's management. Before I did anything foolish, I realized that physically harming them wouldn't change anything."

"I have to be honest with you. If you weren't here, I may've agreed."

"I doubt it. It's not you." Frank looked into her eyes. "You didn't back down over Reed, challenging both me and Erin. Even if you agreed initially, I bet you would've had second thoughts before you reached the tractor."

"Maybe you're right." *The thing is, I just don't know.*

"I'm sure of it, and I'll share something else with you. I never gave up on punishing Interplanetary. I just funneled my efforts more productively. The way to hurt Konklin is through his bank account. My motivation to harness the Marsium121 was, in part, to hurt Konklin. Our application of the city's knowledge will hurt him worse. We'll do it straight-up. Unlike him, we won't buy politicians to have the government do it for us. And we won't turn good people into spies, either."

"C'mon, let's go resolve this Sam situation." She smiled, took his gloved hand, and guided him to the entranceway. Once there, they found that the sun had already set.

"There's another fine, and I'm willing to pay more."

46 | SELLING THE LIE

Frank followed Gretchen through the mobile habitat's airlock, their green spacesuits filthy with red and brown stains they'd carefully applied at the city' edge. With a stern expression carved in her face, she removed her helmet, saying to no one in particular, "I need a shower."

After he removed his spacesuit, Frank entered the galley, grabbed a FieldMeal, and took a seat at a table in the corner.

Sam slid on the bench next to him. "You're back well past sunset, so whatever you found better be worth the fine for breaking regs."

Frank shook his head and swallowed a bite of food, not tasting it. "We found nothing."

"Nothing? C'mon, we all know there's a city there."

"Yeah, it's empty. Long-abandoned. We didn't find the control room or see anything useful—not even a datapad."

"You spent all day poking around and came up empty?"

"Not if you count almost being buried alive."

"How'd that happen?" Sam asked, eyes wide.

"Gretchen opened a two-story double-door and half of Mars crashed down on us. There must've been a hole in the dome somewhere."

"I'm glad the Earther's not my tractor-mate. I warned you to have her practice more in a spacesuit before heading into the wild. She almost got you killed."

Frank hated to hear that sort of talk about Gretchen, but he didn't challenge it. It played into the plan. He swallowed a sip of water. "Almost."

"So what's next?"

"There's pure academic value out there, I suppose. I'm sure archaeologists will go gaga, but there's nothing practical. As far as

I'm concerned, Earth can pay to dig it out themselves. We're not in the charity business. I'll call Chuck first thing tomorrow for instructions. I expect we'll pack up and head to the cavern to mine the Marsium121."

Gretchen entered the galley, hair damp, but dressed in the filthy spacesuit. She stood before the table. "Frank, I'm going to bed down in the tractor. I don't feel like being around people tonight."

"You can't go out alone. It's against regs."

"I don't give a damn about your regs." She turned and left.

"She's not taking it well," Sam said, watching her walk to the airlock.

"She's disappointed. She had lofty expectations, and what we found didn't measure up." Frank wrapped the remainder of his turkey sandwich in a napkin. "I have to go. I can't let her stay out there by herself. No sense breaking more regs."

"Okay, just holler if you need anything."

"Not a problem. And tell the guys to lay off the booze. There's nothing to celebrate tonight. Plus, we'll be busy again tomorrow."

After one last bite, he pocketed the sandwich and left the galley before climbing back into his spacesuit.

* * *

Hidden from the mobile habitat, Gretchen leaned against the tractor's rear hatch and demonstrated a measure of patience she never knew she had. The fatigue of a busy and monumental day helped.

Frank came around the tractor. He pointed to his wrist control pad. She nodded, indicating that she'd reduced her suit's transmission power.

He watched the mobile habitat as he said, "Nicely done. You should consider joining our theater group."

"I was never much for drama, but since coming to Mars, I've gotten a lot of practice."

"Sam bought your performance, no question. While you were showering, I filled in the details. By now, I'm sure everyone knows."

"Good."

"Is everything set?"

"The air mattresses and sleeping bags are arranged in the tractor. I stuffed them with supplies to make them look occupied. And I grabbed two pairs of night vision goggles like you wanted."

As he attached a set of goggles to his helmet, Frank asked, "You look tired. Have you eaten?"

"I had what was euphemistically labeled as a turkey sandwich and supplemented it with a vitamin pack while I set up the sleeping bags. I'll catch my second wind in a minute."

"Why don't you stay here? I can handle this myself."

"Forget it. I won't have you doing this without me just because I'm feeling a little tired."

Frank smiled. "If you ever doubt you belong here, remember this conversation. You're a true Marsee."

Gretchen attached the goggles to her helmet and switched them on. "They don't help that much."

"You'll get used to looking through them in a few minutes. We'll take it slow. I figure the trip will take forty to fifty minutes."

He guided her beyond the leftmost track impression at the campsite.

"Wouldn't it be safer to walk in the tracks?" Gretchen asked.

"Safer? Yes. Smarter, no."

She stopped and put her hands on her hips.

A couple of steps later, he stopped, looked over his shoulder, and finally turned. "All I mean is that Sam isn't going to take a tractor for the same reason we aren't—it would be missed. He'll surely walk in the tracks, for safety, and we don't want him to see our footprints."

47 | REVELATIONS

Gretchen sat beside Frank, back against a building's wall, watching the city's entrance. Their dim interior helmet lights provided a small sense of presence in an otherwise pitch-black nothingness.

She checked her air level and battery life, satisfied she had plenty left of both. She looked at the time on her wrist control pad. Fifteen minutes had passed since they'd arrived. "I guess it'll be a while until Sam gets here."

Frank grunted. "He won't waste a lot of time. Once everyone's asleep, he has to walk here, explore, and get back before anyone wakes. He'll be here soon enough."

"I just want to get this over with."

"Me, too. You've only had a month of Interplanetary's shenanigans. I've been dealing with it for years." Frank paused for a few heartbeats. "Anyway, while we're waiting, I have a couple of items to run by you, so I can submit my proposal to Chuck for the city as soon as we return."

"Go ahead. We have the time."

"I'll transfer from Maintenance to oversee the practical application of the city's technology."

"So, we'll be working together?"

"Yes."

Gretchen closed her eyes. Everything was falling into place. "I can't tell you how happy that makes me."

"So you want to stay on Mars?"

"Of course." Gretchen asked as gently as possible, "Have I given you any reason to doubt it?"

"No, no. I just wanted to be certain."

Instead of sounding happy, Frank sounded worried. "What's wrong, Frank? Is it because I punched Arnold? Be straight. Don't sugarcoat it."

"No, it's not that at all. Part of the reason you want to stay is because of our relationship, right?"

"Of course." She turned to face him. Fear gripped her stomach, twisting it until nausea set in. She readied herself for the news that he wasn't interested in a romantic relationship. "I know where you're heading, so quit stalling and just say it."

"Trust me, you have no idea. I need to reveal what I've been keeping to myself, so you can make an informed decision about the job... about us." Frank set his jaw. "I promised to be straight with you—no hidden agendas, and I'm keeping that promise. All I ask is that you don't repeat what I'm about to say to anyone, ever."

She anticipated his next words, holding her breath. "I won't say a word."

"I'm a Knowledge Keeper."

Seconds passed. The words echoed in her mind, and she couldn't believe a sane, rational man had just spoken them. "You have a strange sense of humor, Frank, and I'm not laughing."

"I'm glad to hear our PR is working so well." He grinned.

She ignored the thought circling in the back of her mind whispering that she might be wrong. "Do you hear yourself?"

"You had suspicions. Some of them, like my music knowledge, were unfounded. But others..."

"Like in the cave when you referred to my unpublished paper."

"A Knowledge Keeper on the journal's staff forwarded it."

There was something about him that caused her to reconsider. Perhaps it was his focus and calm. As crazy as it seemed, she was certain he believed every word he was saying. "You're seriously telling me a secret organization is collecting and sharing knowledge? I don't know what to say."

"Here's the thing. In the beginning, I hid things, and it caused difficulties between us. I don't want anything associated with my Knowledge Keeper activities to come between us."

"I don't think—"

"No, really. A secret like this can become an ever-growing wall, and I choose not to allow that to happen."

"Isn't it risky telling me?"

"I trust you. You need... no, you deserve to know the truth, so your decision to stay on Mars is based on a complete understanding of the situation."

For a few moments, she contemplated Frank's revelation. It didn't change anything about the job or how she felt about him. "In all the times I've heard tales of Knowledge Keepers, I never once heard why they collect and share knowledge. For what purpose?"

"The Order believes that our society is near ruin. Most people have lost the will to create their own futures. Instead of climbing a mountain of laws, regulations, and compliance reporting, they follow the easy path the government has prepared with their needs provided for. It's the recipe for stagnation, decline, and ruin."

"I've heard it all before. Every three or four generations, someone declares we're on the decline."

"That doesn't mean they're wrong. Decline isn't immediately fatal." Frank flashed a quick smile. "We believe the fundamental problem to embrace difficult choices has been undermined because the reward isn't worth the effort."

"Ridiculous. I make choices every day."

"Let me give you a real-life example. Although Marsees aren't subject to Earth's food regulations, your grocery order is verified against your nutritional allowance before it's ordered and delivered. Long ago, you could walk or drive to one of several grocery stores and buy whatever you liked in whatever quantity you wished."

"The system works well. I never had any problems."

"Isn't it a problem that you can't buy entire types of food? Bureaucrats consider foods from potato chips to sushi unhealthy and declare them illegal. If you want them, you must go to the black market. Some make the effort, but most meekly accept the easy path by ordering government-approved groceries."

Gretchen opened her mouth to offer a counter-argument, but exhaled. "Milk chocolate. I buy it on the black market."

"Huh. I'm not surprised. I've yet to see you take the easy path."

Gretchen's cheeks warmed, and she shook her head. "You've failed to prove your point."

"Did I?" Frank grinned. "Tell me about the three-bedroom house you own."

She snorted. "Your information is way off. Check with your Order again. The Housing Ministry assigned me an apartment."

His grin turned into a full smile. "Oh, I know. The question is, why? You've worked steadily and must've made good money. In days past, you could've owned a beautiful house. But these days, you don't because there are so many regulations, inspections, fees, and taxes that ordinary people don't wade through the process. They've neither the time nor the money. Those complications are by design. The easy choice is to live where the Housing Ministry decides based upon its understanding of your needs."

"It works well. It's better than people living on the streets."

"Centuries ago, people bought houses. As they advanced in their careers, they upgraded to bigger and better houses. Those people saw a reward for choosing hard work. However, when the government solved the homeless problem, it did so in a way that erased a reward for hard work as well as giving themselves more power over people."

"Money doesn't hold that much value anymore."

He nodded. "When our society was at its peak, people weren't driven by the idea of having money, as much as how money could get them closer to their goals, whether through acquiring things or investing in their future."

Gretchen contemplated for a moment. "So as the rewards disappeared, the people's motivations to earn more money disappeared?"

"It didn't happen all at once, but slowly, over the course of centuries."

"There are still people who succeed and excel."

"And there always will be. Like you, they love their work, but they are the exceptions, and there aren't enough of them to make a difference."

Most of her archaeology friends jumped from dig to dig, almost as if it were something to do to pass the time. And they were the brightest and most capable. Others did little or nothing at all, living off government programs.

Hawthorne came to mind. His contributions had dwindled once he'd attained eminence in the field. Instead of creating a new pinnacle, he stagnated, only ensuring that he maintained his position.

It was as if dozens of random puzzle pieces she'd barely noticed, had neatly arranged themselves into a well-formed picture. She now understood why she'd bristled under Hawthorne's thumb. She desired to excel, to learn what there was to learn, to be the best archaeologist she could be. Hawthorne had no interest in any of that. He'd merely wanted to maintain the status quo where he was part of the elite.

Quietly, Gretchen asked, "How'll you change things? No one thinks about the types of choices you're discussing."

Frank bowed his head for a moment. "That saddens me more than I can say. The Order constantly searches for a different path, but the prevailing opinion is that we've passed the point of no return. In time, the government will fall because the people producing something substantial will conclude their compensation isn't worth their effort, and they'll quit and live on government-promised benefits."

"But will anyone notice? Many people already spend their lives intoxicated."

"Eventually. Perhaps when they're hungry and there's no food because no one's growing it, processing it, or shipping it. Perhaps when they're cold and there's no heat because no one's operating the power plants."

"Those functions need to be performed."

"They do. When ordinary people stop working, widespread chaos, death, and destruction will engulf everyone as they seek food, water, and heat, and none are available. Mars will be insulated from it, but we'll feel it to a degree. The Knowledge Keepers will step in to guide society along a new path where individuals earn their way through life by reaping the rewards of their efforts. Make no mistake, it'll be difficult, time-consuming, and messy. Many will die."

"That sounds awfully bleak."

He took her gloved hand in his and looked into her eyes. "I'm involved because I want our society to not only survive, but to

THE MUSIC OF MARS

lourish once again. If you can accept my involvement, we have a future. If not, we should keep our relationship to professional matters only... if you decide to stay at all."

For a moment, Gretchen couldn't believe Frank's choices. His passion for the Order's mission masked the inner conflict he certainly felt. True to his word, he wasn't keeping secrets.

"Nothing I heard has changed my mind." She looked him in the eyes, worry filling them. "I want to stay."

"I can't tell you how happy I am to hear that." He smiled. This time, his eyes relaxed.

"You realize there's a new variable in the mix."

"A new variable?"

"With the information this city holds, we can attract the best people from Earth from a variety of fields with an opportunity to learn and develop Bvindu technology, and create a different future on Mars."

Frank shot her a questioning look.

"You just admitted Earth still holds good people. You called them the exceptions." Gretchen smiled. "We need to bring them aboard to shape a different future from the one your Order imagines. At the very least, we have to try."

* * *

For several long seconds, Frank peered into Gretchen's eyes. He'd been reasonably sure she would understand his Knowledge Keeper activities based on her attitude and work ethic. Otherwise, he would never have allowed himself to grow close to her.

But he hadn't expected her to suggest using the city's knowledge to forge a different future. She hadn't merely accepted or rejected his explanations. *Gretchen is considering the problem and attempting to solve it!*

She was one in a million. She possessed intelligence, a work ethic, and drive. Best of all, she would fly under the radar because she doesn't look like the crazed lunatic that the Order proffered to the public.

The Order could use her, and he could train her.

"Gretchen, I have a proposition."

She looked at him coyly.

"Not *that* kind of proposition. And whatever you decide changes nothing about working on the city or furthering our relationship."

Her eyebrows rose.

"I'd like you to consider becoming an Initiate. Think of it as an apprenticeship in the Order. After several years of guidance and training, you'll become a full Knowledge Keeper like me. If you don't want to live in the future we foresee, I can't think of a better place to affect change than with us."

After only a heartbeat, Gretchen answered. "It's the more difficult choice, but it's not a hard decision. I have to take an opportunity to prevent the future you foresee."

Gretchen leaned in, rested her helmet against his, and embraced him.

Never had Frank envisioned taking on an Initiate, but their discussion had highlighted that she had the potential to be an exceptional Knowledge Keeper. In a sense, the circle was complete. His deceased wife, Lori, had taken him on as an Initiate, and now he was taking on Gretchen—his future co-worker and lover. At that moment, he wished to hold Gretchen close, feel her warm, soft skin against his, but such things had to wait.

Sam was on his way.

48 | HUNTER OR PREY?

For the next hour, near the city entrance, Gretchen contemplated the time commitment the Knowledge Keepers might entail. Discussing misgivings so soon after accepting the offer would send the wrong message, though, so she'd see how everything unfolded and deal with the actual situation, rather than her fears.

"Here we go," Frank whispered. "Showtime."

As a light on the ground inched closer to the entrance, Frank skittered to the opposite side of the street, standing arrow-straight behind a structural outcropping. She likewise hid, hoping that Sam wouldn't spot them.

They turned off their interior helmet lights nearly simultaneously. She switched to the expedition's primary radio frequency and increased power to standard, knowing Frank was doing the same. With his hand, Frank covered and uncovered the green status light on his air vest three times. She copied his act. Afterward, she kept it covered like him. *Here we go.*

Based on the light, the new spy, Sam, was scanning right and left as he slowly entered the city. She felt exposed, afraid he'd spot her. She remained as still as possible, trying to not even breathe. Finally, he walked past.

Once Sam was ten yards beyond them, the green light of Frank's air vest became visible. He stepped away from the wall, and she joined him in the middle of the street. Frank turned on both of his helmet lights, and a moment later, Gretchen did the same.

"Sam, stop," Frank ordered. "We know what you're doing."

"Dammit! How..." Sam turned, and his shoulders slumped.

With a zip tie in hand, Frank walked toward the spy. Sam pocketed his flashlight and suddenly sprinted toward Gretchen.

For only an instant, she froze, processing the image of a spacesuited man charging her. She shifted to one side, attempting to avoid Sam's rush. But he managed to seize her left forearm with both hands, then jerked her to the ground.

Gretchen grunted on impact. The deep gray street filled her faceplate. She rolled over and sat up, Sam's helmet light darting along the ground, heading out of the city.

Frank exclaimed, "What the hell!" A split-second later, he knelt beside Gretchen and inspected her spacesuit, starting with her helmet. "Do you have integrity?"

She checked her wrist control. "Dammit, no. It has to be my right knee."

"I see white leak indicator bubbling out. The tear's about four or five inches long," he said, tension hanging on each word. He applied pressure to the rip with his gloved hand. "Get a medium patch."

Her rapid breathing and the sound of her heartbeat filled her ears. In that instant, Gretchen's mind flashed back to Trip's instructions aboard the transport to Mars, *"A spacesuit tear is dangerous, but panic is deadly."*

She purposely inhaled and exhaled. *Focus on the task at hand.*

Gretchen pulled out the patches from her thigh pocket, selected the proper size, and grasped the access tabs with her gloved hands. She pulled the protective film from the patch's adhesive back, after which Frank removed his hands, and she applied it. The blue of the patch clashed with the green spacesuit, which was probably the point. It alerted everyone that the suit wasn't one hundred percent.

"I'll finish it. Run a full integrity test." Frank smoothed the patch, pressing it hard against her leg. Its sealant foam hardened at the edges.

"I have integrity now. Air level's good, too." She exhaled and looked to Frank. Beads of sweat gathered on his forehead and worry etched across his face.

"You hit the ground hard. I want to inspect your entire spacesuit. Keep a lookout for Sam. Use your flashlight."

She swept the beam across the ground, right and left, working
t toward the entrance. Her attacker was no longer around.
Probably making a beeline for the mobile habitat.

"Give me a large patch," Frank said. "Your spacesuit isn't torn,
out the fabric's damaged. The patch'll protect it."

She handed one over. After a few seconds, she felt him
pushing on her right shoulder.

"Stand up, and I'll finish."

Gretchen stood and rolled her right arm to work out a little
stiffness. In a few days, she'd have a couple of bruises, but it
could've been a lot worse.

"You look good," Frank said, his voice filled with relief.

"Okay. Let's get back to camp and take Sam into custody." She
took a step toward the entrance.

"I'm gonna have someone come get us."

She turned. "Won't that confirm we broke the regs?"

"Yep. When we came to catch Sam, I knew we'd break regs and
have to admit to it."

"Wait, my suit's okay, and I feel fine. We can walk back. It's
not a problem, really."

Frank frowned. "Gretch, Sam has to kill us. Otherwise, as soon
as we contact camp, we'll expose him."

"Why didn't he do it right away?"

"He was outmanned, and he knows in a head-to-head fight I'll
kick his ass into the middle of next week. I'm sure he's planning
on ambushing us on our way back to camp. With surprise on his
side, he would take me out, and then kill you."

"Damn." A torn spacesuit wasn't the worst thing that could
happen. "I never suspected Sam capable of murder."

"At this point, I don't know what he's capable of. He's bright,
though, and I'm sure he's worked out his predicament by now. We
need to get outside and radio camp." Frank led the way out of the
city and up the sandy incline toward ground level. He swept his
flashlight in slow, wide arcs.

Gretchen did the same. Sam could be a couple hundred yards
away. Or he could be lurking nearby.

At the top, Frank said, "Bump up your suit transmitter to normal. Also, keep a lookout. If you think you see anything... I mean *anything*, speak up."

"Will do." After adjusting her transmitter on the control panel, Gretchen swept her light around. It found tractor tracks and numerous sets of footprints, most of which were hers from supervising the excavation. For roughly one hundred yards from the excavation site, the landscape was flat. Beyond that were dunes that Frank had created yesterday. If Sam hadn't already headed back to camp, he most likely was hiding among them.

A shrill tone sounded from her helmet speaker. "That's annoying."

"Press the blinking Cancel button. I'm signaling camp. That tone is sounding over the mobile habitat's speakers."

A few seconds passed. "Uh, this is Jackson, east of the Maelstrom Mountains. State your emergency and location."

"Jackie, it's Frank."

"C'mon," Jackie said through a yawn. "You're twenty feet away. Just come inside."

"Jackie, wake up and focus. Gretchen and I are at the city."

"Shit, Frank. You can't travel over unfamiliar terrain at night." There was a pause. "And by *foot*, no less? Bunderbon's gonna have all our asses for lunch, not to mention the Safety Commission."

"Don't worry about it," Frank said. "We're gonna break more regs before the sun rises. Wake everyone up. I want all hands on deck."

"Wait one," Jackie said.

Gretchen imagined Jackson waking up the crewmembers as well as their subsequent complaints. They weren't going to get happier anytime soon.

"Okay, we're here, except for Sam. We can't find him. By the way, you're on speaker," Jackie said.

"Good," Frank replied. "Before we returned to camp earlier this evening, we heard Interplanetary order Sam to explore the city in the middle of the night."

"How'd you do that? You were underground."

"I know this will be a surprise. Before coming into the wild, I suspected Sam of spying for Interplanetary. Everything I said earlier this evening was a lie for his benefit. I'm sorry, but we had to expose the traitor in our midst. Ultimately, we found everything I expected and more. While doing so, we overheard Sam's orders."

"Damn, Frank," Jackie said above several people muttering.

"Once we get back to Mars City, I'll explain everything. Know this—our mission was more successful than you can imagine. The point is, we caught him trespassing. He attacked Gretchen, badly ripped her suit, and ran off."

"Is she okay?" Jackie asked.

"Yes, we patched it. But Sam's current whereabouts is unknown. If he shows up there, allow him in and bind his hands and feet, regardless of what he says. That's an order, my authority."

"Will do," Jackie said.

"Jackie, Reyes, come get us in a tractor. Use full lights and take your time, safety first. If you see Sam, pick him up, if he wishes, and bind him. Everyone else, we're pulling out at dawn and making a speed run to Mars City. We'll leave the habitat in place, but yank the power converters. I don't want it usable once we leave. Jenkins, radio Control with a status report right now. Then, check the habitat's comm system for unauthorized hardware and software. If you don't find anything, check the comm in Sam's tractor. He's rigged something up to communicate with Earth, and I want it as evidence."

"Got it. We'll see you in fifteen," Jackie said.

Frank paused for a few seconds. "Sam, I know you heard everything. The only escape would've been to kill Gretchen and me before we contacted the crew. You certainly aren't taking all of us out now. You have two choices—surrender and face the consequences, or die here alone. You have until we pull out at dawn to decide."

Frank touched Gretchen's arm and pointed to his control pad. He dialed down his suit's transmitter power. She did the same.

"Do you have any problems with this?" he asked, looking in her eyes.

Sam had purposely attacked, intent on damaging her suit—to kill her—but revenge wasn't of interest, only justice. At that moment, she was, once again, thankful that Frank had snapped her back to her senses when the Caretaker had offered to handle Sam. "I don't like leaving him, but it's too dangerous to go on a hunt. It's his choice. I hope he makes the right one."

"So do I," Frank said somberly. He reset the transmission power to full.

After she did the same, they continued searching the landscape. She didn't expect to find Sam, only ensure that he didn't sneak up on them.

Every so often, she looked toward base to see the tractor's lights growing brighter. She hadn't spotted any sign of Sam when it stopped ten feet away.

"We're ready for you to enter through the rear hatch," Jackie said.

A voice called out, "Don't leave, I'm here. I want to go back with you." Sam activated his helmet light and emerged from behind a dune closest to the tractor's path.

Frank met him and secured his hands with a zip tie from his spacesuit. Gretchen opened the rear hatch, and Frank assisted the traitor into the tractor's cargo area. He pulled down a jump seat on the passenger side and buckled Sam into it. Afterward, he bound Sam's feet together with another zip tie. Meanwhile, Gretchen climbed aboard and closed the rear hatch.

"Frank, I'm sorry," Sam said.

"I don't want to hear it. If you want to apologize to anyone, apologize to Gretchen."

"But—"

"I mean it. I don't want to hear your excuses and rationalizations. You and your Interplanetary friends'll do anything—murder included—to keep us down, instead of building a new presence on Mars and competing with us. You disgust me." Frank stared into Sam's eyes for moments that seemed to stretch on. "You nearly killed Gretchen, and you'll return to Earth to answer for that as well as your industrial espionage. I have a recording of a conversation between you and Interplanetary. You trespassed in the city after I explicitly told you it was useless. And I have evidence of several meetings between you and a known Interplanetary spy handler."

As Frank spoke, Sam's expression faded into a blank stare.

Frank shook his head and exhaled. "My only regret is that you'll probably get a slap on the wrist. Count yourself lucky I'm not on the jury."

49 | HARD WORK'S REWARD

In her quarters in Mars City, Gretchen sat on the edge of the bed, strumming a retro-folk song from the late 21st century. She attempted to divert her thoughts from Frank's meeting with Chuck to discuss their Bvindu proposal. She was failing.

Earlier, Frank had assured her their plan was a done deal, but two hours in, she hadn't heard anything. That was a bad sign—Chuck must not have liked something. *But what?*

"Damn." She mis-fingered a series of quick chord changes, creating a noise too ugly to call music. That spot had often tripped her up, and with her attention divided, it'd done so again. She backed up a couple of measures, focused her attention on the music, and tried again. This time, she did better.

The door chime rang.

She placed her guitar in its case and pressed the intercom's Answer button. "It's about time, Frank—"

"Gretchen, it's Chuck."

"Oh. Sorry. Please come in." That sealed it—there definitely was a problem. She pushed the Unlock button and met him in the living area where they sat around the coffee table. "What can I do for you?"

"I came from the Exploration and Mineral Rights Office where I just purchased full rights to the Vault of the Ages and its power generation caverns. It was expensive, but it'll be worth it if Frank is only half right."

Gretchen breathed a sigh of relief, her shoulders relaxing.

"His proposal was convincing. Did you help him with the archaeology portion?"

"Only to flesh out the details."

"I see." Chuck nodded. "It's hard to tell with Frank. Sometimes he surprises me with odd bits of knowledge he has at his fingertips."

Gretchen smiled. *Yes, he certainly does surprise.*

"I want to hire you as our Director of Archaeology. You'll report to me as will the Director for Bvindu Practical Applications."

"That sounds wonderful." Chuck apparently had accepted the proposal, but he'd failed to mention one important aspect. "Is Frank taking the practical applications job?"

"Does it make a difference?"

It mattered, to both of them. But on a strictly professional basis, it shouldn't. "When we first met, I made an issue out of honesty, so I won't lie to you now. It matters a great deal to me. Frank and I work well together. If I were to take the position, I want to work with him. He's perfect for the job."

"Even after your rocky start?"

"Yeah, even after. We've been through a lot, and I trust him."

Chuck nodded. "Thank you for your honesty. You should know I asked Frank to convey the job offer to you, but he said he had a conflict of interest."

"Believe me, I won't allow our personal relationship to interfere with the job. I want to work with him because he's good, not because we're dating." Gretchen leaned back in the chair. Frank should've mentioned how he'd planned to address the situation, so she could handle this discussion with a touch of grace. "This is a bit awkward... Are you comfortable hiring me given the circumstances? You can get a more experienced archaeologist to oversee the project, and one who isn't involved with an employee."

Chuck leaned back in the chair, taking his time before speaking. "Don't you want to explore the city?"

"Of course. It's the discovery of a lifetime."

"Then you're the right person for the job." Chuck smiled. "You have the proper attitude and drive. During our interview, you wouldn't let me gloss over details I preferred not to discuss, even though you were desperate for work. As for a more experienced archaeologist, the number of years doing something doesn't make a person an expert... or a good fit. For instance, I'd never hire Dr Hawthorne. He's too much of an Earther, and what he did to you is a crime. Or it should be."

She didn't feel reassured. He'd completely avoided the relationship issue.

"Strictly speaking, Frank was correct to decline on conveying the job offer. I have no qualms regarding the two of you." Chuck leaned forward. "If being involved with a co-worker were a disqualification, Mars City'd be a ghost town."

Chuck winked.

Gretchen laughed. "Where do I put my thumb?"

Chuck handed her his datapad, and she thumbed off on the job offer. She handed it back, and he added his thumbprint.

I did it! She exhaled. It was done. With that thumb press, she embarked on a future full of amazing and extraordinary possibilities.

He rose. "I'll transmit a copy shortly. Welcome aboard."

"Thanks." They shook hands, and she walked him to the door.

Chuck stopped before opening it. "You know, perhaps I shouldn't say anything, but when we first met in my office, it was the first time in months I saw Frank smile."

"Really?"

"Since breaking up with Erin... Oh, damn, you know about Erin, right?"

Gretchen nodded, holding back from laughing at his discomfort.

"Good. Everyone knows. Anyway, he performed his duties, but his heart wasn't in it. Since you arrived, he's brought a new energy to everything he touches. He probably doesn't realize the difference, but I see it."

"I would've never guessed. He's been creative and energetic since I've known him. I can't imagine him any other way."

Chuck nodded. "You're a good influence. I'm sure he's expecting your vidcomm. Go out and celebrate. We start again tomorrow at 6:00 A.M. in Frank's quarters. There's one last battle to win."

"What's going on?"

"You and Frank did the hard part by securing the Marsium121 and city. We now must stop Bunderbon's power play, so we can ensure MarsVantage benefits from the discovery."

"When do we get to stop fighting for what we've already earned?"

"Honestly, never. Someone will always challenge us. It's been that way since MarsVantage split from Interplanetary. It's not worth getting upset. This challenge, while important, is manageable. Think of it as securing the discovery. It's nothing to worry about. We hold most of the cards. Tomorrow, we're going to determine how best to play them." Chuck opened the door. "I mean it—go meet Frank and celebrate. You earned it."

* * *

Gretchen pedaled behind Frank on Dome 7's Interdome Accessway. To celebrate, Frank had prepared a surprise that required bicycles. As a kid, she'd barely managed to get from place to place, and nothing had changed since.

When they were nearly halfway around Dome 7, she yelled ahead, "Where are we going?"

Frank called back, "It's close. Just keep following."

About five minutes later, they dismounted at a park and walked hand in hand through a stand of trees until the trail forked. They took the left route, and after several seconds, a faint rumble caught her attention. With each step, it grew louder. In the clearing, two oak trees flanked a ten-foot-tall waterfall, which emptied into a lake.

"Oh, it's wonderful!" Gretchen said.

Frank put his arm around her shoulders. "It's not Victoria Falls, but it's a nice addition."

She wrapped her arm around his waist and pulled him close. "You did this for me? Wasn't it expensive?"

"We already had the water circulating equipment to prevent algae build-up. A maintenance team positioned the rocks and redirected the water over them. I understand it's been popular since it opened a couple of days ago."

He removed his backpack. From inside, he laid out a blanket, a couple of FieldMeals, and a bottle of Mars wine with two plastic cups. They sat facing the lake, eating and speaking of many things except work.

He brushed a stray strand of hair from her face, and kissed her. She embraced him, wanting to explore further, but hesitated—they were in public.

When they separated, she sipped from the cup. "Let's go back to your quarters for some privacy."

"We have all the privacy in the world. While we ate, my last order as engineering manager was executed. The park is now in maintenance mode by my old team. We're alone, not even the security cameras are active."

As if on cue, the lights dimmed to twenty percent of their previous brilliance, signaling the beginning of the third shift. She took another sip of wine, placed her cup on the ground, and leaned forward to kiss him again. Her concerns faded away as they stripped out of their coveralls over the course of several minutes. They made love for the first time in the shadow of Mars' lone waterfall, built for her by the man she was falling in love with.

50 | Into the Future

In his kitchen, Frank yawned. He'd had a late night and now an early morning. Though today, the world was clear and in focus. He cracked a fresh Earth egg into the mixing bowl.

"Do you need any help?" Gretchen asked, her wet hair not detracting from her natural beauty.

"Yeah. I'm running behind, and they'll be here soon. Can you get the coffee brewing?"

She sidled up to him and kissed his cheek. "Of course, though I would've preferred to stay in bed."

"That's exactly why I'm running behind." Frank chuckled. "We'll have plenty of time for that. We have to get our house in order. Otherwise, all our hard work will be for nothing."

"I'm on it." A few seconds later, Gretchen opened the coffee container to the sound of a dull thud. "Is this Earth coffee? It smells like my old coffeehouse."

"Yes. And Earth eggs."

"Isn't that expensive?"

"We're also celebrating the Caretaker deal."

Frank whisked the eggs as Gretchen measured out the coffee. After she started it brewing, she grabbed the silverware and mugs and set the coffee table in the living room. They were so close. Everything, the company's future... their future... was within their grasp. They simply had to secure it.

The announcer chime rang. From in the living room, Gretchen said, "I'll get it."

Frank poured the liquid eggs into two small pans on the stovetop and stood in the doorway as Gretchen led June and Chuck into the living room. "It'll be a few more minutes."

"While we wait, why doesn't someone tell me why I'm standing with an archaeologist in Frank's quarters at six in the morning?"

Gretchen looked surprised, shocked, and befuddled all at once.

June added, "Or should I believe the rumor mill that we're surrendering to aliens?"

Chuck laughed. "There's no surrendering. June, this is Gretchen Blake, our Director of Archaeology. Gretchen, this is June Logan, our Vice President of Energy Production and Utilization. Gretchen, bring June up to speed about what you and Frank have been doing."

As Frank returned to cooking, Gretchen recounted the events of the past month. She glossed over some details like how they'd contacted Erin and how they'd survived the airlock sabotage. Around the point where she deciphered the Caretaker's message, Chuck grabbed the coffeepot and returned to the living room. With Chuck's help, Frank delivered four plates of steaming scrambled eggs to the living room while Gretchen described the Caretaker deal.

"I thought all of this was a practical joke," June said, "but you must be serious—the coffee and eggs are from Earth. So, what do you need from me?"

"We need help utilizing the Marsium121." Frank sipped his coffee. "We know we can tap into the transfer cable from the cavern to the city. We want to run a transmission line to the domes. We'll need cable, control circuits, and regulator components. Inventory only contains about ten percent of the cable and a fraction of the rest."

June leaned back and consulted her datapad. "I have a handful of control circuits and regulators plus a stash of cable off-inventory, in case of emergency. And as it happens, I just declared an emergency. The rest of the regulators and control components are outside Dome 5 and 6, in the solar panels. Plus, there's quite a bit of cable there, more than you'd expect. It'll take a fair amount of effort to scavenge it, but it's doable. I suspect we already have close to half the cable we'll need. I'll have Manufacturing fabricate more, starting today."

Chuck nodded, a broad smile forming on his face. "Excellent. That'll save the expense of buying and transporting it from Earth. Now, how long will it take to re-purpose the solar panel components?"

"Two... three months," June answered.

"We'll have to increase our order of fuel cells to replace the loss of the solar panel output," Frank said.

Chuck leaned forward. "Frank, how long to repair the Caretaker's manufacturing capability?"

"It'll take a full crew four to six weeks. Taking the Bunderbon pressure into consideration, I'd like to assign two crews pulling doubles to finish before the next board meeting in two weeks."

"The sooner we get his manufacturing facilities repaired and the ship to him, the faster we get the energy and the city," Gretchen added.

"Can't we tap the transfer conduit before the Caretaker leaves?" June asked.

Frank exhaled. "Technically, yes, but diverting power from the Caretaker may adversely affect departure preparations. Gretchen and I agreed the safest course was to wait until he leaves."

Chuck idly traced the cup lip with his forefinger. "There would be some value if we could get the energy before the next board meeting. Actually, that'd take a lot of wind out of Bunderbon's sails."

"Unless the Caretaker can bridge the gap with equipment, there's nothing I can do to shoehorn our capabilities to the calendar." June crossed her arms. "And *you* need to address Bunderbon, Chuck. He's talking and some of our more weak-spined board members are listening."

Chuck rubbed his forehead. "I know."

"Is it that bad?" Gretchen asked. "We have a treasure greater than humanity has ever seen at our fingertips. We just need a little time."

"Time is what we have least of. Bunderbon asked Security to investigate both Chuck and Frank. They're dragging their feet because Alan's on our side. But he must produce a report," June said, cradling her coffee with both hands, inhaling deeply before taking a sip. "Bunderbon has plenty of damning evidence that he can spin to make you look bad. He can easily assert you overbought land rights and allowed or encouraged Frank to break multiple regulations, compromising safety like traveling at night, which'll result in significant fines."

"The board meeting is the key milestone on our timeline." Chuck looked into the eyes of his friends around the coffee table. "I need to demonstrate value and progress to the board. June, get Manufacturing started on the cable and increase our fuel cell order to compensate for the power loss as we take the solar array off-line. I don't care what non-essential cargo you have to bump to get them here. Hold off on cannibalizing the solar array until we have those fuel cells in hand."

"Will do, Chuck," June said through a broad smile.

"Frank, do everything to repair the Caretaker's facilities and deliver the ship before the board meeting. Use our best people, regardless of their time-in-wild status. Those regs no longer apply since we bought full rights to the city, and it's a permanent structure."

Frank opened his datapad and touched the screen a couple of times. He'd drawn up the order already, anticipating Chuck's decision. "The orders are given. We'll pull out tomorrow at dawn."

"Gretchen, I know you want to go back to the city, but I need your help for a few days to prepare for the board meeting."

"I understand."

Frank said, "Gretchen has a rapport with the Caretaker. Why don't we escort the crews to the city and coordinate the project with the Caretaker and then return? We should be back the day after tomorrow."

Chuck frowned for a moment but nodded. Once Chuck made a decision, he liked to take action. In this case, smoothing the way with the Caretaker would have to take priority over preparing for the board. "That'll work. We'll meet when you get back."

"Thanks, Chuck. I promise we'll both help you when we return. You'll have enough to cut Bunderbon's knees out from beneath him," Frank said.

"Thank you all," Chuck said as he stood. "Please communicate in person about this. No emails or vidcomms. I don't believe interplanetary has any more spies embedded, but I don't want them or Bunderbon getting wind of our plan."

Frank stood along with the others.

June asked, "Where are you getting the spaceship?"

"From Erin," Frank replied.

June laughed as she walked through the living room. "Looks like I have the easy task after all."

* * *

Frank pressed the announcer chime.

"Hold on. I'll get to you," Erin hollered through the door, not using the intercom.

By the sound of it, her day had begun on a sour note.

She opened the door. "Just the person I wanted to see."

Frank entered and followed her into the living area where they stood near the kitchen. Their relationship wasn't in a sit-and-chat place. "What's got you ticked so early, Erin?"

"I had vidcomms from a couple of friends in Operations. Bunderbon's on the warpath over your latest trip in the wild. He's hot to know what you were doing, and people are calling me thinking I know."

"They ought to know better by now." Frank shook his head. "Trust me. Bunderbon'll choke on the answers."

"Rumors are flying. My favorite is that you were abducted and taken off-planet for questioning."

He chuckled. "If it helps, I deny that."

"It doesn't." Erin rolled her eyes. "So why're you here? It's not for small talk."

He'd avoided her since their break-up because he'd been uncomfortable in her presence, yet today, it didn't bother him. "I need your help again. And it'll make a real difference. Are you in?"

"Yes."

"Great." He exhaled and said in an even tone, "I need a ship."

"Where do you want to go?"

"No." Frank stared at her. "I need a ship, for keeps."

"What? Are you crazy? I'm not in the business of giving away ships. If anything, I'm looking to expand and hire more pilots."

Frank nodded. "Of course. I was thinking about that old hull you recently bought for parts. We'll reimburse you the purchase price, and all you have to do is fly it to a location about ten minutes away."

"What's going on? This is the oddest thing since—"

"Since I hired an archaeologist?" Frank finished her thought—like old times.

"Well, now that you bring it up, yes. You're in luck—I haven't scavenged too many critical parts yet. I'll do it, but I have a condition." Erin put her hands on her hips. "Tell me what's going on. All of it—the archaeologist... our two employees... the two Interplanetary nitwits who got charged with industrial espionage... the attempted murders. And most of all, why you want a broken-down relic that belongs in a museum, except they're so common, no museum would take it."

"Anything else?" Frank asked. *A juicy story is as good as money.*

Erin grinned. "I'll let you know."

"Okay. Done." Frank turned to leave.

"Wait, what's the story?"

"It'll all be in the news eventually, though they'll probably get it half-wrong."

She crossed her arms and shifted her weight.

"Hey, no reason to get ticked. After you land, you'll know everything by the time the tractor returns to Mars City."

"I'm going to hold you to that promise." Erin winked. "Remember, I know where you live."

51 | FULFILLING THE DEAL

A head, through the windshield, Gretchen spotted a convoy of six MarsVantage tractors approaching hers, each trailing a plume of red sand. As they passed, Frank, sitting to her left, gave each a small wave.

Once the last had passed, he pressed his earset. "Good work, everyone. You did an amazing job these past two weeks. We'll see you later tonight. The first round's on me."

They were driving over the southern portion of the Vault of the Ages when they passed recently dug sand, its brown color contrasting against the surrounding red. The engineering team had excavated the Baulnsville remains as their first on-site task.

Time had been tight, but those brave explorers' remains had to be handled properly. After coordinating the repairs, she and Frank had trailered their bodies back to Mars City.

In a reverent tone, Frank said, "I read your report about the Baulnsville group's fate. It was spot-on. I submitted it to the Order."

"I assumed you'd suggest changes." Her initial concerns about finding time for Knowledge Keeper activities had been unfounded. Frank's instructions and work all involved some aspect of the Vault of the Ages.

"No. It was well written. You gave the Caretaker's involvement in their deaths a fair retelling, neither blaming nor exonerating him."

"Thanks." She sighed. "I'm comforted that twenty-six of the bodies are returning to Earth, so their descendants can hold proper memorial services and lay them to rest."

He nodded. "Don't feel bad about the other four. They're resting comfortably among the Marsees who've already passed."

"Our ceremony was a fitting send-off for those brave pioneers. I'm sad we couldn't find any living descendants," Gretchen said in an even tone. When she'd attended the service in the graveyard close to Dome 6, she'd looked back on her life, remembering the triumphs and mistakes that had led her here. Rehashing them was fruitless. She wouldn't change a thing—it all led her to this time and place.

They continued to their destination in silence, swaying at times as softer sand shifted beneath the treads. Eventually, Gretchen said, "We're cutting it closer than I like."

"We'll get Erin in the air before the board meeting."

"Barely. I wanted to be there to help Chuck."

Frank glanced over. "Me too, but it wasn't going to happen. It'd make him look weak."

In the distance, a black spot no bigger than a kernel of bird seed traversed the red sand. As they drew closer, it grew into the familiar form of the Caretaker, who skirted around the edge of a massive crater.

"Mars City Control, this is Frank Brentford. Please connect me with Captain Knox."

* * *

"Go for Knox," Erin said from the cockpit of the antique shuttle-class spaceship.

"We're ready for you."

"Copy, Frank. I have clearance. I'll see you in ten." Erin switched off her mic. "Assuming I can keep this hunk of junk in the sky."

She pulled on the yoke and applied power. The spaceship fought its age as well as gravity, clawing its way into the sky. She coaxed it on course and applied forward thrust. It immediately buffeted, which was as bad as flying through a sandstorm. She eased off the thrust, allowing it to build at an unnaturally slow rate. The flight computer now estimated a flight time of twenty minutes. *So much for the quick trip Frank promised!*

She shook her head. For the first time as a pilot, she questioned a ship's flight-worthiness. She also questioned her ntelligence for helping Frank, as well as his parentage. Eventually, she neared the destination, grateful that no more equipment problems had cropped up.

She glanced out the portside window. A crater marred the plain below. Beside it, a tractor sat parked, accompanied by two people in spacesuits and a large black sphere. She added questions to her list but focused on staying aloft, which took most of her attention and skill.

"Erin, can you read me?" Frank asked.

She cycled her mic on. "Yes."

"This is where the fun starts. You need to land inside the crater. It's about twenty feet deep."

"Are you insane?"

"No more than usual."

"You should've mentioned this. I didn't replace the docking lights. I won't be able to see a damn thing."

"There's nothing to see. Trust me, the bottom is smooth and flat, and there's plenty of room."

After turning off her mic, Erin muttered, "Damn grounders don't know a thing about flying." She activated a couple of switches and quickly inspected the controls. "Okay, baby, cooperate with me and everything'll be fine."

She hovered above the crater and locked the controls to Z-axis only. At about a foot a second, she descended into the crater after visually ensuring she hit its center. After ten seconds, the windows darkened, forcing her to rely solely on her instruments to maintain the proper orientation.

A thunk from the right rear landing gear announced her arrival with the others contacting the ground an instant later. She turned off all systems and exhaled for what seemed like the first time since taking flight.

Erin contorted herself out of the pilot's seat, trying not to bruise herself more while exiting the old model's notoriously small cockpit. She entered the lavatory, which wasn't big enough to hold the name, let alone a person comfortably. She wiped the sweat from her face with an ancient towel. "Never again."

After she sealed her helmet to her spacesuit, she entered the cargo bay and opened the doors, switching on her exterior helmet light and scanning the area. She faced a wall of brown and maroon sand, though the ground was so black it seemed as if the shuttle was hovering in empty space.

Because she had already scavenged the loading ramp's motor she jumped from the cargo hold and landed softly after a six-foot fall. "Okay, Frank, how do I get out of here?"

"I see you. Walk sternward for about thirty feet. I just lowered a flexiladder. Come up and join us."

She switched off her spacesuit's mic before sarcastically uttering, "Sure, *sternward*. Come up and join us. No big deal. We do this sort of thing every day."

She found the ladder, a strip of fluorescent green tape reflecting her helmet light as she approached. Slowly, she climbed, careful not to slip and fall. At the top, Frank and Gretchen assisted her over the edge.

Gretchen's here? From above, she'd assumed the person with Frank was from Maintenance.

"Erin, I want you to meet the Caretaker," Frank said. The black sphere she'd seen prior to landing was actually a seven-foot tall, four-armed, metal monstrosity.

Frank's been hiding an alien? Where did it come from? What's it going to do with my ship?

It said, "It has been far too many orbits since I've seen a ship. Thank you all for everything. I'll take matters from here. I ask only for you to withdraw from the city until I depart. You already have my Bvindu-to-English translation, instructions on how to operate the main systems, and a detailed index to our information systems. Before I leave, I'll transmit a message."

Gretchen smiled. "We understand. Good luck with your search."

Erin stood in place, attempting to make sense of everything. And failing.

Frank and Gretchen had taken several paces toward the nearby tractor before Frank stopped and looked back. "C'mon, Erin. It's time to go."

"Okay..." Erin trudged through the Martian sand behind Frank and Gretchen. "I can't wait to hear how you're going to explain *all* of this."

* * *

Erin, we're pressurized," Gretchen said before removing her helmet.

Frank removed his and leaned over, whispering in Gretchen's ear, "I promised to tell Erin the entire story. She isn't going to wait any longer, so you need to drive. Take it slow until you hit Main Street at Waypoint 1. Then, you can open it up."

"I'll tell her."

His head jerked back. "Don't you think that'll be... I don't know... awkward?"

"Mars City is small, and I'll be running into her a lot. It's best for all of us to be friends. We may as well start now." Before he could argue further, she patted him on the knee and squeezed between the seats into the cargo hold.

"Are you going to explain why I flew a ship into a hole for a talking soccer ball with a pituitary problem?"

Frank set out for Waypoint 1 as Gretchen pulled a jump seat down and sat next to Erin. For ten minutes, she described everything from the cave to the Vault of the Ages and the Caretaker. Along the way, she purposely glossed over her relationship with Frank.

"That explains the rumors that we hired an archaeologist. With an entire alien city to explore, we'll need expertise on staff. At least now I know what it takes for Chuck to loosen the purse strings." Erin smiled. "Congratulations on the permanent position."

"Thanks, I'm excited about it. It's an opportunity of a lifetime."

Silence blanketed them as they swayed along with the tractor traversing the landscape. It seemed rougher than when they'd arrived.

The cargo area's temperature seemed to drop a few degrees, too. The last time they'd sat together was outside the landing bay when they had been waiting to meet Frank for the first time. Then, Erin had been uncomfortable—now, Gretchen was.

"So is it true?" Erin asked, her voice softer.

"What's that?" Gretchen asked, keeping her voice low, so Frank couldn't overhear.

"That you and Frank are a couple."

There it was. The conversation she wasn't eager to have, yet one that had to happen. Did Erin still have feelings for Frank? If so, did she want him back? Better to know now what the playing field looked like. "Yes, Frank and I started dating after I accepted the permanent position."

Erin paused for a moment. "Good for you. I wish you every happiness."

"Thanks," Gretchen said evenly. Erin had seemed sincere, but she could be covering her true feelings with politeness.

Erin looked squarely into Gretchen's eyes. "Really, I mean it. By now you've had to have heard Frank and I have a history."

"Frank mentioned it," Gretchen said in a non-committal tone.

"Information like that doesn't remain secret for long. Anyway, we didn't work out because we want different things." Erin leaned closer. "We're just friends now. I only want happiness for him, and if he's happy with you, then I'm all for it."

Gretchen smiled at Erin's honesty. "Thank you. I appreciate that."

Frank hollered back, "Hey, what're you two whispering about?"

They said in unison, "Nothing."

52 | TURNING THE TIDE

At the head of a large cherry conference table, a holdover from when Interplanetary owned MarsVantage, Chuck reviewed his notes on his datapad. Thanks to Gretchen and Frank, he had all the information he could possibly need to refute any Bunderbon accusation. The meeting was as much about the board's confidence in him as it was about his recent spending.

Board members trickled in, taking their assigned seats. A minute before the meeting's start time, Bunderbon entered the room and took his chair, the last open seat.

Chuck stood and forced a practiced smile. "Welcome, everyone. It's no secret that James disagrees with my goals for the company and the past few months have brought our visions into direct conflict. I know he's talked with several of you about my recent decisions."

Five board members looked anywhere except at Chuck. They must be in Bunderbon's camp, which didn't surprise him. They performed well enough in their roles, but those five weren't visionaries.

He had to flip one to land on the right side of a six-to-five vote, though that wasn't his true goal. He strived for a ten-to-one vote—so Bunderbon would think twice before attempting another power grab.

"James, for the record, would you provide the board the specifics of your concerns?" Chuck sat and leaned back in his chair.

Bunderbon stood, looking at his datapad. "As you have read in the mission reports submitted for Frank's exploration of the cave, he broke regulations by traveling by foot at night. That's an expense."

Bunderbon had willingly ignored the reason for breaking the regs. He had to—otherwise, his complaint would sound hollow.

"Their reports are hazy on what was found to justify keeping an archaeologist on Mars. Yet now she's here in a permanent position, no less. Another expense with a doubtful return. I believe Chuck's withholding information for an unknown purpose."

Bunderbon was making inferences based on the reports to concoct a conspiracy. Chuck looked at his prepared remarks. Unfortunately, they wouldn't satisfactorily address wild conspiracy theories.

Bunderbon continued, "Those mission reports indicate a supply of oxygen vests, yet the mission's manifest doesn't record that equipment. Frank misappropriated MarsVantage equipment. What else has been misappropriated?"

Chuck leaned forward. Conspiracy wasn't the only card Bunderbon was playing. He's playing the CEO-without-control-of-his-operations card. *And he's doing a good job.*

"Further, I find Erin's flight over Frank's mission area exactly when he's in distress too much of a coincidence. I believe Frank conducted an illegally encrypted communication with Erin. Any Earth investigation would lead to more expense. The tractor sabotage in our own garage bay is also suspicious. Interplanetary's motivation was to steal Frank's discovery, not prevent it. Who sabotaged our tractors?"

The good news was that Bunderbon didn't have any evidence. If he had, he would've presented it. Unfortunately, he was connecting some dots that weren't meant to be connected.

Bunderbon swiped his datapad's screen. "And lastly, the two teams in the wild for the past two weeks are doing what? They returned the Baulnsville remains their first day along with a suspicious story about their discovery. Their subsequent actions are unknown. This is my division, yet no one is capable of telling me their assignment. Do we really want a rogue group operating in our midst?"

As Bunderbon took his seat, Chuck folded his hands in his lap. "That sounds sinister, indeed. The truth, however, while holding exciting possibilities for the company, is bland by comparison."

Three in Bunderbon's camp gave Chuck their attention. At least they wanted to hear his side.

"I expect all of you read Gretchen and Frank's mission reports, so I won't reiterate facts we all know well. I insisted Frank pack the extra air vests and falsify the manifests. I wasn't taking any chances after Interplanetary failed to recruit her. Many on this board scoffed at the idea of spies lurking within the company, but the truth came to light when Interplanetary attempted to murder our team."

Alan gave a slight nod as he leaned forward. "Security used Chuck's SDA software that ferreted out the spies and handlers to identify a handful of compromised low-level employees. I'm hoping Interplanetary uses them again, so they'll expose their new operatives. Make no mistake—we've stopped the spying cold."

Before Chuck could say anything, June looked to Bunderbon. "Let's not skip over the Marsium121 so fast. It'll power Mars City for centuries at a fraction of our current cost. It's a game-changer."

The look on June's face made Chuck grateful she was an ally.

She continued, "The regs Frank broke were put into place to handcuff us, not protect us. Following them would only have led to death. Chuck and Frank provided true safety. Thirteen years ago, I attended a funeral service outside Dome 6 for twenty-three of us because true safety measures were ignored. We won't do that again. Ever."

Bunderbon's expression had changed from confident to unreadable. He looked at Chuck and said, "Nothing explains the vast expensive plot of sand you just purchased rights to, or what two full maintenance teams are doing there. You should've consulted with us."

"James, you have a point," Chuck said as he leaned on the table and interlaced his fingers. "It's time to brief the board on our lot of sand. Or to be more accurate, what's happening beneath it. Gretchen found a holo in the cavern and teased a message from it. It was an invitation. And before you complain that we withheld it, James, you must've missed it in their reports."

Chuck pressed a link on his datapad to activate the conference room's holo-generator. Above the center of the table, Gretchen's version of the Caretaker's message played.

"We cut a deal with that city's caretaker, and today, w
fulfilled our end. The price was two weeks' worth of repairs and a
antique spaceship for the cavern and the city, including it
manufacturing capability. A small investment for an enormou
gain, and I'm not counting the knowledge of advanced technolog
contained in the city's information archives."

Emily Madsen, Vice President of Transportatior
harrumphed. "You're playing the alien card? Unbelievable."

Chuck looked to Bunderbon. "Do you still insist we foolishl
purchased land rights?"

"Ah... If it's true." Bunderbon had been caught flatfootec
Emily aside, the rest of the board were giving Chuck their fu
attention. *Time to seal the deal.*

Chuck pressed another link on his datapad.

A holo played showing Gretchen in the Vault of the Age
narrating a scene of massive destruction. In due course, sh
pointed out the smashed Baulnsville tractors embedded in th
rubble and the repaired dome overhead. She ended by saying
"Your ancestors bravely explored, nearly finding what generation
had been searching for, if not for an unfortunate accident. We'l
always remember their efforts and salute their dedication an
sacrifice."

Chuck cleared his throat. "We made that holo for the familie
of Baulnsville victims to provide closure. That ought to be proo
enough, but you'll have another round of reports from th
maintenance teams and the city's original exploration crew t
pour through. In the end, there's no reason to lie—it'd only buy m
a few weeks."

Bunderbon said, "Gretchen's interpretation should've bee
included in the mission report. You're acting like a king instead c
a CEO."

Bunderbon was grasping at straws, and Chuck had had his fil
of such maneuvers. "Point to the rule that we need to publicl
announce our interpretation of anything we find in the wild
How's that in MarsVantage's interest?"

Bunderbon remained silent.

"You're right about one matter, though. I've been pursuing a
agenda, not for personal profit, but for the best interest c

MarsVantage. We have a unique opportunity to free ourselves from Earth's stranglehold by becoming energy independent. Everything else in the city—the manufacturing capability and the new technologies—are cherries on the hot fudge sundae. I don't accept Earth's limitations, and I never will."

Chuck stood and closed his datapad. "Now, you must decide our future based on facts, not wild conspiracy theories. Do you want to lead a growing, thriving company or a stagnating one? That's your choice. Choose wisely. Now, do I hear a motion to dismiss me, Charles O'Donnell, as CEO of MarsVantage?"

The five who were on Bunderbon's side at the meeting's start, merely stared at the table, Emily included. For his part, Bunderbon looked as if he'd bit into a lemon. Chuck had done his job better than expected—no one even wanted to vote.

"No motion is presented. This meeting is adjourned."

53 | A New Beginning

On the night table, Gretchen's datapad chimed repeatedly waking her from a dream where she ran on the beach a sunset with Frank. With one eye half open, she clumsily groped until she found it. She pulled the screen open and selected new messages.

The Caretaker's message had finally arrived four months after Erin delivered the spaceship. As time had marched on, she'd anticipated it. Two weeks ago, she felt as if it could happen at any moment. And now, it'd finally arrived.

The message contained only a date and time.

She reached over and shook Frank's shoulder.

He mumbled, "Don't tell me you have an emergency."

"Archaeologists don't have emergencies in the middle of the night." She shook him again. "Wake up. The Caretaker sent his message."

He sat up, rubbing his eyes. "Well, what did it say?"

She handed over the datapad.

"That's twenty-two hours from now. I wished he would've given us more notice."

* * *

The appointed time approached as Gretchen followed Frank and Erin up the stairs, past the farming level near the top of Dome 7. They arrived at a closed access hatch in the ceiling. Frank pushed several controls, and the hatch slid aside. In turn, they climbed into an empty room, which had a 360-degree view obstructed only by six structural girders that met at the center of the room's ceiling.

As Gretchen and Frank assembled various pieces of recording equipment that they'd carried in backpacks, Erin said, "It's a shame Chuck couldn't attend. I wonder what's so important."

"Probably nothing," Frank said. "I think he wants us to enjoy the moment without the boss being around. He asked me to bring by the recording first thing in the morning."

"What do you expect to see anyway?" Erin asked.

"The Caretaker take off in your old spaceship," Gretchen replied.

"According to his knowledge base index," Frank added, "the Bvindu have an advanced propulsion system. I'm guessing he hasn't spent the past four months overhauling the engines we gave him. I'm betting he dropped them entirely in favor of his tech."

"Thanks for inviting me. I wouldn't miss this for the world." Erin nodded to Gretchen, who returned a nod without Frank noticing. He was preoccupied with calibrating the holo recordings.

Earlier that morning, Gretchen had surprised Frank by suggesting that Erin join them. She had pointed out that without Erin's ship, they wouldn't have had a deal, and cementing a friendly relationship with her was in everyone's best interest. It'd taken Frank only a few moments to agree.

With all the equipment set up, Frank dimmed the lights. A few minutes from now the Caretaker would depart, enough time for their eyes to dark adjust.

Gretchen walked the perimeter of the plastiglass-enclosed room, which was the size of an extra-large conference room. In the distance, she spotted construction crews in several illuminated portions of Interplanetary's dome. She walked farther. The protective shield over Dome 4's plastiglass was retracted for a reason she couldn't recall. The streetlights, along with an odd light in a building window here and there, brightened the immediate area. Few people were visible as it was the middle of the third shift and most everyone not working was asleep. Fortunately, Dome 4 would be at their backs when they looked toward the Vault of the Ages.

When she rejoined Frank and Erin, they were discussing Bunderbon's low profile. Gretchen smiled at the progress Frank had made at relating to Erin. Hopefully soon, he'd completely discard his emotional baggage and not flinch whenever Erin's name came up in conversation.

She didn't judge. She understood the pain of a failed relationship. Months ago, she'd decided to help him move past the hurt before it caused problems in their relationship. And it was working, as evidenced by their friendly conversation.

The time specified in the Caretaker's message arrived, and they gazed toward the Vault of the Ages. An ethereal electric-blue glow emanated from the horizon. Gretchen held her breath in anticipation, not wanting to miss a moment of what was to come.

A blue-white spark rose into the night sky and hovered for a moment. A swirling array of colors about the size of Earth's moon appeared. The spark leapt into the center of the swirl, which shrank into nothingness within seconds, restoring the star-filled sky as if nothing had happened.

"Wow," Erin said.

"Frank, you're right." Gretchen smiled. "I think we just witnessed the Caretaker's propulsion technology. What do you think it was?"

"Based on the display, I'd say the Bvindu mastered Heim theory. A group of Earth scientists is researching it again. I figured they were wasting their time because it takes something like twelve dimensions for the math to work. Apparently, I'm wrong."

"Call it whatever you want. I'd like a shot at flying that tech," Erin said with wide eyes, still staring into the sky.

Gretchen's datapad chimed with a message received. It was from the Caretaker.

All the Bvindu was, our knowledge, our history, and our accomplishments, I entrust to you. Use it wisely.

She wished the Caretaker good luck, hoping that he'd somehow find the Bvindu, but expecting that he'd more likely learn of their demise. It was better to know the truth and move on than wait for a time that'd never come.

For her, the future was bright, and she was excited beyond words. The adventure was just beginning, and she didn't know here it would lead. Soon, more archaeologists, including her closest friend, Ashley, would arrive. They'd explore the Vault of the Ages together, and understand the Bvindu technology, philosophy, and history it held.

Along the way, she and Frank, as part of the Knowledge Keeper Order, would provide an example of individuals using their skills and abilities to their fullest potential. MarsVantage would set a brilliant example the Earthers couldn't ignore.

Frank smiled and placed his arm around Gretchen's shoulders. "I've never seen you look happier."

"Hawthorne once told me there were no more big discoveries left." She smiled as broadly as she'd ever done. "We already made one, and who knows how many more are waiting?"

The End

About the Author

George G. Moore lives in northern Virginia with his wife, a dog, and a cat who benevolently rules over all he sees. When not managing a group of software engineers, he writes science fiction and speculative fiction.

He enjoys all manner of interests including golfing, reading, and attending concerts.

From an early age, space and space travel fascinated him. He finds Mars particularly fascinating and sees humanity reaching beyond Earth, to its neighboring planets and eventually the stars.

He previously published three stories:

- Forging Freedom Anthology, Freedom Forge Press (Short story: The Shape of Things to Come)
- Forging Freedom II, Freedom Forge Press (Short story: Unintended Lesson)
- Spies & Heroes: An International Anthology, S&H Publishing, Inc (Short story: Spying Isn't Easy)

For updates on more Mars stories and future projects, check out:

www.GeorgeGMoore.com

@George.G.Moore.Author

@GMoore_Author

**Visit georgegmoore.com/the-music-of-mars/freemiums/
If asked for a password, enter Gretchen.**

If you enjoyed this book,

please review it on Amazon and Goodreads.

Made in the USA
San Bernardino, CA
07 April 2020